1/08

2012

BOOKS BY WHITLEY STRIEBER

*Available from Tor

2012

THE WAR FOR SOULS

WHITLEY STRIEBER

A TOM DOHERTY ASSOCIATES BOOK NEW YORK

2012: THE WAR FOR SOULS

Copyright © 2007 by Whitley Strieber

A Tor Book
Published by Tom Doherty Associates, LLC
175 Fifth Avenue
New York, NY 10010

www.tor.com

Tor® is a registered trademark of Tom Doherty Associates, LLC.

Library of Congress Cataloging-in-Publication Data

Strieber, Whitley.
    2012 : the war for souls / Whitley Strieber.—1st ed.
        p. cm.
    "A Tom Doherty Associates book."
    ISBN-13: 978-0-7653-1896-1
    ISBN-10: 0-7653-1896-2
    1. Extraterrestrial beings—Fiction.   2. Human-alien encounters—Fiction.   I. Title.   II. Title: Two
thousand twelve.
    PS3569.T6955A615 2007
    813'.54—dc22

                                                                                            2007017374

First Edition: September 2007

Printed in the United States of America

0 9 8 7 6 5 4 3 2 1

In Memory of Robert Anton Wilson

PART ONE

AND A DARKNESS OVER THE EARTH

The Soul that rises with us, our life's Star,
Hath had elsewhere its setting
And cometh from afar;
Not in entire forgetfulness,
And not in utter nakedness,
But trailing clouds of glory do we come
From God, who is our home.

—WILLIAM WORDSWORTH
"Ode on Intimations of Immortality from
Recollections of Early Childhood"

There is no supernatural. There is only the natural world, and you have access to all of it. Souls are part of nature.

—The Master of the Key

PROLOGUE
NOVEMBER 21
DARK LENS

MARTIN WINTERS HAD BEEN IN the Pyramid of Khufu a number of times, and he'd always felt the same wonder and the same claustrophobia. The work he was doing here was revolutionizing archaeology, and that was exciting, but this particular journey into the tiny pit beneath the structure was one he had been dreading.

His mission was to collect stone facing from the interior of joins, so that the new technique of mass-average decay dating could be applied and a final mystery solved. Over the past three years, his lab at Kansas State University at Uriah had dated a dozen sites in South America using the technique. For the past nine months, they had been working on the Great Pyramid, and the results were so inconsistent that archaeologists worldwide, eager to dismiss findings that had devastated their theories about the past, were howling that the technique was defective.

What they had found was that the pyramid had not been built in just a few years, but that the work had been done in at least four stages over thousands of years, beginning at least six thousand years ago. The Fourth Dynasty pharaoh Khufu had indeed built the section where his glyph had been found, but the pyramid rested on a base that had been laid three thousand years before Khufu's reign.

Now it was time to address the pit beneath the pyramid, believed to be an earlier burial chamber. It was here that he expected to finalize his study of the Giza plateau, because this was thought to be the first human work that had appeared on it.

He had also worked on another site, a very ancient building called the Osirion, where rituals involving the Egyptian resurrection deity Osiris had been practiced.

His findings were so explosive that he had not yet published them. He wasn't willing to expose his technique to the howls of criticism that would come when his proof that it had been constructed between 18,000 and 20,000 years ago was revealed. He'd also explored dating the Sphinx, but it was carved out of a solid block of limestone, which left him without anything to sample. He needed tiny fragments of stone that had been struck by quarrymen's tools, then soon after pressed against other stone and not moved since.

Before him, the descending passage awaited. The government did not allow the public to go into the pit, and for good reason. More than one visitor had been carried out in a state of panic, and the air was so bad that suffocation was a definite issue. Legends about the place suggested that it had been used by some of the Egyptian priesthoods as an initiatory chamber, presumably where people were taught to overcome whatever fears it caused.

"Okay," he said, testing his flashlight. Then again, "Okay."

Ahmad Mahfouz chuckled. "Okay."

"You bastard, you go down."

Ahmad laughed aloud. "It's not my machine that's driving everybody crazy."

Ahmad was not only one of the finest archaeologists in Egypt, he had an excellent mind for technology, so he understood why it was most unlikely that mass-average decay dating was wrong. It was, in fact, the holy grail of dating techniques: it could tell when stone was last worked, as long as the stone had not been exposed to air, thus the need to go deep into structures like this and drill into joined stones in order to get samples.

In Peru, where the Incas had fitted their stones with a jeweler's precision, this had been easy. In the pyramid and the Osirion, it had entailed careful drilling using sonar guidance. Here, also, so he was loaded with equipment.

The descending passage was narrow, it was pitch black, and madness stalked the people who went down.

"Radio check," he said as soon as he was ten steps in.

"We don't need it yet, Martin. I'm right here."

"I'm sorry, Ahmad. Look, if I get out of here alive, you're buying."

"It's been there for thousands of years—far longer than anybody thought, according to you. So why would it pick today to collapse?"

Feeling like an idiot, Martin headed deeper. Soon, a silence enveloped him that was unlike anything he had ever known, and he had been in some very quiet holes in the ground.

What was different about this silence was that it felt, he thought, aggressive. Like it knew you were there and had been waiting, and now it wanted you. *Like it knew.*

But, of course, that was all in his mind. There was no malign presence here—or anywhere else, for that matter. No ghosts, no gods. This was simply what happens when you descend a narrow tunnel beneath six million tons of stone.

One thing the ancient Egyptians had not been were fools. They had understood this effect, which might be why the pit was here. The conventional wisdom was that it was an old tomb, but that wasn't at all clear. Half of it was an odd, roughly constructed platform with rocky knobs on it. Certainly no place for a sarcophagus, and the rest of the room was just as strange, being dominated by a diagonal cut in the floor about six feet deep. It was, in fact, in the walls of this pit that Martin hoped to find the fitted masonry that was crucial to his success.

He reached the chamber itself. He was now eighty feet beneath the pyramid's foundation. The air was thick and cool, clammy, even. His multi-gas detector was telling him that although carbon dioxide levels were high, he was basically safe. He carried an emergency respirator with an hour's supply of oxygen, more than enough to enable him to withdraw if he used up all the air in the confined space. Or, if the worst were to happen, to suffocate more slowly.

"I've arrived," he said into his radio.

There was a silence. A long silence.

"Mahmoud!"

"Oh, sorry, effendi. I was taking my lazy tea."

"I'm scared down here, man!"

"And I know it, and I'm trying to make some fun for you."

He was a great guy and a fabulous scientist, but there was a cultural gulf between a Moslem who had grown up when this was still Turkish territory, and now had to deal with the Brits. "Remember, I'm an American," he said. This was not the time for practical jokes with the radio.

He took a deep breath, then another. Then he opened his equipment bag and pulled out the radar. It could penetrate limestone to a depth of ten feet, and return detailed imagery of what was there. It could, in other words, locate the joins in masonry construction.

His plan was to send his tiny drill in about an eighth of an inch behind a join, then collect stone right off the join itself.

He did not shine his light around. He knew what was there, and he didn't want to see just how close the walls were. The ceiling was ten feet, though, so he was no longer being forced to hunch as he had when he was in the passage itself.

Back problems were the archaeologist's curse. You couldn't work without hunching and bending, often for hours, often in confined spaces, and the older you got, the more you became aware of this. At thirty-four, he wasn't feeling it much, not with swimming, squash, tennis and— well, Lindy. No, he worked his back plenty, and had two children to show for it at home. He also had a wife who was working to get one of the most extraordinary jobs in the world. Since 2010, when NASA had announced that some UFOs were indeed intelligently guided craft, perhaps extraterrestrial or perhaps from a parallel universe, the International Advanced Propulsion Physics Seminar had been working overtime to understand how they worked.

She was deeply involved in the politics of science, because she wanted to be on that seminar.

How that might be done by a professor from a college so low on the U.S. News list that it was at the bottom of a fold-down page he couldn't imagine. She was driven, though, obsessed with getting us off the planet in a very major way.

For his part, Martin worked deep within the archaeological establishment, which was why the revolution he was, in his own small way, creating was so fiercely opposed. But, in fact, the numbers were clear: human history had to be revised, for the simple reason that all of the most mysterious ancient structures so far tested were far older than had been assumed.

He watched as the radar's computer finally found itself and the tiny screen began to return a sensible image. "I've got picture," he said into the radio.

"Right. You're good on time."

The Imperial Department of Antiquities had given them an hour, from four to five in the morning, when the Pyramids at Dawn tours started. They did not want activity in this area of the pyramid during the time it was open to tourists. Inevitably, somebody would buy their way down, and that would mean big trouble for the poor archaeologist in here trying to work, not to say danger for the rubes with the bakshish coming down here to chant or whatever.

He glanced at his watch. It was exactly four-thirty. It would take a little more time to penetrate the drill, secure the sample and withdraw it. He was not good on time, he was okay on time.

Only a practiced eye could understand the readout that presented itself on the tiny screen of the scanner. He was pressed up against the confined second stage of the pit, attempting to avoid the twenty-foot-deep hole that had been dug in the nineteenth century by Caviglia and after him the English explorer—or was that plunderer?—Howard-Vyse. The green readout shimmered, growing lighter where the stone was more dense, darker where the density was less.

Then he found what he was looking for—a dark, straight line. This was undoubtedly a join of some kind. He couldn't tell, looking at the surface of the wall. For years, it had been assumed that it was carved out of the virgin limestone. Not until radar imagery from above had revealed that there were structured walls down here had it been realized that this particular pit facing was made of quarried stone.

"Commencing drilling."

"Roger that."

He took out the long, thin bit and fixed it into the drill itself. The bit was worth thirty thousand dollars, being diamond tipped and made of the hardest tool steel there was, with a Knoop hardness rating of 920. It was only about the diameter of three pins, so it had to be hard in order to penetrate.

As he worked with it, he wondered how in the world the Egyptians had hollowed out diorite jars with drills that must have been not much thicker than this. This drill would not stand up against diorite. In fact, it was being challenged by this granite, and he stopped to let it cool. Although he carried three of the bits, he certainly didn't want to chew budget by using them up. He had plans for digs all over the world. Lindy might be taking us to the stars, but he was revising history, and that was important, too.

It was then that he noticed the vibration. The sensation was coming up through his shoes.

"Ahmad?"

"Go ahead."

"There's something . . . happening. I feel a vibration."

"The drill set up a harmonic?"

"Possibly, but it's off now."

As he stood there, the vibration became a pulsation. It was quick, regular, machinelike. If he did not know it to be an impossibility, he would have said that a compressor of some sort had turned on somewhere beneath this chamber.

What he must be feeling was some factory in Cairo starting its motors for the day. The entire limestone plateau might be set to vibrating by something like that. "I got it, it's a city sound. Some factory."

"A new machine tool plant is a kilometer from here."

"That would be it." Vibration, a new variety of pollution. He predicted that it was going to be playing hell with the archaeological district. He returned to his work.

Now, with the bit cooled down, he made better progress by just touching it to the surface, rather than pressing. Farther in, also, the stone was softer. He had been working for some time before he realized that there was dust coming down from above. Once again, he stopped the drill. He shone his light around, following the dust to its source, which proved to be the ceiling.

He was astonished to see that the finished ceiling of the chamber was spitting little geysers of dust, as if it was being compressed, or pressed from above.

"Ahmad?"

"Yes."

"Anything going on topside?"

"Interestingly enough, I saw a jackal. I thought Cairo had run them all out by now."

He returned to his work. He was bare millimeters away from getting his sample—and the drill was moving—and there! Now to withdraw and go in with the collecting tool, a tiny claw made of the same hardened steel.

He took the silver tool out of his case and plugged it into the zinc-air generator he was using for power, then inserted it into the narrow hole made by the drill. Or rather, tried. The pulsations made it harder than threading a needle.

"Do we know if that machine shop ever shuts down?"

"Come out, Martin."

"Why?"

"Because I'm starting to feel it up here, and that should not be."

Bits of stone were now dropping from the ceiling, and he knew that this was no ordinary event. The reason he knew was that the floor was clean and the room intact. Therefore, this was something new and Ahmad was right, he needed to get out of here right now.

He was millimeters from finishing, though. He watched the now vibrating screen, manipulated the instrument.

"Martin, are you coming up?"

"Hold on."

"Are you pulling out? What are you doing?"

He didn't answer. The pulsations got bigger, *whoomp . . . whoomp . . . whoomp* and he struggled, trying to catch just the tiny bit of stone he needed.

There was a crash and a piece of ceiling that must have weighed a quarter ton plunged past him into the Caviglia pit.

"The police are here, they are saying come out."

"On my way."

But still the instrument wasn't set. Watching the screen, he maneuvered it frantically now. The weight of what was above pressed down on him like a great, suffocating hand.

He thought of Lindy and Trevor and Winnie, and drew the instrument out. Another block fell, and he knew that it was over. He started to gather his equipment.

Whoomp! Whoomp! Whoomp!

This wasn't an earthquake, no earthquake felt like this. There was a machine down there, there had to be.

A series of sounds like shots being fired came echoing down the passage. In the dust, his light revealed cracks appearing along the walls.

He dashed for the passage, hunched, half running, half crawling, tearing his knees and hands to ribbons, racing along as the whole tunnel twisted and swayed like a rubber tube in the hands of a mad giant.

Screaming now, he burst upward. The floor crumbled beneath his feet, showers of stone fell around him, his progress slowed. The pulsations were huge now, great, shuddering seizures of the ground itself.

And then there were arms, people dragging at him, and he was coming out, he was free—and they were outside the pyramid. Coughing, his eyes closed by a thick layer of dust, he staggered and tried to collect himself.

What in the name of all that was holy was going on here?

"Run, Martin!"

He felt somebody tug at him, managed to wipe his eyes enough to see, turned and observed the strangest thing he had ever seen in his life.

Looking up the north face of the gigantic structure, he found himself watching huge ripples. It was as if the stone blocks themselves were liquefying and threatening to pour down on them like some kind of bizarre flood.

He mouthed the words, too astounded to speak them: *The pyramid's collapsing.*

Sirens started wailing, one and then more, until the sound filled the air. In the distance, a line of tour buses on their way to a Pyramids at Dawn experience began making clumsy attempts to turn around in the roadway.

Martin followed Ahmad and the three policemen, running toward the wall that controlled access to the archaeological zone. Behind them there was a noise. It was a howl from the very throat of the world, screaming like a jet going down, like a million madmen burning alive.

Martin turned and saw that the pyramid was now bulging, as if it was becoming a huge block, its pyramidal shape disappearing as the stones that had been there for thousands of years burst from their rest and flew out into the sweet of dawn.

All across Cairo and up and down the Nile, people looked toward the sound, toward Giza. What they saw was unrecognizable to them and completely incomprehensible, a great, black column gushing into the sky, its walls flickering with tan dots.

Each of these dots was a stone weighing between one and three tons. Each was the size of a large automobile. And all were about to fall on the helpless millions of people who jammed the city of Cairo.

Martin understood this quite clearly. His belief, at this point, was that terrorists had detonated an atomic weapon under the pyramid. It had been his extraordinary misfortune to be inside it during the moment when the ages-old structure, the most important construction on earth, met its end.

As the great fountain of stones reached its apogee at an altitude of over two miles, Martin lay down beside the wall. He was not a religious man, and was surprised by the deep feeling of peace that had come over him. Death had come to him. This was quite certain.

But then a paroxysm of fear made him grab his head, made him scream into the continuing, expanding roar of the vast unfolding explosion.

Then he stopped. He brought before him an image of Lindy, the most beautiful woman he had ever seen, one of the wisest human beings he had ever known. He decided that he would die like this, with her filling his mind.

And then he heard Trevor's voice as clearly as if he had been standing there say, "When's Dad coming home?" And Winnie replied with prim care, "Trevor, you're so impatient. He'll be home when he's finished."

It seemed the most natural thing in the world to be able to hear them, and then the big clock in the hall was ringing the hour, eight deep bongs.

A whistling sound turned to a scream turned to a hoarse roar, and a stone crashed down into the desert thirty feet from where he lay. The ground leaped and knocked the breath out of him. He saw Ahmad, his eyes glazed with shock, his lips pulled back from his teeth, staring straight at him.

Another block hit, then another, then it was raining stones and there were screams and above them the clanging crunch of stones as they struck buses and cars, and the distant roar of the ones hitting the Nile, and explosions as they bombed Cairo. A row of houses a quarter of a mile away disappeared in dust, the road was smashed, cars ran into the desert weaving crazily, a bus, careening away from the scene, was struck in the rear and lifted up as if begging for deliverance, and then exploded in flames and desolate, shattering screams.

It went on and on and on, for what seemed like hours, then days, then it was as if it entered a sort of eternity, an endless explosion. Always, there would be another stone from the sky. Always, another chorus of screams, always another bone-shattering jolt.

Until that was no longer true. What he heard now was a silence even deeper than the one that had oppressed him in the pit. In part, it was because of his stunned left eardrum and the ringing in his right ear that would not go away for days. In part it was the shock of seeing what looked like a cliff where Ahmad had been, just feet from his face. Beside it, one of the policemen lay sprawled on his back, sightless eyes staring at the sky, dead from shock. A German tourist wandered about calling out, "*Morgen hat gebrochen, Morgen hat gebrochen.*"

Morning has broken. And, like thunder out of the east, the sun rose behind the storied plateau of Giza, wreathed now in smoke, choked by rubble.

Martin got to his feet. He was staying at the Mena House just across from the pyramids, and he began walking toward it now. He realized that he was staggering, but it didn't matter, the other ghosts on the ruined plateau were just the same.

In contrast to the plateau, the gardens of the Mena were still verdant. Half a dozen huge blocks were embedded in the golf course, looking as if they had been there forever.

The hotel itself was undamaged, the staff and guests outside, looking up at the great, black column that hung in the sky, blowing slowly south with the prevailing winds of the season. The British and Egyptian Royal flags flew in stately splendor, as unaffected as the hotel itself.

November in Egypt could be so lovely, with even Cairo enjoying a few crystal days.

Martin went through the upper lobby and into the Khan el Khalili. There was a waiter there, standing at a window. "I would like a cup of coffee," Martin said. The waiter did not move. Then he did, he turned. His eyes streamed with tears. Martin realized that he was crying, too. They embraced, and the two men wept together like children. "I lost my friend," Martin said.

"I lost my Egypt, our heart is broken now, sir."

Later that day, Martin went onto the roof of the hotel, to see for himself what everyone was talking about, everyone who was not fighting fires or cleaning up the bombed city, or looking helplessly at the great stones that had shattered her.

Before him stood the plateau, and where the pyramid had been there was a new object, a gigantic black lens. It was afternoon now, with light made delicate by the dust.

He stared out across the space that separated the hotel from the pyramid complex. Here and there, figures could be seen moving around it, for the most part Royal Egyptian Police in their green uniforms, and British soldiers in khaki. A resplendent Rolls Royce stood in the road in front of the Mena, and the Governor General could be seen striding amid the huge blocks, followed by a crowd of officers.

Martin gazed long at that lens. It appeared to be perfectly round and convex, perhaps twenty feet high at its center. He cast across his memories of the past, trying to find in the encyclopedia of his mind some point of reference.

There was nothing. The past had not portrayed this. But he did not think it an accident that it had emerged immediately beneath the Great Pyramid. Of course it wasn't an accident.

Had the pyramid, then, been built to block it, or perhaps to conceal it?

These were mysteries, but the even greater mystery was, what was it for? Clearly, it was the product of an advanced technology—and not only that, a very old one. The Giza Plateau had not been disturbed in thousands of years. Certainly, nothing this large had been buried here after the pyramids were built.

It was old, it had to be, but its construction must have presented more than just a structural challenge. The energy needed to blast all of those stones into the sky would have to be enormous. And yet, in all the years that the ground beneath the pyramid complex had been probed with tunnels and shafts, and examined with sonar and radar, no sign of the lens or of any sort of explosive device had been observed.

In fact, very little had been found. In the 1950s, the two so-called "solar boats" had been found buried in the boat-pits along the southern side of the Great Pyramid. But nothing else had ever been located—a few shadowy areas that suggested caves, but that was all.

God, but look at it! Gleaming in the light. Ominous as it could be.

The air was filled with the mourning of sirens. He thought of the British Empire as being ramshackle and overextended, but the Cairo Emergency Service was certainly well supplied with vehicles. He wondered about the hospitals, though. Had they as yet extended the National Health System to the protectorates, as well as the outright colonies? He didn't know, but if not, then the hospitals here were liable to be primitive and he was damned lucky not to have been hurt.

Even his ears had stopped ringing.

He turned away, unwilling—or unable—to stare any longer at the gaping dark eye that had replaced that great wonder. Eternal pyramid, built for the ages.

How long had it taken to destroy it? No more than five minutes.

He'd started back downstairs when he hesitated. This was a nightmare of some kind. He wasn't awake.

But he was.

He turned back, and there it was again. Nothing to call it but a lens. Huge, glaring darkly upward at sky into which it had spit the pyramid.

As old as it must be, it seemed perfect, fresh and new, come up out of the earth like some demon's eye that had opened after a sleep that had crossed the ages.

Which was exactly what had happened.

ONE
NOVEMBER 22
DANCING IN THE DARK

GENERAL ALFRED WILLIAM NORTH ENTERED his superior officer's luxurious suite in the Pentagon. General Samson had been appointed Chairman of the Joint Chiefs of Staff last year, and had taken Al with him into the stratospheric world of high-level military politics.

General Samson's orderly had not been present to announce him. Given the present state of chaos within the military, that wasn't too surprising. He was probably on some detail or other within the vast building, and there hadn't been anybody available to spell him.

They were due at the White House in ten minutes, so Al didn't stand on ceremony. Knocking once, he entered the office. Al had met Tom Samson when he'd been promoted to Air Force Chief of Staff. He'd been a very efficient officer, and personable.

That, however, turned out to apply only to superior officers. Now that he was Chairman of the Joint Chiefs and Al was still vice chairman, things had changed. Tom was a cold, charmless yeller, he was intolerant of failure, he was extremely demanding. Al still believed him to be a good officer, but his approach to the job was often too rigid. Truth to tell, Al had expected this promotion to be his. Counted on it, actually. What had happened had been a serious humiliation and a sad end to a great career. He had known the president for years, and he could not understand why he'd chosen Tom over him, frankly. He'd carried out his responsibilities with excellence.

The difference between the two of them was that Tom had served in fighters and Al had trained in them but served his entire career as a staff officer. Tom had a Purple Heart and an Air Medal. Did Al, who had never heard a shot fired in anger, envy Tom his participation in the Cuban Troubles?

Short answer: damn right. If it had been him, his career would not have stopped just short of the pinnacle.

"Tom, I'm here," he said. Tentatively.

Silence.

The bathroom door was ajar, so Al walked toward it. "Tom?" he repeated.

There came a shuffle of sound from inside the bathroom.

"Excuse me," Tom replied, an angry challenge in his rumble.

"Tom, I'm sorry, Lenny's not out front—"

"Get out of here!"

"Sorry!"

As Al headed for the door, he noticed, open on Tom's desk, a silver box about the size of an old-fashioned cigarette case. Inside were six narrow golden cylinders. Lying beside them was a hypodermic, silver, that tapered seamlessly from a wide back with a socket in it that would obviously fit one of the cylinders, to a needle with a point so fine it almost appeared hairlike.

Al hurried out, his mind racing. That outfit—was he an addict of some sort? A cancer victim? And what strange looking equipment.

A moment later, Tom slammed his office door with such force that the entire room shook.

Al hardly heard. If Tom was an addict, very frankly, that could be good. Worth knowing.

At that point, Lenny reappeared.

"General, let me announce you," he said.

"He knows I'm here."

Lenny went white. "He does?"

Al nodded. Nothing more was said, and a moment later Tom strode out, resplendent in his uniform, his gray eyes staring straight ahead, his face expressionless.

Lenny snapped to attention.

"We need to talk," Tom snarled at him as he passed his desk.

"Yessir!"

"You bet, yes sir, young fella." He went stomping off into the outer part of the suite.

Al followed him, and together they descended in his private elevator to the basement garage, where his staff car awaited them, rear door open. All of this was done in silence. In point of fact, you just plain did not talk to Tom unless he spoke first. He wasn't responsive to social chatter, jokes, gossip—anything like that. In fact, the most amazing thing about him was that he held this most political of all military appointments. How the bastard had managed it, every single general on his staff would have loved to know—if only to help find a way to hurt him.

Historically, the Joint Chiefs was a solid, smooth-running organization. Not under Tom. Tom had made it into a rat's nest full of spider webs. Men who had worked together for years now fought like what they were—creatures in a trap.

In the year since Tom had come, there had been five "resignations." All, in fact, firings, brutal, mean spirited, often mysterious. Worse, they had been followed by vindictive little appointments to posts designed to humiliate the victims. General Halff had been Army Chief of Staff. He was now serving out his time as commander of Fort Silker in Mississippi. Fort Silker was being decommissioned, so Harry's basic job was to arrange for environmental cleanup and the sale of assets.

Al settled into the car. He knew that this meeting was important, but he wasn't quite sure what it was about. He supposed that Tom knew, but Tom wasn't saying. Perhaps Al was on the chopping block. Perhaps Al was due to be caught unprepared in front of the president, a certain prelude to destruction.

Except for one thing: Al had known James Hannah Wade since they were roomies at the Academy. In recent years, the friendship had necessarily become arm's-length, but the two men were still close enough that Jimmy would on occasion invite Al to hammer squash balls with him. This usually happened when the going in this very difficult presidency got really rough. But Jimmy was flying high right now, so no squash with his old friend. And, as both of them knew, betrayed friend.

The car turned onto Fourteenth Street, headed past the familiar emerald arches of a McDonald's, then entered the White House grounds.

"We're listening today," Tom said. "An intelligence report."

"What's the general area, sir?"

Tom turned toward him, then turned back again. A moment later, the car stopped, and they were walking through the White House to the Cabinet Room—but then they passed the Cabinet Room and the Oval and headed through Deputy Chief of Staff Morrisey's office into the Presidential Study.

It was an improbable place for a large meeting—except that it wasn't a large meeting.

"Hi, Al," the president said. Al could feel Tom stiffen. Good sign, maybe the president had finally realized that the appointment had been the mistake that Al had told him it was—practically the only political thought he'd ever shared with him. He turned to Tom. "Good morning, General."

"Good morning, Mr. President."

A moment later, National Intelligence Chief Bo Waldo came in, followed by two aides, who proceeded to hover over the TV.

Waldo spoke. "Yesterday, there was a massive explosion in Cairo that resulted in at least a hundred thousand deaths and property damage on an extraordinary scale. The explosion destroyed the Pyramid of Cheops."

"And?" Tom snapped.

The president gave him a sharp look.

But his impatience was understandable. The Cairo disaster was on every news channel in the world. You couldn't find anything else on TV, radio, the Internet—you name it. Al thought, *they know the terrorist group responsible, and they're about to inform us that the Brits are going in with a hit.* We were being asked to provide some sort of support, no doubt, and the problem with this kind of thing was always the same: how did you do what one empire wanted without angering another?

Waldo cleared his throat. "We haven't had another one in half an hour, Mr. President," he said.

Al's mind whirled. *Another one?* What was he saying, here?

"How many are there, at this point?"

"Including the one that just came up in Cambodia, that would be fourteen."

Al wanted to ask what in the world they were talking about, but he couldn't without revealing his ignorance. Tom's glare showed that he was thinking along exactly the same lines. The Joint Chiefs controlled no fewer than five uniformed intelligence services, in addition to the Philippines Colonial Agency and the Cuban Intelligence Corps, so how was it that they hadn't been briefed by their own people? Tom would want that looked at, and for once Al would be in total agreement with him. It was an inexcusable lapse.

The president said, "And they're all—it's the same? Distance, all that?"

"Each one is exactly six thousand two hundred twenty miles from an axis point eleven hundred miles from the north pole. They've all appeared in the middle of ancient ruins. The Institut Indo-Chinois de Culture has already started testing the one in Preah Vihear. Thus far, it has a hardness number of at least three thousand, just like Cairo. Clearly, the same substance, and by far the hardest thing on earth. The only weapon that might affect these objects would be a hydrogen bomb."

"Do we have any of those?"

"We do, Sir," Tom said. "Well hidden from Royal Air Force mandatory inspections, but we do."

The Brits were rigorous enforcers of the Non-Nuclear Pact between the five empires, of which the U.S. was the smallest and the most lightly armed—and therefore the only one that actually needed to obey the damned pact. Certainly, the French didn't. And as far as the Czar was concerned or the secretive Japanese Emperor, who knew what they might be doing in their hidden lairs? There might even be a Chinese warlord with a nuke of some sort.

The president went to the window. "I've worried about one coming up here in Washington. Should I?"

"Unless there's another phase," Waldo responded, "this thing has the look of being completed. But you know, of course, what's odd—every single location was an ancient sacred site."

"So they knew," the president said, turning suddenly, staring first at one of them and then another.

Al saw a plea in his eye, as if the American people were there, pleading through him for knowledge.

"Lenses," Al said. Tom gave him a sharp look, but he continued. "Lenses reflect and they refract. Do we have any idea which it is that these are supposed to do?"

Waldo shook his head. "So far, they're simply there. According to MI-3, the one in Cairo isn't emitting or absorbing any known energy. The Institut says the same about the one in Cambodia."

"Any idea if they're natural, then?"

"We don't think they're natural, Mr. President." Waldo replied.

"But it's a good question," Al said. "If they're manmade, who constructed them and why?"

"That is an urgent question," President Wade snapped. "Possibly the most urgent question in the history of the world." He looked from one of them to the other. "You seem unimpressed, Tom."

"Sir, if we don't know anything about them, how can we make that assessment?"

The president stiffened. "It's instinct, goddamn it!"

"There's something else you need to see," Waldo said hurriedly. "Roll the imagery, please."

The TV screen flickered, came to life. Al saw people walking through a rather pretty countryside. They were dressed oddly, some in nightclothes, others in underwear, one or two in coats, one completely naked. There were men, women, and children.

The group was being followed by green and white checked police cars, with their blue light bars flickering.

"What are we looking at, here?" President Wade asked.

"This is in Gloucestershire," Waldo said.

"Shot when?"

"It's live," Waldo replied. "During the night, these people were struck by a bright light that emanated from objects overhead that were disk-shaped in structure. They've been walking due north ever since. They've come fourteen miles in eleven hours."

"Are these things related to the disks we've been seeing for years? The ones NASA claims are intelligently controlled?"

"We don't know. We really don't know much of anything."

"Bottom line, though, these people can't be stopped, am I right?" Tom asked, his voice full of sarcasm.

"They cannot be stopped, General Samson," Waldo snapped back. "They can be demobilized only by being drugged. An examination of one of them completed at a hospital in the area showed a normal physical specimen. But a brain scan revealed a different picture. The brain function was about a third normal."

"They've lost something, then," Tom responded. "Their intelligence?"

"We don't know," Waldo replied.

"Do we have any imagery of the attack?" the president asked.

"Witnesses report disks glowing dull orange."

Al had a thought. "Where is the nearest lens, in relation to Gloucestershire?"

"What relevance does that have?" Tom asked. "If I may be so bold, General?"

"No, it's a good question," Waldo replied, "and the answer is, the nearest lens in the Tassili Desert in Algeria. And what I was about to add is that there's a Foreign Legion report that a burst of orange fireballs was emitted from the lens there. But the event took place just four minutes before the Gloucestershire attack, so—"

"They're related," Al said. Instantly, he regretted it. He'd spoken in haste.

"General, I fail to see—" Tom began.

The president interrupted him. "I agree. Whether the things that struck in Gloucestershire came out of the lens in Algeria, God only knows. But there is obviously a relationship of some kind between all of these things—the disks we've been seeing for fifty years, the ones that attacked those people, and the lenses, and I might add that I think we need to assume the worst, here."

"All I see are British and French problems," Samson said. "Unless some of these things are in the Japanese Empire. Are they?"

"No, so far only British and French imperial territory is involved, and some South American countries."

"Then I say we wait," Tom announced, his voice taking on the tone of the pulpit. "Maybe it's some kind of a secret weapon. Nothing to do with us. The Czar's supposed to have some doozies, and he wants African possessions. He'd like Egypt, in fact, to annoy the Turks, if nothing else."

The president turned on him. "Why are you here, Tom? Why in hell do you think you're here? Something is wrong. *Goddamn* wrong." He gestured at the screen. "This will spread, you know."

Tom held his ground. "We have no evidence of that, Sir."

"It will spread!"

"It's not an attack on the United States. And there's no evidence that such an attack is imminent."

"Tom," the president responded, "as soon as you get back to your office, you are to go to DEFCON 1 and issue a War Warning to all commands, worldwide."

"Sir, I—"

"We're under attack, you damn fool," the president said. "The blue, white, and red, damn you! Not just a couple of the empires and a few banana kingdoms. Us!"

Tom went stiff. His eyes seemed literally to glitter with murderous rage.

But the president wasn't finished. "Gentlemen, I've got a military background, and I know when my enemy is probing my defenses. That's what happened in that little town in the very heart of the most powerful empire on earth. Bo, I want you to liaise with the Brits, the French, all the empires on this, and I want CIA to watch the streets worldwide for other, similar incidents."

Al could smell the fear in the room, and found himself hoping that President Wade was not acting in the haste of panic.

"Al, you're to organize a task force. You are ordered to find a way to destroy those lenses, all of them. I want it fast, and I want a one hundred percent certainty of success."

"Sir," Tom asked, "is an attack on them wise? We're in the region of the unknown here."

"The man with the medals suggests retreat," the president said. "Okay, I hear you. Al, when you're ready to attack these things, inform me at once. Directly." He pointed to a telephone. "Directly," he repeated.

"Yes, Sir. We only have four bombs, Sir. We'll need British and French support."

The president sighed. "Waldo, how many nuclear bombs do I have?"

"Twenty-three, Sir. Four in the hands of the military, the rest underground at—"

"Tom, Al, you understand that you had no need to know on this."

"Sir, I beg to differ," Tom said. Al could see that his neck was red, his veins pulsing. "We had a need to know. Strategic planning, war games—of course we had a need to know!"

"And I have a need not to find myself face to face with a quartet of outraged imperial ambassadors all demanding that I hand over my nukes. You leak, Tom. Nobody on your staff likes you, and that makes for security issues, doesn't it?"

Al fought his face. The least trace of the smile that his enjoyment of this was urging to his lips would get him fired before sunset.

One of Waldo's aides listened to his earpiece. He nodded to the intelligence chief.

Waldo said, "Mr. President, we have a party present at this time who might be able to help us. There was an archaeologist inside the pyramid as the explosion developed. His working party was killed, but he got out. He's here."

"Excellent work, Bo," the president said. "Now, you listen and learn, Tom. Bo here wants to impress his president. This is what I like to see. You might take that under advisement."

Tom bristled, then plastered a rigid grin on his face. A dusty young man, handsome but looking profoundly exhausted, came wide-eyed into the room.

MARTIN HAD BEEN GIVEN EGGS and a whole lot of coffee on the plane. It was quite incredible—Air Force private jets all the way from Cairo to Le Bourget, then here. He had been able to talk to Lindy and the kids via videophone from the plane. In normal times, incredibly fun. Now, not so fun. He was heartsick about what had happened, still trying to accept it as reality. The Great Pyramid, gone, replaced by that . . . thing. Lens, they called it—he'd called it that, in fact, for the BBC, which had interviewed him just before he left Cairo. In fact, he'd probably started the use of the word.

Now here he was in the White House, in the West Wing, no less. He was a reeking mess, he supposed. Nobody had bothered him with such niceties as a change of clothes or a shower. He still had Giza dust in his hair, as a matter of fact.

A man in a black suit took him to a book-lined study. He'd hoped to see the Oval Office, but this was apparently the inner sanctum of the Great American Fool, President Jimmy Wade. He'd gutted National Academy of Science budgets, he'd pulled grant money out of dozens of universities, Uriah included. He was a man willing to spend billions supporting American trade associations in their perpetual war with the larger imperial economic systems, but his education program was a sham, his entitlement system was a mess, and his interest in the sciences appeared to be, if anything, negative.

Under Wade, even NASA's exobiology and alien culture programs were languishing, and now that it was known that UFOs were intelligently guided, these two programs seemed to be doing some of the most important science in the world. Not to mention the Advanced Propulsion Physics Seminar.

Still, he was the president, the leader of the American people and one of the more powerful world leaders, and seeing him here, all human and vulnerable, was an odd experience. He came to his feet and put out his hand. Martin shook it, and looked into the strange, empty eyes of the professional leader.

Another man, bald, big—dominating the room, in fact, despite the presence of two resplendent generals—pumped his hand, drew him past the president, and sat him down. "We know you've had a shock," he murmured. His hands were soft, his eyes were not full of fear like the president's. They sparkled. They watched. Martin recognized Bo Waldo, of course, he was all over the news all the time.

"Doctor Winters—may I call you Marty—"

"Martin."

"Okay, Martin is a distinguished member of our country's archaeological community. He's managed to cause a small revolution of his own."

It wasn't small, it was huge, but Martin couldn't say that.

"You lived through the pyramid?" the president asked. "Where were you, because I've been in that thing, and it's not easy to get around."

"I was in the burial chamber a hundred feet beneath the surface."

"How could you have been there and survived?" one of the generals asked. This was a man with a narrow, almost cruel face, and small, ugly eyes, gleaming as black as obsidian.

Martin decided not to even address the question, it was so impertinent and, frankly, so stupid.

"What General Samson means is—"

"I meant what I asked, Al!"

The other general went instantly silent. Obviously, the tall man with the mane of white hair was the lesser of the two. He had a better face, aquiline, aristocratic, and, Martin thought, sad.

"I survived because I was so deep. We picked up unusual pulsations about three minutes before the structure blew, so I had time to withdraw."

"Doctor Winters, if I tell you that these same lenses have appeared around the world at fourteen different sites, all the exact same distance from an axis point near the north pole—"

The room became distant, the voices like memories.

"Doctor Winters?"

He fought to pull himself together. The first one of them he saw was the beady-eyed general, gazing at him like a guard might at a dangerous prisoner. He swallowed, looked around for water, saw none. "All right," he said, "I know what that would be. That's the Sacred Circle. You'd have Ollantaytambo, Easter Island, Preah Vihear—are you telling me that all of these sites have been destroyed?"

"All," the president said. "Our interest is this. Are these lenses a matter for concern, as I certainly think they are. If so, would you be willing to speculate on defense implications?"

Wade was portrayed by the media as an idiot, but that was an impressive question. "Sir, we know that there was some sort of advanced civilization on earth fifteen thousand years ago, that abruptly disappeared in a catastrophe. All of those sites except the pyramid are later structures built at specific geodesic points. The why of that, we have never known."

The snake-like General Samson almost spat his words. "I think this is largely speculation."

"General Samson," the president retorted, "you're here to gather information that'll help you execute your orders. Thank you, General."

"This man's work is highly controversial," Samson snapped.

"Actually, um, it's not," Martin said.

"Well, I read my share of science journals and I say it is!"

Martin didn't know how to react to a yelling general. It made him mad, though, the rudeness of it.

The president asked, "Doctor Winters, tell us what you think these lenses might be?"

"From strictly an archaeological point of view, I don't know. But if you read old chronicles, a lens like this could have been the mechanism of destruction."

"Of what?"

"The civilization. It ended in a day, you know. In a matter of minutes. It happened on an afternoon in June, actually. Over five minutes, perhaps a little less."

That silenced even the blustering general.

"What is our risk now?"

Martin recognized his responsibility here. "I've been, frankly, a little thrown, here. I—you know—the shock, and now this . . ."

"Let me rephrase," the president said. "Do you see a possible risk now, and, if so, on what do you base your speculation? Is that a little easier to handle?"

"There is a calendar—the Mayan—that marks the end of this age as being this coming December 21. The winter solstice occurs on the day earth crosses both the galactic equator and the solar ecliptic. A highly unusual conjunction."

"What's so absurd about this," Samson said, "is that it assumes that the ancient Maya knew about galaxies. A bunch of blood-soaked headhunters. The very idea is ridiculous."

Martin decided that he loathed this man, a rare intensity of emotion for him. He reserved his intensity for love of wife and kids. He did not indulge hate. But General Samson invited it. "The date is there," he said. "And no matter what the Maya knew or didn't know, the position of the earth is there, too."

"What does it mean," the president asked. "You're telling me a whole human civilization was killed in a day, Doctor. What should that be saying to me in the here and now?"

An aide finally produced water and Martin drank all of it at once. "I've still got the desert in my throat," he said.

"All right," the good general said. "You can do this, you can say it."

"Yes. This prophecy—the 2012 thing—it's always been a mystery that it was so exact. And it required tremendous calculational ability— the whole Mayan long-count calendar—and apparently a knowledge of the position of the earth in relation to the rest of the galaxy—and I'm sorry if that gives offense—"

"Which astrophysicists are still arguing about," Samson said.

"Tom, will you stop interrupting him?"

"I'm trying to help, here, Mr. President!"

"Doctor Winters, please continue," the president said.

Martin swallowed. His throat was dry again. He was not used to in- tensity like this. There was terror in every eye, and the stink of sweat rising in the room. "Yes. I'm looking at these things coming up out of the ground, and thinking about the fact that so many ancient cultures speak of beings that came through gateways—"

"Aliens, as per NASA?"

"Not aliens, as from another planet. Given the distances involved, present thought leans more in the direction of UFOs being projections of some sort from parallel universe or universes. All right here, right around us. Now."

"Aw, come on! Mr. President, we don't need this kind of speculation," Samson said.

The president exploded. "General, for God's sakes, will you shut up!"

Samson would not be silenced. "I think this man needs to be re- moved, he's obstructing—"

"You listen to him, Tom, god damn you!" The president roared.

Samson's mouth snapped shut.

"Go on, Doctor," Bo Waldo said softly.

"Uh, the, uh—the Sumerians called them Annunaki, the Babylonians Akpallus, the Hebrews Nephilim—the list is long. Always, they were powerful, dominating people—somewhat human looking, but with a reptilian cast of eye—who came from another reality. Some were hos- tile, others more benevolent. Almost as if there were two warring fac- tions, with different agendas for us. They fought among themselves, at one point, and then were no longer present here."

"And this relates to our situation?"

"Maybe the reason that the end-of-world predictions in the old calendars are so exact is that there is something in the astrophysical situation that opens these gateways. Maybe that's what the lenses are. If so, then we can expect that they're the worst things it is possible to imagine."

Silence.

He didn't say it, but as he spoke the words, they just tasted right. He paused, then decided to take the plunge. "Um, I would therefore say that a machine has been turned on. I think, between now and December the twenty-first, we can expect them to become increasingly active, and on that day, to destroy human civilization. Attempt to."

The president stood up, went to the window. "Bo?"

"Sir, we don't have any information like that."

"Tom?"

"This is—I can't call it a fantasy, obviously. The things are there. But I think we need to wait a little longer. If we have to fight, we also need to know what to fight, and how."

"Al, I want to revise your orders. I want you to do the following. You execute a nuclear strike against the most isolated of these things—"

Tom Samson leaped to his feet. "That's out of the question!"

"Tom, you already have your orders."

"Sir, not if I'm seeing this dangerous, impetuous tack you're taking—no, sir, I will not!"

"Al, will you execute?"

"Sir, I'm a notch down in the chain."

"I want you people to understand something here. I am not hearing what I need to hear. And I'm not just going to be asking for resignations. In just another minute, I'm going to be carrying out arrests. Here. My Secret Service, your ass!" He glared straight at Tom, and Martin thought that he would not like to be in that man's shoes.

Al came to his feet. "Sir, I'll get the strike going at once."

"And you'll continue to fulfill your oath, Tom?"

"As I understand it."

" 'I will faithfully execute lawful orders . . .' That's the part that's relevant here."

"Sir, I will issue the alerts and the War Warning. But I urge you to address this other matter to the National Security Council and to Robbie. Don't leave your Secretary of Defense in the dark. And for God's sake, let the British and the French know—all the empires. Don't surprise them, Sir."

"Nobody's gonna be in the dark," the president muttered. "Now, let me tell you something incredible. You know what I have to do right now? I have to go out into the Rose Garden and slap a smile on my kisser and pardon a goddamn turkey! Happy Thanksgiving."

He left the room, and Martin thought he would follow that man anywhere. He had completely revised his opinion of the president. He was smart, decisive, and a master of the art of managing powerful men like the ones in this room.

They followed him out. Martin was left behind, completely forgotten. His role in this meeting would probably be lost to history, but he understood what he had done. If they were going to stop what was about to happen, immediate, decisive action was essential.

It had been a year since NASA had made its announcement about UFOs, and he wondered, now, if that had been a good idea. If they were aliens from another planet, it appeared a harmless enough thing to say. But if parallel universes were involved, whether or not we believed they were real might have a lot to do with their ability to enter our world. The mind might play a part here, a very unsuspected part. Our belief might be essential to their ability to use their gateway, meaning that NASA could have unwittingly opened a door that had been closed by the wisdom of the past, then sealed with the sacred sites that had just been destroyed.

He pulled out his cell phone. Would there be a signal in this place? Yes, good. He called Lindy. "I'm coming home, baby."

"I thought you were on a plane!"

"I took a detour. A quite incredible detour." He looked around, saw a man in the doorway, a Secret Service agent, apparently his minder. "Excuse me, I need to get to Kansas City," he said.

"National Airport. TAT and Braniff both go to K.C."

"Actually, I was brought here on an Air Force jet, and I thought—"

The agent smiled. "Our job was to get you here. You're here."

"And that's it?"

"That's it."

"Martin, what's going on?" Lindy asked. "Who are you talking to?"

"I'll call you from the airport, let you know when I'm getting in."

He swallowed the terror that had been building in him. He just hoped to God he could make it home, that there was still time.

TWO
DECEMBER 6
THE LAST GOOD NIGHT OF WYLIE DALE

WYLIE DALE TRIED TO STOP shaking, could not. He thought he might be more scared right now than he ever had been in his life. He was exhausted, his story had been running through his mind like some kind of out-of-control hallucination and he thought that it was not a story, it was real.

This was because of the fact that he'd been unable to stop his hands from hitting the keys. He'd watched them like an outsider. No control.

At least they were no longer moving. He glanced over at the clock. "Holy shit!"

"What?" came Brooke's sleepy voice from the bedroom.

"I'll be there in a sec."

Wiley had been in front of his laptop writing for an incredible sixteen hours. He knew what had been written, but not as if he had been the author. It wasn't creation, it was transcription. He wasn't creating a novel, he was writing a history and it was a very scary history and he was afraid it was real, and it wasn't just a history, it was a warning.

He turned on the little TV set that sat on the corner of his desk. He watched Fox News for a while, then went up to MSNBC, then back down to CNN.

Just more of the usual bullshit, an actor gunned down by a posse of outraged fans, a combination hailstorm, tornado, and flood that seemed to have flattened every trailer park in Arkansas. The European empires were gone, and there was nothing about any weird lenses coming up out of the ground anywhere at all, and certainly not under the Great Pyramid.

He flipped through what he'd written—and found over fifty pages.

What the hell, you don't write like this, nobody does.

What in God's name had happened to him? It's hard to create fiction, it takes hours, sometimes, to get a single sentence out.

His damn knuckles hurt from the pounding.

He read more. If this wasn't fiction, then what was it? There was no President Wade, there was only one moon in the sky, and there was certainly no czar.

This was reality from a parallel universe, somehow bleeding over into a susceptible mind—his.

The creatures he'd seen in his woods five years ago—the subject of his notorious book *Alien Days*—had been scaly, and Martin had described the ancient biblical Nephilim as having a reptilian appearance. There was nothing like that in our Bible, but he'd certainly seen scaly faces, right here in these woods, not a quarter of a mile from here.

Brooke slipped into the room and put her hand on his cheek. "Wiley, it's time to come to bed."

The spell broke, and his body took over. It had been in this chair for a damn long time, and there was a bladder involved and the bladder had just come to its senses.

He ran like hell.

"Wiley?"

He hit the john just in time and opened up. "Thank you, God."

She followed him in. "What's the matter with you?"

"Nothing, now!"

"You've been in there since breakfast, do you realize that?"

He finished his business, opened the medicine cabinet, and drank a couple of slugs of Mylanta. Chased it with Pepto Bismol. "Nectar of the gods," he said.

"It's late, it's time to go to bed." She caressed him from behind.

"I need a breath of air. I'm gonna take a walk."

"The book is making you crazy."

"No."

"Yeah, it is, and I'm not ready to go through that again, Wiley. That alien book, that was enough for one lifetime."

She referred, of course, to the hated *Alien Days*. He hated it, too, for that matter. It wasn't fun, being a laughingstock. "The book I'm writing is not about aliens."

"I know you, Wylie Dale, it's about something weird or you wouldn't be so crazed. No more saucer crap, that's bedrock, boy!"

"It isn't about aliens, and neither was the other book. I only thought it was."

"*Alien Days* was about a writer being very crazy in public. Embarrassment, that's what it was about."

"There are no aliens."

"At last, he faces the truth."

"What's happening is much stranger than the arrival of aliens from another planet. And this book, it's—wow—it's possessing me."

"You write fiction that you come to believe is real and in the process you drive this entire family crazy, and I'm sorry, no more."

"Brooke—"

"No more! End of story! Books that possess you, that drive you nuts—no, I'm finished, I've had it!"

"Mom? Dad?"

Nicholas appeared, looking bleary and pissed off.

"Wonderful," Wiley said.

Brooke said to their son, "Dad has a sour stomach."

"You're fighting."

"I love your mom too much to fight with her. I just obey." He made a steeple of his hands and bowed toward her.

"Except you don't, Daddy." Now Kelsey had arrived, his gorgeous little girl. "He has cigars hidden in the woods."

"That is not true!"

Brooke folded her arms. So did Kelsey. Brooke glared. "The aliens you go looking for in the woods, Wiley Dale? Would they be from Cuba?"

"The cigars are Matt's," he said.

"And he's out there right now, isn't he, smoking a Monte and sucking on a bottle of Beam, and that's the real reason you want to take a walk—to make yourself sick on cigars and hootch."

"Cubans are the best cigars in the world."

"You're coming to bed with me. And scoot, you two, the sandman's gonna be furious."

"I'm past the sandman," Nick said.

"I'm not," Kelsey told him. "I'm just a little girl, and I still believe."

"Meaning, don't rain on your sister's parade."

"No, Sir."

Wiley went into the bedroom and fished his flashlight out from under the bed where he kept it alongside his shotgun. "I need some space, hon. This thing I'm writing, it's getting to me, for sure, and I agree with you, we need that not to happen. It's about us and about people who live in another version of this house in a parallel universe. I think that's what it's about, anyway. I'm sort of more of a reader than a writer, here. Reading as my fingers write, as it were."

"About us in what sense?"

"Well, like this conversation. This will be in the book. Because we're part of the story, somehow. I'm not sure how, yet, but we're part of it."

"Not our names again!"

Uh-oh. He had to tread carefully here. "Well, uh . . . hm. The people in the parallel universe aren't us. They have different names. They live in their version of this house and the town is called Harrow, too, but the people are not the same."

"I am so tired of this."

"Whoa, slow down. The parallel universe is obviously different. Their McDonald's has emerald arches. Their Target target is blue. The president's named James Hannah Wade and the family's named Winters. We're the Dales, if you hadn't noticed. And here, McDonald's has golden arches, obviously. Plus there is no British Empire, among numerous other things. They have two small moons rather than one large one."

"In the part of it that's set in our universe, what are the characters' names?"

She knew him well and she was not dumb. Far from dumb. "Well, of course, I'm using ours—"

"NO!"

"Well, uh, it's us. They're us."

"My kids' names will not be in another one of your books. You know what Nicholas said? He said you really are the most embarrassing father in the world, and he was right! Saying you were taken aboard a UFO was bad enough, but you included him! When he was all of seven years old. Wiley, where do you get off?"

"The names are—are—like, they're just place markers. After I'm done, I'll change them."

"Because it's an act of vanity to write novels about yourself!"

"Brooke, goddamnit, that's a betrayal. You know it happened."

"It hurt this family so much, honey. I just can't go through it again. The kids can't. Especially not your son. He is so brave but he suffers."

"What do you mean?"

"The kids eat him alive! His dad got a rectal probe. You try living that down at the age of twelve."

"The laughter is the failure, not the book. It happened." He paused. "It just wasn't what I thought." There came to him, then, a feeling—a sort of pull, really. To go back to the office, to sit down . . .

But not after sixteen straight hours, he'd be in heart attack country. Stroke country.

"Thing is, this book—I'm not its author, babes, I'm its prisoner."

"You will be responsible, Wylie Dale. You *will* be!"

"All right, that's it! I'm going walking. You'll be asleep when I get back, God willing."

"If I smell the least trace of cigar smoke—"

"Kelsey's gotta have Indian blood, the way she follows me and I never see her. But neither one of us is an Indian, my dear, so how do you explain that?"

"By the fact that you're two hundred percent hot air and half baked." She came to him. "Which are two of the many reasons that I'm so damn crazy about you."

She kissed him. He was furious at her, but he kissed her back, and she felt so vulnerable and so—so Brooke. He held her tight.

Noisy though it was, this marriage was a good fit for Wiley Dale. He needed someone willing to come up the side of his head on occasion, and Brooke had no compunction about that. But he was not going to change any names in any part of the book, this one included. "You're so nice," he said.

Little feet went scurrying away. Kelsey could be heard whispering, "We have a kiss. Gawd!"

Wylie and Brooke managed to swallow their laughter.

When he went downstairs, she sort of tried to stop him, but he promised to come back soon. He really did need that air. If he didn't get away from that keyboard and let this thing die down, he'd be up all night.

He left the house, glad to enter his familiar woods beneath the familiar starry sky—and that good old moon up there, good old friend. It couldn't be very romantic to have two moons.

He sucked the air deep to rid his head of the fog that the writing had invoked. He shuddered. It was a mild night, but he felt cold in his blood.

He had lived Martin's sense of suffocation down under the pyramid, had cringed in anguish of terror with him as the blocks smashed down around him, had *actually not known* whether or not he was going to be annihilated.

Creepy enough, but even creepier was the fact that he could still feel Martin's presence. See him, sort of. He was down in Harrow, and things had gone very bad since his visit to the White House just—what was it—eleven or twelve days ago?

He was down in Harrow and he was living in absolutely amazing terror, and Wylie knew that, as soon as he returned to his office, he was going to live that terror, too.

Thing was, he could sort of see into the lenses, and what he saw there was another parallel earth, a third one, and it was bad news. Real bad.

He couldn't see it clearly, but he could feel that it was a fallen world, a real, living hell, and it was seeking to escape itself. He could sense its ravening hunger to escape the ruin it had made of itself.

Amazingly enough, they'd done even worse than we had. "They're old," he muttered to himself, returning to one of the lines of thought that he'd been worrying for years. He thought he might now know the secret of the bizarre creatures he had encountered in these woods a few years back, that were the subject of *Alien Days*. They weren't aliens at all. They were *from here*. But in their version of earth, the dinosaurs had never gone extinct. Instead, that dark reptilian brain had grown and evolved and changed until these sleek creatures had come about—tough, brilliant, and utterly heartless.

Oh, God. God help the human beings.

With our compassion and our softness of spirit, we were not going to be a match for brilliant reptiles, not in Martin's universe or in this one.

They were going to take it all. They really, really were.

The woods were dead quiet, the early December night touched by just an edge of crispness. As always, he found himself moving along the old foresters path that crossed the top of the little draw where, five years ago almost to the day, he'd noticed that odd light.

He stopped, looked down the draw. He had encountered them just there, just fifty feet down. It had looked like an old witch's cottage that he'd never seen before. Glowing, infinitely sinister.

Curious, thinking maybe he had squatters in his woods, he'd walked up to it, and the next thing he knew, he was grabbed by scaly hands, he was being glared at by the most terrible eyes he had ever seen, he was being manhandled—and yes, the infamous rectal probe had taken place—and then he was on the ground, the little cottage was gone, and there was a crackling electricity in the air.

At least, that's what he remembered in his conscious mind. His dreams were a different story. In his dreams, there were towering emotions of loss and longing, and Brooke was involved, but she had sworn that she'd seen nothing that night, heard nothing.

He moved up the dark path, shining his light ahead, looking for the cigar cave. A smoke was what he needed. He had a gargle station in the garage, which he'd use before he got in bed with Brooke. Cigar breath and he'd be on the couch, and he was way too tired for that.

He shone his light on the trees that loomed around him, the oaks with their golden leaves, the red maples, the gnarled pitch pines that began to appear as he climbed farther up the ridge.

He was maybe fifty yards from the cave when he became aware of a more solid shape up ahead.

He stopped, peered into the dark. Matt was on duty tonight, so maybe it was a deer. And yet, the form—it looked like a man standing real close to the trunk of that oak.

Oh, shit, what if the reptilians knew that he was writing about their invasion, and they didn't like it?

Hardly daring to do it, his hands shaking so much he could barely manage it, he got the flashlight pointed in the direction of the figure.

—which did not move.

Was it a branch? What *was* that?

He stepped closer. "Hello?"

It leaped out at him.

He fell back, he lost the light, and then the figure was on him, glaring down at him—and laughing.

"Godddamn it!"

"Oh, man, Wiley, Wiley, oh Christ, this is rich! It's rich!"

Wiley got to his feet. "You call yourself a cop? Out here wasting tax-payer money like this—what if there's a lost kitten or something down in the town? What *will* you do?"

"That flashlight! How many batteries in that thing?"

"A few."

"Beka says to me, who's got a searchlight up on the ridge behind the Dale's house? That's what it looks like. I mean, they were concerned over in Holcomb, they thought we had a fire goin' up this way."

"Holcomb is fifteen miles from here."

"I rest my case."

"You saw my flashlight from your house?"

"Absolutely."

"And you got out here in what—five minutes? I don't think so. You've been out here for a while, because you're raiding the Cubans, you shit."

"You're raiding 'em, too, you shit. Otherwise, why would you be out here yourself?"

"Bastard."

"You're the bastard, because you can afford the damn things and they're a precious luxury to a poor cop."

"I'm hardly rich."

"Your kids are in an exclusive private school in K.C. Not to mention the Jeepazine with which you convey them to said school daily."

"It's moderately customized."

"TV in a Jeep is very froufrou for rural Kansas, buddy. Look, let's go down to my wife's roadhouse and get hammered. We can take cigars with us, the place is closed, nobody's gonna know."

"Brooke's gonna get suspicious if I stay out here too long. And as for coming home drunk, that's been done one too many times."

"Man, I have to admit I'd like to be pussy-whipped by your ball and chain."

"You think?"

They began to wander back, both of them planning future cigar raids, hopefully more successful ones. The point was to smoke more than half of the cigars. The guy who did that was the winner.

As they reached the ridge that overlooked Wiley's house, he noticed, in his office, a light. It came, glowed bright, then went.

He stopped. "You see that?"

"Actually, yeah."

"Given that my family's asleep, I'm concerned."

The light came again, flickered, and was gone.

"Looks like you got a short workin' in there."

As he scrambled down the ridge to the house, Matt stayed right with him. He was a reprobate, but he was also a dutiful cop.

They arrived at the edge of Wiley's yard. His pool stood still and silent. The light flashed bright, and there was a sputtering sound from the open window.

They went in through the screen door. Matt dug the fire extinguisher out of the closet while Wiley dashed up to his office.

He looked at the desk, at the cords running down behind it. Nothing was sparking.

"So what is it?" Matt asked, coming in.

Could it have been the reptilians, maybe here to wreck the book? They'd broken through before, for sure. Sort of broken through.

Matt bent down and brought up a frayed cord. He shook it and it sparked. "Sadie do this?"

Their Burmese cat was a notorious cord chewer. "I forgot to close the door."

"She could've burned down your family, buddy."

"Thanks for helping me, Matt."

They said their good-byes, and Matt went clomping off down the stairs.

Wiley started to leave the office, but was stopped by sounds that should not be there. Footsteps. Somebody pacing in the bedroom. But Brooke was asleep.

He realized that he was hearing Lindy Winters.

Their world was not an inch away, not a millimeter. If the physicists were right, they were infinitely close, and yet it would take more energy than existed in both universes together to enable them to make contact.

Except . . . the physicists appeared to be wrong, didn't they?

Wiley sat down in his chair. He leaned back and closed his eyes, and when he did, Martin's universe seemed to settle around him, caressing him like a living, complex fog.

The lenses were hooks, and they had hooked into Martin's world, and it would not be long before they hooked into this one, too.

When he opened his eyes, nearly two hours had passed. It was nearly one. He needed to sleep, but he felt kind of sick inside, like somebody in a crashing plane would feel, waiting for the impact.

They were coming. That's what this was all about.

In the other human world, NASA had announced that UFOs were real. Apparently, that had changed the balance, enabling the reptilians to enter on a tide of belief.

So far, that did not seem like anything our NASA was likely to do.

Now he understood why the government denied the obvious UFO reality. Somebody down deep in its secret corridors must know that belief counts, that it is the oil in the hinges of the doors between the worlds.

He heard another sound, coming in from outside. Metallic. Very faint, though. What *was* that?

It came again, faded again. He went to the window, leaned against the screen, trying to hear more clearly.

And there it was again, more distinct this time, and this time he could tell what it was—the unmistakable ringing of church bells. On a good day, you could hear them from out here in the hills, but who would be ringing them at this hour?

Matt lived closer to town, maybe he could hear better.

He picked up the phone, then hesitated. It was late and he was going to make Matt mad. But how could he not? Matt was the police chief and, at the moment, the town's only cop. If somebody was ringing the bell of one of the churches, maybe it was because he couldn't make a call.

He dialed, listened.

"Yeah?"

"Hey, I wake you up?"

"I sit by the phone all night waitin' for you, you stupid fuck. So what in hell do you want?"

"Would you do me the favor of going to your window and tell me what you hear?"

" 'Course not."

"You're a cop, aren't you at least curious?"

"Not at all. Good night."

"Matt! MATT!" And suddenly it wasn't funny. *He had to know.*

"Yeah?"

"Just do it."

There was a silence. It extended. Eventually, Matt came back. "Nothing."

"You must have heard something."

"The faint plink of leaves falling. Possibly, the snuffling of a possum, or it could've been a coon."

"No church bells?"

"No, but I did hear something connected with church bells, actually. With belfries. Bats. In your belfry, squeaking like sonembitches."

"Somebody is ringing bells down there, my friend."

"You wake me up again, I'm gonna come out there and cuff your ass and put you in the tank."

"The drunk tank's rusted closed. You told me so yourself."

"For you, I will apply Liquid Wrench."

Wiley hung up. He flipped on his police scanner and watched the red LED race across the little screen. The scanner emitted a slight burp of static each time it crossed the county sheriff's carrier wave.

Lonely sound. Lonely out here.

He'd damn well heard those bells.

Not in this version of Harrow, Kansas, though. If Matt had heard them, he would have gone down into town to check things out. He was too conscientious to dismiss something as odd as that. At best, it was going to be vandals, but at worst—well, maybe a fire, who knew?

If he could sit down at the laptop—if he dared to do that—he might find out. He turned it on. His hands stirred, moved. His fingers fluttered above the keys. Then they touched them. It was like watching a machine turn on. The hands were not his.

His fingers pounded keys. Stopped.

Then he looked down at what he'd written. "The masters of the sky were on the earth in those days—and also afterward—when the sons of God went to the daughters of men and had children by them."

Was that a quote from the Bible? Or an ancient Hebrew text, maybe?

He googled the passage, came up empty.

But the masters of the sky had been the Nephilim, creatures who had come out of the air to rape and pillage, who had caused the devastating war portrayed in the ancient Indian Vedas, with their stories of sound-guided missiles, flying saucers, and nuclear bombs.

In legend, the coming of the Nephilim had marked the end of the last age.

As, indeed, according to the ancient Maya, December 21, 2012, marked the end of this one. The Mayan date 13.0.0.0.0.

All the new-age gurus were howling that it was going to completely blow the mind of man. Wiley figured it was another Y2K, when the coming of the year 2000 had been expected to cause an outbreak of chaos, but which had actually been a lot of overhyped nonsense.

When he closed his eyes, it seemed as if the office did not have his desk in it. Instead, there were two recliners with reading lights beside them. Where he kept his little TV, they had a bookcase full of science tomes, archaeology and physics. He saw the books so clearly that he could almost read the titles.

The bells were now joined by the long wail of a warning siren.

He found himself uttering a prayer for the other Harrow, and all whom she was losing on this night, right here, right now, December 1, 2012.

Near him, he could sense movement.

He tried to open his eyes, couldn't. *Really* tried. Could *not*. He called Brooke, but nothing came out.

The room in Martin and Lindy's house became more clear.

He could see a woman—Lindy. Kind of pretty. Scientific looking. Not gorgeous like Brooke.

She, also, had heard the bells ringing, and had come in to listen at the window. She was haggard and had a shotgun in her hands—not a good one like his, but rather an old ten-gauge that had seen better days—much better ones.

Then he noticed that he was typing. The damndest thing, he hadn't even realized it. His eyes were closed, but he could hear it. Feel it in his fingers.

He tried to draw his hands away from the keyboard, couldn't.

"Lindy," he said. Sweet name. She drew her head back from the window and started out of the room.

The phone in her version of the room rang. Wiley couldn't see it, but he heard it so clearly that he froze, his fingers stopping just above the keys. He could hear her breathing, gasping almost, between the insistent rings.

From down the hall, he heard a murmured sigh as his Brooke tossed and turned. Was she aware, at least dimly, of the sound of Lindy's phone?

Lindy put her hand on it. She tightened her grip. Her face reflected a torment that was horrible to see. She picked it up.

THREE
DECEMBER 1
THE NIGHT WATCH

ON NOVEMBER 29, 2012, WHAT had started so strangely in Gloucestershire on the 21st had become a great terror that had, on that night, struck millions of cities, towns, and villages across the world, and expanded from there. Now, on December 1, the White House that Martin had visited was long since evacuated, Washington was in chaos, the world was in chaos. The stories from the great cities were beyond horror. Rather than face what was happening people by tens of thousands had gone out of windows in New York and Chicago, leaving heaps of untended bodies in the streets. The country's communications had broken down, fuel and food had ceased to move along highways choked with refugees, and worse had happened, much, much worse.

Harrow, Kansas, however, had not been struck. All the towns in the area had organized themselves and were as prepared as they could be, but so far the problems had not affected Kansas—at least, not this part of it. However, with communications down, they really had very little idea what was happening past thirty miles away.

Martin was on watch in the steeple of Third Street Methodist when, just before one in the morning, he saw light flicker in the clouds that choked the dark west. As he looked more carefully, the clouds lit up briefly. But there were thunderstorms out there, so there would be lightning, of course.

Another flash slowly dwindled and was gone. He knew archaeology, not meteorology, but he had never seen lightning that lingered like that.

He turned on the little radio that he'd brought up with him, just in case there would be some signal from somewhere, but the world remained as silent as it had been these past three days. No radio, no TV, no Internet, GPS mostly not working. Landline telephones were sporadic, cell phones were local only, and then only occasionally. There was no TV, and even the shortwave radio consisted of static, and in the higher frequencies, endless streams of what sounded like some sort of singsong code, a machine language.

Another flash, this one going close to the ground, then expanding and getting brighter.

He became aware that his heart had begun to thutter. He faced the fantastic reality: *They* had come to Lautner County. That light was over Holcomb, not twenty miles away.

Nobody had ever seen them. The only thing known was that the fourteen lenses, when night fell on them, disgorged thousands of dully glowing bloodred disks, which fanned out spreading the most appalling and bizarre form of death ever known to man.

He picked up his cell phone and called the town's police officer, his friend Bobby Chalmers. "Got some bad-looking flashes in those clouds, Bobby."

"I'm lookin' at 'em."

Next, he phoned Lindy. Attempting not to alarm her, he kept his voice casual. "Hey, Doctor Winters."

"Hey, Doctor Winters."

"Sorry to rouse you from your beauty sleep, but, uh, why don't you go ahead and get the kids ready? I think you need to come over here. Looks like we could have some activity coming in from the west."

She didn't get a chance to react before his phone started beeping in another call. He clicked over. "Hi, Bobby. Where are you, BTW?"

"On my way to you. Ron Turpin over in Parker—"

Parker was between here and Holcomb, a scattering of trailers and a tumbledown convenience store at a crossroads. "I know Ron."

"Yeah. He's sayin' there's a formation he can see in the flashes, moving with the clouds. And nobody's answering the phone over in Holcomb."

"But they're working? The phones are working?"

"They're ringing. No cops, no sheriff, no paramedics picking up, nothin'."

"Dear God."

"You better get down outta there, now, Martin."

Immediately, he clambered down the four flights to the choir loft, glanced out across the dark church, and then went down the stairs to the entrance. Bobby had arrived and was going into the electrical closet as Martin reached the foot of the stairs. Bobby hit the power switches, lighting up the nave, then all the external lights.

Martin flipped open his cell phone and called the minister. "Reg, we could be getting hit tonight, looks like."

"That can't be true."

"It looked like Holcomb was getting it a few minutes ago and now Bobby can't raise them on the phone. Disks passed over Parker coming this way. We're the only town in this direction for eighty miles, Reg."

"I'm on my way."

Martin stepped outside. "I called Dennis Farm," Bobby said. "We—" His phone buzzed. He flipped it open, listened a moment, then closed it. "That was Larry Dennis screaming for help, they got Sally, the light's coming down like rain—then the line—" He held out the silent cell phone.

In both of their minds was the same thought: it couldn't be happening here, it was something you heard about, a big city thing, a European thing, a Chinese disaster.

"Wake 'em up," Bobby said, "we're under attack."

Martin went back into the church and started the bell. There was a whirring sound as it began ringing, its stately tones trembling off into the night. His finger hesitated over the siren. It hadn't been sounded since September, when it had been turned on for the tornado that had taken out the Conagra silo and the Kan-San Trailer Park.

He flipped the switch, and the siren began as a low growl, quickly increased its volume, then filled the air with its wailing. Across the street, Sam Gossett came to the door in his pajama bottoms and yelled, "Is it for real?"

"Holcomb and Dennis Farm just got it," Bobby said. "It's for real, all right."

The Wilsons and a family Martin didn't know except to nod to arrived in SUVs and went hurrying into the church. They must have been sleeping in their clothes. As he passed, Timmy Wilson said, "They're coming up Six Mile, slow and low."

His words made Martin feel literally sick. He telephoned Lindy. "Hi, hon, what's your situation?"

"We're leaving the house."

"You need to hurry, Lindy, they're over Six Mile Road."

"Oh, God, Martin."

According to Homeland Security, people alone did not survive, none of them, not ever. Groups supposedly had a better chance. They still got flyers dropped from time to time. He speculated that Bo Waldo might have something to do with that. There was a man who was not going to be beaten, unlike those two generals, who'd been edgy, bitchy thoroughbreds.

"Lindy, cut across the Walker place to the highway."

"I'll wreck their garden."

"Do it now!"

She closed the phone—unless something else just happened. A wave of nausea almost made Martin gag.

"You okay?" Bobby asked.

"Lindy's out there with the kids. Where's Rose?"

"Same thing, coming in fast as she can."

"But not down Six Mile Road."

"Goddamn, buddy, that's right."

Bobby, who had been his friend since their boyhood in this community, met his eyes. Bobby had stayed, Martin had gone on to university. But he'd returned in the end, discovering after Berkeley and Stanford that one did not leave Kansas so easily.

"I never thought this would come," Bobby said as the two of them watched the sky and the people now hurrying into the church.

"We're not in Kansas anymore, Bobby. Kansas is gone with the wind, I'm afraid."

"You think it's gonna be all of us, Martin?"

A wave of what could only be described as woe swept over Martin. He said, "The pamphlet says that more survive if we congregate." It had been dropped by Homeland Security last week.

"What I feel like doing is hiding. That's what feels right."

"I would assume that we can't hide."

The pamphlet, which had been dropped from a Goodyear blimp, of all things, was the only defense the government had offered. In fact, the most terrifying thing about the whole business was the silence from Washington and Topeka.

George and Moira Fielding came huffing up, she in a slip and bra, he in baggy boxer shorts and flip-flops. "There's screaming coming from down the end of Constitution," he gasped.

Serenity Lodge. Forty old folks. Martin looked at Bobby. "You want to go over there?" He thought to himself that Lindy and the kids must pass right in front of the place on their way in.

"I'm needed here."

It wasn't cowardice, it was simple truth.

Across town, Martin could see the steeple of the First Church of Christ light up, and heard its bell join theirs. Saint Peter's was invisible behind the huge oaks that stood along Evans behind Main, but he knew they'd be lit up, too. They didn't have a working bell.

Emma Heard got out of her car. "There was that light just like they say, it was horrible, *horrible*!"

"You were at the home?"

"I was in my office when—oh, Jesus, I tried to help them, they were all in their rooms—" She broke down in sobs and Martin looked off down Third, looking for some sign of Lindy's blue Dodge truck.

"Did you see any actual attacks?" Bobby asked.

"When I ran out, I saw the light coming down on the building, out of one of those things, the disks. It looked like some kind of goop, a glowing membrane—really bright—like on *Nightline* that time, that video of it. I got the hell out of there, lemme tell you." She lowered her eyes. "I saw it slide down in the windows, and I heard—I *heard*—oh, Bobby, the *scream-ing*." She paused, then added in a tiny voice, "They're all headed north now, every single one of them that can walk, and in their pajamas, poor things."

Then she noticed Martin. She came close to him. At forty, she was still beautiful. She'd been his older woman when he was fourteen and she twenty. They had cuddled and touched, and he'd learned mysteries from her that still inspired the deep, deep joy he took in women. In Lindy, now, only her.

She clutched at his shirt. He took her by the shoulders and turned her toward the church. "Go inside, do it now." She walked away with a curious, gliding motion. Martin watched her. "You sure she's not . . . affected?"

"Nah, that's just shock," Bobby said. "Right outta the book."

"Jesus will help us," Mrs. Oates said as she came up the walk. "Never you mind, Jesus will help us." She went past them, unseeing, glassy-eyed with terror.

"The Lord sure hasn't been helping us much lately," Bobby said, but softly, as if it was a kind of dirty secret—or, what he was more likely to think, a blasphemy.

As a scientist, Martin had grown past his childhood piety. Nowadays, while he wasn't against religion, he just didn't see the mechanism of the spiritual.

Bobby and Rose brought their kids here to Methodist every week. Martin and Lindy had chosen not to visit the burden of organized religion on Winnie and Trevor. Trevor had been delighted at not having to join the acolytes of the Anglican Communion in America. He'd dreaded Latin.

People everywhere were taking the horrific business that was unfolding in the world to mean that the soul was real. No less a luminary than the physicist Sir Roger Penfold had called it "the profound organ" because of the way it appeared to control memory and emotion. Given that it consisted exclusively of electrons, the belief that it was immortal had turned out to be entirely correct. Energy is indeed immortal. But could it be conscious in its own right outside of the body, or remain a coherent structure after death? Martin didn't understand how that could be, and he doubted that anybody else did, either.

He did understand the extraordinary irony that the attack on the soul was what had led to its discovery. The scientific community's soul blindness had only been lifted when the human soul began to be taken, and we could see, hear, and feel the consequences.

To Martin, as a scientist, this did not mean that the gods were therefore real. But the average person had taken proof of the soul to mean that his particular gods, also, existed. So churches and temples across the world were jammed day and night with people pleading for help from their deities.

Martin viewed things differently. He was fascinated that this plasma could be drawn out of a human body, as shocked as everybody else at the changes that resulted. But as far as it being the ka of the Egyptians, the jiva of the Hindus, the hun of the Chinese—any of those concepts—the folkloric soul—well, that remained unproven. It was simply an organ of a type they had not previously recognized, with a profound function, most certainly—in fact, a function that explained why we were different from animals, because of the way it preserved memories and delivered them to the brain for processing. But it had not confirmed the reality of the gods, at least not for this intellectual, nor was it clear that it survived in any coherent way after death.

Clearly, though, the removal of the soul was hell on the organism, and it was hell here in Kansas tonight, and maybe across the entire country, but before communications had failed, the real hell had been unfolding in the jam-packed, exposed third world, with swarms of the disks gushing each night like vast formations of locusts out of the fourteen great, black lenses that ringed the world, and people by the millions being torn apart in this strange new way night after hellish night.

He pulled his worn copy of the Homeland Security pamphlet from his pocket. "Approach damaged individuals with extreme caution. Their state is unknown and, while generally passive, they can be unexpectedly violent."

Martin had seen some of the people who'd been disensouled, as the media had called it when the media still existed, a cluster of six of them ragged on the roadside, stragglers up all this way from the Garland, Texas attack that, for America, had signaled the beginning of the nightmare. They'd been walking in a rough line. They were filthy and stinking, sewer drinkers, carrion eaters, muttering and growling to each other as they shuffled aimlessly along, aware, perhaps, of some loss, but no longer understanding what it was.

He had stopped his car because he hadn't been able to resist at least observing them from a little closer, despite the Homeland Security warnings. They hadn't seemed dangerous at all. Far from it. Up close, they were more like migrating elk or something.

He'd spoken to them. Nothing. There had been two men, three women, some children, one on the back of one of the men, the others hand in hand with their mothers. He'd walked beside them, touched a woman's shoulder, and asked her, "Could you tell me your name?"

She had turned to him, and what had happened was the most dreadful thing—she had smiled at him. But such a strange, strange smile. All wrong—so bright that it was empty. Not cruel at all, but relentlessly innocent, like the smiles of poor Jim Tom Stevens had been when they were kids. Jim Tom was retarded, though, and he had not had the feeling that these people had been made stupid.

No, it was much stranger than that. They had not lost their intelligence, but rather their information, and not how to count or how to read—oh, no, the information they had lost was much deeper. What they had lost was what distinguishes us from animals—the arrow of consciousness that points inward. They still knew and saw the world. The information that they had lost was that they *were*, and for this reason had ceased to be human. They had become brilliant animals.

For all of Jim Tom's intellectual poverty, he was not this lost. He knew that he was. When you called his name, he did not simply come to a familiar sound as an animal might. He turned to you with an expression in his face—the fundamental human expression that says, *This is me.*

Martin had been reminded of a line of poetry, "With its whole gaze a creature looks out at the open . . ." and sees nothing of himself at all. Has no self.

They'd hurried off, moving in the general direction that all wanderers moved, at least around here, which was north-northwest.

He had sat on the terrace all afternoon watching the leaves run in the yard, and trying to make sense of what he had seen.

He had told Lindy that they had reminded him of Jim Tom, who had been so innocent that he would eat raw roadkill if he happened upon it hungry.

"If you taught them," she had asked, "do you think they could learn?"

"How to drive a truck or something, sure. But not concepts. No."

"Then they've been made stupid."

"I didn't get that impression."

"What impression did you get, then?"

He'd considered his reply for some time. Finally, he said, "The difference between us and a brilliant animal is that the animal understands what *is*, but not what it *means*. I think they'd been returned to what we were before the discovery of our being made us human. They weren't human, Lindy. They were just sort of . . . there."

As a scientist specializing in the past, he was well aware that the human body and brain had evolved a hundred thousand years before civilization had appeared. We'd been brilliant animals for a long, long time, and in the dark back of his mind, he feared that whoever was here was not really destroying or capturing souls like people believed, not at all— it was much simpler: they were manufacturing slaves, and the reason the wanderers all went off in the same direction was that they weren't wandering at all, they were moving to a collection point.

As far as the souls were concerned, pulling them out of the body was like letting the air out of a balloon. They became part of the general electromagnetic flux. In effect, they disintegrated.

People swarmed into the church now, in pajamas, in underwear, in whatever, coats thrown over shoulders, hats jammed onto heads. The one thing they all carried was a gun, many of them more than one. Pistols, rifles, shotguns, a few assault weapons. A formidable arsenal.

May Whitt got the organ started. It burbled for a moment, then blasted into a brave rendition of "What a Friend We Have in Jesus."

A moment later a scream pealed in the street, the sound rising above the wail of the siren, the tolling of the bell, and the hymn. Ten-year-old Chrissie Palen pointed at the sky. At first Martin saw only first moon, pale and serene, speeding in ragged clouds. Then Tom Palen raised his 30-06 and fired, and Martin's eyes followed the muzzle flash to a simple ovoid, dull orange against the sky, as motionless as if it was fixed to the ground.

Martin scoured the street for Lindy's Dodge. He put in a call to her, but could not get a signal.

"We need to get out of the street," Bobby cried. "Everybody, run, run NOW!"

Despite his lack of religious belief, Martin found himself begging God in his heart to bring his family to him safely. He breathed the words in and out, in and out: *God, please, God, please*, and tried to send some sort of protection to his beloved and their kids, his striving pre-teen boy and his darling little girl.

The object slid over Rite Way Drugs, then backed off to the Target end of town.

Then Lindy was there, getting out of the car with Winnie and Trevor—and the disk was there, too, sliding back across the sky as if it was on a tabletop.

"For God's sake, RUN," Martin screamed at them. "Shoot at the god-damn thing, Tom, shoot at it!"

The rifle cracked, cracked again—and the thing slid away into the darkness. Bullets were rumored to slow them down, but not for long.

Lindy and the kids came toward Martin as if in a slow motion night-mare, like ballet dancers executing a *pas de deux*, like a little boat drift-ing in a calm.

The thing reappeared, speeding into view at rooftop level. Electric fire crackled along its edge, spitting sparks into the air. The Palens raced into the church, and Martin realized that his family was not going to make it. He ran toward them, his blood pumping, his legs going fast but not fast enough, as the thing dipped low over Main Street not a hun-dred yards behind them, and began moving forward. It was about to hit them with the light, he knew it.

"Run, Lindy!"

Whereupon Lindy, God love her, turned and shouldered her bird gun and let go four blasts of buckshot.

The thing seemed unaffected—bullets delayed them slightly, but buckshot apparently not at all.

The kids reached him. "Get in the church!" he shouted to them, pushing them toward the lighted door. Lindy, he saw, had returned to the car for a backpack of provisions.

The bell tolled, the siren moaned, and the congregation sang in ragged chorus, ". . . he'll take and shield thee; thou wilt find a solace there."

Bobby yelled, "MOVE! MOVE! MOVE!"

Lindy came out of the car. She seemed to be under water, she was moving so slow. And then Martin saw why: she was falling, she'd tripped. He ran toward her.

Reg Todd called, "We're closing the doors!" Winnie and Trevor realized what was happening and began to shout, "Mom! Dad!"

"Martin, it's right over you, it's starting to glow!" Bobby pulled out his service revolver and fired at it. The street around Martin began to turn red. Still he ran toward Lindy, he could not conceive of abandoning her.

Her skin was red in the red light from above. He threw an arm around her and began pulling her forward. As they got to the church steps, she gained her footing and began to help him. As she fell into the foyer, Maggie Hastert came to her rescue, and the two women staggered into the last pew as Bobby and Martin slammed the doors.

"Mom," Trevor shouted.

"Mommy!" Winnie shrilled, the littlest finally realizing that something was not right in her world.

"Momma is all right," Lindy managed to gasp.

"You're crying," Trevor said.

"We're all crying, Trevor," Martin said.

"Are we supposed to be crying?" Winnie asked.

Martin moved into the pew with Lindy, with their kids clinging to them, and the Hasterts made room for them. Given that Rose had arrived with their kids, Bobby and his family were okay, too—for the moment.

Reg Todd went into the pulpit. Martin liked him, had hunted with him when they were boys. "Everybody's praying now, all over the world, calling on the power of God to defend the soul. There is wisdom for us in the Bible, the book of the soul written by God, written for this time when we are discovering our souls because we are losing them. So you listen now. If the light comes—"

There was a scream. Everybody looked around, but it had come from outside, from above the building. It was repeated, and children all over the small nave began screaming, too, and Peg Tarr cried out, and Bobby tried to calm her down and she shook him off. "It's my husband," she screamed, "I know it's him, I can feel it!" She backed away from her neighbor, pushing into Doctor Willerson. "Where's the Air Force? Where are the planes?" she bellowed. He shrank away from her, fumbling as his glasses flew from his face. "The planes," she screamed, "the planes!" She grabbed his shoulders and yanked at him so hard she ripped his coat, and he reached back and slugged her, which snapped her head to the side and made spit fly, and made a sound like an exploding lightbulb.

Then the scream outside repeated. It was a human sound, and involved such extraordinary anguish that everyone in the church screamed with it, a roaring agony that, in embracing it, only made it more terrible. Children collapsed, their mothers going down with them. Ron Biggs of Biggs John Deere, fourth generation in tractors, emptied his twelve-gauge into the ceiling, a Remington notched with the lives of forty-one bucks and happy days.

As bits of plaster and angels and clouds rained down, a hideous scraping sound slid along the shingles, ending with a thud in the side yard.

Silence, then, followed by little Kimberly Wilson singing: "A-hunting we will go, a-hunting we will go, heigh-ho the derry-o . . ." until her mother hushed her.

Total silence. This was not what they had been expecting. Now, a murmur among the congregation. Bobby looked to Martin. "Any idea?" Martin shook his head. This wasn't supposed to involve people being dropped onto roofs, but that's what it had sounded like. "Doctor," Bobby said, "let's you and I go out and take a look around."

Rose said, "No!"

"Rose, I—"

"Bobby, no! You stay in here."

There was a silent look between them. She knew Bobby's duty, and finally turned away, her eyes swimming.

Bobby and Doctor Willerson crossed the room, went out the vestry door. The body—if that's what it was—had fallen down that side of the church.

The congregation stood in silence, waiting, some bowed in prayer, other people simply staring.

When they returned a moment later, the doctor said into the silent, watching faces, "I believe it is Mayor Tarr. He's dead from a fall. He had a rifle. I believe he was on the roof trying to defend us, and lost his footing."

Peg fainted.

As Ginger Forester and her boyfriend, Lyndon Lynch, who had been sitting with her, moved to help, there came more screaming, fainter, but from many more throats.

One of the other groups was under attack. Bobby went to the main door, opened it for a moment, then returned. "It's Saint Peter's," he announced.

Mal Holmes said, "This is insane! What are we doing just waiting like this. Tarr had a point, let's go outside, let's put up a fight. For God's sake, *let's fight!*"

"Our fight is in our prayers," Reg shouted.

Mrs. James cried out loudly, then, and shook her fist, a gesture that must have been repeated billions upon billions of times on earth over these past terrible weeks.

"I want to read now," Reg called out. "I have a text. And then we will pray. We will pray all night and the children can sleep in the pews."

"No way am I going to sleep," Trevor said.

"Me neither!" Winnie added.

"Okay, kids, hush," Lindy whispered.

Winnie pulled on Martin's pant leg. "I'm real thirsty," she whispered.

"I've, uh—oh, it's in the street," Lindy said. "When that thing—"

"We have plenty," Jim said, producing a bottle of Ayers water.

"This is from the Book of Isaiah," Reg announced. "Listen to this. Isaiah fifty-five, you can turn to it in the pew Bibles, it's page four hundred and thirty-five." He read, " 'So shall you summon a nation you knew not, and nations that knew you not shall run to you, because of the Lord, your God, the Holy One of Israel, who has glorified you. Seek the Lord while he may be found, call him while he is near. Let the scoundrel forsake his way, and the wicked man his thoughts; let him turn to the Lord for mercy; to our God, who is generous in forgiving.' "

At that moment, the lights went out. There was a roar from the whole congregation, ringing loud, shrill with terror.

"Let us pray," Reg called into the din. "LET US PRAY!" Voices dropped, flashlights came on.

But there also came another light, crawling along the tops of the stained glass windows of the birth, youth, and ministry of Jesus that lined the west wall.

Martin watched, unable to turn away, transfixed with horrified fascination.

As the congregation realized that it was there, silence slowly fell. Became absolute. They watched it coming down, this most terrible weapon that had ever been in the world, and yet so strange, so unexpected.

As a scientist, Martin tried to use what skills of observation he could muster. It moved like a thick liquid, this light. We had slowed light down, stopped it, reversed it, but had never created anything like this.

When it began to come in, there was a sigh in the room, just the softest of sighs, no more, and a little girl's voice piping, "Look at the pretty, Mommy, the pretty is on Jesus!"

The painted glass with the bearded figure on the cross, the rough rocks, and the praying virgin in her chipped blue glittered with new life as the light ran along them, seemed to pause as if it was looking out across the congregation, evaluating them, scanning them, tasting of them . . . and then it came on, glaring on their upturned faces.

"Dad, is this an alien being?" Trevor asked.

"It's Lucifer," Winnie said. "Be quiet or he'll come after us."

Some children began to cry, and a ripple of panic spread. Parents held them.

Martin saw immediately that the thing moved like something alive— and something that felt no need to be careful, not the way it came surging in the windows, filling the room with its slicing glare. He was fascinated by its motion, he couldn't help himself. It was a little like the spread of a membrane, he thought. But then it came forward so quickly that there were shrieks of literal agony, the terror was so extreme.

Old Man Michaels dropped to the floor with a thud. He went gray, and Martin thought he'd probably died. A stench of urine and feces filled the air. Children broke away from their parents and began running toward the doors, in their terror imagining that they could escape. Mamie Leonard dashed after Kevin, but the boy reached the vestry door and threw it open.

Glare literally gushed in. The boy cried out and jumped back, but the light swept around him. Martin observed only a flicker, and the child went still, standing in the body of it, surrounded by it, his jaw agape. His mother raced to the far side of the nave, and stood there shrieking again and again, sorrowing cries that dominated the room.

Reg cried out, " 'For my thoughts are not your thoughts, nor are your ways my ways,' says the Lord. 'As high as the heavens are above the earth, so high are my ways above your ways and my thoughts above your thoughts.' "

The light moved and expanded, crossing the sanctuary and flowing down into the nave. People got up on the pews to keep their feet out of it, but Martin knew it was useless, it would do its infamous bloom any second, and then, well he could not imagine it. He just could not.

There was no sign of any biological material. It was definitely a plasma, he could see that. But it had the stability of a highly organized membrane. He tried to think of any bas-relief, any wall painting, any sculpture anywhere in the world that reminded him of this, and could not.

This was new, he was pretty sure, to the experience of mankind.

"Pray now," Reg said, "pray and hold the children and be ready with the guns."

Martin put his arm around Trevor and Lindy picked up Winnie, and Martin felt the pistol in his pocket. He'd loaded it with hollow points. A shot to the head would destroy a child instantly, but Martin did not frankly know if he could do it. God willing, Homeland Security was right about the value of congregating and they would survive.

"Shoot it," a voice said. "God help us, shoot it!"

"Don't do that!" Bobby shouted. "That spreads it, we all know. That—"

They were suddenly surrounded by the strangest thing any of them had ever experienced, a flickering mass of colors that hurt and felt good against the skin at the same time . . . and felt like somebody was watching you, not with malice, but with a sort of evaluative skill that seemed almost . . . professional.

Martin thought, *we are destroyed, a destroyed species. This is how we end, killed in a way we do not understand by something beyond our knowledge.* And then also thought, *But it's the way cattle die every day, or used to.*

He glimpsed a man, lean, dark hat over his eyes, face of a snake, sliding toward him. He shook the hallucination off. They'd all heard stories about this phenomenon, it was the mind trying to force the impossible into some form that it might be able to understand and thus to fight.

Now Trevor closed his eyes. "Dad, I'm seeing a sort of snake." He opened them. "In my mind. Watching me in my mind."

Children's voices were raised, "There's a cobra, Mommy, a dragon,

Daddy, a python . . ." and he knew where the ancient tale of the snake originated. It was how the mind of man gave form to disincarnate evil.

There came a dull sound, like one of those deep thuds that never seem to find an explanation, that one sometimes hears back in the woods. But something had changed. Reg had changed. Where he had been in his pulpit with his Bible in his hand, wearing an old gray suit with no tie, now stood a man who appeared to be wearing the most intricately beautiful colored coat ever devised. But it was not cloth, the colors came from tiny, exquisitely detailed memories, each one full of life and motion, swarming around him like living jewels. He threw back his head and roared like a maddened gorilla.

A passage from the Bible occurred to Martin, the one about the coat of many colors. He understood the message: Joseph's coat had been his soul. The old biblical authors, therefore, had known what souls looked like. They were seeing Reg's soul being sucked from his body the way a monkey might suck the pulp from an orange.

Nobody made a sound now, nobody dared. But every single one of them hoped in his heart that this would be enough for it, this would be an end of it, after Reg it would go.

Reg began to physically distort, his face growing long, his eye sockets stretching into bizarre vertical ovals, his lips opening, mouth gaping— and then all over the room others did the same, their faces twisting, colors oozing like gorgeous pus out of their bodies. They pissed and shat and howled and writhed, sinking down, tearing at their throats.

There was a deafening *wham* as Milly Fisher blew her boy Tim's head apart.

"Mother," Winnie shouted into Lindy's face, "what is this, *what is this?*"

Crackling became screeching became sucking, deep, the sucking of a chest wound, of a woman of the night, and the congregation became a blur of light and struggling, writhing people, some of them clawing at themselves and howling, others with guns in their shaking hands, trying to kill the ones who were being destroyed—as if it mattered, as if it would help.

It remained like that, people crawling, leaping over one another and running for the light-choked doors, wading in it, pushing against the warmth of its ghastly fleshiness.

Then came darkness, then silence, broken by a single wracking sob.

The chandeliers flickered, and with their return came the sense of a storm having passed.

The minister still stood in his pulpit. From a middle pew somebody asked, "Reg? Reg are you okay?"

The Bible dropped from Reg's hand, hitting the floor beside the pulpit with a crack like a shot. In the pews, some people shook others, calling into blank faces, shaking them until the spittle flew.

"Angie, honey, Angie, you're okay! She's okay, it didn't do her—"

Martin saw Angie Bright, Carl Bright's wife of thirty years, looking at him with the blank innocence of a newborn.

Others began to growl, to laugh, to back away toward the walls. As the minister did this, he laughed softly. His face was still his own, but it was empty, the eyes glassy, staring.

Bobby came to the center aisle, then trotted up to the pulpit. "Okay, we have the law on our side, we need to do this, people."

"My baby, my baby is fine. Lucy, you're fine. She's fine!" Becky Lindner shook her twelve-year-old. "Lucy! Lucy, don't you playact!"

The girl, who had been plastic like a catatonic, lunged at her mother, biting as a dog bites when it is cornered and cannot get away. Becky cried out, falling back into the Baker family, and young Timothy Baker caught her in his arms.

Then Carl Bright screamed as he realized that his teenage son Robert, also, was among the wanderers. Martin's heart was torn by all he was seeing, but the families like this one were the hardest. The Brights lived back in the hills in a comfortable house. In fact, it was only a few miles from their own place. He was a technical writer, she ran an online crafts business.

Without so much as a murmured warning, Mrs. Haggerty leaped on Lindy's back like a lioness leaping on a wildebeest, and she lurched forward into Martin, and the three of them went down with Mrs. Haggerty ripping Lindy's hair out in handfuls while her husband, crying out, dragged her off and took her into the aisle.

"Kids, don't look," Martin shouted as young Haggerty shot his mother dead.

Lindy and Winnie and Trevor turned and moved to the back of the church. Martin was confused by this. "Lindy? Hey."

Another shot from the back of the sanctuary, and one of the Desmond boys stood over his father's body, looking down out of tear-flooded young eyes. "Momma, I did it, I did it," he cried, and his mother took him to her, and buried him in her embrace.

Phil Knippa, whose wife was gathering at the back of the church with the others who had been ruined, asked Martin, "What happens?"

Martin ran to his family. "Hey, this—"

His Lindy had reached the door. She stood with the others. "Lindy? Oh, no!"

Bobby came up to him. "Hey, come on, guy."

"But they didn't—nothing happened to them!" He laughed. "She's in shock. Hey, Lindy!" He went down to his kids. "See, they're fine, Bobby, they're just following their mother. Winnie! Trevor! Stop this! Stop this!"

Phil said, "In that day the Lord with his sore and great and strong sword shall punish leviathan the piercing serpent, even leviathan that crooked serpent; and he shall slay the dragon that is in the sea."

The new wanderers crowded the entrance, pressing against the doors, slapping them and Lindy and Trevor and Winnie were doing it, too, and then Bobby put his hand on Martin's shoulder. Martin turned, and when he saw the gun that his dear old friend was offering him, the anguish that ripped his heart caused him to throw his head back and cry out, and in that quiet part of him that is in us all and sees and knows all, a voice said, "This has happened. This is what you have, now."

Lovers, wives, husbands, children—all circulated among them, trying to communicate with them, and the church was filled with their tears.

Bobby got the door open for them, and they went out into the street . . . and joined many others, a shocking number, all walking away into the night. Martin thought that it was more than half the town. Three quarters.

They shuffled silently off toward the low water crossing and the back roads that led up into the Smokey Hills, hardly hills at all, but wilder than they looked from a distance.

A few people ran after them, two husbands, a wife, some others who had exchanged death promises. "If it happens to me, don't let me be like that." Pacts made in blood and love.

Martin ran, too, touching his love, calling to her, calling to his babies, "Kids, come back here, this is Dad, this is an order!" And to his wife, "Oh, Lindy, wake up, love, wake up, love."

But they did not wake up, none of them woke up. An arm came around Martin's shoulder, the arm of somebody he knew vaguely but who now seemed like a savior, and he leaned against this man and wept, and in the street the little clusters of those left behind wept, and the wanderers went on down the street, disappearing into the dark.

Martin ran after them again, and then he stopped, and he went to his knees and he howled her name, "LINDY!" He cried in rage and in anguish as she went off without even a backward glance, taking his babies and his love and all that meant anything to him with her into the night.

The shattered town sank away into the horrible small hours, with weeping in the churches, and the bodies of the destroyed dead lined up with what little dignity could be managed on the lawns. Most of the ruined, though, were not killed, because people did not have it in their hearts to rip the life out of the familiar and the beloved, no matter their state. So they went away, absorbed by the night. When daylight came, people would seek them out, taking water and food to the empty shells of their loved ones, trying to feed them, to talk to them. And they would smile, the wanderers, or sometimes lash out like scared animals, but the followers would stay with them, begging, pleading, praying, trying anything to bring them back. It is an extraordinary anguish to say good-bye to your dead while they are still alive, and many, many people could not do it.

Martin went to his feet. He would not be a follower. He vowed that. He would be a fighter. Somehow, he was going to rescue his love and his children, he was going to go out there into that darkness, and whatever it took, whatever was needed, if he give his blood or his life or his own soul, it mattered not a bit, he would rescue his family.

Toward dawn there was a fall of dew, and morning came pearled with it, on the leaves of autumn and the yellowing late grasses, on the neat houses, the empty streets, and on the wanderers, too, far out in the rustling fields, shining on their pale skin, pearl upon pearl.

FOUR
DECEMBER 2
THE POISONER

WILEY LEAPED UP FROM THE computer, threw open the bottom drawer of the desk, grabbed the booze he kept in there, and just plain poured it down. "Christ, you dummies, can't you see it's a damn trick?"

But they had not seen, not even Martin and Lindy. They'd gone to the church, too, they'd made themselves sitting damn ducks and they'd— oh, God, the poor Winters family, and poor Harrow. All those good, decent people.

Wanderers. It was worse than dying. But why was this being done to them and where were they going? He thought that Martin was right about one thing—they were certainly on their way to designated locations. Collection points, though—he was just guessing about that. Maybe they were going to gas chambers or something, God forbid that such a fate would befall Lindy and Winnie. He was crazy about them, that sweet, bright little girl, her mother so full of love and brilliance.

"This is not real," he said, "I refuse to let this be real."

Maybe he wasn't recording events in the other human universe, but creating them. Maybe he was an instrument of the reptilians, and maybe that was why they had came into his life five years ago. They had done something to him. Prepared him. But how?.

He knew that supple movement between parallel universes was involved with belief and the lack thereof. By continuing to deny that UFOs were something real, our own version of NASA had saved us—at least, so far. But not him. Maybe not him.

Thing was, the closer we got to December 21, the easier it became to get through the gateways. And on that day, all hell was going to break loose in the other human universe. That had to be what this was all about. Preparing for the invasion . . . and maybe here, too, no matter what our version of NASA denied or did not deny.

He clicked through the pages he had written. He knew both more and less than was in the laptop. For example, he knew what was happening in the Far East in Martin's world, which was a catastrophe so vast that it was, quite simply, unimaginable. He knew, but he couldn't access any detail. Couldn't see much. Could feel it though, the terror being experienced by billions.

What would happen if everybody became a wanderer?

He took a deep breath, let it out slowly. Damn Brooke and her rules. A cigar would go very, very well right now.

Maybe Martin was right and it was a harvest of slaves. Might not six billion slaves be worth something in the parallel earth of the reptilians? But if the souls were being taken out, then what was happening to them? Martin thought they were just disintegrating, but Wiley wasn't so sure of that. He had no idea what to think. He'd never really believed in the soul or God or any of that stuff. Like Martin, he'd been to Stanford, and had come away, also, with a strong rationalism and fundamental disrespect for unprovable assertions.

Those monstrous creatures wanted the bodies, he was convinced of it.

Unless . . . how many parallel universes might there be? If the Many Worlds interpretation of Hugh Everett was correct, then this oppression could be coming from any one of literally uncountable numbers of parallel universes.

He thought not, though. He thought that the reptilian forms that the people in the church had glimpsed were the final telltale. He was right about the creatures and he was right about their world. He could feel their need, could see their glaring, relentless eyes the same way he had on that night five years ago when they'd tried to—what had they tried to do? Had they really somehow captured him?

No, something was wrong with that picture. He'd written a whole book about it, but he was increasingly aware of a missing element. Because what had happened to him on that night had been hard, but—there was just something missing. Tip of the tongue. Couldn't quite remember.

Maybe it had something to do with the fact that there were three earths involved. A triad.

Buckminster Fuller had called the triangle the building block of the universe because of its structural integrity. There was a reason in conscious life, also, that notions of trinity made structural sense. A triad had a positive side, a negative side, and a balancing side. If the two-moon earth was the positive side, then the negative side was the reptilians with their evil hungers.

Oh, Christ, he was not the balancing factor. I mean, well, let's face it, a middling writer with a burr up his ass about aliens is not the right guy to bring things into balance.

In other words, not up to the job of—what? So far, he wasn't really doing a whole lot beyond writing a history that his world would take to be fiction. He wasn't helping anybody.

He closed his eyes. If there was a god anywhere out there, may he now deliver his servant Wylie Dale from the curse of this writing.

But even as he tried to push away the other human world, his mind slipped back toward its suffering. There, this house was now cold and dark, not nicely heated and cozy with a lovely family inside.

As dawn broke here, the phoebes started their sweet calling, the very essence of peace in the country. Over there, though, the people left alive were crying together, their sorrow unspeakable. Wylie was crying, too—in silence, though. Brooke and the kids mustn't hear.

Then Brooke was there. She had come quietly and he had not heard her, but she was there, standing in the door of his office, and he thought she was an angel come down, and he turned to her in his creaky old chair, and slid out of it and to his knees, and embraced her waist, and buried his face in the sweet and sour scent of her.

Her hands came around his head, and he felt cradled. She said, "You need to come to bed, love."

"What time is it?"

"The phoebes are starting."

He'd been in here for close to twenty-four hours. "Oh, man."

"Wiley?"

He looked up at her in her nightgown, so pale in the thin light that she might have been a ghost or a memory. "We're travelers on the long water," he muttered, "you and me, sweets, you and me." Her hand came into his and it was warm, and he kissed it and it smelled like sweat and remembrance.

He went to his feet and took her into his arms, and she settled there. He closed his eyes and sailed in the comfort of her closeness.

"You were crying," she said.

"Mm. My story."

"It's really getting to you, Wiley."

He nodded against her shoulder.

"Your imagination is supposed to be a tool, not a weapon, especially not against yourself."

"Oh, honey," he said.

"Wiley, it's not real, remember that this time. Don't get yourself confused."

He nodded again. Her hands swept his thighs, then her long fingers probed at his pants, but playfully, quickly. He felt himself stir. She was his home, Brooke was, the home of his soul.

She'd been there that night five years ago. It had been the two of them. And it—was it—not what it seemed?

"Let me show you a little reality," she whispered in his ear. "Let's do dawn patrol."

That's what they called it when they made love in the early hours, which they often did. This is the time when childrens' sleep is deepest and parents are least likely to be disturbed, and, for Wiley, when his body called him to the ocean of his wife.

But as they walked arm in arm to the bedroom, he heard a door open and close downstairs, and then the voice, low and full of sorrow, of an invisible man. The man went into the living room and became silent there. "Did you hear that?"

"The warbler? He just started in."

"Not the warbler."

She guided his hands to the familiar pink ribbon that was tied behind her neck, and he untied it, and the nightgown floated down. Her matchless curves shone in the rising light, her nipples blushed pink and coming tight, and she was the loveliest thing that he knew, a beauty that, when it surrendered itself to his big hands and arms, seemed as if it must bear some sort of strength in it that was connected to eternity, or it would have melted into shadow at his touch.

As she unbuckled his belt, she made a familiar tune in her throat, "Never grow old, never grow old," a line from the old hymn that was a theme in the music of her life. And they would not, not in a love like the one that had possessed the two of them. And had possessed Martin and Lindy, too, and been destroyed, just freshly, along with the children that had been woven out of its flesh.

They lay with the windows open, their bodies close in the cool morning breeze, and came together while the birds called softly, the phoebes and the tanagers and the doves, and the first sun spread across the floor.

When he should have been completely absorbed in her, when his body was radiant with pleasure, his eyes drinking her face, his power-ful hips pumping and making her cry out softly, then, at that grand pri-vate moment, he heard another voice cry out, and knew that it was his own and not his own, a broken, bereft voice from downstairs and a uni-verse so close and so very far away.

He went plunging on, but then heard the back door slam and the voice screaming, but faintly, faintly . . . and yet so terribly that it shat-tered everything and caused him to go twisting off her.

He flopped onto his back, gasping.

"Honey," she said, "oh, honey," and came to him. But he leaped out of the bed.

"It's him," he said.

"Who?"

Out in the back yard, he was screaming. Wiley ran downstairs. "Martin," he yelled, "Martin!"

He went through the living room and out the back door into the dewy grass.

"Wiley, for God's sake!"

Then he heard them, their shuffling walk, the wanderers coming up from Harrow. He stood in a shaft of hazy light as they came closer, and saw the branches shake, and then heard their voices murmuring, and heard Martin screaming and screaming.

The murmuring came closer, got louder. "Hear it, Brooke?"

"What?"

They were right in front of him now, murmuring, breathing, their feet shuffling. "Brooke, look at the grass!"

"Honey, oh, for *God's sake*!"

The footprints came closer and closer.

Then he reached out, and he touched the air where one of them must be. He felt a shoulder, part of an arm.

And then he saw them. Where he touched them, he could see a knit shirt, part of a neck, then a muscular forearm. "My God, look, *look*!" He reached, he touched the face—and saw glazed, empty eyes, a slack mouth—male—but the man went on, the man did not seem to be aware of him at all. "Winnie," he cried, "Lindy! Trevor!"

Then he heard Martin, heard him close, heard him whispering "baby, baby please, please wake up baby—"

He reached out—and there, under his hand was a khaki jacket, then a face—Martin, richly alive, totally there! "Martin! Martin, you can't help them, you were all tricked, you should hide, *you need to hide*! Oh, Christ, somebody in the government is on the dark side, Martin, can't you see that, *they want this to happen*!"

But Martin was gone. All around him, the wanderers continued passing, and he kept reaching out to them. He touched Mrs. Sweet from the drugstore, her gaping face, and the old pastor Reginald Todd, and then Doctor Willerson—the town doctor, reduced to this. "Oh, Jesus, Jesus—"

Then Brooke was there, and she slapped him so hard there was a flash and pain.

He grabbed her wrist. "What the hell's the matter with you?"

"With *me*? You're naked in the back yard, for God's sake, and look, you have an audience—"

There, face pale in his bedroom window, stood Nick, staring down on the scene. His expression was grave, like a judge at a sentencing. Martin took the robe she'd brought and covered himself, and went in through the shuffling sounds of the wanderers, and Martin's cries, and the pleading, praying voices of the followers, and the last thing he heard was a child's voice calling for his mother and his father to stop, in the choked tones of a twelve-year-old trying to be brave.

"Get in here, Wiley, you're scaring me!" She tugged at him and he went with her. As they returned to the house, he waved up at his son. Inside, she threw her arms around him. "Wiley, what is it? What's happening to you?"

"The story's got me. It's drowning me."

"Wiley, you were warned."

"I can't stop it!"

"I want you to see Doctor Crutchfield. I want you to see him today."

"He's a wanderer."

"A what? What does that mean?"

"No, of course not, that's Doctor Willerson in the two moon world, I'm sorry. I'll call him."

"What in hell is a two-moon world?"

"A place of great beauty, my wife, that is being raped by creatures without mercy." He grabbed her shoulders. "And they are coming. They are coming here."

She stepped back. She went pale.

"In your heart," he said, "you know."

"I do not know!"

Then Nick came downstairs. He looked up at them. "I dreamed awful things," he said, "then I woke up and it was worse."

"What was your dream, son?"

"I dreamed we left, Dad. You tried, but you couldn't go where we were going, and we couldn't stop, and then I woke up and you were in the yard, and what's wrong, Dad?"

Brooke gave Wiley a hard, hard look, and coming from his gentle Brooke, that meant a lot. It meant she thought he had hurt her boy.

Then Kelsey came down, flitting along in her pink nightie, her curls bobbing. She looked just as darling as the most wonderful little girl picture ever taken, and he opened his arms and lifted her to him. "I had a bad dream," she said, "I dreamed me and Mommy got leashes put on us and we had to walk all night and forever and I got so tired but I couldn't stop, and you ran along behind us praying and he had a bottle of Ayers water. I thought we didn't get bottled water. I thought it was too expensive."

"Now, see," Brooke said, "that proves it was just a dream, because there's Evian and Perrier and Ozark and lots of other kinds of water, but there is no Ayers water."

"There isn't?"

"Not in this universe," Wiley told her, and kissed her button nose. As best he could, he concealed what was almost a sickness of fear. In the other universe they had Ayers water, he'd seen bottles among peoples' provisions in the church.

But how had Kelsey known about it? How indeed, unless the wall that separated the two human universes was also breaking down, just as he had feared it would, and hell was getting closer fast.

They all went into the kitchen, and he turned on the radio and he and Brooke made breakfast. His mind was completely focused on one thing—how had Kelsey known? What might be about to happen?

"You're staring," she said.

He shook his head. "Don't be mad at me."

"No."

"It's not even a big deal in physics. Parallel universes are real."

"I'm sure they are. I'm also sure that they don't cause people—just generally speaking, I mean—to leap around naked in their backyards. Your appointment with Crutchfield is at eight-thirty, so you'd better get rolling."

"Eight-thirty? You're kidding."

She looked at him, and the fire in her eyes actually reassured him. He wanted to feel like somebody was in control, because he was not in control.

He gobbled down the last of his eggs and went up to dress. Maybe this would be actually be good, maybe all that was happening here was that he was losing his grip—which, frankly, would be a hell of a lot better than what he feared.

Moving fast, he managed get to town just in time.

As he drove along the familiar streets, he kept expecting to see little knots of tragic people, but all he did see was a small Kansas community in its mild prosperity, a gentle bustle in the streets, even a recent addition, the Starbucks. Nobody seemed strange, nobody had a vacant look.

He drove past Third Street Methodist. The church was closed, but it looked perfectly normal. Sylvester was on the walkway with a trowel, turning soil in a flower bed. Wiley slowed down and waved. "Hey there, Syl."

Syl waved back. Nothing unusual.

Of course not, you fool. Things are fine in this universe—for now.

When he arrived at Crutchfield's office, which was a walk-up above the Danforth Meat Market, one of the few small businesses hanging on in downtown, it was twenty to nine. "Sorry I'm late, Marla."

"Brooke says you've gone around the bend."

"That would be true."

"Then I'll remind you that I've got Mace."

He'd come on to the girl with the porcelain skin and the bright green eyes. But all in fun, of course. He would never cheat on Brooke. But with that black hair and that creamy skin, Marla did inspire.

Crutchfield looked normal, also. White hair, tiny glasses, a sense of therapeutic fog clinging to him.

"So you were capering around in the back yard naked. What say we start there?"

"Look, I've got—oh, Christ. I've got something happening that I can't even begin to understand."

"I think Brooke is having exactly the same problem."

"It feels to me as if something enormous is happening that has to do with what I am writing, and it is not good, this huge thing, but I cannot stop writing about it even if I want to. I'm a sort of infernal machine."

"You're a machine?"

"Not in control of my own body. Not channeling, it's not like that. I sit there and I type. Automatic typing. I've abandoned my Corona and I'm just working on the computer. But the book isn't mine. I can write without thinking. Read, watch TV, close my eyes, it doesn't matter. My fingers just type away on their own."

"If your work isn't yours, whose would it be?"

"That's a hell of a good question. The answer is, I have no idea."

"But you're not involved in the writing?"

"Well, I am, of course, sort of. In the sense that I can see their world, hear their voices. Shit! You moron. Moron!"

"I'm a moron?"

"I'm a moron! You don't tell a shrink you hear voices."

"The voices don't want you to tell me about them?"

"Aw, shit. Sheee-ut! Goddamn it, the voices don't care."

"So what do they say?"

"They cry. They're suffering. Some of them came up through the yard, and when I touched them I could see them—see the hands, the faces that I touched. Does that sound plain crazy, or spectacularly crazy?"

"Sounds like I might as well get that new Lexus I've had my eye on."

"Do you know what a parallel universe is?"

"Something that exists deep inside the CERN supercollider for a few billionths of a second?"

"I'm not paying you to bait me, Henry. We're deducting three minutes of money for that little flippancy."

"You're afraid I'm laughing at you, but that isn't what's going on."

"What is?"

"I'm trying to make sense of what you're saying."

"Would it disturb you to know that in a parallel universe a doctor very much like you called Frank Willerson is currently walking off toward the northwest with most of the other people in this community, and he has no soul?"

"We're probably all better off without that soul mythology, anyway. Let's you and me deal with who and what we know we are, which is us in this room together. Or are you here? Are you a projection from a parallel universe, Wiley? Is schizophrenia the problem, here?"

"Look, I had a close encounter with creatures from a third parallel universe a few years ago, and because that happened—well, I'm doing what I'm doing."

"Which is?"

"I'd say I have no fucking idea, but I'm beginning to have an idea. I'm the balancing force between the positive and negative earths."

"Ah, of course, that makes complete sense. Would you be God, then, or just Jesus?"

"I'm Napoleon, you fuck."

"Not interested, Wylie. Every psychiatrist reaches a point in his career where he has to draw a line. No more Napoleons. I reached that point a while back."

"Am I insane?"

"Of course you're insane."

"What can I do about it?"

"Come here a lot. Keep paying your bill."

"You are a cynical man."

"Yes I am."

"Look, I'll apologize to my wife for going out in the back yard naked. If that's a compromise, here."

"Is it a compromise?"

"When you're bored, you turn the patient's statements into questions. You're doing that now."

Henry lifted his arm, drew back his sleeve, and looked at his watch. "I'm relieved to say that we've come to the end of our time, Wiley. You can reschedule with Marla."

"Can I fuck her, too?"

"If you want to continue treatment with me, no."

"You don't like me very much, do you?"

"Do you want me to like you?"

He left the office without making another appointment. What was the point? The good doctor didn't believe a word he said. Hell, *he* didn't believe a word he said.

Driving back in the Jeepazine, he made a decision. He would change it. He'd simply go back and alter the text. Because if he changed it, maybe he would also change events. No more ruined Winters family, no more ruined world.

He drove faster, and faster still, thinking only of his computer, of the urgent need return to his writing—which was returning to him and fast, roaring into his head like some kind of a dam-break flood blasting down the stream behind his house, a flood of words—

—and then there were lights, bright, back windshield.

Damn, he did not need another ticket, he was gonna need to take a damn compulsory driving course, which would take hours and piss him off in a mighty way.

"Hey, there, Matt, I'm sorry, I guess I was a little fast, there."

"Wiley, you were doing a hundred and eleven."

"Oh, that is bad."

"Well, you know, I don't usually stop town people. But—"

"How's Beka?"

"Aw, shut up."

"Uh, I could buy you a box of Partagas? Or just hand over the fifteen hundred bucks they cost? Cash, now?"

"I'll take money and smokes. But I'm still gonna have to write this up."

"Aw, fuck, Matt. Damnit, *fuck*."

"Why were you going so fast? I mean, damn."

"What can I tell you? I'm crazy."

Matt wrote the ticket and handed it in for Wiley to sign. "This is gonna four-point you, but this is town, you're in town, and we just—a hundred and eleven is not good, Wiley, I'm sorry."

Four points added to the eight he already had would mean not only compulsory driver's ed, but also a court appearance.

"I'm gonna call George Piccolo and tell him you harassed me."

"You do that and I'll beat your ass, boy."

When they were kids, Matt had always won. He was heavier, he was faster, but Wiley was capable of getting more pissed off, as he did now. "Gimme the goddamn ticket, and for the love of God don't tell Brooke or I'll get my ass whupped, serious."

"Well, you might like that."

"Tell you what, I'm gonna drive home at thirty miles an hour and then I'm goin' back to the cave for a smoke. I'll call you on your cell to share my enjoyment with you."

"Smoke my cigars, you're gonna eat the butts. Remember that, because I get off duty in an hour and I *will* check."

Hiding the ticket carefully, he drove on. He'd find a way to hide the fat check to the county in Quicken. Somehow or other.

Once back in his office, he pulled out the bottle of Woodford Reserve he kept in his bottom-drawer liquor stash and sipped at it.

What seemed like the next moment, voices caused him to come awake. Had he been sleeping? What had just happened? For a disoriented moment, he had the horrifying sense that he'd crossed into the parallel universe. But then the voices resolved into familiar ones. Brooke was coming in from the garage with the kids. She'd brought them home from school.

He looked at his watch in stunned amazement. It was four-thirty and the sun was on its way down. He'd been sitting here all day. Writing? He had no idea.

He listened to Brooke, to Kelsey's high voice full of excitement about a snake in show and tell, to Nick's thumping tread on the back stairs.

Then silence fell, and what he listened to now was the silence. Soon, the words came again, the *words*—whispering, shouting, demanding, from the other universe.

It was Martin, and he was talking to himself, and Wiley knew why. The poor guy had stayed here at the house, and was trying to force himself not to follow his family, and was agonized about that.

Martin was crying out, Martin was more desperate than any human being Wylie had ever known.

FIVE
DECEMBER 3
THE BUNKER

AND NOW, SUDDENLY, WYLIE WAS looking at trees. At grass. He knew that he was far from Harrow, Kansas.

He wanted to return to Martin. He could feel the poor guy's mind just racing for solutions, could feel his hunger to give up and blow his poor damn brains out, and his agony that he could not because those he loved could not.

He took a deep breath, closed his eyes, and saw that he was in a dark meadow in a pine woods. There were vents low to the ground, humming softly. Two deer, their ears turning this way and that, ventured out from the shadows.

Then he thought maybe he knew what this was. Martin had followed his family after all. He would have loaded his car up with food and water and set out through the woods and across the fields of his beloved Kansas, and that's where this was.

But no, it was too quiet and too—well, the word was *creepy*. It had an evil feel to it. Nasty. The deer were uneasy, flipping their tails, their great eyes wary.

Night was falling here, the west was dense with clouds . . . and there was flickering in the clouds. A sign, he feared, of the disks.

Then he wasn't in a meadow anymore, he was in a gray place that was softly rumbling. There were walls here, a long corridor lit by bulbs in wire cages.

Footsteps came, somebody moving fast, and a man in uniform wheeled around a corner. General Al North moved along the hallway in what appeared to be a military bunker of some sort. As the general came closer, Wylie could see that his fatigues were dirty, his face was sheened with sweat, his eyes, which had been gray and full of resolve in Washington, were now the flitting eyes of a rat.

So, he had survived the attack. Wiley had wondered about what had happened to these people. This was a huge thing, involving the whole world, and Washington had taken one of the early hits.

Al burst into Tom Samson's office. "Does the president know about this?" he shouted, throwing a crumpled sheet of paper down on his superior officer's desk.

"How dare you!"

"You're telling them to *congregate*? To gather in groups? Are you insane?"

"God damn you."

"Oh, shut up with your bluster, Tom. You're in way over your head and you never should've been appointed and we both know it. But this—this isn't just executive ineptitude. This is treason and I want an explanation that satisfies me, or I'm gonna arrest you, General."

"You? You don't have the authority."

"This is war. We're out of touch with higher authority."

"The president of the United States is two offices away."

"And I'm carryin' and you're not, and I'll shoot you as soon as look at you unless you explain this goddamn thing. How many people have received this?"

"Pitifully few, given that I'm forced to deliver it with blimps, trucks, Cessnas, and word of mouth."

"Let me go in another direction with this. We got a communication from Fort Riley about three hours ago, to the effect that a group of small towns northwest of Topeka took a terrific hit last night. They had your pamphlet. They congregated in their churches. And eight out of ten of these people are now wanderers. Thank you, Tom. I thank you for them, for their families, for the country. And what's this Kansas deal? Why did you even leaflet these people? Did you somehow know that Lautner County was gonna take a hit?"

"Of course not."

"Oh, no, you did. Because you singled it out. Two days ago, you directed a blimp run over the whole area."

"Routine."

"Really? Why not hit Topeka? Why not hit K.C.? But instead, you just go to this one little county. So I have to ask you, Tom, who's side are you on?"

"Don't be ridiculous!"

"Our chains of command are busted all to hell, Tom. We're going down in damn flames, worldwide. Bases raided by the disks time and again, desertions by the tens of thousands—we're done, man."

"We have a weapon."

"What? Stealth bombers? Nukes like the one that failed to do jack shit to the lens on Easter Island? Now, there was a good move. We nuke 'em and as a result they pick up their pace a hundredfold. So I'm not so sure I even want to hear about this damn weapon."

"You want to hear about it."

He picked up the crumpled pamphlet. "I want to hear about this, Tom."

"Aw, Christ. Has anybody ever actually told you what an extreme asshole you are?"

"Please," Al said.

"You talk about failure of discipline—speaking of Kansas, you belong in Leavenworth."

Should Al just draw the gun and shoot? How would the president react to that? "Tom, you should've told them to hide, seal themselves in spaces where no light can reach. Force the attack to be executed in detail. Takes more time that way, and we already know that they withdraw at dawn."

"Fish school because mathematically the survival rate among large populations being attacked by predators is greater than that for isolated individuals. Same goes for herding animals. And under these circumstances, my friend, the same exact principle applies to us."

"Let's put it to the president."

"The pamphlets are being distributed as fast as we can manage it, and that's going to continue. Do you know why we were concerned about Lautner County?"

"No."

"Your friend, the little man, the archaeologist—he's there. And they want him dead, I can assure you."

"They? I'm dealing with lenses that emit these bursts of disks every night that go out and wreak havoc. There is no 'they.' "

"Somebody's behind the lenses and behind the disks, never doubt it, and your man is a danger because he has the smarts and the knowledge of the deep past to maybe figure this out, and maybe—just maybe—to figure out a vulnerability. And they know it, and they are after that man."

"Did they get him?"

"Don't know. The place is in chaos, communications are down."

"Why doesn't that surprise me?"

"You still ready to shoot me?"

Al was silent.

"Then you start respecting my command. You salute me, and you call me *sir*."

Al shook his head, laughing to himself.

"Do it now, goddamn you!"

The two men glared at each other. Al did not salute.

"I'm doing my job, Al. Best I can. Under the worst conditions any American general has ever experienced."

Slowly, as if his arm itself was unwilling, Al raised his hand and saluted. "Yes, Sir," he said.

"Okay, I have an appointment with the president. I want you in attendance, Al."

That surprised him so much he almost gagged. He'd seen himself as being on the way to Diego Garcia for a tour managing the fuel dump. As if there still was a Diego Garcia, let alone a base, let alone fuel.

Face time with the president was a gift. Normally, he couldn't go on his own unless called, and Wade was not in the mood for squash, although there was a good court down here, he'd looked it over when they first came in and this was all exciting and interesting, and they were gonna nuke those suckers to glowing dust balls and go back home in triumph.

As they went along the hall together, Tom put a hand on Al's shoulder. "We're not friends."

"No."

"But we need to put our personal battle on hold. We've got warfighting to do, and we are in trouble. You're about to hear a report that is going to disturb you. Maybe also give you a ray of hope. But I want you to maintain strict military discipline in there. He will ask for your opinion. It will mirror mine."

"Yes, Sir." He realized that this was how it had to be. He just hoped to God that Tom was right. That business about congregating still sounded wrong. It sounded like intentional sabotage.

They went through the outer office. No pretty furniture here, this place was constructed for work and work only. If the president was here, a catastrophe was unfolding. Communications equipment dominated. Secret Service agents with machine guns lined the halls, young men with stricken eyes, all watching the generals pass. Angry, bitter eyes. Mostly, the families of these people lived in places like Arlington and Bethesda, and those communities had been worked for a full week, all of them, and the fleeing lines of cars had been worked out on the interstates.

Whoever was doing this knew exactly how to proceed. If you break the enemy's organization, you neutralize his warfighting capacity even before he's aimed a weapon. Of course, down here there was no question of the light being a threat, but this was obviously a special place.

There were numerous corporate and private bunkers as well, he knew, not to mention government facilities all over the planet, but with all satellites fried and most land-based switching stations so loaded with atmospherics that they'd shut down, there was little communication except by messenger—and they could only run during daylight hours.

They entered the presidential office, and Al was horrified at what he saw. The president looked like he'd lost fifty pounds. His eyes were dark, brooding shadows. Trapped, animal eyes.

He looked mean, in the same way a struggling cur looks mean when you're trying to stuff it into a cage and be done with it.

He raised his head, and at once the misery in the face was replaced by a beggar's grin. Now he was a used car salesman who'd spun his last lie. "Sorry," he said, gesturing at papers on his desk. "Signing death warrants. Line of duty desertions, hundreds of them."

"You're ordering executions, sir?"

"Do me a favor, Al. Call me Jimmy. You guys. Should I, you think? Yeah, it's total bullshit, isn't it. They came from CIA, not DoD. There is no DoD, of course. And Bo Waldo's gone. This shit's from staffers." He crumpled one up. "Kids like to kill."

"They're operating out of a unit in Maryland," Tom said. "Above-ground, so it won't matter much longer, be my guess—Jesus, what was that?"

The president looked up, they all looked up. There had been a sound coming out of the ceiling, a low noise, loud enough, though, to drown conversation.

"Call the contractor," the president said, acid in his voice. "Try flushing my toilet sometime, you want a hell of a damned surprise." He sighed. "I wish I knew where my wife and kids were. Do you fellas know where your families are?"

"I've been divorced, Jimmy—oh, long time," Al said. Sissy had packed it in when they were still base bums, shuffling around the world. He'd never bothered to remarry. The air force was his wife, his kids, his mistress, all that and more. As far as his rocks were concerned, he got them off the way monks did.

"My wife is whereabouts unknown," Tom said.

They'd worked together a long time for Al not to know that Tom was married. But it had never come up. Come to think of it, they'd never even shared a round of golf together, or a game of squash, or had a drink. Then again, maybe Tom didn't drink. Addicts don't, do they?

The sound came again, and this time it was in the wall—moving down from above.

The president stood up. "Is that normal?"

"It's the plumbing," Tom said. "What we need to talk about is I want to reach out to this man, Martin Winters. I want to reach out to other people with knowledge of the deep past. I have a list, Graham Hancock, William Henry, Laurence Gardner, John Jenkins—all leading experts who used to be considered wrong. I want them all located."

The president went to the wall, felt it. "There's heat," he said. "That should not be."

"Call security," Al said.

Tom gave him a look that said he had just overstepped his bounds. Don't speak unless spoken to.

"I have come to believe that what's happening has to do with the deep past," Tom continued.

"That's not news," the president snapped. "Tell me something I can use, please! And don't ask me for permission to convene meetings. I don't care who the hell you talk to, just save our asses, here, Tom! For God's sake, Homeland Security—what's left of it—tells me we're losing a half a million people a night just in this country. Wanderers—well, they aren't wandering. They're all heading to three points: northern Nevada, central Nebraska, and northern Indiana. Now, why? You might ask, right, Al?"

"Yes, sir."

"Yes, sir . . . The FBI is in total meltdown, so that leaves military intelligence. So, here's my question to you fellas, do you have any assets working?"

"We've got assets," Al said.

"Oh, good. Then reach out and get me reports." He laughed a little. The beaten-dog look returned—beaten dog turned mean. "Or just tell them to fucking nuke themselves. I mean, why wait around? Wandering's hard on the tootsies, I hear." He took a fabulous silver-clad forty-five automatic out of a desk drawer. Laid it on the desk. "Can you guys imagine what it is like to be a pregnant woman now? Out there?" He sucked air through bared teeth. His color had deepened so much that Al thought he might be having a coronary. "My God, but it was all so very, very beautiful. And how odd that we didn't know it. All that yelling, all that scheming, the money, my dear heaven, the *money*—and what was it, in the end? I have come to this: a single child seeing one single leaf that has turned in the fine autumn air means more than all of that. A child clapping because the leaf is red and it was green."

"Mr. President—"

"Of course I've gone mad, Tom. For God's sakes, in this situation, madness is sanity. Millie, where are you, baby, are you out there walking the dark path with all the others? Oh, Millie. Forty-four years she walked beside me, fellas. Forty-four years. She gave it all. Everything she had to give. And I can't even think about Mark. Somewhere, I trust. My poor boy." He picked up the gun. "Gentlemen, would you like to join me in a bite of bullet?"

"Mr. President!"

"Al, you know what? You are the nicest man I have ever known." He laughed. "That's why I gave shitheel here your job. He can do it, he's a real bastard. I'm sorry, Al, but you came along at the burnt-out end of the age. No more room for good men." He sighed. " 'What rough beast slouches toward Bethlehem . . .' I had a great-uncle who knew Yeats. Met him by simply going up to his door in Dublin and knocking. Oh, my God, the voice of the man! The voice of Yeats!" He wept, and Al almost wept with him.

There came, then, a sort of chuckling sound. It was really a very strange sound, so strange that Al knew at once that it was no noise ever heard on this earth before—at least, not in this cycle of history.

The president's head snapped to the left. He stared at the wall. Then he turned back, his eyes liquid with pleading. "Why?"

He was pleading with Tom. But Tom didn't need to be pleaded with, he was an underling.

Something then happened that must have looked to Al like the arrival of the Spaniards on their horses must have looked to the Aztecs. Something was in the room that could not be there, that had come from nowhere—not out of the wall, but out of the sound in the wall. He could not say exactly what it looked like—a shell so black that it absorbed light, or a machine propelled on enormous legs, or a gigantic spider, even. The sort of thing that comes out of the closet when you are four, and eventually recedes on the expiring tide of childhood.

He heard a voice, *"Agnus dei,"* Lamb of God, sounding so pure that it was as if sounded from the highest, the farthest of all voices—a voice beyond telling. Wade ascending.

"Qui tollis peccata mundi," the president whispered, *"who takes away the sins of the world."*

The roar of the gun was like a blast of Satan's breath, so ferocious that it made Al cry out, so enormous that it seemed to gather the whole bunker in its strength and crush it to rubble.

Al had him in his arms before his body, which had slapped into the wall, had even begun to slide to the floor. He stank of raw blood, his left eye was shuddering like the wing of a wounded fly, then green and bloody vomit pumped out of him with a furious, questing seizure that parodied sexual passion.

Secret Service poured into the room. One of them lifted his machine gun, braced it at Tom, who stood quite calmly, the very least of smiles on his face. He did not even glance at the young man with the gun, or any of the young men frozen in the doorway.

"I have a mission for you, Al," he said. "Put him down, you'll need to leave at once."

Al laid the president—Jimmy—on the thinly carpeted floor. He went to attention. "Yes, sir," he said. He saluted his superior officer, now the leader of the free world.

SIX
DECEMBER 3
WANTED

MARTIN DROVE HARD, IGNORING THE thudding of his tires and the screech of harvest stubble scraping the sides of his truck. In the east, dawn burned orange, so he didn't have much time before the lights of followers would become invisible and he'd lose his chance to catch up, maybe forever.

Last night, he'd driven out to his house to be in their path, but hadn't been able to find his family. Wanderers had gone past, but there had been so many of them, far more than he'd realized, and his family had escaped him.

He consulted his compass. He was no navigator, but was trying to drive as straight in a north-northwesterly direction as he could. Wanderers went in straight lines, so people said.

At first, he'd tried to reason with Lindy. He had picked up Winnie and carried her to the car—and been bitten for his trouble. He had not been able to find Trevor at all, which had only added to his sorrow.

All around him, there had been screaming people, begging their loved ones not to go, trying to wake them up.

They'd gone off down Third Street and between two boarded-up stores. Behind those stores was Oak Street, then behind it Linnert Lane, then the plains, and ten miles out, the Smokes, and beyond them the high plains, then Canada. And somewhere, he felt sure, whatever fate was in store for them.

Martin had trotted over to his jeep and got in—and then Bobby was there. "Hey, guy, we need to do this another way."

Martin had looked at him, and it was like looking across a great, black river to a man whose life was unfolding on a better shore. He fought the tears down, but when his friend reached in and put a hand on his shoulder, he broke down. Bobby stayed with him until there were screams, then shots, off in the direction of Oak Street. A follower was killing a wanderer, probably based on an agreement. It was a common thing, these days, not considered murder. "Gotta go," Bobby said. "You stay right here, you're comin' home with us."

Martin had waited for a couple of minutes, but then he had turned on his car and moved off toward Linnert Lane. He had seen, out in the fallow fields, a slowly moving cluster of lights, disappearing into the night. There were voices, too, cries and pleas echoing in the silence, and then a voice, high and full of something Martin guessed must be faith, "Yea, though we walk through the valley of the shadow of death . . ." then lost to an errant wind and long thunder out of the west.

Martin had not returned to Third Street Methodist. He had not been able to face going home with the Chalmers family.

Instead, he had driven out into the night, going up 1540 into the Smokes. He knew every inch of the hills where he lived. As a boy, he'd hunted the Smokes with his dad, taking whitetail deer and turkey. He'd hunted across the very land where he'd built his house. Nowadays, he didn't hunt, largely because Trevor wasn't interested. He preferred the intricacies of fishing, and just Saturday before last they'd driven over to the Kaw River and fished for cats with cut shad and done well . . . except, of course, Lindy and Winnie had thought them insane to use shad as bait in order to eat catfish, but they were women and—oh, hell, he'd had to pull over, he was just plain overcome.

By the time he'd gotten home, he'd known that he was in serious shock. He needed medical attention. But Willerson was the only doctor in town and hadn't he gone out with the wanderers? Martin had taken a couple of the Xanax he used to mainline during bill-paying time.

He'd wandered his own home like a ghost, pacing from room to room, hugging Winnie's beloved stuffed elephant she had named Bearish and burying his face in Trevor's pillow. He had ended up in his own bed clutching one of Lindy's nightgowns to his face, and had stayed there until the sun was well up.

There had come a buzz from the front door. It was Rosie with food, the sort of casserole you brought to the bereaved.

"Harrow's formed a committee," she had said. "Followers. You're welcome to join. They're going to be taking food and water. Some plan on going all the way."

"Do we still know where they are?"

"Helen's out there with a walkie-talkie. They're about twelve miles out, moving at three miles an hour. North-northwest, just like all the rest. They're about a mile from Holcomb's wanderers, and it looks like the two groups're gonna meet up about noon. That'll put it up to about two thousand people."

"Two *thousand*!"

"Hon, there's just eighteen intact families in Harrow. None in Holcomb. In fact, Bobby drove over there and he's telling us the place is entirely empty."

Then she added, "We also lost some kids. Children of folks who got hit. The little ones stayed around, but a lot of the older kids—fifteen to twenty or so—we can't find them. They aren't wandering and they aren't here anymore."

Another unknown was a cold, frightening thought.

Rosie had helped him pile the jeep with every bit of everything edible and drinkable in the house—a six-pack of Dr Pepper, two bunches of celery, beer, milk, half-and-half, orange and cranapple juice, Winnie's soy milk, all the cereal, the Lean Cuisines, everything he could find, even unbaked refrigerator cookies, and seeing the Pillsbury Doughboy on a half-used tube of cookies had brought more tears, angry tears.

He had driven out just after noon, going down 205 to the Holcomb crossroads and then out into the fields. He'd crisscrossed the countryside for hours, finding not a sign of anybody. Increasingly afraid and frustrated, he'd driven harder and harder, bounding through fields, screaming around bends, and in all that time not come upon a single human being, wanderer, follower, or free.

Now he was here, sitting on a bare quarter of a tank of gas with the sun going down. He realized that he was at Dennis Farm, one of the places that had been hit before the strike on Harrow. Well, he knew the Dennises, and he decided that he could go ahead and borrow some of their tractor gas. He drove the jeep over to the pump and tried to turn it on. No good. He went around the side of the barn and fired up the generator, then returned and filled his tank. He looked across at the dark house, and after he'd cut off the pump and the generator, got in the jeep to continue his quest.

He thought he heard something, though, and went over to the house. He approached it warily, not sure what to expect. The Dennises had raised about ten kids, but they were all gone, doctors and lawyers and corporate executives and other things that were not farmers.

He heard it again, a sort of mechanical chuckling sound. Was it coming from inside? He couldn't be sure. Could be around the side of the house. "Hello? Anybody there?"

No response. Then the sound returned, more distinct this time, and he realized that it was coming from two directions, out behind the low hill that separated the house from their north fields, and then again from down near the pretty little stream that was one of the reasons they'd put the house here.

For all the world, it sounded like two dirty old men chuckling at him over his plight. "Hello?"

Then he heard something in the sky, *whoosh . . . whoosh*. He looked up, but clouds were coming in and it had turned inky black.

His mouth went dry, his heart began the peculiar, twisting beat that came when his fear increased. He ran to his car and jumped in and locked the doors. Who knew what might be out there? Aliens, even, the concealed architects. What was it some old scientist had said, "Aliens when they come will be stranger than anything we have ever imagined, or can possibly imagine." Words to that effect. Beings from a parallel universe might be even stranger . . . or strangely similar.

He got out of there fast, driving as close to northwest as he could, blasting his way through the stubble-choked, furrowed fields. How very ordinary it had all seemed just a month ago. Driving out this way to pick out a Thanksgiving turkey at Smeal's, he had seen Old Man Dennis working his harvest, thought how sad it was that, out of all those kids, he couldn't find a single one willing to continue the tradition. Word was they were going to sell out and move to Florida, but he'd thought at the time, *No, the Dennises are gonna die on that land.*

The sun slid behind the clouds, and with night came an increase of loneliness that was so deep it amounted to a new kind of emotion for him.

He drove on, searching blindly, trying his best to stay on course.

It was some moments after he'd seen the glow on the horizon that he realized that it meant headlights in the distance. He stopped the jeep, got out, and clambered up on the roof. About two miles ahead, there was a slowly moving cluster of lights—the cars and trucks of followers. Couldn't be from Holcomb, they had all been disensouled. So that had to be the Harrow contingent.

Lindy was out there somewhere, his Lindy and his Winnie and maybe Trevor. He looked up into the black sky and wondered if those were dead bodies out there, and if his family's souls had gone somewhere better. *Oh God, please help them. Help me help them, God. If only you're there, we need you. We need you.*

He got down and drove ahead, keeping his own lights off so he could see the caravan. He closed quickly. They weren't going fast, obviously. Soon, he was in among them, about five vehicles. It had been more. The wanderers had lost many followers.

"Hey, bone collector," a woman's voice yelled.

"Helen!"

She leaned out the back of the Turpins' mangled Buick. "Got supplies?"

"I got 'em!"

"My Reg likes Oreos, you got Oreos?"

"I've got some Pillsbury chocolate chip cookie mix."

"Well, hell, I'll try it on 'im. I think he sorta recognized John Twenty-four by the way, so I'm lookin' for a comeback."

"You folks seen Lindy?"

Another voice called, "Sure thing, Martin. We fed your family twice. Your girl's happy when she gets soy milk." That was right, oh God, that was Winnie's favorite.

He scoured the backs that were visible in the car lights, but there were so many of them, it wasn't a small crowd, it was enormous, it stretched on and on.

He stopped and got out. He grabbed soy milk and orange juice, they would need strength and fluids, they would be in shock and they'd been walking continuously now for close to twenty hours.

"Be careful, there," a voice said as he sprinted among the vehicles, then out into the darker crowd of wanderers. "Winnie," he called, "Soy milk, soy milk! Trevor Winters, Dad's here, Dad's got cranapple."

Then he saw a back, familiar hair. He doubled his speed, pushing past people who were breathing hard, who were staggering. What was going to happen, would they be walked to death? Why not kill them outright and save everybody this terrible, terrible suffering?

"Lindy! LINDY!"

A head turned, and he found himself looking into the empty grin of Beryl Walsh, the local bank manager. He went on. "Lindy! Trevor! Winnie!"

There was her hair again, and this time he was sure. "Oh, Lindy, hey, hey, it's me, babes, I'm gonna take you home, I've got the truck, I'm gonna take you guys home!"

He came up beside her, and it was definitely Lindy of the green eyes and the straight, proud nose, Lindy of the bobbing blond hair. "Oh baby, I got you. Thank the Lord." He looked around. "Where are the kids? Winnie? Where's Winnie?"

Not a glance, not a word. He sprinted in front of her, walked backward as he talked. "The kids, Lindy, where are the kids?"

She came straight on, her face expressionless. Unlike some of them, she didn't even have a smile left in her. She strode like a Valkyrie, though, a powerful, healthy woman . . . whom, he thought, was going to make an excellent slave.

Would they be taken to another world, like the slavers took people from Africa? How similar that must have felt to this, to the people who watched the ships sail away. It had been history to him before, but those millions of lost families were now part of his heart.

And he thought, the Nephilim, those strange rapists mentioned in Genesis, called the fallen ones, they had enslaved us before biblical times, had they not? Enslaved us, and then gone. Mysteriously.

In recent years, as his data piled up, he had become more and more willing to entertain the notion that there might have been some sort of human-alien interaction in the distant past, which had led to the catastrophe of 12,000 B.C., when the makers of the great stone monuments had abruptly vanished.

Had it been a war? Had it been, perhaps, something like this? And therefore were these people going to some far place destined to suffer a fate that maybe not even God could know?

Then, a miracle. He saw Winnie. She was trundling along, she had a bit of a limp. He ran to her, swept her up in his arms, cried out, buried his face in her little-girl sweetness—and then realized that her legs were still moving. She was still walking, in fact, she hadn't stopped walking even when she was picked up.

Pointing her back toward the car, he put her down. She took a few steps, then, as if she was controlled by some sort of inner gyroscope, she turned abruptly and continued on with the others. He hurried along beside her. "I've got some soy milk for you, honey," he said. He fumbled in his pocket for a box of it and held it out to her. She took it and drank it down. "Thank you, baby," he found himself saying, "thank you." Then he cried out, "Trevor! Trevor Winters! Dad's here, I've got cranapple. Dad has cranapple." His throat constricted and he had to stop. He controlled his emotions, fought them back, and kept on. "Trevor Winters, Trevor Winters."

He moved back and forth in the crowd, and suddenly there was a light in his eyes. "Martin! Hey, buddy!"

"Uh—you're—"

"George Matthews, I'm that damn plumber."

"Oh, George, for the love a—yeah!"

"You're looking for Trevor?"

"Yeah, actually. I got Winnie to drink some soy milk."

"That ain't Winnie anymore, and Trevor's not here."

"Not here?"

"Nah, Trevor's not wandering."

He grabbed the man's shoulder. "George! George, are you sure!"

"There's something else going on. There's kids gone."

"Are they—are they okay, George?"

He could feel George's eyes on him. "Dunno. But my girl's one of 'em. Wife's out here."

"And you're sure they're not—Trevor is definitely not here? You're certain of it?"

"Not certain of anything in this world, bro, but I've been out here all day with my Molly, and I've seen Winnie and Lindy plenty, but not him, and I did see him—you know, after the church—and he was going out toward the Smokes with my daughter and some of the middle-schoolers. He wasn't wandering, Martin."

Martin turned around with the intention of going back to the house immediately—and it was then that he saw the thick column of light drop down like some kind of bright shroud on the cars of the followers.

"Oh my God," he said.

George turned, too, and saw it. "God almighty." He began to run, loping ahead to the wanderers, who continued on at their steady and oblivious pace. Martin's first impulse was to follow him, but a golden shaft came down, razor-thin and quick, and George sparkled for a moment, and then dropped back, joining his pace to that of the other wanderers.

It had been that quick. Martin forced himself not to run, he forced himself to fall in with the wanderers, to pretend to be one of them. As he had on many a hike, he walked beside his wife. The screaming behind him told him that the light was doing all the followers. Their compassion and their love had been used to trap them.

Then he saw little Winnie fall and cry out, and his whole heart and soul longed to help his child, but he kept on walking.

The wanderers never slowed their pace, but every so often, he saw one or another of them fall down. The others simply walked over them.

It was a brutal—and brutally efficient—selection process, he thought. Only the strong would make it, and only the strong, obviously, would be wanted. Overhead, he once again heard the *whoosh*, *whoosh* of . . . something. Could it be that a big old barn owl was shadowing them? But the owl's wing is silent.

Ahead and to his left there was leaping movement. A voice rose in a frantic salad of words, babbling and shrieking, then going silent. He looked neither left nor right, but kept on, leaving the struggle behind him. Soon the voice was silent, replaced by that odd, mechanical chuckling he'd heard in the woods around his house. Eventually, the sounds faded.

He was aware that Lindy was just beyond his touch, and that Winnie maybe had fallen aside. He forgot all his careful intellectualizations about God and prayed the Jesus Prayer over and over again, the prayer out of J. D. Salinger's *Franny and Zooey*, which had been a favorite of Lindy's. It was the repetitive prayer from *The Way of the Pilgrim*, "Lord Jesus Christ, have mercy on me, a sinner."

As the stars wheeled in their generous majesty, Martin walked to the rhythm set by repetitions. From time to time the light dropped down on another follower it had discovered in the mass of wanderers, and ripped out a soul.

The rhythm made it easier for him, but by the time two hours had passed, he knew that he could not keep up with the pace of the wanderers much longer. He was contemplating this danger, letting the prayer drop into the back of his mind, when he heard a distant voice. It had an echoing, mechanical quality to it. He listened—and then, incredibly, saw its source. A police car stood on a roadside ahead, it's light bar flashing. Beside it stood a state policeman with an electronic bullhorn. He raised it to his lips and blared, "You are trespassing on a wildlife preservation zone. You are required to leave this area immediately. Please come up to the roadway, ladies and gentlemen. You are trespassing—"

A tongue of light snicked down out of the clouds and there appeared around him the loveliest spreading glitter of little stars that Martin had ever seen. From this distance, you could see exactly how the light made the soul literally burst out of the body. He thought that a human soul was truly a universe all its own, as the stars that had been that man's memories, dreams, and hopes flittered into oblivion. The trooper dropped his bullhorn and turned northwest.

Martin had reached a point of crisis. He had to stop. No choice. Already, he was visibly dropping back, he couldn't help it. "Good-bye, Lindy," he said in his heart, "good-bye my love, and good-bye Lindy's soul, wherever you are, and god rest you, my baby Winnie, my poor little girl never even had a life." Then he let himself fall forward like an exhausted wanderer. He did not close his eyes, but rather continued staring straight down at the ground.

Soon, the last of the wanderers had passed him by. He heard the intimate whistle of a night bird. Then something else—that chuckling again. It was close, and there was a lot of it. Now he thought it was like a flock of geese in flight, honking back and forth to one another as they ploughed the sky.

The aliens. That must be it. This sound represented the elusive aliens, coming along behind their human herd. Drovers. Cowboys.

Then something stepped on his back. It was heavy, and it had a sharpness that penetrated his jeans and entered his thigh. He had to force himself not to move as this sharpness very painfully twisted inside his flaring muscle.

Then it was gone, and he could just glimpse what looked like the leg of an insect touching the ground beside his face, then another, and then the chuckling had gone on ahead, and with it the faint whooshing and whistling in the sky.

Then he knew that there was light all around him. He felt the most incredible rage at his defeat, and then waited to feel the light, to know what it was like to lose your soul. Did you go with it, or stay in your body—or, as he thought—just disappear?

But then there was something in his ear. Snuffling. And an odor, a familiar one. He opened his eyes, turned his head, and found himself face to face with a very large skunk.

As the tail rose, he rolled, then jumped up and ran like hell, and the skunk ran, too, wobbling off into the light, which was not the light of death, but that of dawn.

He stood up in the sunlight. It was golden, low still on the horizon, but so pure that it must be as sacred as the old Egyptians had thought, and he turned toward it and knelt as he might to God.

Then he went back along the long series of low folds in the land, heading toward his truck, hoping to find Winnie's body somewhere, a little snatch of clothes somewhere in the prairie.

But he found an adult instead, blood-soaked, dead. This was no fallen wanderer, this person had been done violence. He looked down. The school jacket, the smoothness of the backs of the hands—this was just a kid. He turned him over, and leaped back when he realized what he was seeing, and when he fully realized it, screamed.

Instantly, he stifled it. The light did not come during the day, apparently being rendered ineffective by the sun, but there had been other things out there and he wasn't so sure that they were particularly nocturnal.

He thought that this pitiful ruin must have been a boy. He was, at most, fifteen or sixteen, and he had been horrifically mutilated. His lips were gone, his mouth open and his tongue removed. His eyes had been gouged out, and his lower body was bloody. Martin didn't examine him too closely, but it looked as if he had been castrated, too.

He forced himself to open the shirt, to look for the familiar mole that would mean he had found his son.

The cool gray skin was unblemished.

Martin stood up and ran a short distance, then came back and picked the poor kid up, and carried him in his arms. He carried him across a field and into an empty farmyard, and put him down in a porch swing.

"Hey! Anybody home? Hey!"

Not a sound. He went inside and found eggs in the fridge, and cracked six of them raw into his mouth. He also ate cheese and crunched into a head of lettuce. He drank warm grapefruit juice that nearly made him puke.

Then he went on, walking until the sun was high and warm, and the gladness that it brings even to the most oppressed human heart made him close his eyes and lift his face to it. "Lucky old sun," he said.

Whereupon he found his truck . . . which he had left running. He jumped in and pulled the key out.

He'd damn well burned out all his gas, damned fool that he was. Fool!

Well, not quite all. There was a hairline between the edge of the gauge and the red line, so there was still a mile or so in it.

He walked back to the farm, but this was a hobby place, there was no gas tank here. Returning to the jeep, he got in and started it. He headed back toward Harrow, and had the town in sight when he ran out of gas.

He never passed Dennis Farm, but he'd been looking for it. Never saw a trace of it, must have been too far east of it, he figured.

He walked for half an hour, finally crossing the last field and climbing a final fence. Then he was in a backyard. He went down the driveway beside the house and into the dead-empty streets. A flicker of curtain in this house or that was the only indication of life here.

He was passing the bank when a familiar car pulled alongside him. "Bobby!"

Bobby just looked up at him. His eyes were strange, and for a moment Martin had a horrible thought. "Bobby?"

"Yeah?"

"Your family okay?"

He stopped his car.

Jesus, his family had gotten it in the night. "Oh, buddy, did you lose 'em?"

He shook his head.

"Bobby, what's the matter?"

He held out a flyer. Martin took it. He was astonished to find himself staring at his own face. "This man is wanted dead. Name: Martin Trevor Winters. Last seen in the area of Lautner County, Kansas. This man is extremely dangerous, and carries a bounty of ten million dollars, upon satisfactory proof of death being provided."

Martin looked at Bobby, met his eyes, saw them flicker away. His face said it clearly: this was not a joke. "Homeland Security dropped them about half an hour ago."

"But I—there must be some mistake!"

"Buddy, you know I love you. But I got this job, here, and half the town, they are looking for your blood."

"But what did I do? Why has this happened?"

"It doesn't say what you did, but we all know you were over there in Egypt when the pyramid went, and it must have something to do with that, which is why I'm arresting you, buddy."

"Bobby?"

"I'm not gonna read you your rights. Because it's a patriot arrest, you don't have any rights."

"Bobby, hey!"

But Bobby cuffed him and took him off to the sheriff's substation, and put him in the one cell, which had been cleaned of file boxes for the occasion. He drove through town telling them that Martin had been caught, and they had to meet at First Christ to vote on what to do with him.

SEVEN
DECEMBER 4
THE TRAP

WILEY STARED AT THE WORDS on his computer screen. This damn nightmare was way out of control.

He'd come back from the shrink determined to just erase the whole thing, but he hadn't done it, and now look what had happened, it had gotten so much worse so fast. Winnie was probably dead and Trevor—God knew what had happened to him, and look at poor Martin. He was going to be killed by his friends.

But it wasn't only what was happening to this one little family, it was the whole vast scope of the thing, an entire world being destroyed.

That bastard Samson was part of it. Al North was right, he was a traitor. But the fool hadn't shot him. Stupid fool. Nice guys sure as hell finish last, General North.

Wylie had CNN on continuously now, waiting for any sign of anything odd happening at any sacred site in his own world.

So far, this dear old place was quiet. But would it be forever? They knew we were here, or we wouldn't see UFOs. They just needed one more little push, he suspected, and they'd be in. Let NASA announce that UFOs were real. Let the Air Force admit that it couldn't explain some sighting or other—and bang, here come the lenses, dark goddamn things blowing the same fourteen sacred sites to hell here as they did in the two-moon world.

When he wasn't writing, he did research and he thought. He thought about the number fourteen. It was the Osiris number, the Jesus number, the resurrection number. Seven was a complete octave and a complete life. Fourteen was a life and a life beyond. It was the number of the goal of man, which was the projection of human consciousness into eternity. Osiris had been cut into fourteen pieces. The passion of Christ had fourteen stations.

Destroy the man, build the man.

Might that be true, also, of whole worlds?

He sighed, blew air out. Was he tired? He was beyond tired. More exhausted than he'd thought it was possible to be.

He did not think he could imagine what the suffering going on Martin's world was like. By now, every single human being on the planet who was not himself a wanderer had lost at least one loved one. The sheer scale of it was beyond imagination. Appalling.

What could he write about it? That it brought tears to his eyes, made his mouth dry, made his stomach fill with fire?

Describing this was beyond even a great novelist's skill, and certainly beyond his.

Fourteen. He kept going back to it. The fourteen sacred places were there to enable us to recover the knowledge that made man immortal. Giza, Tassili, Ollantaytambo, all the way around to Easter Island, Sukothai, Persepolis and Petra—to enable us to recover the knowledge, and also to protect us from our ignorance.

In Martin's world, they had failed. Too late—just. He had been close, but not close enough, not in time. That was why Samson was after him. The knowledge he possessed was still dangerous.

It was evening now, on this earth, on Martin's earth, presumably on all the earths in all the universes that filled the unimaginable firmament—including the world of the reptilians.

He'd never seen it. Glimpsed it, perhaps, down in the draw that night—felt the delicate hands of the monsters, felt them raping him.

He thought he knew why it had been done. They needed a communicator to spread belief in them. Problem was, they chose the wrong guy. They needed a Nobel prize winner or a great political leader, not a horror novelist.

Too bad, suckas!

Voices shrill with excitement reassured him that all was still well, at least in his neck of the woods. Nick and Kelsey were playing normally outside. Brooke was downstairs making one of her stunning pot roasts.

The kids sounded very happy together, and that was not always the case. Even though she was eight and he thirteen, there was still plenty of sibling rivalry to cut through.

In another year, Nick probably wouldn't be willing to run around like that with his little sister, but he was having old-fashioned childhood fun now, oblivious for once to the fact that he would soon, at thirteen, no longer be a child.

It was a dark afternoon, with some heavy fall weather on its way in from the northwest. Typical Kansas, a little late for the season was all. He glanced at his weather radio. The light glowed green, meaning that it was on and hadn't picked up any alerts.

Still, blue flickering came from the sky, and thunder rolled in from far away. The storms were still the other side of Holcomb, maybe fifty miles out. Probably they'd arrive during the night.

He didn't like storms. He feared that the disks might come, might be hiding in them.

But no, the lenses were the anchors. Hooks in the gills of the fish, as it were. And there were no lenses here. He kept telling himself that.

Then he would think, what if there were just one or two? Tassili was in the middle of the desert. Nazca was isolated; so were a number of the other sites. Most of them. They had been created so long ago that they were all centered on a north pole from God only knew how far back in the past.

He wanted a drink so badly that he dared not open the liquor drawer. No way.

He stared at his words on the screen. Lindy and Winnie destroyed, Trevor gone, Martin about to be locked up . . . which he could still see taking place. Even though he had stopped writing, the story still unfolded in the bright hell of his mind. In it, Martin was watching his old friend lock the cell door, and Bobby had tears in his eyes as he did it.

No, this was too much, this had to go, and now was the time.

He selected the chapter and erased it—and wow, there were some blood, sweat, and tears down the drain. So okay, that was done and it should be done. He'd rewrite it with a more bearable scenario.

The blank page confronted him, and he told himself that he actually preferred blank pages.

Bullshit, this was awful, killing his work like this. But he had to, he could not see his people suffer this much.

So he started a new chapter. Then he stopped. He didn't feel like just plunging into it like this, and he was sick of using the laptop, which he closed. Writing on the computer was an addiction, and he already had too damn many of those, drinking the way he did and sneaking cigars, and wanting to do a lot more than that.

He put his beloved old Corona back in her place of honor. Now, this was a writer's tool. She clattered like an old freight train, churning out the words, engraving every mistake in stone. Everything he had done—everything real—had been done on this fine old typewriter. Early days, he would lie in bed writing through the night on yellow pads, then transcribe them onto her in the morning. Civilized way to work.

As he rolled in a sheet of paper, he noticed that the laptop hadn't gone off as he closed it. A defect due to the short, no doubt.

Intending to shut it down manually, he opened the clamshell.

There were words. He scrolled down. It was all there, right up to—here. He typed. These words appeared on the page. He erased them. As he did so, they reappeared. He did it faster, but the faster he worked, the faster they came back.

Okay, this appeared to be insanity at work here. This could not be. He erased the chapter again.

The process sort of made the words bounce, then they were back. He erased it again, then yet again and again, until erasure did nothing at all. Not even a flicker.

All right, this was crazy. This was not a possible thing.

He closed *2012*. Time to go nuclear. On his computer, he had a program called Zztz, which would destroy any file completely. It used the same sophisticated techniques approved by the Defense Department for the destruction of classified files.

He opened Zztz and dragged the entire *2012* file into it.

"Neutron bomb," he muttered, setting Zztz to Defcon 12, its ultimate destruction level.

So, he'd write another novel, big deal. Late or not, he'd come up with something.

Even as he watched Zztz work, the file came back. He destroyed it again. It came back again.

There was no level in the program higher than Defcon 12. But there was one other way to go about this. He went into the DOS prompt and typed "erase *.*"

By the time he was back in Windows, it had all returned.

He stared at the screen. This was proof of something, because if you can't make the erase function on your computer work, things are crazy.

"Brooke," he called.

From their kitchen, "Yeah!"

"Could you come up to my office for a second. It's important."

"Wiley, I've got a million balls in the air."

"Brooke, please!"

"In a minute!"

He found himself shaking, feeling the clammy coldness of fever or fear. Because this was proof, right here staring at him, that all these nightmares and all this craziness had something real about it. *It was exactly as real as he had feared.*

He jumped up and got out of the office like the place was on fire. He ran downstairs and threw his arms around Brooke. He kissed her forehead, her lips, her neck.

"Hey! I'm cuttin' up a stew, here, fella."

"Never leave me, for the love of God, never leave me!"

He took her in his arms, and this time he kissed her hard, pushing her head back, pulling her body to his until she was collapsed against him, her breasts compressed against his chest, their genitals pressing through their clothes.

When he let her go, her eyes were soft with pleasure. "We're gonna have a long night, I hope."

"I'm gonna break you in half, you gorgeous thing." Then all of his fear surfaced, and he held onto her as he might to a life preserver in the wild ocean. "I love you with all my soul," he whispered, his voice hushed in his truth.

Probably she didn't quite understand what had inspired this, but she didn't need to, the intensity and the honesty were there. She stroked his head, and her hand against his advancing baldness felt as soft as the wings of a butterfly. He remembered the yellow porch lights of his boyhood, and the moths there, their fluttering the only sound in the quiet of a summer night.

Thunder rumbled, long and low. It was accompanied by a distant flicker of lightning—and he reacted with a surge of terror so great that he all but pissed himself. He raced into the living room, cutting off lights as he went. The sky was alive with flickering.

He went out onto the porch, looked up into roiling high canyons of madly flickering clouds. And then at his kids running around in the eerie light.

"Kids, come inside, please."

"Aw, Dad."

"It's lightning, it's dangerous."

They continued to play.

"What's going on?" Brooke asked.

"Look at the sky!"

"Yeah, so what?"

"You don't understand!"

"Honey, it's miles away, you can hardly even hear it. Let them play."

"No, please, for me. Because I'm so scared for them, Brooke. I am scared for my kids and you need to help me."

"I think Crutchfield needs to help you."

"Okay, look, if you would deign to come upstairs for just a few minutes, I can prove to you that something is wrong around here. Very wrong."

She followed him.

"Okay, now. I erased Chapter 7 of my book just now. And it reappeared. Then I erased the entire book. And it reappeared."

"You erased your book?"

"Absolutely. From the DOS prompt. Absolute erasure."

"Goddamn it, we need that money."

"We need—I don't know what we need, here, exactly, but I do know that these people on the other side, they're having a hell of a bad time, and if I can erase this and rewrite it, maybe things will get better for them, and maybe for us, too, because there is a nightmare over there, and it is about to invade us, too."

She sat down at his desk. "Oh, this is nonsense. Here's your book right here."

"Erase it."

"I will not!"

"Okay, then, watch this—" He moved in front of her—and she grabbed his wrist. Her grip was strong, shockingly so.

"You will not, Wiley Dale. You will finish this and turn it in or you will lose me and your children."

"Excuse me?"

"How much self-indulgent bull crap can one woman take? Answer me that? Because I am personally at the end of my tether with you. I can't handle this anymore. How dare you bring me up here and terrorize me playing games like this. We could lose everything! End up on the street! I'm sick of being the wife of the rich writer who is actually a poor bastard."

"Never tell anybody I'm broke."

"Then write a book that sells and you won't be. Put food on the table, God damn you!"

She got up and stalked out. "Dinner in ten minutes," she called over her shoulder.

"There's obviously food on the table," he muttered—but very softly. Then he went back to his desk, put the Corona aside, and opened the laptop. He began to type.

Outside, the electric sky flashed.

He worked steadily. Thunder began rolling, as the source of the lightning swept closer, rumbling across the gathering night. Outside, the kids, now wearing sheets, swooped in the dark.

It was as if death echoed in the thunder, for he knew that this same storm, across the divide between the worlds, brought with it the body thieves.

Downstairs, Brooke began singing, as she usually did after they'd fought, "Listen to the mockingbird sweetly singing, singing over her grave . . ."

She knew, that was why she was singing a death song like that. That was also why the kids were playing ghost, they knew in their secret hearts that their counterparts in the other universe had lost their souls.

"Supper's ready," Brooke yelled, "and you might think about coming down in a reasonable time for once, Wylie."

He thought of Martin in his prison cell. Looked, in his mind's eye, and saw him standing there, just standing in the steel and concrete chamber.

He knew that Martin could hear his friends, most of whom he had known all his life, in the next room—what was left of the town crowded into that small space—arguing about whether or not to kill him.

They didn't care about the ten million bucks. What was that, anyway, at this point? But they had this warning from the authorities, and they still trusted their authorities.

"You idiots," he yelled, "he knows something, that's why General Samson wants him dead. The man knows!"

"Shut up and get down here, your supper's getting cold!"

"Yessum!"

Texas Max, the local *contrabandista*, had gotten in some fine absinthe recently, which Wiley had bought, of course, and put in the back of his desk drawer after giving it a taste. Hideous stuff, but it did pack a pop. He got it out now, unscrewed the bottle, and chug-a-lugged.

Fuckaroo.

He went down to his dinner, and ate in silence.

"What's that smell, daddy?"

"What smell?"

"Ew, Daddy's been eating licorice."

Brooke eyed him, but said nothing. In hope of disguising the smell, he gobbled pearl onions. He'd left the damn absinthe on his desk, too. He needed to get that back out of sight. In the past, there had been serious fights over his various excursions into the world of drugs. After discovering that there was not a single official opium den left on earth, he'd set one up in the garage. He'd needed to see what opium was actually like for a book. When she'd found him and Matt out there stupefied, and Matt still in his cop getup, she'd hit the ceiling. And as far as his crack pipe was concerned, even he wasn't crazy enough to try the stuff, but he had the pipe. Again, research. Like the dominatrix. It had taken some real fast talking when that damn Amazon had burst in on them one night demanding cash for pictures. But it hadn't looked like him in the contraption, thank God.

Lila hadn't fazed Brooke. "If you want to get into leather, I'm your girl," she'd said. "But be careful, because once I start, I ain't stoppin'."

She was back in the kitchen starting in on his job, which was the washing up. Kelsey joined her, still in her ghost robe, and their voices as they worked together created in him a joy so gorgeous that he thought he might levitate. He loved this family of his so very, very much.

"Let me do that," he said, getting up. He took the stew pot from her and set about scouring it. She was not a Teflon user, she preferred iron and copper—anything, in his opinion, that increased the workload of the cleanup crew.

So be it, though, she was one master cook, she could turn twelve carrots and a few pounds of beef into manna, as she just had.

As he worked, he did not see the face that appeared at the window so briefly, the dark mirrors of eyes, the terrible eyes. None of them saw it.

EIGHT
DECEMBER 6
IN THE DEEP OF A MAN

GENERAL AL NORTH WOKE UP to find that his head had been forced back and something was being shoved down his throat. It was a struggle just to draw breath.

Instinct made him try to scream, but he gagged against what tasted sour and cold, and must be metal. His eyes focused on the only thing he could see, which was a white film of some sort. He looked at it, trying to understand what it might be. It undulated slightly, perhaps being moved by a draft. And then he realized that it was a white sheet—that his own bedsheet was drawn over his face.

Every muscle in his body twisted and tightened, until he thought they were going to knot and pop like rubber bands. His lungs bubbled, he began to feel air hunger, and then was lost in a hell of gagging, as the thing in his throat was twisted round and round.

It got dark. There was no warning, no flicker of lights. It simply got dark. Al couldn't tell if he'd been blinded or the lights had been turned out.

Then he saw a small red glow. He smelled tobacco smoke.

"Who are you?" he tried to ask around the thing in his throat. His voice was a pitiful, choked gabble.

Something brushed against his naked body, first on his face and neck and chest, then his shoulders, his arms, legs, genitals. A soft tickling, like the fingers of a mischievous woman. Then came the most exquisite sensation, an extraordinary, profound relief: the hard, pulsing thing was drawn out of his throat. He felt air roar in, heard gargling, then there came a sound, high, shattered—which stopped when he snapped his mouth closed, determined not to shriek like that, not a general in the United States Air Force.

In the thousand places on his body that the tickling was present, there began a stinging. This sensation deepened fast, and as it did, subtle fire seemed to race through his skin. He groaned, willing the raping fingers to quit, but they would not quit.

Voices murmured in an unknown language, a strangely soft tongue with a twanging music in it, full of lisps and peculiar whistling sounds mixed with ugly gutturals. It was complex with nuance, trembling with emotion, not human.

A face came into view, peering at him, waxy with makeup. The face was female, but the eyes—gold, oddly metallic—stared with a reptile's empty fury. Implacable. He thought it must be a mask. Yes, plastic. Or no, it was pliant, it was alive, but once again there was a reptilian effect—a shimmering smoothness that suggested that it was composed not of skin, but scales, very delicate ones. The eyes began snapping back and forth like the weak eyes of an albino. They looked like actual metal, like gold teeth might look. They were sickening.

As the figure moved in and out of view, black, curly hair bobbed prettily. It was a woman, he was sure, and she'd just had her hair done.

He did not want to die like this, in ignorant agony, like some lab animal being dissected alive on behalf of an experiment that it could never hope to understand.

He tried to speak, but nothing came out but puffs of air. Then he felt something against his head—spikes. They seemed to drive into his skull. The golden eyes fluttered and darted, the voices pattered on, rapid-fire. He felt, then, something entering his rectum, more as if it was crawling into him than being thrust in.

She said something—"Waluthota." Said it again, louder. Speaking to him.

"I can't—"

The thing was pushed back into his mouth, down his throat, he could feel it in his stomach, could feel it meeting the thing that had been sent up his colon, and now there was a sizzling sound and a taste like burnt bacon, and smoke came out of the sides of his mouth. It didn't hurt, but he thought they must be killing him and he struggled, thrusting himself up, trying to somehow expel either of the things that were doing their work inside him.

Laughter came, high, quick, unmistakable for what it was.

And then there was something—yes, plans. He saw plans. Now they came into clearer focus: pages and pages of reports, of e-mails, of orders. *I'm downloading*, he thought. He was seeing every report he'd read over the years, every plan he'd examined, every specification he'd approved.

He thought they were looking for something in his mind, but he could not follow the pattern of the search. He'd overseen a lot of construction in his career, most of it innocuous, but not all, and they were soon in his memories of work done at the Cheyenne Mountain facility, and that was very secret.

Stifling heat was what woke him, a great wave of sweating misery drawing him out of what felt like death itself, a sleep so deep that it had no door.

What had just happened?

He crouched in the humming silence, feeling the pressure of the air-conditioning against his back. Then he stood up, went into the head, and stared at himself in the mirror. Hollow-eyed, haunted man.

His mouth tasted of something toasted and sour. Burnt vomit.

He opened the medicine cabinet and found some mouthwash, swilled it, and spit it—and watched in loathing as hundreds of writhing black threads went swarming down the drain. He spit again, a mass of them, ferociously alive, squirming and struggling, making a sound like spaghetti being poured from a pot.

He cried out—and then saw that the sink was clean and the mouthwash still in the cabinet. He was dreaming, that was what was going on here. He started to feel relief—but then noticed that his billet was thick with tobacco smoke, and he did not smoke, he loathed smoking.

He sat down on the side of his bed. The smoke seemed real, but maybe it wasn't, maybe he was still in the nightmare. Or maybe somebody nearby was smoking, and the odor was being carried into his room. It was possible, of course. In just the short time they'd been in occupation, it had become obvious that the place had been constructed out of cut corners.

The smell was fading and he was beginning to feel a little better. He tried to think back on what just happened, and see if there had been some pattern in what had been looked at in his mind.

When he tried to inventory the flashes of memory, though, he found something odd. They really were not very important, just the debris of his years as a military executive. Of course, some of them were secret, such as the floor plan of the Cheyenne Mountain facility, but they were easily obtainable without revealing to a senior officer like him that they were of interest.

What was odd was the curious feeling that it was something other than the information that was important. He looked down at his own hands—craggy now, once as soft as a surgeon's. He'd never flown in combat, but he'd read that great aces like Albert Ball and Bubi Hartmann had such hands.

Hands reveal people, he'd always thought that, and he wondered now why this thought was even passing through his mind. But as soon as he did ask himself the question, he knew.

He almost cried out, then he felt a gnarled agony in his gut and understood that his soul had not been stolen from him, but rather that it had been raped.

And he knew that his loves and his secrets had been turned inside out, that his most private places had been seen, that *what he was* had been violated.

It wasn't a nightmare. They'd been here, and they hadn't been looking at floor plans. They'd made a map of his naked soul. His lips twisted, he sucked breath, forced back the screams. This was violation at its deepest, its most profound, violation of the secrets of the sandbox and the playground and the blushing first love, of the sweaty experiments, the discovery of girls and the long descent of his wife, and his losses, so precious to him, mocked and tossed aside by snake-faced monsters.

He had been evaluated and measured by somebody so darkly evil that their most neutral touch was a corrosive horror.

He thought, *It's a negative civilization, a whole world ancient in its days, that has become corruption.*

And it had work for him to do.

NINE
DECEMBER 8
HUNTER'S NIGHT

WHEN MARTIN HEARD BELLS, HE leaped off the cot in horror, thinking that the disks had come again. It took another moment for him to become aware that sunlight was slanting in the barred window of the little cell. Despite everything, he had been asleep.

The bells were being rung over at Third Street Methodist, bells that Martin had been responsible for ringing just a few nights ago. And now here he was in this hideous situation, and with no idea why this had happened to him. Somebody in the government had done this, but who? And why ever would anybody consider an archaeologist dangerous?

He had thought all night about it, reviewing his published work, his experiences in the pyramid and in the White House, and he had reached the tentative conclusion that there must be something in his knowledge of the past that made him potentially dangerous. So dangerous that, even when their world was collapsing around their ears, they would still reach out for him.

It wouldn't be supposition. They would *know*.

His thought was that the lenses and the disks represented some sort of machine. He knew that a great human civilization had fallen in about 12,000 B.C. It had not been a technological civilization like ours, but it had possessed profound scientific knowledge, including—and especially—a science of the soul. It had also left a very precise prediction, that the present age would end on December 21, 2012. The Maya, possessing fragmentary knowledge from this far more ancient culture, had integrated this date into their system of calendars. In fact, they had started with that date and worked backward, that's how important they believed—or knew—that it was.

They had gotten the date, he felt sure, from a city that was now deep underwater off the coast of Cuba. This immense metropolis was probably the capital of what legend called Atlantis, and there was something quite strange about it. What was strange was that the British Navy had been guarding the site, and the Canadian archaeological group who had made the discovery ten years ago had been prevented from returning.

It should have been a scandal, but the profession was just as happy that the discovery was being suppressed. Its revelation would overturn a hundred years of theory and wreck dozens of important careers.

Martin had lobbied various institutes to open research in the area. He'd even published a letter condemning the military action in the *Archaeological Record*. He'd demanded explanations.

They weren't trying to kill him because they thought he was to blame for the disaster. They were trying to kill him because he was one of the few people in the world who had any chance of understanding it.

The bell stopped with a suddenness that seemed almost to shudder the dew that clung to the three yellow leaves he could see through his bars. He saw cars go past, heading for the church. They were gathering there, then they would come for him.

He felt like a rat, exactly like a rat, except that a rat only wanted to escape, and he was tormented by thoughts of his family. All night, he'd suffered over Lindy and his poor little Winnie who had been limping, and his lost son.

The things that had appeared behind the wanderers after dark—he thought that they must be a sort of cleanup crew, destroying the stragglers. That mangled boy had been their work.

Was Trevor, also, a mangled boy?

Sounds came from the office, a voice raised, then dropping. Bobby's voice. Sounded angry. Then he blustered in. "Fifty-six to fifteen," he said, not looking at Martin.

"Hey," Martin said.

"I have no idea how to hang anybody."

"Use your pistol."

"Martin—" He had to stop. He swallowed, pulled himself together. "We gotta go now. We're gonna do it over by the bank. There's that tree there."

"Christ, you're not serious about this?"

"They're getting rope. I'm sorry. So damn sorry."

This was actually going to happen. "Bobby, I haven't done anything."

"I know it." He raised his eyes. "But what if you have?"

"Oh, for God's sake!"

"Martin, please don't make me—you know, drag you."

As Martin came out, Bobby took his cuffs off his belt.

"Bobby, come on."

"Martin, it's regs."

"Okay, if you put the cuffs on me, I am going to need to be dragged every inch of the way, and I am going to scream, goddamn it, because I have lost everything, and now even my life. My *life*, Bobby, and for nothing. Not a thing. Zip."

Bobby put a hand on Martin's shoulder. "Come on, let's deal with this."

They would not know how to hang anybody, and so would tie the rope around his neck and drag him up, where he would die in a slow fugue of suffocation.

Bobby had been a friend not to cuff him, and he noticed, also, that he wasn't exactly holding onto him as they crossed the square where, in happier days, the Lautner Super-Regional High School band had performed in the bandstand.

Those afternoons had been so damned good, with kids and dogs running around underfoot, and women from the churches selling brownies in the shady park. World without end, amen.

They approached a sullen, miserable little crowd. Nobody wanted this to happen, Martin could see that. They were looking away from him. "Bobby, you gotta shoot me, don't try this hanging thing, nobody knows what they're doing."

"Martin, I can't."

A car door slammed, and Rosie got out. She strode over to them. "Come on, Bobby, we're going home right now."

"Rosie, this is law, here," Bobbie said.

"It's murder!"

"I have a wanted notice. It's official. So this is law."

"Then something's wrong, because Martin's probably the one person in the world who can help 'em get this thing straightened out, so why do they want him dead? It doesn't make sense." She turned to the others. "Go on home now. Go on, all of you!"

Malcolm Freer and his wife and two boys went over to their old station wagon and got in. They drove off without a word.

"See, at least somebody around here has some sense." Then, in a lower voice, "Bobby, this is wrong, this is just dead wrong."

His hand dropped away from Martin's shoulder. Bill West stood waiting, wearing his butcher's apron, with a big coil of rope in his hands. Nobody spoke.

Martin realized what Bobby had done. He knew that he had a few seconds, but only a few.

He had also understood something back in that cell. He was indeed unique in the world. Something he knew, or could potentially do, was so dangerous to the enemy that they wanted him dead. That's why this little corner of Kansas had been scraped the way it had, and why the leaflet had been dropped.

He was not a runner. He'd never even been in the army, or run a marathon or—well, he didn't even jog.

Bill and Mary West both jogged, he saw them all the time. Will Simpson was a black belt.

Nevertheless, Martin took his chance. He turned and ran wildly toward the far side of the square.

A shot, shockingly loud, whinged off into the trees.

Rosie's voice rang out. *"Bobby, don't you dare!"*

Bobby was too good with a pistol to have missed at this range, and Martin reached the corner of the bank still intact. Behind him, though, he heard engines start up and feet slam on pavement. They all had guns, too, and most of them were skilled hunters.

He sprinted across to Harper's Café where he'd eaten a thousand hamburgers, then went out the back and into the alley. He was completely at a loss. Then he saw a pickup sitting next to the wall, its bed full of sodden boxes of what he thought had once been vegetables, and he realized that there must be dozens of abandoned vehicles around town. He went up to the truck, but there were no keys. He heard an engine snarl nearby. A car was turning into the alley.

He jumped into the cab of the truck and crouched down. The car came slipping quietly along. In it were Bill West and his son Coleman, both with deer rifles.

How could Bill set a boy of thirteen to hunting a man? But they were so scared now, they weren't themselves, none of them, that's why they were willing to engage in this insanity. The savage was never far from the surface, not in anybody, and frankly, he needed a gun, too. And a damn car.

The best place to find a car with keys left in it would be around one of the churches. People arriving late would have been in a panic, and might well have left their keys, and might well have ended up wandering.

The nearest was First Christ, and that was where he would try to go. He didn't think he was capable of eluding them long enough to get farther away, over to Saint Pete's, for example.

He was just getting out of the truck when another vehicle appeared, nosing along even more quietly than the Wests' Lincoln. It was Mrs. Tarnauer's Prius. He thought that he might get her out of it, he even thought that he could snap the old woman's neck, but he stayed below the edge of the window as she passed. She wanted to kill him, too, did Jesse Tarnauer. She'd been a teacher, then a librarian.

As soon as she'd gone, he crossed the alley and went into the back of the Darling Dixie children's store, long since driven out of business by big chains. Nobody bought lacy dresses for their girls anymore, and boys wore T-shirts six sizes too big, not little gabardine suits with fake handkerchiefs in the breast pockets.

Carefully, he approached the display window. Across the street was the First Christ parking lot, which was indeed full of cars. There were a number parked askew, doors opened, as if the occupants had been very late and had jumped out and run in.

He heard a sound, then, the snarl of a really big engine. He listened. What could that be? Nobody would be chasing him on a tractor, surely.

He trotted across the street and got into one of the badly parked cars, a Buick Lucerne that smelled of cigarettes and the floral perfume that

Louise C. Wright wore. Her daughter Pam worked as a manager at the Target. Louise was a lush, professional grade.

The car started normally, thank God. He drove out of the parking lot and headed north up Elko. He turned down the Makepeaces' driveway and went through their backyard, then across the Morgans' east field, with the car slipping and sliding in the dusty furrows. He broke through a barbed-wire fence and drove onto the same dirt road where he and Lindy had come to neck when they were kids.

As he went down the road, he floored the gas, then hit the brakes to make a turn onto 215. Anybody who saw him would assume that he was heading toward the interstate. Two-fifteen ran straight for about five miles to a long bend, and he forced the car to give all it had. It accelerated to ninety, then a hundred, then 106.

As soon as he reached the bend and was out of sight of anybody behind him, he braked, then took Farm Road 2141, which headed toward the Smokes and home.

Yet again, he made a turn, this time onto Six Mile Road. He followed it up into the Western Division where Louise lived. Her little place was familiar enough to him. She tutored French, of all the improbable sidelines, and Trevor had been among her pupils. Like his father, he was not good at languages.

And suddenly Martin was screaming and hammering the steering wheel and kicking like a lion in a net. He was stunned, he had no idea that this rage was in him. For a moment, it seemed as if it was happening to somebody else, but when the car began swerving across the highway, it didn't, and he had to fight to regain control.

He caught his breath, choked back another roar, and thought, *There are deep things inside us that we aren't even aware of. Deep, deep things.* He was extremely sad, but it was a dullness in the pit of his stomach, not the savagery that had come boiling up just now. He thought, *Not only can I kill, I want to kill.*

His people had turned against him so easily, just on the strength of a piece of paper dropped either by the enemy himself or by traitors in his employ.

Unfortunately, he was fairly sure that the enemy was overreacting. He had no idea what he might do to defeat them. In fact, the modern world was about as prepared to deal with all this as the Aztecs and In-cas had been prepared to deal with the Spaniards. It had taken the Aztecs weeks just to figure out that the horses and the men riding them were two different creatures, and they had not understood how guns worked at all. Of course they had considered their adversaries gods. They had observed them working magic.

The Aztec was overwhelmed by the gun, we by the light. We did not understand what we were seeing, either, any more than the Aztecs had understood the actual way the horse and man worked together.

The Aztec—also using a version of the Mayan calendar—had first en-countered the Spaniards on the day that their reverenced god Quetzal-coatl had been prophesied to return. So they were even more certain that they were gods. They fit right in to the Aztecs' cosmology.

Somebody, working thousands of years in advance, had known when that would happen. But who? How?

Did the answer lie a mile beneath the sea off the coast of Cuba, and had the Brits been obstructing exploration to make sure it was not found?

This, he thought, was true. Had to be. Coupled with the attempt to take him out, there was now no question in his mind but that the en-emy had subverted world government, and had done so years ago.

What had been that general's name? Samson. General Samson, Chairman of the Joint Chiefs of Staff. That man had been evil.

But there was another, deeper truth, wasn't there? It was that the Spaniards were far more vulnerable than they had seemed. They hadn't defeated anybody. The Aztecs had been defeated not by the Spaniard's strength, but by their own ignorance. In fact, Spanish technology had not been that far in advance of Aztec technology, and in many ways be-hind that of the Incas. Perhaps far behind. Perhaps we were still behind.

He pulled into Louise's driveway and was careful to park the car in its usual place. Then he got out and went around the house and back into the stand of trees behind it. He needed to get out of sight and stay out of sight, but this was Kansas and these hills were low, their woods were sparse, and they were full of meadows and grassy glades. If any-body realized he'd come this way, they would be likely at some point to spot him.

He moved through the trees and up toward the ridge line that would lead him, after about half a mile, to the old road where he used to bring his archaeology students to search for remains of the stagecoach that had crashed there in the nineteenth century.

He'd also searched the area for fossils and arrowheads, which he'd found by the dozens, even some Folsom points ten thousand years old. He'd searched these hills with Trevor, teaching him the skills that he knew, of finding things that normally would not be found.

He clambered up the ridge, and from here had a long view across to town. He could pick out the white steeples of the churches, the roof of the bank, the roofs of houses, and the top of the Burnside Building above the tree line. He knew this spot well, he'd been coming to it since he was a boy and out hiking alone, come and wondered here about time and chance, and what life might bring.

He thought, *Whoever is here is stripping away the people but leaving everything else intact.* What the enemy was going to have was an empty but intact world, and millions upon millions of slaves.

Thus he knew that the enemy might be more technologically advanced than we were, but he had a more primitive culture. No modern human society used slaves, or even needed them.

He wondered what manner of creature might come to this same spot in the future, and contemplate those steeples.

Then, incredibly, he heard a familiar but unexpected sound. Somewhere nearby, a helicopter was moving slowly from east to west, paralleling the ridgeline but out of sight, therefore below it in the draw where the Saunders River flowed.

Who would have a helicopter? Certainly not Lautner County. Could it be the state police? That had been a state cop who'd showed up last night, completely oblivious to the danger, so maybe they were still functioning.

The sound faded. He waited a moment more, then moved along the ridge. If Trevor had survived, Martin thought there was a good possibility that he would have gone home. No question. If he had been able to make it, he'd be there right now waiting for the family to reassemble.

The helicopter came roaring up as if out of the ground, not five hundred feet away. He dove off the ridge, down into the tumble of rocks that bordered the path. He hit heavily, felt pain clutch his left hip and leg.

The thing thundered overhead. Sweat broke out all over him, and his muscles literally twisted against themselves, so strong was the urge to run. He told himself that fear, above all things, kills. Fear makes you a fool. And so he did not do what he so desperately wanted to do, which was to roll another few feet down and run crouching along to see if he might find one of the shallow caves that honeycombed the ridge.

No, they would have motion sensors. In among these sun-warmed rocks, infrared spotting devices would not work. So he stayed still, and the helicopter went slowly off along the ridge.

It was black, and the windows were black. He'd hardly dared look, but what he had seen was nothing but reflective glass.

For twenty minutes, he waited. Finally, he could bear it no longer. The chopper had been gone for a long time, and he was so eager to find Trevor that he almost couldn't bear it.

His worry now was dogs. If they were indeed looking for him, they might have understood that he'd parked Louise's car in her drive and come on foot. If so, dogs would follow soon.

Warily, he got to his feet. His thigh ached, but he hadn't broken anything, thank God.

He knew that he would not be able to stay at his house. He thought he might not even be able to approach it. But he had to know if Trevor was there, he could not leave the area without knowing that.

As he trotted steadily on, his thirst increased fast, and his fatigue exploded into a crippling weight. He thought that his only chance was speed. There was too much power arrayed against him. The people of Harrow were more than enough to defeat him, but there was yet more strength here, and he thought that it wasn't the state police or the U.S. military, and he thought that they might have a lot more dangerous things than highly sophisticated helicopters.

Then his house was there, his and Lindy's beautiful home which they'd built when he got tenure. He was proud of it, the lovely new house, Craftsman style, that blended so well with the older houses in the area.

The windows were dark, but the house was not silent. No, there were vehicles there—two pickups. He didn't recognize them.

So people were waiting for him. Well, he could wait, too. He'd wait until the locals left. He'd wait until the military left. And they would leave. In time, they would all leave.

As he moved closer to the house, he heard the sound of breaking glass. Then he saw a window shatter and his reading chair come through and smash into one of Lindy's flower beds.

They were looting, of course. Oh, God, please don't hurt Trevor if he's in there. He stared across at the storm cellar. Could Trevor have gone down there? It was certainly possible. But there was fifty feet of yard between here and there, and he didn't dare cross. He thought that the people in that house would shoot him on sight, no question.

Then the helicopter came back. It hovered over the house. The people inside did not appear. It came lower, and when it did, he thought for a moment that it was not a helicopter at all, that it had another configuration entirely. It also made a strange sound, he noticed, hissing like escaping gas rather than chuffing like helicopters usually do.

He watched the helicopter circle the house, then fly off fast in the direction of Harrow.

They hadn't even landed. But surely they weren't in radio contact with the people in the house, not with townspeople. So what were they really doing?

The destruction inside his house went on and on. At least he was fairly sure they wouldn't set it on fire. It was the dry season, and a fire would spread up and down the ridge. The volunteer fire department would be in a shambles, if it even still existed, so no, they wouldn't do that.

He saw books coming out of Winnie's bedroom window, her old treasures, *The Winter Noisy Book* and *Cat in the Hat* and *Jennifer and Josephine*. He heard clanging as Trevor's Yamaha keyboard was smashed.

The day wore on, the sun crossed the sky, and still Martin lingered, unable to leave the sacking of his home, in despair, in sorrow, and wondering—hoping—all the while that Trevor was hiding in the crawl space or the attic or the storm cellar.

Finally, at a quarter past three, the two trucks departed.

He waited. He scanned the sky methodically, all of it he could see. He was practiced at spotting tiny objects in sand, and the sky was not so different from a featureless wasteland in Tunisia or Libya.

He was just starting toward the house when he heard, from very far off, a sort of sighing sound. Immediately, he faded back into the stand of trees.

High in the afternoon sky, there was a black dot.

They were still up there.

He waited, listening to the faint sound of the thing, never moving from behind the tree where he hid.

By the time the sound had gone, the sun was setting. He stepped out to the edge of the yard he'd mowed a thousand times.

Maybe they had left somebody hiding in the house. He hadn't really seen them, after all, just the trucks.

He moved across the grass, aware of its whisper beneath his feet. Dear God, but an abandoned home is a lonely place.

Martin searched the storm cellar. He pulled open the door and peered down inside. Then he climbed in. Things appeared unchanged—there was the lantern, there were the candles in their box, the two gallons of water, the box of PowerBars, all untouched.

Martin was surprised at how much sadness weighed on him to know that his son had not been here.

He crossed the yard to the front porch. The door stood open. He entered, careful to look first for wires across the entryway, and not to move the door at all.

He looked, amazed at what confronted him. "Trevor," he whispered. Then shouted, "Trevor, it's Dad! Are you here? Trevor!"

He bent down to the ruins of the dining room table. How could this be, wood destroyed like this? He ran his hand over the lumpy, twisted mess.

The wood had been melted, there was no other explanation.

This hadn't been done by townspeople, or any people. People couldn't do this, we couldn't melt wood. And look at the books, all turned to powder, and the knives in the knife rack, drooping like melted candles.

"Trevor!" He opened the crawl space, looked inside. "Trevor?"

No sign of his boy.

He went upstairs and opened the hatch to the attic. "Trevor, are you up here? It's Dad." He pulled down the steps and went up. It was a complicated attic, and he was careful to look in every nook and cranny. A twelve-year-old could make himself very small if he wanted to, and Trev was expert at hiding.

When he understood for sure that he wasn't there, Martin felt himself just run out of steam. He sat down on the floor. He was suffering now more deeply than he would have thought a human being could suffer. This was what they called anguish, this searing, agonized sense of helplessness. Every time he thought of Lindy walking and walking like that, and his precious little Winnie toddling and limping, his insides twisted against themselves. And Trevor—the sense of him being somewhere in the wind, scared and alone, made him feel more helpless than he'd felt in the jail.

He suppressed an urge to go up on the roof and scream his name, even though that might actually work.

Trevor knew these woods well. He could be hiding back in there somewhere close enough to hear.

Martin headed downstairs, and as he passed their little office, he stopped. He stared in confusion. What was this? Increasingly confused and amazed, he went inside. His papers hadn't been taken, they'd been methodically shredded, and not simply ripped up, but turned into masses of what looked like thread. Books turned to dust were strange enough, but this was just bizarre.

His laptop lay on his desk. He touched it—and snatched his hand back when the edge of the screen collapsed under his fingers. He touched the keyboard, and the whole laptop simply disintegrated. He was left with more dust.

He understood that he was seeing firsthand the work of the enemy. Whoever had been in those two pickups had not been human.

He raced downstairs, threw open the gun closet—but Lindy had taken their only gun, her little shotgun. It was still at Third Street Methodist.

He cursed bitterly, and as he did so heard something. At first, it sounded like that strange chuckling he'd heard when he was among the followers, and it came from the woods behind the house. But then that sound was covered by another, the rumble of a huge engine, the same sound he'd heard briefly in the streets of the town.

He ran into the hall and down to his and Lindy's bedroom where he could look out into the driveway.

As he watched, three huge, black Humvees came trundling up to the house, and black-clad soldiers jumped out, their faces covered by dark plastic. It looked like a Ranger team right out of some military movie, but he knew that these were not Rangers.

He was face to face with his enemy.

TEN
DECEMBER 11
INNOCENT

WILEY CAME HOME TO A very subdued household. "What gives?" he asked Kelsey as he carried his new laptop into the kitchen.

She called out, "Mommy, he's back."

Nick appeared, his eyes scared. "Why did you chop up your computer, Dad?" There were tears in his voice.

"It had to die. Its life was over."

"Children, go upstairs."

As they hurried off, Kelsey said, "Daddy is insane."

Brooke lifted a box onto the kitchen table. In it were the remains of his old laptop.

"What's the big deal?" he asked.

"The big deal is, you went after this thing with a hatchet, and I want an explanation for that behavior, because it's too far from the norm and I'm considering getting my children out of here. That is the big deal."

He tried to sound reasonable. He even smiled. "The hard disk was fried. Nothing would erase."

"So you went after it with a hatchet?"

"I did that to make sure the files could never be recovered. You can't put a computer loaded with files you can't erase in the landfill. Next thing you know, your life is gonna be on the Internet. So, my love, I have acted rationally, and I do not think I've given you reason to take my kids away from me."

She shook her head. "Oh, Wiley, it's so hard. It is *so hard*, honey, and I'm getting tired in my soul."

"Now, hey, this is us! Me and my girl!"

"Goddamnit, go upstairs and set up your computer!"

He went to her instead, and took her in his arms. She felt pliant and indifferent, but did not try to pull away. "Please, Brooke, bear me. You're all I have. Bear me."

She shuddered all over, then buried her face in his shoulder and sobbed bitterly.

"Don't start yelling," he whispered, "remember the kids . . . remember the kids."

And slowly, there in his arms, she composed herself. She drew back from him. They met each other's eyes. They kissed.

From halfway up the back stairs came Kelsey's excited whisper, "We have a kiss!"

So the troubled ship of the Dale family sailed on, tossed on a dark ocean, lost to navigation, but still afloat.

He'd bought a top-of-the-line laptop, fast processor, huge memory, massive hard disk, every bell and whistle known to man.

"It's nice," Brooke said as he put it on his desk and plugged it in.

"It was actually somewhat inexpensive. Ish. But it has room to grow."

She sat down at the desk as he crawled around hooking it up to their home network. He had an Ethernet. Out here, wireless was unstable because of all the electrical storms.

"What's this?"

"What?" He came up from behind the desk.

"*2012,*" she said.

"Died under the hatchet, I'm afraid."

She stood up, gestured. He looked at the screen and saw words there, neatly typed: *2012, The War for Souls.* It was his title page.

He reached out, ran his fingers down the screen.

"But you—you—oh, Wiley, this is weird, this is scaring me!"

"It's scaring *you*? I went at that hard disk with a hatchet, and this computer has never been near this house before. It's brand new, look at it, I just took it out of the box."

"Now listen, because I am going to believe you. I am about to believe you. And if you are lying, and you did this to impress me or make me crazy or for whatever convoluted Wylie reason, then we are over, no matter how much we love each other, because I can't—I can't—I don't like things that are weird like this, Wylie, I do not handle this stuff well. As you know."

"Brooke, on my honor, on my soul, on all that I hold sacred, I brought this machine in here clean and clear and empty. I made no effort whatsoever to put those words on it, and I really and literally cannot imagine how they got there."

She nodded. Then she kissed his cheek. "Wylie, I choose to believe you. Because I saw you hack that computer up and the hard disk is still in it, and you are telling me—assuring me—that you didn't first put *2012* on an external drive—"

"Absolutely not. What external drive? I don't even own one."

"I know that. So I think we have to now escalate this whole thing. This is genuinely strange, it isn't just Wylie weirdness. And my instinct is this. It is to protect my kids. Very, very carefully."

"I can't argue with that."

She sighed. "I want to show you something that I wasn't planning to let you see. But I think you need to see it and I'm sorry I hid it from you."

She passed him the second section of the Lautner County *Recorder,* and there, on the first local news page was a fantastic and disturbing story. A man who lived about thirty miles south of there had disappeared while riding a four-wheeler near Coombes Lake. "Local residents who wish to remain anonymous claim that he was seen ascending in a shaft of extremely bright light. A search thus far has turned up no sign of William Nunnally. Dogs have been unable to gain a scent except from the abandoned vehicle itself."

He read it. Read it a second time. Then he grabbed his phone. "I gotta make a call."

Matt was off his cell, so he called him on the official line.

"Police emergency."

"It's me."

"Not on this damn line!"

"Then turn on your cell, damnit!"

"I don't want to turn on my cell, you'll call me and call me and bother me with trivia while I'm trying to work."

"This isn't trivia."

"I'm out there gettin' that drunken shit Joe Wright to stop going after his sainted wife with a cheese grater of all the damn things, and *you* call. Happens every time. Or I'm trying to eat. Then, for certain, it's gonna be you."

"Speech over?"

"I'm hanging up."

"I have a police report."

"If this is about a skunk, possum, or coon, please call the FBI."

"It's about a possible UFO attack down in Melrose County."

"I'm hanging up."

"Call down there and then call me back, can you do that?"

" 'Course not. It's not police business."

"A man has disappeared. That's police business."

"The fact that this tragedy is of interest to you is what isn't police business. Now, I've gotta go, seriously. I've got a call out on Mr. Leonard's god-for-damned-big fuckin' snake got away again."

"Don't hang up, damnit, do this! Hello? Shit!" He slammed down the phone. "He has to go catch a snake."

"That thing. Who in the world would want a fifteen-foot python for a pet?"

"I thought about a python at one point."

"And then I had children."

The phone rang. Brooke picked up. She listened, handed it to Wiley. "Look, the truth is I got an assignment down there, and I'm leaving in a few minutes and I guess you can tag."

"You're kidding."

"No, and I'm not waiting, either. They want me to look over the dogs, the dogs are acting up and I've run a fair number of 'em. So I'll pick you up in fifteen."

"What about the snake?"

"Screw the snake. A man's life is at stake here. I'll pick you up in fifteen."

He hung up the phone. Brooke looked at him. "And?"

"I'm going down there with Matt."

For a moment, she returned to the paper. Then she looked up. "You know that I love you very much," she said. "Never forget that."

He reached out to her and took her hand. "I've thought—lately, you know . . . it's been hard. I know I've been tough to live with."

"You have yet another book that's making you crazy and I'm a writer's wife. My skill is to keep you from going around the bend until it's finished and we've got our money. Then you can go around the bend until I miss my guy, then you have to come back."

"Do I come back?"

She squeezed his hand. "You come back."

He looked up, looked at Brooke. "Where are the kids?"

"The kids are in their rooms cowering."

"Oh, yeah."

She put her hand on his forehead. "You're not going anywhere, you're on fire."

Matt honked.

"I'll take a couple of aspirin, I'll be fine."

"You've been up working almost continuously for days, and a couple of aspirin aren't gonna do it."

Matt came in. "Hey, Wiley, I haven't got all day!"

Brooke went between them. "He's sick as a dog, he's not coming."

"Jeez, musta come on all of a sudden."

"He's exhausted, he won't sleep!" She took him under the arm. "You're taking a pill and going to bed, and that's final."

"Sorry, Wiley, feel better."

He shook her off.

"Wiley, you can't do this!"

"I have to! HAVE TO!"

"You don't belong getting mixed up in this."

He gestured toward the computer. "I need to look into it. It could be related."

"YOU LEAVE IT THE FUCK ALONE!"

Silence. The faint sound of plaster falling from the ceiling. And a decision of stunning intensity. "I have to do this," he said quietly, "or it will be my soul."

She wept, shook away the tears, and nodded. "Good-bye," she said in a whisper.

"Brooke—"

She shook her head, stepped back, then suddenly turned to the sink and started in on the dishes.

As they rolled out, he heard them clanking, and saw her in the window and thought to himself that something, indeed, was being lost between them. It was like a quicksand pit had appeared in the middle of the marriage. Everything you did to save yourself made you sink a little deeper.

He rode in silence beside Matt, who also said nothing. They'd been friends a long time, and there are times when friends just don't talk.

They drove through Harrow, then into the cropland to the south. "Storm's comin'," Wiley said, "look at that mutha."

The western sky was choked with great towers of clouds, and Wiley knew that, if there was a storm in this universe, then in the other universe there would be one ten times worse, and he felt for them, he worried about the wanderers out there in the rain and the wind, he wondered about Martin on his desperate quest, a brilliant archaeologist who sensed that he could save his dying world if only he could connect a few more dots, who now wanted only to reconnect with his son, and somehow save them both.

The worst of it was that he couldn't help them. He could know of their suffering, but could not lift a finger.

He could not warn Al North about Samson. He could not help Martin find Trevor. He could not give a single wanderer back his soul.

So why in the name of all that was holy was this happening to him?

They drove in silence. Matt followed the GPS onto more and more isolated back roads.

"Where is this place?"

"Middle of nowhere. I've got them figured for trailer trash."

"Trailer people."

"Still trash in my business, buddy, till I've actually pulled the knives outta the gizzards. Then they're perps and vics."

Wiley heard the voice, but only vaguely. He wasn't interested in banter anymore. He was beyond banter. "The guy went up in a column of light?"

"And the dogs can't catch a scent off anywhere except the seat of the four-by-four."

"Which means it did happen."

"Which means the dogs need checking out, which is what I am doing."

They turned into a driveway.

"Here we are," Matt said.

They pulled up in front of, not a trailer, but an exquisite, ultramodern house, an architectural gem. There were half a dozen police vehicles of various kinds parked in the yard, a couple with their light bars still flashing. Other than the clicking of their switches, the silence was profound.

"Nice place," Wiley said.

"I'll say."

As they came to a stop, a woman appeared. She was as stark as her ultramodern home, reminding Wiley of one Andrew Wyeth's immeasurably sad paintings of the model Helga Testorf.

Closer, Wiley saw that her face was a tear-stained shambles. A teenage boy appeared in the doorway behind her. He wore baggy jeans and a black T-shirt.

She came up to Wiley. She stood silently, so close to him that he could smell sweat and the sourness of her breath. She leaned into his chest and clutched him.

"I'm sorry for you," Wiley said, "I'm so sorry for you."

She looked into his eyes. "I know you."

Holy Christ, this was not what he needed. "I'm from Harrow. You've probably seen me around."

"No, from your book. You said they were good. In your book, you said they were."

"I said they were very strange."

"They are not good. No, Mr. Dale, they are not good. He had all your books, you know. He was trying to come into contact. He went up the ridge to meet them. And this is what happened."

"Mrs. Nunnally, we have to understand that we have very little idea about what's going on with the aliens—even if they are aliens. That's why my book doesn't give answers, it asks questions. Because we do not understand."

She put her hands on his shoulders. Her eyes were like fire burning into his soul. "There was light," she whispered. "Two nights ago, the whole house was surrounded by it."

Oh, Jesus. "And this light," he asked, "what did it do?"

"Lit up everything. Then suddenly it's gone and there's this clap of thunder but no clouds, see. When it went away he says, 'It's them,' and the next afternoon he went up the ridge, and it came again, and he went up in it."

This wasn't the killing light, then, it was something else. But what? "And that's what the farmers saw?"

She nodded. "You're in touch with the aliens, it says so on your Web site. I want you to call them!"

Nick and his friends had created a Wylie Dale website. It was very slick, but he hadn't seen anything on it about him still being in touch with aliens, and there had been many books since the one about the close encounter.

The boy came out. "Please, Mr. Dale, tell them to bring my dad back home." He was perhaps seventeen, a gangling kid with anguish in his face. He looked like he was in physical pain—as, Wiley felt sure, he was.

Wiley realized that he'd been a damned fool to come here.

"Call them," the boy hissed.

"I don't think I can."

"Don't say that!"

At that moment, a state policeman appeared around the side of the house. He came up, his face grim. "Mrs. Nunnally—"

"No! NO!"

"Ma'am—"

"Oh, God . . . God . . ." She twisted as if at the end of a rope, and then turned and clutched her boy.

They came out then, from a wetland a thousand feet behind the house. Wiley watched the play of sunlight along the silver bars of the gurney, and the blackness of the body bag in the sun.

"Mrs. Nunnally, we need to get an identification."

She heaved with grief, but made no sound, which made it more awful, somehow, this silent, gagging, shuddering woe.

A man in soaking jeans unzipped the bag, and Wiley then saw something so unexpected that he cried out. He saw the head of a man, but with black sockets where the eyes should be, and teeth grinning from a lipless mouth. "Can you recognize him?" one of the troopers asked.

"Dad," the boy shouted. "What happened to my dad?"

"It's rapid deterioration . . . because of the wetland he was in."

"Don't be ridiculous," Mrs. Nunnally shrieked, "it's a mute, Mr. Dale, a mute! They mutilated my husband just like they do the cattle!"

Wiley was well aware of the mysterious cattle mutilations that had been going on for fifty years. Cattle would be found by farmers and ranchers with their lips, eyes, tongues, and genitals removed and their rectums cored out. Often, they looked as if they'd been dropped from above, and huge lights were seen in the fields the night before they were found. Between 1970 and 2010, over fifty thousand cases had been reported, all blown off by the government as coyote attacks, which was clearly a lie, and now here was this human being, killed in exactly the same way.

A hideous thought came tickling into his mind, *I have a beautiful home in an isolated area. What if they were looking for me?*

One of the state cops said, "Ma'am, you need to say if this is Mr. Nunnally."

She nodded. Nodded harder. "I think so. I think so. Ohh God, God—" She clutched at Wiley. "Help me! Help me!" It was horrible to be near her, he could smell her sour sweat. He feared that he would throw up on her.

The boy, his face streaming with tears, said, "What if they come back, what happens to us then, Mr. Dale?"

What, indeed?

He could not be silent, but he had no idea what to say or do. He remembered the creatures he had seen, and the figure Al North had seen in his room, that delicate, hard face, and he knew what this was, what it must be: they were trying to cross the barrier into a universe that had not accepted them as real, and this was a side-effect of their struggle.

The boy leaped at him and suddenly he was on the ground being hammered by powerful fists. He tried to protect himself, but the kid got through his flailing, incompetent arms.

Matt and one of the state cops pulled him off.

"My dad wanted to meet them! Well, he sure did, he sure did, you *bastard.* Liar! Liar! BLOODY LIAR!"

"Get him out of here," one of the cops said to Matt. "For God's sake, get that freak out of here!"

"I thought it would help. He knows about this stuff."

"Come on, Matt, please," the state cop said. Then he confronted Wiley. "There's no law against the kind of crap you dish out, Mister, but I have to tell you, there has to be a special place in hell for scum like you, lying *scum!* This man died we don't know how, but it wasn't little green men, God damn you!"

"No," Wylie said, and the quietness in his voice drew the attention of all of them. "I am not a liar. And the real shame is, maybe if I had understood this better, or taken it all more seriously, this man would not have died."

He went to the car, got in, and closed his door. For good measure, he locked it.

Matt drove them away. Wiley looked back at the fabulous house in the middle of nowhere.

"I saw somebody," Matt said, "at your house."

"You're kidding."

"Last night, buddy."

"I didn't see anybody."

"You were downstairs."

"But—where were you?"

"On the ridge. I was goin' out to see if you were fuckin' with the cigars, and I just happened to see this guy come across your yard. Came right up to the house, looked in the window at you, then went around the back, and a few seconds later your computer comes on."

"When was this?" Wylie asked.

"About eight."

"Eight! The whole family was up!"

"Nobody did a thing. He was quiet, man, and fast."

"Was it an alien? Could you tell?"

"It was a person."

He turned onto the highway. The storm was closer now. He punched a couple of buttons on his police radio, and a mechanical voice began to deliver National Weather Service warnings. High winds in Hale Center, roofs off houses in Holcomb, tornado sighted in Midwood County, fast moving, dangerous storm.

He increased speed.

"You think we're gonna take a hit, Wylie?"

"That's a big mutha out there, you got that right."

The storm towered, its base black and flashing with lightning. "Matt, I'm so scared it's beyond scared."

"I hear ya."

"You say he was a person? Like us kinda person?"

"He looked like a kid. Nick's age, twelve, thirteen."

"So it was a townie? Or someone looking for Nick? Some friend of his, maybe."

"No. This kid, he steps back, he looks at the house, he peers in windows."

None of the town kids would do that. There were only maybe a hundred twelve-year-olds in the whole community, and Wylie knew them all. "No kid from around here, then," he said.

"Absolutely not. He looked—I don't know, Wylie, but the word is confused. Looking and looking at that house. Like he was trying to figure something out and couldn't."

"He couldn't've been trying to get in. The place is unlocked until late. He could've just walked in."

"He went in and went into your office and came out. Then he went down toward the Saunders. So I followed him. I'm right behind him. I thought he was some kid from town, was my impression. But when he walks up to the river bank, he did not cross the stream. He disappeared."

"Disappeared?"

"Swear to God."

"Why didn't you come into the house?"

"You guys were doin' a screamer."

"But he disappeared? I mean, in what sense?"

"He took three or four steps into those little rapids. The shallow place where it's easy to cross. Right in the middle of it, he just simply was gone. Gone, Wylie."

Dear heaven, it had been Trevor. He'd crossed the boundary between the worlds and he probably didn't realize it. He'd been going home, but come here instead.

For a long time, Wylie had entertained the notion that the weir-cats people saw around here—the black panthers you saw back in the woods every once in a while—were from a parallel universe. They were animals that had evolved an ability to pass between the worlds as a defense mechanism.

There'd been a book called *The Hunt for the Skinwalker,* written about a ranch in Utah where scientists had documented the movement of such animals—not between this earth and Martin's world, but yet another parallel universe, one in which creatures from our ice age still roamed freely.

Wylie's mind wanted to race, but he didn't know where it should go.

Silence fell between them. Wylie's thoughts turned to the poor mutilated guy. What was that about? Something *they* were doing in their effort to enter this world. No question, but what was it?

They'd cut the guy up—therefore, had taken parts of him.

He shuddered. He had a feeling, if he waited, he was going to find all this out, and it wasn't going to be good, not at all.

The storm, when it came, brought long, heavy gusts of wind, and the police radio began to burp trailer calls, as they were known. As everybody in Tornado Alley knows, trailers actually attract twisters, which was why the Kan-Sas Trailer Park had been the only thing destroyed by that tornado back in September.

"I know something's wrong," Matt said at last. "I just don't want it to be this—oh, crap, Wiley, this *weirdness* that seems to follow you everywhere you go. I never told you this, but when we were kids—eleven, twelve, about—I was out on my bike late. I used to like to ride past Sue Wolff's house and hope I'd see her on the porch and we'd get to talking or I'd get up the courage to ring the bell or whatever, and I turned onto Winkler, and there is this goddamn huge light over your house."

"Jesus."

"I thought the place was on fire. But then I felt the thing, Wiley. I felt it looking back at me. And, you know, it did not want me there."

"When was this?"

"Summer of, uh, eighty-eight, I guess."

"No, what time?"

"Oh, late. Coulda been after midnight, even. 'Cause I couldn't risk her actually seeing me, of course. Not fat me, mooning after a cheerleader and all."

They arrived at Wylie's place. As he got out of the car, he saw that Matt had tears on his face. He said nothing about them, only thanked him for the ride and watched him leave.

Storm or no storm, he clambered down to the Saunders, moving among the heaving trees.

The little stream flowed normally. Some rain along its path somewhere had sped it up a bit, but that was the only thing in the slightest out of the ordinary.

"Hi, Dad."

"Nick!"

"I saw you coming down here."

"Yeah, I—"

"The kid is from the other world."

He was absolutely so stunned that he couldn't talk.

"I've read your book, Dad, and I know it's real."

Nick was a private sort of a kid. Smart, as his grades revealed, but not by nature very social. Wylie and he had a good relationship, though.

"You've been reading my book?"

"I read all your stuff."

"And this kid? You've seen him?"

"Come over here, Dad."

Nick led him a short distance away. They were right before the little rapids. Thunder rolled and wind gusted. Leaves raced past, yellow and red. It was quite amazingly beautiful, Wylie thought, but also completely normal.

"Watch," Nick said. He picked up a river stone and sailed it out over the water, as if he was trying to skip it but coming in too high.

In its flight, the stone did a very strange thing. It sort of jumped. Not a lot, but it jumped in the air.

Nick tossed another one, and this time his aim must have been better, because the stone completely disappeared. Never hit the water. Was gone.

"My God, Son, when did you discover this?"

"He did it this afternoon."

"He was here?"

"In your office, Dad. Dad, he's all dirty and he looks really scared, and I think he's Trevor. He started reading your book."

The world heaved, and it wasn't the storm. "Oh, my God," Wylie said.

He turned and ran back to the house, Nick following.

"What's going on," Brooke yelled as they burst in, "don't you two know it's raining?"

"They can use it!" Wylie shouted as he dashed upstairs. "They can use the book!"

"Who? Nick, what's going on?"

Nick hesitated on the stairs. "The closer we get to the twenty-first, the wider the gateways are opening, and there's one down on the Saunders, right at the rapids. It's between our world and Martin's, and they're using it. We think his son is. We think it's Trevor. He tried to come home last night, and came through the gateway instead."

Wylie said, "If they can read the book, honey, think how it can help them! We can let them know that Samson's evil—"

"Dad—"

"—we can help them find the wanderers, maybe they can turn this thing around!"

"Dad, I think Trevor came here by accident. That's why he was so confused and afraid. He thought he was going home. He couldn't understand why all the furniture had changed, why there were strange people in the house, any of it. Then he stumbled on the book."

"But he'll be back. Of course."

"We can't know that, Dad."

Wylie went into the office. Sat before the laptop. "There's something larger at work, here. Whatever created that gateway. Whatever prevented me from destroying this incredibly precious book."

"Um, Dad, that would be me and mom."

"Excuse me?"

Nick nodded. "She has a USB drive she keeps in her pocket. She saves it on that." He paused for a moment. "Don't be mad at me, but I wrote the code that prevented you from erasing it."

"You can program? I didn't know that."

"It's a few lines of code."

"We need to find Trevor. I need to write about him. Tell him where his dad is, give them a plan of action."

"It's better not to talk about this." Brooke stood in the doorway. She had the drive in her hand.

"But you—we—"

She put her finger to her lips. "Don't talk about it, either of you. Just let it lie."

Kelsey came in. She came to her daddy, crawled into his lap.

Silence fell among them. Wylie understood that all was not as it seemed. In fact, nothing was as it seemed. "What's going on?"

"Wylie . . ."

Kelsey stuck her face in his. She held him by the ears. "That's what we don't ever, never talk about, Daddy." She shook her head. "Ever, never." Then she gave him a wet kiss and ran off laughing down the hall.

Nick and Brooke gazed steadily at him. He thought again of poor Nunnally, and how very close to this house that attack had been.

The reptilians had reached Nunnally, and they could come here, too. Five years ago, they'd opened a gateway not far from this house. What would prevent them from following Trevor through the gateway on the river? "We could be in trouble, here," Wylie said.

"You've got that right," Brooke said.

"But I don't know what to write about. I don't know where to take it."

Brooke said softly, "Trevor. Just think about Trevor."

Wylie closed his eyes.

"Let yourself happen," Nick said. "Just let it flow."

He saw a face. White hair, gray eyes, all crag and grandeur. "Christ, I don't need Al North!"

Then it came, a flood that blanked his mind, that broke his thought and his will and took him over completely.

Throwing back his head as if he had been slugged hard, he started to type. He watched his fingers fly across the keys. He stared, finally, at the words that were pouring out of him. "Al," he whispered, "it's you, it's gonna be you."

Outside, the thunder rumbled and sheets of hail came bouncing down, and the trees moaned. Inside, Wiley's helpless shouts at a man who could not hear him echoed through the house, in the dark of the storm.

Brooke got water for him, and tended him as she always did, while he worked.

Nick went downstairs and saw to the guns.

ELEVEN
DECEMBER 11
MOUNTAIN OF LIES

THE DEEPER INTO CHEYENNE MOUNTAIN Al went, the better he felt. This mission mattered, it was progress, and it might yet bring them a win. He'd had a hell of a time getting out here, but he'd made it at last. The problem hadn't been finding a jet that worked or even a crew. It had been gathering enough fuel.

But this place, this was the Air Force as it ought to be. These people didn't feel a constant sense of threat, and you could hear the difference in the firmness of a step, or an easy ripple of laughter in the canteen. Morale here was very far from the redoubt in West Virginia, where the whole dismal picture was on everybody's mind all the time. These people were winners. They were used to victory. They had no idea they were on the damn *Titanic,* and he tried to project confidence he did not feel. Nothing must disturb morale like this.

A young captain led him down into the test area. She looked maybe thirty, she was clean and well groomed, she smiled and she moved along ahead of him, her static-free shoes whispering against the pavement.

It was in this test bed that human beings would, today for the first time, remove a living soul from the body that contained it. Once the soul was extracted, they would find its frequency and destroy it. This would be the first such execution. The prisoner was a monster, presumably from the Federal ADX in Florence, Colorado, and after this death, not even what of him that had been eternal would remain.

This might have extended benefits, because if reincarnation was real, it would mean that this horrible soul would never return to life. Maybe the reason that crime was always with us was that the souls of criminals returned just like everybody else, and were criminals again. Maybe, if the war was won, we could learn to pick and choose who would survive in eternity and who would not.

But this was only one aspect of the experiment. Of greater importance was understanding just how souls and bodies connected, so that some defense against the light could be devised. The disks were methodically following the night around the world, striking the entire planet all the time, and so far no attack, not with hydrogen bombs, not with neutron bombs, not with any form of conventional weapon, had affected them.

The British and French had concentrated on the most isolated lenses, exploding nuclear ordnance over them, in the ground near them, pulsing them with electromagnetic waves, even firing artillery shells into them.

The U.S. had concentrated on the one on Easter Island, going back again and again and with full imperial approval, but with equally dismal results.

A unit of Marines had deployed around the lens and opened fire when the disks came out, but they were themselves made of light and ordnance simply passed through them.

Now, however, all that was ended. Communications had been jammed, planetwide. Satellites were dark, broadcast transmitters had been disrupted by artificially induced changes in the earth's ionosphere, and landlines by powerful electromagnetic pulses being continuously emitted from deep space. The objects responsible ringed the planet, fourteen of them, each one twenty-two thousand miles above one of the lenses. Even though they weren't in precise geostationary orbit, astronomers using old-fashioned backyard telescopes, which were the only ones that still worked, said that they showed no sign of moving off course. Military communications had been reduced to single sideband radio—sometimes— and a couple of fiber-optic networks that had pulse-hardened switching stations that so far were impervious to the electromagnetic energy being beamed from above.

The beautiful young captain paused before a steel door, input a number code. The door slid open.

Beyond it was a tunnel with a pronounced downward slope. At the head stood a small stainless steel car. It was mounted on a black strip that descended, it seemed, into oblivion.

"This is the railhead," she said as she got into the car.

It looked like an amusement park ride, he thought, but when she closed the door, the seal seemed very tight. He found himself looking out a small windshield at a concrete tunnel with conduit running along its ceiling.

She pressed a button, and the car began moving with startling silence and smoothness.

"What propulsion?"

"Maglev."

He'd never seen any of this before, but just the scope of it all, riding this silent, efficient little train deeper and deeper, made him dare to consider again the possibility of victory.

"We've reached cruising speed, Sir."

"Which is?"

"Two hundred and eighty clicks, Sir."

"You're kidding!"

"Sir, you're gonna see a lot of wonderful machinery today. I mean, some of the stuff down here—Sir, this is a new world."

He glanced at his watch, calculating in his head. Two hundred and eighty clicks an hour was a little over four and a half kilometers a minute, so they'd gone almost three miles. He made a note of the time.

"What's your first name, Captain?"

"Jennifer, Sir. General Burt Mazle's my old man. I'm third-generation Air Force, Sir."

He'd never heard of Burt Mazle, but all generals were supposed to know each other. The mythical first name club. "Old Burt," he said. "Sure."

Whoever he was, old Burt had surely produced a handsome specimen of a daughter. Bright, too, or she wouldn't be in the Mountain. Al had not thought about sex in a long time. He'd been attracted to many women, but every time he tried to start a relationship, he just lost direction.

He still kept his picture of his Sissy in his wallet, with her brightness and her smile, looking up from their table in the Wright Pat Officer's Club where they used to go dancing. Her expression held surprise at being photographed, her eyes joy. Her skin shone with sweat, because they'd just come back from a vigorous rumba. A year later she had said, "Al, I need you," and fallen over in the middle of the bedroom, dead before she hit the floor. It had been a massive aortal aneurysm. She was thirty-eight years old.

"You doing okay, General?"

"I'm fine."

"You weren't need-to-know on this part of the project, were you?"

"Apparently not. I thought I was need-to-know on everything."

She smiled at him. "Then look at this as the adventure of a lifetime, because that's what it's going to be."

"What about our prisoner?"

"Gonna die die, that's what we call it."

"What's his crime?"

"Dunno, sir. Bad boy, though. Not a friend of ours."

"No, I suppose not. Do we know for sure that the soul persists outside the body?"

"For sure, Sir. We've taken them out and put them back in."

"Really!"

"We're making strides, Sir. Catching up fast. We know for certain that when the body is killed, the soul does not die or lose its integrity. It can be destroyed, though."

"How?"

"Certain frequencies make it fly apart. Trillions of electrons. All organization gone, tiny bits of consciousness flying off into space forever."

He had to think that this progress was brilliant. They were racing against time down here, but at this rate they might just learn enough to actually win this thing. "Could we give the wanderers back their souls?"

"It's conceivable."

"That would be a hell of a victory, right there."

"It'd ruin somebody's day, for sure."

"The God-for-damned enemy's day."

"That would be true."

Another glance at his watch: they'd traveled seven miles, meaning that they weren't under Cheyenne Mountain anymore.

He put his foot against the footrest and leaned back. The little transporter, about the size of a jeep, was now passing under the thickest conduit he'd ever seen, a black, endless river affixed to the cut stone of the wall with heavy steel wrapping that flashed past hypnotically as they sped along. On either wall were light fixtures about every fifty feet, but glowing so softly that they did not completely penetrate the darkness. Looking ahead through the windshield, it was as if an endless stream of lit portholes were coming up on either side, then speeding past the side windows as a continuous streak.

"That conduit carry power?"

"A lot of power. You need it to change the patterns of the electrons. Disrupt the frequency of a soul, it becomes confused. Then you just keep ratcheting up the power until—bang, it flies apart. Humpty Dumpty."

"You've killed some down here before?"

"Couple dozen."

"But just the bodies? Not the souls?"

"Taken them out. Soul surgery. Today's our first try at a kill."

"But the ones you took out—where did they go?"

Her face clouded, and she fell into what he could only interpret as a sullen silence. It was as if he'd insulted her, but how? What was the big deal if there was some part of the thing they didn't understand yet?

They were now eighteen miles in. Eighteen goddamn *miles*! Where was this place? Who had built it and when? He recalled that on September 12, 2001, the Secretary of Defense had announced that the Defense Department had "lost" a trillion dollars, and he thought that projects like this might be an explanation.

They'd been working on this a long time, then, because facilities like this take years to construct. Hell, generations. And trillions of dollars, for sure.

Twenty-two miles.

"We're also descending, aren't we?"

"Yes, sir."

"And?"

"We're at six thousand meters at this time, sir."

Holy God, that was twenty thousand feet! Eighteen miles in and four down. "Why so deep?"

"You don't want the souls getting away. And they are slippery, sir. Very slippery."

"They know what's happening to them, then?"

"They're alive. Never forget that. If you start messing with a soul, it wants to get away from you. And it's smart. If one escaped, the enemy would see it immediately and know what we were up to. So we're deep. Best place for us to be."

"What kind of lookdown do you have?"

"Sir?"

"Satellite lookdown. Guardianship."

"None since last week. But we're guarded by a unit of Air Police and fully sensor protected."

In other words, the facility was totally exposed. If the enemy got so much as an inkling of what was happening down here, they were coming around, and right now.

The car slowed to a stop.

"We've reached stage two, sir. Time to move to the lift for the rest of the trip. Stay seated, there's gonna be an equalization."

The door sighed, and there was a jarring *pop*, and Al's ears rang. "What in hell is this?"

"We're at four atmospheres down here, Sir."

When they stepped out, the ceiling was so low that Al had almost to crouch. The chamber was hewn out of solid basalt—gleaming black walls scarred by drill trenches. It was also very, very confined. He was aware of the miles of stone overhead and all around him. It was like being in a coffin.

How could anything have been drilled this deep in a military facility without the Joint Chiefs being told?

"How long have you been down here?"

She glanced at him, but said nothing. She ushered him into an elevator that looked like some kind of meat locker. It was heavily insulated, with a very small cab. It contained bench seating for four people around its steel walls. There were seat belts.

He asked her, "Are these needed?"

She buckled herself in. "Advisable."

There was a clank and a whirring sound, then a sucking whine and Al was practically lifted against the ceiling. Scrabbling hard, he got the ends of his belt and managed to strap himself in.

"We're going down a further three miles," she said.

Three miles straight down, after another thirty-five laterally and nine down—it was inconceivable. There was no technology he knew of that could accomplish this. But, obviously, somebody did know, and they had been experimenting on souls down here for a long time.

"It's a Manhattan Project for the soul instead of the A-bomb," he said.

"That's right on the money, sir. Need-to-know's spread very thin."

"Samson?"

"Project director."

The man was a shit, but he surely knew how to keep a secret. "Impressive. I never guessed."

The elevator hummed and jostled slightly as it descended. Confinement disturbed him. And, truth to tell, the closer they got to actually doing it, the more uneasy the idea of killing a soul was making him. He was not really seeing how even the worst criminal deserved destruction like this. It felt like they were intruding into God's business.

Actually, he wished he could call Samson and request that this be at least postponed. Even if he'd somehow managed the call, though, Tom would never allow it. He'd consider the request treason, and he wouldn't be wrong. We had to learn everything we needed to learn to defeat that light, and if some criminals were denied eternal life in our quest for answers, then that was too damn bad.

The elevator stopped. "Gonna be another pop," she said. "Open your mouth."

She pressed a button and the door slid back. This time there was a loud thud and a sensation of being hit in the chest with a medicine ball.

"Wow!"

"Seven atmospheres," she said.

They walked out into a tiny chamber with black, sweating walls. It was maybe five feet wide, seven high. Not much bigger than the interior of a coffin. On the far side was a door, equally black. "What is this, the entrance to hell?"

She laughed. "It is."

He followed her down a steep corridor, then deeper still, down a winding metal staircase so narrow that he could hardly manage to negotiate it. They descended for easily twenty minutes, and he thought that coming back up was going to be a battle.

Now the two of them were in a chamber that really was the size of a biggish coffin. Embedded in one wall was another black door, this one with a round window in it like the bulging eye of an insect.

"You'll need to disrobe, please."

"Excuse me?"

"Take off your clothes, General. You'll be provided with a special suit. So it won't kill your soul, too, General."

"What about you?"

"I stay out here, sir."

He took off his tunic, his tie, his shirt, while she watched impassively. He waited, but she did not turn around. Finally, he removed his shoes and trousers. He waited again. "Ma'am, could you give me some privacy?"

She turned, then, and faced the wall. He could understand her reluctance—she now had a face full of basalt.

When he was naked he faced the door. It was eerie, the way the dark porthole seemed almost like something alive.

"The prisoner is ready," she said. And the door began slowly to open.

Before him there appeared the most astonishing thing he had ever seen. The room was painted vividly, with images right out of the interior of a fabulous Egyptian tomb, lines of men, a god in a golden headdress, prisoners standing stiffly, strange objects that looked like giant vacuum tubes.

"What the hell is going on here?"

Then he saw a stack of what looked like the same vacuum tubes in real life. There were men in the room, too, dressed in black uniforms without insignia.

"Excuse me, gentlemen, but I need something to wear."

Nobody took any notice of him. They were clustered around the vacuum tubes, which were attached to thick cables that came out of the walls. He saw only backs.

Some of the rigid figures in the relief painting had cables thrust down their throats, and the tubes attached to the other ends of these were brightly lit. Others still were being intubated, their heads thrown back, their guts distended as black-painted soldiers just like these men pushed the cabling down their throats. Others waited, their faces turned away.

"Look, I need that coverall now, please, gentlemen."

Behind him, he heard a loud thunk. He turned toward the sound, which proved to be the door closing.

The young captain had come in after all. Ready to explode in her face, he turned around—and just plain stopped dead.

Her eyes regarded him with a doll-like emptiness that did not look alive. Immediately, he remembered his dream of two nights ago—that face, geisha-like, staring at him.

It was her.

She smiled a little. "Hello again."

He threw himself past her. She didn't try to stop him. On the contrary, she stepped aside with the grace of a matador.

He sought some way of opening the door, sweeping his hands across its smoothness. There was no handle, there was no lock. She watched, completely impassive.

He stopped. His heart was hammering so hard that he thought he might simply drop dead from the shock. He tried to talk, but his mouth was too dry. He hesitated to think who these people must be— but he did think it, they were the enemy, that was why the blackness of the uniforms was so bizarre, as if they were literally dressed in night.

A powerful realization came to him, of the sort that will come to a dying man. It told him that it was sin that generated that blackness, that they were not in uniforms at all, but were as naked as he was.

"Your soul isn't going to be killed," she said from behind him. Her voice was—well, it was musical. And yet, there was something else in it, something that he could only think of as rage, and maybe deeper rage than he had ever heard before.

Or no. He *had* heard that rough, bitter tone before. "Samson is one of you."

"Indeed."

She put her hand on his shoulder. "Come on," she said. "You can make this easy or you can make it hard."

She was wary. She knew that he was dangerous. "I don't want you to imagine you have any chance to get out of this," she said.

And then she shuddered for all the world like a dog shaking its hide.

The uniform fell away, and he saw that it wasn't actually a uniform at all, but something thin and now dry. It looked like skin shed by a snake.

Her real skin shimmered, and her face changed. She blinked her eyes, and the sockets were round, blinked them again and they were long. Now a nictitating membrane came across the eyeballs, and when it retracted he found himself face-to-face with the most beautiful and awful thing he had ever seen.

The face was that of a snake or a lizard, but flattened and extended so that it covered the front of a human-sized head. It was softly angled, sleek, with a snake's fixed lips. There was a smile, though, sparkling in the golden eyes, which were an incredible contrast to the human eyes she'd been exhibiting a few moments ago. These eyes were sparkling with life and humor and, he could see it so clearly—glee.

There was an earthly equivalent to these creatures. They were chameleons. But these—they were far, far more evolved than any earthly shape-shifter. And he suspected, also, now, why Samson carried his syringe. He wasn't an addict. To live on the surface, they must need some kind of support. Allergies, diseases—he'd probably never know what endangered them there.

"Now, I want you to try to stay calm, Al. The less you fight, the less this will hurt. You need to understand that we have no mercy, Al. We have no mercy." The eyes twinkled. "So it's up to you. This can be a terrible agony for you, or it can go smoothly. Up to you, Al, up to you."

The others were working with their equipment. Al watched the nearest one turn toward him. He was as black as night, his skin had the polish of a jewel. It shimmered as he moved, sleek muscles rippling within. He drew a black tube out of the wall and approached Al. As he moved forward, the tube made a faint hissing sound. The end, which appeared to be made of copper, glowed with a curious green light.

"We've already tested you on this," 'Jennifer' said. "We know it's going to work."

A huge emotion filled him. This wasn't just death, it was worse, it was the absolute end of his being. Soul murder.

He hadn't practiced his martial arts in years, but he called his old skills up from the very depths of his being, moved to a back stance and tried a side kick.

The creature caught his foot and slammed him to the floor.

He took the hit, tried to shake it off, failed. The female made a string of sounds. And then, unmistakably, they all laughed. It was quiet, easy laughter, the laughter of men running a slaughter line, joking about something else as they slit the throats of the pigs.

The one who had taken him down turned away and continued his work, which involved screwing a copper fitting onto one of the strange glass tubes.

Al got to his feet. He was feeling a dull, hopeless sort of determination. His own greed had brought him here. He'd taken the assignment from Samson despite the fact that he knew damn well that something was very wrong. He had done this out of eagerness for promotion, and that even though the entire system was hopelessly broken and none of it made a bit of difference.

They had seen his ambition, and used it against him to lure him very neatly into this trap.

He had been more than willing to come down here and kill another human being's soul, so why was he now being so careful of his own?

But he was. He had a touch of eternity in him, he could feel it clearly, and he did not want it to die, he did not want it so much that this time he really lashed out at the female, who had come close to him. His blow connected, and her head bounced to one side as he gave her the hardest knuckle slap he could manage. Then he waded in, fists pounding. But each time he struck a blow, less seemed to happen. It was like fighting wet cotton, and she watched him impassively as he slowly became unable to move at all. Just like the victims in the relief, he was soon standing frozen, arms at his sides.

One of the males now strolled over to him.

The female pointed at a particular painting and spoke a few words. The painting showed a prisoner having his eyes gouged out.

One of his captors went to it, looked at it for some moments, then opened a black case like a thick pocketknife. There was a *pop*, followed by hissing. The thing became like a tiny star in his hand, fiercely bright.

He approached Al. His eyes were emptier than hers, narrow and yellow-green, not gold. As Al watched, the nictitating membranes slid quickly over the pupils, then disappeared back into the orbits.

The star was brought close to his face. It was hot, and he tried to turn away but could not move a millimeter. Now it began to burn around his lips. Then there was a sizzling sound and he tried to cry out, but instead found himself gagging on his own blood.

When the light was withdrawn, blood poured down, spattering on the floor, washing his feet and the fleshy remains of his lips in thick, red sheets.

His mind blanked. He knew that he was being slaughtered. Was aware of it but distantly. Shock does that, even to a soldier.

An instant later, what appeared to be a red serpent's tongue darted out of the object, striking his left eye, causing a bright red flash in his brain. He heard muscles pop and felt torment in his neck as his body literally tore itself to pieces in its effort to move against the invisible restraints that bound it. He did not understand that he had been placed on an electrically charged plate that neutralized his nervous system, stopping all communication between brain and body. He also did not understand that all this equipment was not only old but simple— simpler by far than most man-made circuitry. He did not understand that these creatures were not advanced beyond man in most science, but only in *one* science, the science of the soul, which made these exhausted, half-starved and poverty-stricken beings appear like dark gods to him, as the Spaniards—sick, starving, and far from home—had once appeared to the Aztecs.

He never dreamed that the operators were tired and bored and longing to be home with their own wives and lovers, and did not, themselves, fully understand why they were here or what they were doing. He did not know that the young female's happiness came from the fact that she would get a great deal of credit and power if the monster she was creating was successful. He didn't even begin to understand what it was—that it would be used to penetrate into another universe and end a threat that had appeared there.

It was a human universe, and one that they had known about for thousands of years. They could even enter it, to some extent, but not so completely that they could actually do something there as complex as finding a computer file and destroying it.

They could enter that universe only with clumsy thrusts, not with the kind of precision they now needed.

The world went black and he wanted to howl out his rage and his absolute terror, but those abilities were not available to him. Nothing was available to him. He was a bright spark called Al, that was all—that, and pain, waves of it, gushers of it, boiling oceans of it.

Then he felt fingers moving his genitals, and then yet more pain, this time radiating up from there, and he knew that he had been castrated.

Through the agony, Al began to get the odd feeling that he was rocking, as if he was in a boat or on a swing. He had no way to know that the surgery he had just undergone had shattered the specialized nerve-endings that bound the electromagnetic organ that was the soul to the physical one that was the body. This was one way to do it. The shearing light was another.

The moment the coring and cutting was complete, the rocking became a bizarre, sensationless lurching and the room seemed to race past him, the figures in it whizzing and spinning as his vision, freed from the limitations of his eyes, saw everything around him at once. He was manipulated as casually as if he had been a moth captured between the fingers of a cruel child.

And yet, the connections between body and soul remained strong, and when one of the creatures thrust his thumbs into the base of Al's jaws, he felt it pop as his blood-gushing mouth gaped.

The next sensation Al felt was very like what he'd experienced during his nightmare the other night—the same choking, gagging sense of being invaded down his gullet. One of the thick cables with its frayed, cracking insulation was being brought up and pushed down his throat. It hurt a thousand times more than what had been done the other night, and what happened to his mind was similar but a thousand, thousand times more powerful. He gagged, his body tried to choke the thing out of him, but strong hands pushed it deep.

The other night, they'd been sifting his thoughts to see if he would come to understand who they really were and what they were doing, and therefore if he might betray their plans on his way into their trap.

He gagged furiously, he tried to make sounds, he tried to scream out warning to the world, that the United States was actually under the leadership of the invaders.

That traitor Samson's flyers were indeed intended to deceive people into congregating, and Samson had used some sort of mind control to induce the president to commit suicide, and now Al was down here being destroyed, the one person who might have been able to get in Samson's way.

He was here because he'd been about to figure out that Samson was one of them.

Like pages from a book, the living pages of his soul swept from his body and into a new state. Around him, he saw blue glass, and beyond it, the lithe and gleaming figures moving in the extraction chamber where his body now lay in a bleeding heap. He saw them take the parts they had cut off and push them into a hole. He was stuck to the filament inside one of the huge glass tubes. The filament was inside him, and his whole soul was on fire, his soul was burning.

"Nice," the female said in English. "We're done, General."

The tube was now filled with him: a plasma of electrons that shimmered with a million different colors, sparking and recoiling when it hurled itself against the glass wall again and again.

The captain made a series of statements, speaking in her soft, swift voice. Two of her helpers lifted the tube as the third pulled the cable out of its worn bronze socket. They placed the tube into a larger socket in the floor. Al could see them, but he could not speak, he could not scream out, above all, he could not get out of the tube.

He watched them slide his body into an ordinary military issue body bag. Then two of them lifted it onto their shoulders and carried it out. As the door slid closed behind them, Al saw them taking it off into the depths of the facility.

When the door closed, darkness came, absolute. Then, not quite. There was a glow, fitful, that he realized came from this tube. What light was left in this dark chamber of hell, was the light of his soul.

PART TWO

THE RUIN OF SOULS

Saint Michael, the archangel, defend us in battle, be our defense against the wickedness and snares of the devil. May God rebuke him, we humbly pray, and do thou, O Prince of the heavenly host, by the power of God, cast into hell Satan and all the evil spirits, prowling throughout the world, seeking the ruin of souls.

—POPE LEO XIII
Prayer to St. Michael the Archangel

This is the Hour of Lead—
Remembered, if outlived,
As Freezing persons, recollect the Snow—
First—Chill—then Stupor—then the letting go—

—EMILY DICKINSON
"After Great Pain, A Formal Feeling Comes"

TWELVE
DECEMBER 18, EVENING
CHILDREN OF MYSTERY

MARTIN HAD BEEN LYING SO still for so long that he had lost sensation from the waist down. His legs were not there at all, his torso was as cold as a corpse. He was famished and freezing. He'd been on the move for days, going from house to house, sleeping in attics and storm cellars, anywhere that offered a decent seal against the return of the light.

He was home now, hiding in his own crawl space.

All of this time, he'd been looking for Trevor. He'd given up on Winnie and Lindy. They were beyond his help now, given that following was a trap.

As an American, he had not felt vulnerable in the same way that so many people did in this world, perpetually frightened that their loved ones might simply disappear some night.

That didn't happen here, and he had not anticipated the extraordinary emotional wear and tear that losing your loved ones brought. It was so emasculating that he had to fight just becoming passive.

He did this by creating a goal for himself. His goal was Trevor. He'd searched half the houses in the Smokes by now. He was planning a night raid into the town, soon, too. Night after night, the light had scoured Harrow, Kansas, and he doubted that many people were left by now. The same was true of the Smokes. It came here every night, seeking and probing, and those other things came, too, the shadowy things that he'd encountered when he was a follower.

Thunder bellowed. Another storm was coming. Soon, there would be more rain. Methane releases from permafrost, the collapse of the Greenland and Antarctic glaciers, the flooding of polar oceans with fresh water from the melt, the wild state of the sun—all of these things were combining to make the weather turn dangerous just when this horrific attack occurred.

For years, the U.S. had pleaded with the empires to curtail pollution, but they would not touch their development zones. Industrializing regions of Africa and South Asia had completely overwhelmed the planet's ability to maintain balance.

More planning on the part of these invaders? He feared so. He feared that they might have infiltrated every colonial administration on earth. No doubt they would turn out to be comfortable in an atmosphere choked with what we thought of as pollution.

Despite the sodden cold of the crawlspace, he sweated.

The silence was deep, now. His watch told him that sunset was not far away. He had a mission tonight—aside from avoiding the light and the other menaces. He intended to track down a sound he'd heard off and on, that came from down toward the Saunders. Drumming, he thought. Somebody down there, perhaps.

Of course, in this world it was impossible to tell. Could be anything. Some creature from hell, or an alien machine. Or it could be people, and if so, there were more than one or two of them.

He stirred a little, just moving his body slightly. Then he waited. There was no sound from above. He raised his left hand and pressed it against the trapdoor.

After a moment, he pressed harder, causing the door to move just slightly. When there was no reaction, he pushed the door all the way open.

He made his way through the dining room, then the living room where he had spent so much time in his chair reading, where he had read to his kids, where he had listened to the music he loved.

The front door gaped. As he went through, he tried to push it closed, but it was no use, they'd torn it off its hinges. He stepped into the grass, in the long shadows of evening. He listened, heard nothing.

No, it was a night sound, that drumming, and finding its source was about the only thing he could conceive of that would draw him outside after the sun went down.

Then he heard another sound, a great whooshing overhead that was familiar to him from his night as a follower. He glimpsed, turning hard against the clouds that raged above, what looked like a gigantic bat.

He could feel it watching him. Knew that it was. And then he heard from the woods behind the house that familiar mechanical clatter.

The sun was not yet down, but the alien animals were already stalking him. The bird was the spotter, and whatever was in those woods, he suspected, was there to tear him apart.

He scrambled down the hill toward the stream, and then moved along its bank, rattling the dry autumn brush as he went through it. Tears swarmed his eyes, he was that afraid, as above him the wheeling bird wailed, and the woods behind him and around him echoed with the noise of whatever monstrosities were there.

He came to the little lake, really just a widening of the Saunders, where he sometimes swam in the summer, and ran out onto its pier. Forcing himself not to dive, he slipped into the frigid water and moved under the pier, clinging to one of its slippery pilings, concealed by the three rowboats that were there, old Mrs. Lane's little white dingy that she used to fish for crappies, and his boat that could be fitted with a small sail and go racing across the thirty-acre lake, and the third boat, a duck hunter's craft, camouflaged, that had not been used by anybody in years.

Then he heard his pursuers, their feet splashing softly, and heard their sounds, mutterings, clatterings, small whistles that he realized were a language and a complex one, and he wondered, then, if these might be the real aliens, or if they were creatures that had been trained like dogs or were smarter than dogs, and then if they might be constructed things, machines brought to life.

There came tapping, a claw tip on the wooden dock above his head. He heard the eager whisper of their breath, and the more intimate clattering of what he thought now must be mouth parts. There was a whisper in that clattering that suggested knife blades, steel against steel. From high overhead there came the long wail again, and he could hear in it quite clearly a tone of angry question.

Had they lost him?

Something slid into the water. It was clear and deep, the little lake, with tall water weeds that rose up from its darkness, and he saw, sailing below him, a huge shadow, blacker than black, with eight great legs outstretched around it.

He watched it sailing above the gently waving fronds, coming toward him, and felt as it came closer, more frozen, more helpless.

This was his death, then, his ugly destiny, and he'd done nothing to deserve it.

The thing in the water made a graceful turn and then came back toward the dock. He watched the shadow glide closer.

He'd lost, he'd been captured, and now, he thought, his lot must be to share the fate of the mangled boy he'd seen in the field. Perhaps he should fight more, but he didn't know how. If he swam, the thing would be on him in a second. If he got out, he'd have to confront the ones crowding the dock.

Something brushed his leg, feeling like a whipping frond of water weed, and he saw the shadow darting there. It was closing in, it was about to strike.

He shut his eyes. Waited. Heard a sloshing sound, very light. Sick with fear but unable to bear the feeling that he was about to sustain an attack he opened them again.

There was a girl in the water beside him.

She cocked her head and raised her eyebrows, then held a long finger across her lips. She looked sketched by a Dutch master, she was so flawless, so full of glow. And also, she looked familiar, very much so, but he couldn't place her.

He was trembling with the cold of the water. She reached a hand like a sparrow to his shoulder, and warmth came from it, soothing him and bringing him a startling sense of protection.

She raised a finger beside her ear and shook her head. Don't listen, the gesture said. Then she held her hand out before her, palm toward him. The message was clear, don't listen and don't move a muscle.

But how could he not listen to that hideous wailing in the sky? It was the most terrifying sound he'd ever heard. And the mechanical chuckling of what appeared to be gigantic spiders gnashing their mouth parts—it caused sickening dread, visceral terror as it conjured thoughts of agonizing mutilation.

She frowned at him. What was she getting at, and who *was* she? So familiar, the face.

She smiled softly, and he thought that certain female looks define the very essence of beauty for the male, and she reached out as if she had heard that thought, and touched his cheek so very kindly, and his mind went to Lindy, and his heart almost broke in half.

This all happened in an instant, during which time she touched her temple and nodded and smiled, and that gesture, one he had seen her make before, caused him to realize who she was. This was Louise Wright's daughter Pammy, manager of the Target . . . and he thought she could read his mind.

He noticed, also, that as he had become distracted by her, the things in the water seemed to have lost track of him.

There was a crackle, a huge noise. Electronic crackle.

Pammy Wright frowned.

A voice echoed, electronically amplified. "Martin Winters, I am Captain Jennifer Mazle of the United States Air Force. Please come up on the dock."

Pammy shook her head. Then she pointed downward, and disappeared.

"Doctor Winters, I am Captain Jennifer Mazle of the United States Air Force. The situation has been stabilized and it's safe to come out. Please come up on the dock."

He saw Pammy's pale body disappearing down among the water weeds. She swam right through a line of black shapes, which simply hung there, not moving.

He followed her, going deep, swimming as hard as he could, struggling and, he was sure, drawing attention to himself. He swam toward the creatures, which all spread their legs and began closing in on him. He dropped down into the water weeds, into the dark and the pressure among their roots, glimpsing a great fish, then Pammy again, far ahead, deeper yet in the lake.

How could she do it? How could she possibly manage? Waves of frantic air hunger were already coursing through his body and he was going to have to surface, he had no choice, it was essential to life, he could not manage another second—

—and then she was there, coming up from below, and she had with her a blue cylinder. She offered him a rubber tube and turned it on when it was in his mouth. As he gulped oxygen, tingling, exquisite relief filled his lungs, his blood, his crashing heart.

She flitted away as a great, rough *something* whipped his back. He didn't turn to look, he just followed her. He couldn't suppress his fear now, not when he was swimming for his life.

But what had that voice been? Was the Air Force really out there? Maybe he would've been safe if only—

Pammy stopped, turned, and yelled in bubbles: *NO!*

He went deeper, following the disappearing form. The water was dark here, the pressure was making his ears ring, and his lungs were bursting again.

Somebody else was beside him, a young man as naked as Pammy had been, swimming hard, his eyes behind goggles also. He had the oxygen, which Martin took in huge gulps.

He was being rescued by the town kids who had disappeared, and Oh, God, maybe that meant Trev.

He swam hard, and soon found himself in a narrowing, dark space, a tunnel. Where he was he didn't know, but they were ahead of him and he swam for all he was worth.

Then something like steel springs grabbed both of his legs, and he began to be dragged back out of the tunnel, and he knew that it was one of the things and he kicked and kicked but the harder he tried, the tighter its grip became. Also, air was getting short again and he was in too confined a space, nobody could reach him here. As he began to be dragged back, he clawed at the walls, he kicked with every ounce of his strength, but still the grip on him tightened and he knew that he had lost this struggle.

He began to be pulled backward out of the tunnel. Going faster by the second, he could soon see again. As he was pulled back into the body of the lake, light grew around him.

The walls of the tunnel were stone, he could see them now, and he had a last chance, here. He understood spaces like this, tunnels, tombs, and such. With all the strength that was in him, he thrust out his arms and the leg that wasn't in the grip of the thing that was dragging him. As the thing met sudden and unexpected resistance, he felt a flash of pain in the ankle it had been gripping. Immediately, he kicked. Kicked again. Kicked a third time, and felt himself come free, then kicked harder as the legs or grippers or whatever they were scrabbled around his feet.

He pulled himself back into the blackness and narrowness of the tunnel, until he could barely move and had to breathe and knew that it would be water.

And he did breathe and it was water, it came sluicing down his throat and gagged him, causing him to cough and involuntarily draw in more.

It hurt to drown, it was not magic, he saw nothing of his life before his eyes as he died, only agony, only a frantic need that could not be ful-filled and then dark.

Dark. Dark.

Air, sweet in him, filling him, air but maybe only the air of wishes, the air of dreams.

"Come ON!"

"CPR him, hurry!"

Pressure on his back, a cough, water coming out, flowing out, then another breath, deep and good and he was fully conscious again, wet, aware of how miserably cold he was.

Dappled autumn woods, larks singing in the last, high light, Little Moon racing in the clouds, beloved star wanderer. And her—Pammy—standing over him and the young man, the boy—also familiar but no name, not yet.

They dragged him to his feet. "Hurry!"

High overhead, a long, chilling wail shattered the noise of the larks.

"Don't listen!"

"Why not?"

"They home in on fear. If you're not afraid, they can't find you. Come on." As she spoke, the young man sprinted away.

She tugged at his arm. "We've gotta go. They're realizing they made a mistake." She smiled shyly, her cheeks and neck turning pink. "Some-body just said, 'Who's back at the lake?' and now they're all looking at each other." She lowered her eyes.

"You understand their language?"

She hauled at his hands, then slipped away as easily as if she had been born to the forest, her pale face glowing in a dark that was being brought by clouds that were speeding out of the north like hungry pan-thers, flashing and bellowing.

She had already disappeared, and he ran to follow her—and was stopped by a devastating blow from behind. And then he saw the ground, felt cold leaves in his face.

"I want you to be calm." It was the Air Force officer, Jennifer Mazle.

He cried out in the direction the girl had gone. "Help! Help me!"

"I'm a scientist, too, Doctor Winters, I'm not going to hurt you."

"Then let me up."

The weight lifted, and Martin pulled out from under her. She wore a camouflage vest, a rumpled hat, and heavy glasses with a split lens. Her eyes were big with sadness. "This mission isn't going right," she said. "I need you to come back and help us."

"What are those things? My God—"

"You need to help us understand, Doctor Martin."

"They were trying to kill me. The government was, too."

She touched his hand, then gripped it. "There's a lot of fear out there."

He glimpsed movement behind her. She started to turn, but was struck, and hard, by a piece of wood. She turned quickly back.

Her face was distorted, the skin on the cheek where she'd been hit imprinted by the wood.

She moved to one side, her skin rippling, turning cream-colored, red where the board had hit.

What in the world was wrong with her?

She snarled, came quickly toward him. Seen full on like this, her face was—oh, holy Christ, it was—the skin was ripping like a crazy jello, the eyes were weird in the eerie cloud light, weird and gold.

He turned and ran. He didn't think, he was beyond that. He just ran because what he had seen was so terrible that his mind had been com-pletely stripped away, replaced by a terror so raw and so deep that this educated, civilized man was thrown back in an instant to the days when men were hunted things.

A thunder of slashing jaws rose up all around him, as overhead the wails came again and again, exultant now, joyous now, the sky, the very air vibrant with their triumph.

His fear was the beacon, but he couldn't help it, she'd turned into a monster when that kid had hit her, and that had been the single most shocking thing Martin had ever seen, more shocking even than the explosion of the pyramid, which involved an inanimate thing, not the face of a living creature like that.

And then Pammy was there, looking down at him from a ledge. She motioned to him and he clambered up beside her.

She lay flat and he did the same.

"Blank your mind," she said calmly. "Concentrate your attention on your body. Don't think."

Lying on the sun-warmed stone, he concentrated on his aching lungs, his crashing heart. Below them, he heard movement, then quiet voices. Above, the wailing came and went as the great birds began to patrol.

"Come on," she whispered, "fast!"

The instant she spoke, there was a rustling sound, and a black-gloved hand gripped the ledge from below. He turned and ran, following her, putting all the strength he had left into his effort.

The trees shuddered and the thunder echoed, and great gusts of wind swam down from the north. Martin ran behind the fleeing girl, deeper and deeper into the woods, and rain came in sheets, a yellow deluge. Behind him he heard the cries of the strange birds and the crackle of alien voices.

"Come on," Pammy urged.

He could remember this part of the woods. They were past the Saunders and about a mile down from his house. This was state land, part of the Prairie Heritage program. The forest here was as thick as it got in Kansas, and when you dropped down into the hollows, dense with brush. The hunting back in here had been excellent when he was a boy. Wild pheasant, plenty of turkey.

Times gone by. He'd discovered here that Trevor was not going to be a hunter, that he felt too bad for the animals. He and Lindy had come back in here when they were first married, and walked naked here, hand in hand, in some sort of sacred contact with the land that they could not articulate.

It was miserable here now, though, soaking, the rain pounding down, wind roaring. A storm like this could easily bring a tornado, too.

Then she seemed to drop down, as if into a hole. When he followed her, he discovered a tiny glade, and in it a camouflaged tent. He recognized it. They'd been on sale at Hiram's Sporting Goods. She darted in. He approached more warily. Close to it, he could hear drums in the sound of the rain. Then the flap opened and she gestured frantically. He went in.

The first thing he noticed was that the drumming was much louder, the second that the air was stifling. As his eyes adjusted, he saw that the space was filled with children and young people, perhaps twenty in all. He knew at once that these were the kids who had disappeared when their parents and siblings had become wanderers.

He looked from face to face, seeking recognition, not willing to taste again of his hope.

When he did not see Trevor, he swayed, staring, helpless to either stand or sit. He had reached the end of his tether, he was going to collapse.

Unable to defend himself from his own tears, he dropped to his knees and covered his face, and fought to keep his tears silent.

A hand came onto his shoulder.

"I'm sorry," he said. "I'm sorry." And the tears became a helpless, humiliating flood.

"Dad?"

He'd heard the word, but—

"Dad?"

He raised his face and saw standing before him somebody he did not recognize.

"Dad, I'm Trevor."

Then he did—behind the dirt, behind the dark cast of his eyes, behind the wild hair and the muddy camouflage suit, he knew that it was his son.

Trevor had changed fantastically. He was not a boy, not at all. His expression contained an adult's knowledge of the world—that and more—and the change had been so abrupt and so total that in just these few days he had become unrecognizable to his own father.

The heart, though, the heart sees, and Martin's heart saw his son before him. He opened his arms and Trevor came to him, and he closed them around his son's narrow body. His heart and mind may have grown, but this was still the same boy, fragile, almost, but with the long legs and big shoulders that said that he would soon grow much taller.

"Trevor," he managed to rasp. "Trevor."

Trevor pushed gently at him but he clung more tightly. He could never let him go, not ever, he could not do that again. "Dad—um—" He managed to look up into his father's eyes. "Dad, nobody else here has any parents left."

For a moment, Martin didn't understand. Then he did. He was the only parent who was not wandering. He looked out across the expectant faces, the eyes that he was realizing all had the same strange shadow in them, some of them touched now by tears, others wide with sorrow, others resigned.

"I'm sorry," he said.

"I'm George," one of the older boys replied. "Glad to meet you." George held out his hand, shook formally. Others followed, most of them teens, some as young as ten. There were twenty-two of them, two more boys than girls. Each in turn introduced himself. It was so formal. Oddly formal. But there was no precedent for such a meeting, was there?

Through all of this, the drumming did not stop.

Trevor glanced away from him, then murmured, "It drowns out the sound of the night riders, so the little ones won't get scared."

Just hearing his son's voice, Martin felt another wave of joy.

"Dad!"

"He can't help it," a little girl said.

"Can you hear me thinking, kids? Is that it?"

"We sort of pick up thoughts, but it's not like you'd imagine, Dad. People don't think alike and thought patterns are even more different than faces. You can't figure out what somebody else is thinking unless they know how to organize their thoughts to communicate, and we're still learning. But they can all feel your feelings, and you're . . . it's embarrassing me, Dad."

"I can read thought," George said. "I'm getting kind of okay." He looked quickly at Martin. "Not you, sir! I'd never do that."

"I better not catch you in my mind," a girl warned him.

"Oh, I'm not, Sylvie! I'm not!"

"Of course you are. Anyway, *we* have no trouble reading you morons, any girl can do it, you don't need to have gotten zapped. You're transparent from birth, gentlemen." She leaned her head against George's shoulder. George crossed his legs.

"What's this getting zapped?" Martin asked.

Silence fell. "Dad, we want you to try."

"Try what?"

"Don't ask him, Trev, he has to!"

"Shut up!"

"What's going on here?"

"Dad, you remember the night when it happened?"

"How could I ever forget it?"

"Mom was holding Winnie and I was standing beside them. You had your hand on my shoulder, you were squeezing so hard you nearly broke it."

"I'm sorry."

"No, no, it was good. The light missed you. It hit Mom and sort of splashed on me. I went out of my body and up in the air. I saw you down there, I saw us all. Then I was out in the sky, up above the church. I saw Mom and Winnie, they were gold in the light—gold masses of sparks—and they were rising fast. But my shoulder hurt so much, I went back down.

"At first, I was in shock. I went to the back of the church with Mom. I saw you but you seemed far away. You were hollering at us. You—I never saw you like that, Dad. I felt so sorry for you. *So sorry!*"

"I want your mom back. I want my girl."

Another boy shook his shoulder. "We're gonna win, Doctor Winters."

Martin recognized him as Joey Fielding, son of George and Moira, who ran Octagon Feed. "That doesn't seem possible," he replied, trying to keep his bitterness and his resignation out of his voice.

"Every one of us had the same thing happen. We were in pain when the light hit us, and it didn't take all the layers. Who we were stayed with our bodies. What we lost were the lies, the hopes, most of our education, what we wanted, what we thought of ourselves, our hopes. We lost all the baggage."

One of the little ones said, "We're like, fresh. We're new again, like we were—"

"Look at him, you're scaring him," a girl hissed.

"I'm not scared," Martin said.

"Yes, you are. We're weird and you're scared!"

"He doesn't scare easy," Trevor snapped. "My dad has courage."

"He's gonna need it if we do this."

Martin was aware that this conversation was happening on two levels, one he could hear and another that he couldn't. "I think I need to know what's going on."

"What's going on is we need you to try to become like us."

How would he do that? It seemed like some sort of side effect of a failed attempt by the aliens to strip away a soul.

"That's it," Trevor said.

"I thought you couldn't read minds."

He looked down at the smashed grass that made up the floor of the tiny chamber. "Um, you're easy, Dad. 'Cause I know you . . ."

George said, "It's getting dark."

Trevor looked at him sharply, shook his head.

"Trevor, no. NO!"

"What is this?"

Trevor threw his arms around him. "Dad, they want you to leave!"

"Leave? I can't leave!"

A boy of perhaps ten or eleven produced a pistol. He handed it to one of the older kids. Martin saw that it was a .45 automatic. He didn't exactly point it at Martin, so much as leave it visible.

Martin stared at it. He looked from the barrel to the young face. Those eyes again, all shadowy. These kids had *changed*. He gentled his voice. "Look, I need a break here."

The boy thrust the gun toward him.

"Trevor! Trevor, tell them, I'm a good father, I'm—I'm—kids, listen. I'm needed. You need me. Yes. Oh, yes. I can be—can replace—replace . . ."

The boy racked the slide.

"You helped me, Pammy! Hey, you just helped me escape, now you want to do this? This is crazy!"

"Dad, if you don't go—" Trevor pulled in his words. He was choking with tears, Martin could see it.

"Trevor, tell them, I can't survive out there. Nobody can!"

The boy got to his feet. He had a dusting of beard, barely visible in the gathering dark. He held the gun in Martin's face. "Doctor Winters," he said quietly, "you get out of here."

"Oh, God, listen, please—I've been running and running, I can't run anymore. Trevor, please help me! Help your dad!"

Trevor looked at him out of his strange new eyes, and Martin saw the truth of it: the horror they had seen had made them monsters, all of them, and Trevor was a monster, too.

But then Trevor reached out a hand and touched his father's cheek. It was not the gesture of a boy, but of a man of maturity. "Dad, it's survival of the fittest. The reptilians are going to find you. You can't hide from them, not anywhere, not like we can. If you stay here, you'll lead them right to us."

Martin backed away from the gun. "Get that thing out of my face!"

"Dad, you have to do this." Trevor threw his arms around his father. Martin held him, felt his body shaking.

He looked to Pammy. "Why did you save me? How could you be so cruel?"

"She's a damn asshole," the boy with the gun spat.

"Ride the storm," a voice said from the back. "Same as we did."

"Doctor Winters—"

"Pammy, call me Martin, please."

"Doctor Winters—"

She pulled back the flap of the tent. Outside, Martin saw rain sweeping in almost continuous lightning, and shadows in the nearby clearing that did not look like any shadows he cared to see. "This is crazy. I can't."

"Dad, do it!"

"Trev, no, absolutely not!"

His son was standing before him, looking up at him, his face stained with tears. "Get out," he said. He turned to the boy with the gun. "Give it to me," he said.

"Why?" the boy asked, raising his eyebrows.

"Because I'm the only one who can handle this!" He took the gun and held it to his father's face. "Decide," he said.

Martin looked straight down the barrel. He could see muscles working in Trevor's hand, could see his finger tightening. "Trevor?"

Trevor screwed his eyes shut. "Now, Daddy!"

Martin tried to think—some argument, some appeal, but there were no more arguments, there were no more appeals. That weapon was going to go off in another second, and Trevor was going to have to spend the rest of his life an orphan like all these other orphans, but knowing, unlike them, that he had taken the life of his own father.

Martin raised his hand. "I'm going," he said softly. "I'm going, son, and I want you to know that I don't understand, but I don't blame you."

"Just go."

"I know you have to look out for each other, that you can't risk the group—"

"Damn you, GO!"

Trevor's voice was not the same now. He'd been so gentle a boy that he couldn't shoot a pheasant. Now here he was ready to kill his father, and his voice was low and hard, scorched with the pain of somebody who could.

Martin went out into the lightning.

THIRTEEN
DECEMBER 18, MIDNIGHT
A FAMILY AFFAIR

WYLIE STOOD BY THE QUIET waters of the Saunders, trying to get the courage up to try and cross into the other world. If Trevor could come here, then surely he could go in the other direction, and that was urgently necessary, obviously.

He paced, he looked for some sign of the gateway. Martin was out there right now in those deadly woods, and somebody had to save the guy, and Wylie thought it might as well be him.

He could bring Martin across. If nobody over there wanted him, he could live here. Impractical though he was, professorial in a way that Wylie found infuriating, nevertheless the guy didn't deserve this to happen. His own son, doing that to him? Good God.

Why would they save him, then just discard him? And how could Trevor—too gentle to hunt birds, for the love of Pete—ever be that hard on his dad?

Over there, it was storming. Over here, the sky was clear. The moon near the half rode high. It was close on to midnight, and from the house he could hear Brooke singing. She'd once had vocal ambitions, but life and children and a certain lack of volume had kept her away from an operatic career. Her voice was too delicate for the stage, but on a quiet night like this one, it was an angelic wonder.

He knew that she was sitting in a window looking at the moon, waiting for her man to return. She never protested his midnight walks, but they made her uneasy. It was as if her voice was meant as a kind of lifeline, reaching out to him in case he strayed too far from home.

She sang an old lullaby, one that she had sung to Nick and still sang to Kelsey, a song from her deep past, his woman of the tribe of the Celts. It was called "Dereen Day," the little song, and it floated across the softly muttering water like a breeze.

He tossed a stone into the moonlight, listened to it splash in the deeper river. Where was the gateway now? Did it open and close? According to some of the more *outre* stuff he'd been reading about *2012,* there were gateways all over the world, especially at the points where what were called *ley lines* met. He was not sure what these lines were. Planet Energy Lines would probably be the simplest definition. New Age Bullshit Lines was another contender.

He stood just where he and Nick had been, and tossed another stone. It gleamed in the moonlight, then splashed gently down.

"Damn."

He heard something, though. He listened. It was on the other side of the river. He'd never heard anything quite like it before.

He listened again.

What *was* that?

Then he knew, and his blood all but froze in his veins.

That slashing noise could only be an outrider, and it was actually *in* the gateway, hanging between the worlds.

He hadn't brought a gun, he'd been afraid that shooting it in the other universe would bring on some sort of catastrophe. He'd read all he could about parallel worlds, but little was actually known, except that experiments showed that they were actual, physical places. There was no scientific speculation about what might be in them. He thought that he was the only person who had ever speculated that certain animals must be able to cross this divide, that they had evolved the ability as a threat avoidance mechanism.

Had to be true. He'd seen a weir cat himself, and not far from here, when he was a kid. Damn big, damn black, and damn scary. Then gone—poof—right before his eyes.

The slashing sound grew louder. Came toward him.

Brooke stopped singing. Her voice floated across the night. "Wylie?"

Jesus, he needed to get back to the house, he needed to get his hands on a gun. Nick had been right to get them ready. That was a smart kid there. He had foresight.

The slashing was now right in front of him—but he couldn't see it. It was loud, it was deafening—and then he could feel tickling, then pricking against his face, his neck. Crying out, he lurched back.

He fell against what felt like iron bars. Where he touched them, they became visible, and he saw that they were not bars, but the legs of what the kids called an outrider. And now the slashing sound was overhead. He was *under* the damn thing!

He rolled. The slashing came down toward him. He lashed out at it, kicking furiously toward the sound. Where his foot struck, he saw a section of the creature—a gleaming abdomen striped yellow, then a complicated eye, then a hooked claw on the joint of a leg.

Screaming now, he rolled.

There was a pneumatic, liquid hissing and boiling yellow sludge sprayed the ground around him. A stinger the size of his arm slashed his jacket and was gone.

But it was coming back, he could hear the mechanical slashing of the jaws, but more he could *feel* the thing probing with its legs, and he knew that the next time it attacked, that stinger would impale him.

A roar, huge, echoing off into the woods.

Silence.

Nothing there. Nothing at all.

"Dad?"

"Nick!"

His son scrambled down the hill that dropped to the riverbank. He carried his 10-gauge. He wore pajama bottoms and one house shoe. Behind him came Brooke. "Wylie! Nick! What's happening?"

The moon sailed in splendor, the night birds called, the sacred peace of the Kansas night enclosed them, and the sweet little river rolled on.

Nick threw his arms around his father as Brooke came running up, seeking with her hands, almost hitting him, enraged with fear, then choking back sobs, then holding both of her men.

"An outrider," Nick said. "I heard it and I saw it attacking Dad. Sort of."

Brooke nodded.

"Martin's in trouble," Wylie said.

"We know," Brooke responded.

"We just read it, Dad."

"I was trying to get to him. To cross over."

Faintly, from the house, they all heard Kelsey's voice call out, "Is anybody home?"

"We're coming, Baby," Wylie called, and they all trooped back to the house, where she waited at the kitchen door, her hands on her hips.

She hugged her brother. "Thank you for saving our daddy." Then she went into her mother's arms.

Wylie was not too surprised at what his family knew. Kelsey was eight and an excellent reader. She was probably reading the book in everybody else's downtime.

Brooke put on water for coffee. "I think we need to tell Matt," she said. "We need some support out here."

"Fighting them is acknowledging them. Believing in them. And the more we do that, the stronger the link to their reality becomes. So getting a posse out here might not be such a good idea."

Brooke poured water into the coffee maker. "Then we need to not try to use that gateway at all."

"She's right, Dad," Nick said.

"But Martin—he's dying out there. Right now."

Nick gave him a long, searching look.

"What?"

"Dad, just let it happen. You're fighting and we can't fight. We have to just write and hope they find it, and hope that it helps them. If one of us takes so much as a single step into that world—"

Kelsey's eyes were wide, and Nick dropped it.

Brooke poured three mugs of coffee and sat down. Kelsey came into her lap.

"Nick, should you—this late?"

Nick gave him another of those searching looks. "You don't remember?"

"He doesn't," Kelsey said. "He can't."

"Remember what? What am I missing?"

So softly that it was almost inaudible, Nick said, "I'm the guardian, Mom is the facilitator, you're the scribe." He glanced toward Kelsey, whose eyes were heavy. "She's the sentinel." He raised his eyebrows. "Remember?"

It didn't make a bit of sense, any of it.

Nick stared into his coffee. "Our sentinel woke me up when she heard the outrider. If she hadn't, you'd be dead now."

He owed them his life. The bond that he felt with his family at this moment was the strongest thing he had ever known, the biggest emotion he had ever had. "Thank you," he said.

Then he heard from upstairs, low voices.

Kelsey had closed her eyes now, and Brooke began singing "Dereen Day" again, her own voice as soft as a breeze, too soft to drown out the conversation Wylie was hearing.

He looked toward the dark stairs, then toward Nick—who jumped up and ran upstairs.

"Nick!" Wylie followed. Brooke only glanced at them, then continued singing.

Nick stood in front of Wylie's office, his shotgun ported in his arms.

Wylie had known that there wouldn't be anybody there. He went into the office. The voices were louder here, more distinct.

But nothing was breaking through, not here, not this far from a gateway.

"It's my story," he said to Nick. "My story's calling me."

FOURTEEN
DECEMBER 18, LATE
THE MONSTER

WYLIE SAW REPTILIANS, GORGEOUS LIKE snakes are gorgeous, their scales shimmering in a bright room with white tile walls, fluorescent tubes lining the ceiling, a metal autopsy table.

Where was it?

Then he knew, and he wrote: The entrance to their lair is in Cheyenne Mountain, but the place itself is right here, right beneath us. It has to do with the mass of the planet and the power coursing through its veins, which are the ley lines, and the great confluence of lines in this place.

Twelve miles from this house lay the geographical center of the continental United States. In the other human world, their base was beneath it. And in this world, if there was anywhere that they could break through, it would be in this area, where the veil between universes was thinnest.

Wylie's hands flew. He hardly noticed that Nick and Brooke stood behind him, with Kelsey asleep in her mother's arms.

The little team rode thus deep into the night, on the tide of Wylie's words.

He watched his own hands, then watched the screen as the words appeared:

General Samson injected himself, sucked air through his teeth as the familiar agony spread up his arm, then burned through his chest, then invaded his face and head, his whole body. It was a hateful, miserable thing to have to do every day.

Today, he did not expect to expose himself to the human earth's atmosphere, but he was doing it under an order that he could quote precisely: "You will maintain a physical state that allows you free movement in existing planetary conditions at all times." There was nothing about not being prepared for a day because he didn't expect to be in their raw damn air.

"Time?" he barked as he entered the abattoir. His feet squished in blood. The place stank of raw human meat.

"01044," Captain Mazle replied.

Lying before them on a steel table was a body. Samson looked down at it dispassionately. General Al North, big deal. He'd despised the eager creature with its idealism and its pathetically uninformed mind.

He looked at the mouth, noted the drying along the raw line where the lips had been removed and the clotted blood in both eye sockets.

"Mazle!"

"Yessir!"

He gestured. "If you fail—"

"We won't fail."

"It's you, Captain. *You*. You will fail or you won't."

"Don't threaten me, General."

She came from a powerful family. He didn't like it, but he must not forget it. "I'm doing nothing of the kind."

"You'd like to, though. Anyway, I've already told my father what a complete piece of shit you are."

He tried not to take her threat to heart. Her father could order death to a man in Samson's position. "Captain, I'm sorry if you don't like my style."

"Your *style?* You have all the charm of a skerix, and you smell a lot worse."

"It's the anitallergens, as I'm sure you are aware. Please be reminded that my responsibilities leave me no choice." He gestured toward General North's ravaged body. "If we're going to get this thing through that gateway, we have no time, so let's get started, Captain, if you don't mind."

"You'd be delighted if I failed, General, of course. But I'm not going to fail."

"This whole operation is in danger of failing, and if it does, not even your father will be able to save you. We still don't have enough slaves and we can't get the personnel in to control the ones we do have because the lenses are old and barely functional. We're losing 20,000 humans a minute and we need another billion in four days."

"Well, that's not my issue, General. My issue is this little writer sitting in the other human earth—you know, the one you people haven't been able to enter usefully *for the past fifty goddamn years!*" She strode over and slapped the chest of the inert human. "If we don't succeed in this, we will both stand before Echidna herself. You and me, General Samson, and not all the power of Abaddon will save us."

She crossed the room, moving toward a male who stood in silence, waiting. "Doctor," she said to him, "it's time for you to do your duty. Assuming that you can."

The doctor gleamed in the light, his scales tiny and creamy. She didn't know his name, but his appearance confirmed his class. She would be polite to him. He'd no doubt paid a lot for this job, in hope of sharing in the spoils of earth.

However, the doctor didn't do anything.

"Let's get moving, okay?"

Samson chuckled. "The loyal retainer. Your personnel are as promising as your plans."

"I need more power," the doctor said. "Forty thousand volts at least."

"Do it with twenty."

"Captain—"

"You do it, all you have to do is use care instead of brute force to cover your incompetence. So do it with twenty or you're going on punishment report. I'm sick of your excuses."

"Captain, for this to last—"

"We don't need it to last, we need it to work for a few hours."

The doctor threw a look of desperation toward General Samson, who did not react.

"Okay," Captain Mazle said into her phone, "how much can you give him?" She looked at the doctor. "Compromise: you can get your forty, but only for one minute."

"I applied for two, Captain."

"Do it! Now!"

The doctor drew a narrow silver case from his pocket, opened it, and took out an instrument with a black, tapering handle and a long blade so thin that it was no more than a shimmer in the air. "This specimen has mild arterial damage from cholesterol," he said, "typically associated with advance of age in this species. Do we want to invest—"

"*This species*," Jennifer snarled. "Where do you get off? It's the only other intelligent species we've found across a billion parallel universes and throughout our own." She gestured toward the remains of Al North. "This creature, if it can successfully do what it's being designed to do, could save us all."

"I hardly think—"

"Because, Doctor, have you heard the news from home? Have you heard what's happening there?"

"It's an aged specimen."

Samson broke in. "I don't want you two sniping at each other, not when we're working against time and there's so much at stake. We are behind schedule *so MOVE*."

"I won't be responsible if I'm rushed!"

"Doctor, I'll hand you over to the soultechs."

The doctor's scales shuddered and flushed yellow. Everybody feared the soultechs and their skills to capture the soul and to destroy the soul.

"Under what regulation? You have no right."

"Maybe and maybe not, but I will do it, of that you can be sure."

"You ought to do it anyway," Mazle added.

"Shut up, bitch," Samson said, his voice deceptively mild.

"How dare you!"

"Gonna tell on me again? Daddy's getting old. Daddy's not who he used to be. So maybe Daddy loses his power soon, and I get to kill your fucking little prune of a soul."

"Talk about a hollow threat."

"Are you willing to take the risk?"

"All you do is talk, but the clock doesn't stop, does it, General? You're easily distracted. You're failure prone. Daddy says." She curtsied.

"This thing of yours probably won't even work."

"A mix of biological material from both earths. It's bound to."

"Well, great, because if it doesn't we can all kiss our asses good-bye. We fail here and we die here—in this facility, fifteen hundred cubits beneath gorgeous Kansas."

The doctor began to set out his instruments. "Get support services in here," he said, "if you want this done."

"I'll be your support services. This is extremely classified."

"Nothing like a military idiot for a nurse-assistant," the doctor muttered.

"Maybe I'm better than you think. Maybe I've even been trained."

"I bought my job and your Daddy sure as hell bought yours. If I'm lucky, I might be able to flush a child's craw. Very lucky."

Jennifer opened the small box she had brought in with her, in which there was red liquid. "Look at it, Doctor. This is living material from the one-moon earth."

"You're kidding."

"There are humans crossing between the two worlds," Samson said miserably.

"That's ridiculous," the doctor replied.

"We believe it was a lucky accident. But that might not be the case. The union's hand might be in the matter somewhere."

Mazle, suddenly interested, strode up to him. "You didn't tell me this."

"You didn't need to know," he replied.

"This casts everything in a very different light."

"In what sense?" the doctor asked. He had a stake in the matter, too. They all did.

"If we're defeated by enemy action, Echidna might not be so—well, so hard."

"Harder, never doubt it," Samson said. "I've had experience in the palace."

"I grew up with her last crop of children," Mazle said. "My egg was honored with a place in her basket."

"I've seen them running eggs through that exalted basket. A new clutch every ten seconds."

Mazle turned on her hireling doctor. "Get to it," she shouted at him. "Get to it now!"

He lifted the lid of the black lacquer box, looked at the blood-covered material within. "Won't this explode, if it touches this air?"

"It's not going to happen."

He drew out a long, wet object. A lip. "This is dead."

"So is the cadaver, but we've got its soul."

General Samson thought of the millions of them collected deep under this room. The harvest of bodies had a certain value when terraforming began, but the harvest of souls was truly valuable plunder. It wasn't the doctor's business, though, or the Captain's. For Samson, it was a guarantee of wealth beyond imagination, the kind of wealth that bought an endless supply of perfectly cloned bodies, and with them the sort of eternal life that only the highest nobility enjoyed.

The doctor unrolled his instruments, taking a fleam in his long, narrow fingers, and drawing it along the line of one of General North's eye sockets, removing the dried flesh from the edges of the wound.

Then, using instruments like two golden chopsticks with splayed ends, he drew out a bloody ball. "This eye is not in acceptable condition."

"Acceptable for what, Doctor?" Mazle asked.

"For use!"

"It won't see?"

"Oh, it'll see. For a while. Somewhat. But—look at it, look how it's deteriorating."

"Why is that?" General Samson asked.

"General, I know you go topside because I prepare your allergy kit. Think if you entered their world without your serums. You'd disintegrate, and this eye is disintegrating."

"But if we get it back to its home world, then the rot will stop, won't it?" Mazle asked.

"This is all ridiculous. This can't work."

She persisted. "Can you attach it to the cadaver?"

"Um, sure."

"THEN DO IT NOW GOD DAMN YOU!"

He began using his instrument to touch the left eye socket, gingerly, experimentally. As the doctor touched the socket just with the tip of his probe, his fingers working with a pianist's virtuosity, immense generators that drew their energy directly from the planet's core started up deep beneath the facility.

Tiny sparks appeared around the eye, until the whole rim of the socket was shimmering as if with millions of little stars, each one of which was actually an enormously complicated object in itself, a whole miniature universe consisting of billions upon billions of stars no bigger than dust motes on a gnat's toe.

"Is the tissue going to explode?" Samson asked.

"No," Jennifer said.

"I can't be sure," the doctor responded. "We'll have to see."

"We'll have to *see*? We could all be killed!" Samson shouted, backing away from the table where the operation was taking place.

"Good," the doctor said. He then rested the instrument in its case and took the eyeball between the gloved fingers of his left hand.

"How dare you say that!" Samson hissed.

"Look, I'm here because I have to be. This whole thing—taking this planet like this—it's wrong. These creatures don't deserve this kind of treatment because of the avarice of a bunch of developers, and to be drafted by the military to do the work of a greedy few, it's sick and it's evil, General, and I don't give a rat's ass who knows what I think." He inserted the eyeball, which settled into the socket with a sucking *plunk*. "Well, whaddaya know, it didn't explode. Too bad, we live on."

"I ought to have you disensouled," Samson muttered.

"Ah, the hollow threat again. You two are certainly expert at tossing those around. Problem is, you can't do without a doctor, therefore I'm not in any danger, am I?"

He inserted the second eyeball, then attached the lips. The doctor stared for some time at a photograph.

"Hurry!"

"The lips are too fat."

"Thin them, then!" Samson glared at Mazle. "Time?"

"01048."

Still staring at a photograph of Al North, the doctor pressed a glittering cloth against the lips, the contours of which gradually grew more and more to resemble those of the general.

He then addressed his attention to the genitals and rectum, which were taken out of the box and attached to the body. In the end, it appeared fresh and undamaged.

Finally, he stood back. "It's completed," he said.

"Bring up the soul," Samson said.

Jennifer Mazle spoke into a fist-sized walkie-talkie, and in a few moments two of her soultechs appeared carrying between them the enormous glass tube that contained the living soul of Al North. The light inside the tube no longer flashed and twisted, but clung close to the copper filament, which glowed deep red. "You think this will actually work?"

"Postoperative reensoulment isn't exactly gravitic science," the doctor said. "If you could stuff him for me, Captain."

Jennifer drew Al's body up, and hung the head back over the end of the table until his mouth lolled open. She sprayed into it from an aerosol can gaily painted with hieroglyphics, in colors familiar to anybody in any of the three parallel worlds, because all three of them had evolved Lysol spray. Then she lifted a thick, black cable that was coiled on the floor at the head of the operating table, and pushed it deep down Al's disinfected gullet.

"This soul's been cut the way you want it cut, right, General Samson?" the doctor asked.

"I approved your pattern."

"Because with all these shittily completed new connections, once the soul goes in, the only way you're gonna get it out again is by tearing this body to pieces."

"Am I going to want to do that, Mazle?"

"It's been debrided of every thread suggesting independence."

"And the brain?" Samson asked.

"Its memories have been erased back to two days before it entered Cheyenne Mountain," Mazle replied.

One of the soultechs held the tube, which was about four feet across at its top, tapering to a diameter of perhaps nine inches at its base. Another inserted the cable into the socket.

"How old is that equipment, Mazle?"

"My dad's company buried it in the Egyptian desert, at a place called Dendera."

"When?"

"Eight thousand years ago."

"What cheap bastards you people are. What if the humans had found it?"

"Not too likely."

"Still, eight thousand years, and we have to rely on it. That's criminal irresponsibility, in my opinion."

"The objective is to create wealth for garbage like you to enjoy, General, not spend it on extravagant equipment we can do without. And I can't help it if my family has been running a successful enterprise for twenty generations and you're a propertyless consumer."

The body began heaving. "Don't lose this, Mazle."

She raised her eyebrows. "Doctor?"

"Normal," he snapped.

"Fill it," she said to her soultechs.

One of them began raising the impedance in the tube until the soul was a purple spark dancing on the end of the filament.

The body heaved again, then again.

"You're sure these seizures aren't a problem?" Mazle asked the doctor.

"You can't expect this to work like modern equipment."

Samson snorted derisively, but made no comment.

Slowly, the color of the filament went from purple to violet, then to white. The body's eyes flickered open, the chest gave a great, oily heave. The muscles rippled, the skin flushed, and there came from the gaping mouth a noise, earsplitting, like a hiss of gas escaping a broken pipe. A scream, Samson realized. That had been a scream.

And then Mazle said, "Look."

The tube that had contained the soul was as black as a shroud. Al North's eyes were open, though, wide open.

General North was crying.

FIFTEEN
DECEMBER 19, PREDAWN
THE STALKER

THEY'D MADE A SORT OF evil Golem, a monster that would be incapable of disobeying its orders. But it was more than that. Wylie saw the idea behind it. They had used the eyes and lips and tongue and the other parts they had managed to cut out of poor John Nunnally from down the road, and grafted them into the body of Al North. Because the result was mixed of flesh from the two earths, they probably hoped that it could move more freely in our world, and get around the fact that, because we ignored them, they could not enter freely here.

Unlike the outrider and the wanderers from the other earth, it would be able to enter this world fully.

So far, the only person who had managed that, seemingly without any restriction, was Trevor. But now there would be another, and this one would come with blood in his eye, a monster in the truest definition of the word.

Wylie wanted to stop writing, he wanted to warn his family, but his fingers moved relentlessly on, taking him where they chose to take him, on a journey he could not stop and could not control.

He was aware that dawn was coming, but he could not stop, he could not speak. He couldn't even turn away from the keyboard. Nick slept in the easy chair that stood in the corner. Brooke, he thought, was in their bedroom.

The problem was that this monster was intended to cross the gateway and come up that hill and come to this house and kill them all, and now they were asleep and they were not reading and so they could not see this warning, and as hard as he tried, he could not call out to them, and he knew that time was of the essence.

Then he was swept away, far away, to the last place he cared to go, almost as if some larger force was at work, a silent wizard controlling the whole horrible catastrophe.

Here, he saw dark, complicated heaps up and down sidewalks, bits and tatters of paper and clothing and all manner of debris blowing in a north wind, and there was a smell, thick, sweet, that he recognized as the odor of many dead.

He was in New York, the New York of the two-moon earth, and these were people who had leaped from their apartments up and down Fifth Avenue, and there were more of them, Wylie was sure, on every single street everywhere in the city.

Detail struck him—an Armani purse lying open on the sidewalk, a doorman who had shot himself at his post, his brains hardened on the wall behind him, his kind old face crossed by a path of busy ants, a bicycle lying neatly against a lamppost.

He moved with a dreamer's gliding ease but the horrible precision of reality, into a side street. Here was a little restaurant called Henri's, all of its sidewalk tables bare, a full bottle of Cliquot champagne standing on a waiter's station beside a copy of the *Times* for the day New York got hit, December 6. Headline: BIZARRE TRAGEDIES SHOCK WORLD.

There was a flag snapping before a brownstone, and he could see that it was an art gallery, but he didn't go in, not in this storm-tossed, broken morning.

He fought to stop his hands, to pull away from the laptop. He could feel Al North standing, moving on wobbling legs, coughing, gasping, staggering, see him held up by sleek, creamy Mazle and black, gleaming Samson with their lithe bodies and long claws and their cruel reptile faces.

New York gave way to the ocean, big green waves involved with complicated little waves, and off through the bounding whitecaps the heeling dark shape of a great liner. She wallowed in the storm, and as he drew closer he saw that her bows were well down, and every time a wave struck her streaming flank, a great spray of water shot up, pushed across her by the driving wind like her own private rainstorm.

The people had disappeared from the deck like so much sea foam, but he was not long there, he was inside in the great sweep of a restaurant with chairs waltzing to the roll of the ship. But there were also others there, men in tuxedos, women in long dresses standing at the tall windows of what he supposed was the main restaurant. What was so appalling was that they had been made wanderers here, and had simply starved to death. He could see trenches in the carpeting under their feet. They had continued to walk after hitting the wall. He could see their sunken, gray faces.

I have to get home! Somebody help me!

And then he was on a twisting street, there were pushcarts everywhere, little motor bikes, signs in an unknown language and dogs barking and monkeys chattering in the blaze of day. But the streets were empty, and not only that, water was coming, and the buildings were heaving like women beneath the plunging weight of the night. And small, intricate waves came farther each time the place shook, the careful water licking the motorbikes and the paper signs and the cold sidewalk bakeries where *naan* had been sold for a few rupees.

India, some great city, and it was dead and it was sinking.

He was alive in it completely. Standing at an intersection. Down the street a luxury building in the chaos—a Four Seasons hotel with curtains blowing out the windows. He looked down at the sloshing water, how very carefully it licked his bare feet, how clear it was despite being floated with cigarette ends and Fanta bottles and plastic bags and sodden, gray disks of *naan* from the dead bakery.

Then he was in woods. His woods. And he saw a man.

Nick! Brooke! Kelsey! For the love of heaven, wake up!

Al North was walking and his movements were strange, purposeful but odd. He was flickering as he walked, like he wasn't entirely there. When he blundered into brush, he would mutter and groan, and there would be blue flashes all around him. Where his feet touched grassy places, there was flickering blue fire.

"Mommydaddy! Mommydaddy!" Kelsey flew in, throwing her arms around Wylie—who still could not stop typing. And Nick slept on.

"Daddy, Papa Bear is in the woods."

At last Nick woke up. He shook his head. "Hey, Baby," he said to his sister. "Daddy's busy."

Look at the book, Nick! Look this way!

Kelsey went into her brother's lap. "Yeah, Kelsey, it's Papa Bear," Nick said. He reached over and shook Wylie's shoulder. "Dad, you want to stop for a second? A little girl wants to say good morning."

"There's a papa bear in the woods, Daddy."

With every ounce of strength in him, Wylie tried to react. But his hands swept the keys and his voice remained as paralyzed as it always was when this seizure-like state was upon him.

Look at what I'm writing, for the love of all that's holy. He tried all caps, LOOK AT THIS! HELLO, NICK, IT'S AL NORTH IN THE WOODS!!!!

"Why don't we pull out the guns today, Dad," Nick said, the sleepy calm of his voice revealing that he had NOT looked.

"Oh, no, Nick, it was just *Papa Bear!*"

"We need the guns to be ready, Kelsey."

"Mommy, Nick is scaring me!"

"Nick!" Brooke came in. She glanced at Wylie. He could feel her looking at the screen—but then Kelsey ran to her and she was distracted.

DANGER DANGER DANGER!!!!

There was a change, he thought, in the way they moved.

"Dad, we're gonna go downstairs now."

The three of them left. A moment later, the clattering of the keyboard stopped. He tried to move his hands—and they pulled away.

At last!

He leaped up and dashed down the stairs. "Get the guns out," he shouted, "Al North is in our woods!"

They were in the family room, the three of them. The gun cabinet was open. The Magnum lay on the coffee table. Kelsey sat on the couch with her thumb in her mouth and her knees pulled up under her chin. She had saved them all, Wylie thought. He went to her. "What did Papa Bear look like, honey?"

"He'd been eating strawberries!"

"And how do you know that?"

"His mouth was all red."

The crude surgery.

"Dad," Nick said, "He was just here. He came right up to the house. I thought he was going to come in but something either went wrong or he changed his mind or something."

"Because he didn't come in? You're sure?"

"Of course I'm not sure! Maybe he's in the crawlspace, maybe he's in the attic, maybe he's invisible or something. I have no idea."

"But you didn't hear him come in?" Wylie went to the window.

Nick came beside him. "There," he said after a moment.

"I don't see him."

Then he did—a splash of red in the shadowy woods. His crude surgical wounds. Then he saw also a flash of metal.

There was a figure back among those trees, most certainly, and in its hand was a very big, very ugly gun.

SIXTEEN
DECEMBER 19, MORNING
SOUL HUNT

MARTIN HAD CIRCLED AROUND AWAY from the clearing where he'd seen the moving shapes of the monstrous spiders the kids called outriders. He'd gone up along the ridge line that led eventually to his house. But not in that direction, no way. The idea of going anywhere near that misshapen ruin sickened him.

It had been raining hard, but now that had stopped and second moon was low on the horizon, casting its glare over the tumble of rocks and twisted little trees that he could see below him.

He was trying very hard not to think about the future, of which he obviously had none, and above all not to feel angry at Trevor.

Of course, the son he'd loved, little Trevor, was no more. The strange being who had taken his place knew the world in a whole new way. "But I love you," Martin whispered to the silence. He always would, the little boy whom he had held tight in the scary nights, who had looked at him with joyous, dependent eyes, who had so admired his dad.

No matter how far beyond the edge of the known world Trevor went, Martin would follow in his heart, trying to understand, trying still to give what he could of love and support.

Then it hit him again: *He threw me out.* He *did it*. And he asked himself, *what could set a son to do such deep evil?*

He had never believed in the devil myth. He'd seen that the Christian devil was the horned god of the old witch cult of Northern Europe, nothing more than that, and the horned god was the old Roman god of festivals, Pan. In other words, a pagan deity had been made into the enemy of the new god. Similar things had been done throughout the history of religion, the gods of yesterday becoming today's demons.

Still, it did seem as if something had tipped the balance against the good of the world, and that was why Trevor had done what he had done, and why his own soul was about to be captured or, more likely, to die, and his body to become somebody else's property.

Thunder clapped and the rain came again, and in the lightning Martin saw deer. Then he heard, high above, the cry of a nighthawk. Dawn was coming, but these new clouds were so thick that it was, in effect, still night.

He clapped his hands over his ears, then turned and pressed his face against the rock. The cleft he was in wasn't even two feet deep and hardly longer than he was tall. Rain splashed against his back, and the wind, now wintry cold, now storm heavy, came in under his torn windbreaker.

He was as miserable, he thought, as it was possible for him to be. And maybe, he thought also, with an upwelling of sorrow, maybe it was, quite simply, time for him to go.

Lindy and little Winnie were gone, something that he was beginning to think of as an always. It had been hard to accept, and Trevor's rejection on top of it was rawest agony.

But how do you manage to commit suicide when you dare not move a muscle? Perhaps if he tried to force his way back into the tent, the kids would shoot him. But how could he make Trevor participate in such a thing?

Another cry came, full of eagerness now, trembling above the rumble of the thunder. Martin shifted, and looked out across the clearing. Somewhere out there was the Saunders, and the Saunders might be running high. When it flooded it was as dangerous as hell, and with this rain it was going to be doing just that.

If he dove in, the rocks would knock him senseless before they broke him to pieces. Hard, but better than gnawing his wrists open.

In relation to the stream, then, where was he? Directions were guesswork, but if he moved down the long slope of the land and stayed in the folds and meadows rather than crossing the ridges, eventually he had to reach the Saunders. Unless, of course, he was taken first.

He looked out across the dark land, and it was an alien place, the surface of another planet, it seemed—this little woodland where he had hiked and hunted all his life, where he lived.

These same trees, these rocks, this speeding storm—all would continue after he ceased to exist. Beetles, hungry in the grass now, would soon find a feast.

He stood up into a sheet of rain, then set off running into the roaring dark. The wind made him stagger and the thunder made him cringe as he plunged along. He would have been blinded because of the rain and the dark, but there was so much lightning that it enabled him to find his way. He heard another sound, then, that he could not quite make out. It was deeper than thunder, an enormous sound but with hiss in it, and booming, faint but strong enough to shake the lungs.

Lightning flashes revealed a wall of haze. He stopped running, because he was going toward it. Then he glimpsed its shape—it was a thick funnel cloud, immense, and probably not more than a few miles away, whipping toward him across the broken prairie.

He threw back his head and screamed and laughed at the same time, and saw in the storm a black shape sailing easily, a nighthawk. It seemed to be circling him, and he ran toward a stand of trees, to get in where a thing like that couldn't go.

"Oh, God, Lindy, I'm so sorry. I am so damn sorry." He should never have taken them to that damned church, he should have followed his own instincts and hidden his whole family in the storm cellar.

Another flash revealed shapes around him. It was only the briefest vision, but it made him howl like a frantic dog. He whirled round, but they were behind him, too, and closer there. But also, rising into the sky now like a great wall, was the tornado, a looming pillar of death, with darker objects speeding in its funnel. He saw cars, roofing, trees, bodies like akimbo swimmers. He ran toward the storm—then saw just ahead what appeared in the inky rain to be tall bars, and slung among them, a black thickness striped with yellow. A claw of lightning flailed in the clouds, revealing by its silver flicker that he was looking at the raised forelegs of a spider the size of a small horse.

Then he was down, his breath gone, his head smashed against the ground so hard the crack of his jaw sounded like a shot and he saw flaring stars in his stunned eyes.

What breath he had left was sucked out of him as the ground shook, and in another flash of lightning he saw the thing that had been menacing him shoot off into the sky like a demon flying, or rather, sucked away by the advancing tornado.

Light slipped down from the darkness with the shuddering grace of an aurora. Lying on his back, the rain swarming in his eyes, he nevertheless saw his death coming in the great detail with which legend tells us we see our ends, the way the light quested downward like syrup dropping quickly, white and alive, and raindrops when they touched it making hurrying patters of smoke.

But no peace came, not with this strange numbness—and then the seeing, *the seeing*—a great alteration of vision, and he felt a kind of ecstasy in his skin, and saw a forest of tapered furniture legs, and knew that he was seeing out of his own infant eyes, his mother's room where he had taken his first steps, and it was like flying, this wonderful new state of walking on two legs, and the happiness, oh dear Lord in heaven, childhood is the kingdom, it is the kingdom.

And he saw how very valuable this commodity called memory was, all the gold of his life capable of being tasted, touched, and smelled, feeling just as if it was happening again and always, and he knew that the human being is a device that records perfectly the rustle of every leaf and every sweated passage, the happy flying days and the gray ones, and his last thought was how grand, how incredible, what a miracle and no wonder it took the old earth five billion years to create us.

And then: *I am to be boxed, cataloged, and sold like dope to somebody who has lost all happiness, all joy, all decency, and is more hollow inside than death and the zero cold of space. I—my eternal being—is to be sold.*

Red. Voices—a voice, a voice of gold, an angelic, perfect voice.

The red became noise, rushing, slapping. Became fire. Fire on his hip. Somebody sanding his skin, no, worse, cutting. They were cutting and they were sliding the knife between the muscle and the skin.

He was being butchered in the field.

Trevor's face beaded with rain, swimming with tears. Trevor, ancient being, journeyer.

Like me.

Journeyers together, father and son.

The wind screamed, rain and hail struck like bullets, and Trevor screamed, "Dig in, Dad, *dig in!*"

He clutched the ground. All grew silent. It seemed as if the last possible bit of air was pulled from his lungs. He felt his legs rising, heard the deepest rumble he had ever known, and saw the ground just ahead suffused by electric green light.

Whereupon there was an earsplitting roar and a truck crashed down from the sky, its lights as they flashed drilling into the rain. It was huge, an articulated thirty-two-wheel poultry mover.

Then chickens were everywhere.

The clucking, squawking, crowing clumps of feathers and terror flounced like great, fluffy snowballs in the rain.

The weight left his back. He turned, and a figure was helping him up, a strong male figure. He could not see the face.

"They'll be back any second, they won't stop!"

Trevor ran off into the dark and Martin did not stop to think or even try to understand what had just happened. He followed, running with all his might, and he found that he could see in the dark of the storm just by wanting to, and could run like an angel with the wind at his back, and he could go and go, his heart ticking like a slow engine.

Trevor stopped, grabbed a couple of chickens, and ran on. Martin did the same.

They went into deep and deeper woods. The storm passed, bringing with it first moon, tiny and bright and with it stars, but also, to the north and west, another massive tower of clouds. They never seemed to end, the storms, as if the unbalanced universe itself must expend energy at every level until equilibrium once again prevailed.

Martin heard drumming, and it was soon clear that they were moving toward the tent.

"Trevor, they'll shoot—"

"No, they won't." He snapped the necks of his chickens and laid them next to the tent wall. Martin did the same, then put them beside the others.

At that instant, there was a soul-freezing scream, then another and another and another, and a dozen great shadows dove at them. One of them swooped right into Trevor's face. It screamed, its red eyes burned—and it flew around him, wheeling tight, as another made the same maneuver.

Then Martin was enclosed in cold skin that reeked like garlic and embalming fluid, and claws came against his chest, slicing his jacket and his shirt and slipping into his skin as a knife does into hot wax.

It was fear, they had said, fear that the things used as their beacon. Very well, he would take his fear and put it in a box inside him, and close it.

The thing glared at him, its eyes so close he could see the fire inside, its mouth open, the white tongue shuddering as a maggot does in the sun.

He found, somehow, Franny Glass's Jesus prayer and breathed it again and again, and it took him away from his fear, no matter that he was not a believer, it still bore its power to distract a terrified heart.

The thing leaped back, giving him a look out of the side of its eyes that was mixed of regret and rage, and a touch, even, of humor that this miserable little man had bested it.

Pam held the tent flap for them as they went into the candlelight and the drumming. There was not a lot of light, but Martin could make out Len Ward and Claire James beating the drums. He noticed Harrow Cougars emblems on the skins.

He saw so clearly, every detail, the eyes of the others gleaming in the candlelight, and he recognized their youth in their scent, the young, powerful smell of his son, the blooming scent of the girls, and he saw them, really *saw* them—and he knew that only at a few moments in his life had he ever seen people with this clarity, this love, and the abiding compassion that he felt now.

Michael Ryan, the Cougars' star tackle said, "Hey," and looked up at him with those strange, shadowed eyes they all had.

Then Pammy began to clap. Trevor threw his arms around his dad. Except for the drummers, they all clapped.

"What's going on?" he asked.

"Dad," Trevor said, "please try to understand" Tears streamed down his face. Martin embraced him. Then a girl he thought was called Crystal something came over. She had a mirror in one hand and a candle in the other.

A face looked back at him. It was dirty, wet, thin and covered by a day's old growth of beard. It was the face of a street person, a hobo, somebody from the lower depths, a miner in the dark of the earth.

The eyes looking back at him gleamed darkly, very darkly, in the yellow candlelight. In fact, they were as black as coals, his eyes, just like those of the kids around him, and his son.

His soul seemed to fill the air of the tent, to mingle with their souls, and it was like picking up a song you'd known always, and singing again.

Martin understood, now, what had been done to him—the same thing that had happened to these kids when the light tried and failed to take him.

Something was gone, though. It had certainly taken something. Not his essence. He was still Martin Winters. He felt lighter, though, and far more in touch with the world—not the world of streets and companies and archaeological digs, however. Rather this world of the here and now. The rain, the trees, the kids in the tent.

He was alive, Martin was, more alive than he had ever been before.

They hadn't discarded him, not at all. Rather, they had done to him what natural human societies had always done to their shamen and their priests, their healers. They had made him face death, and so come free.

That was the difference. The kids in this tent had not been captured by the light, but rather made free by its failure to capture them.

Martin was free, too. Trevor was smiling at him. His son's face was soaked with tears. It had been a near thing out there. It had been real. He might not have made it.

"Thank you," he said to them all, and to his son. Trevor came to him, and leaned against him, and instantly the exhausted boy was asleep in his father's arms. Martin slept, too, and the lives of the kids swept on, racing toward the destiny that awaited them, now, in just a matter of hours, that would bring them new life, or extinguish forever these last few sparks of the human soul.

PART THREE

ABADDON

And they had tails like unto scorpions, and there were stings in their tails: and their power was to hurt men five months.

And they had a king over them, which is the angel of the bottomless pit, whose name in the Hebrew tongue is Abaddon, but in the Greek tongue hath his name Apollyon.

One woe is past; and, behold, there come two woes more hereafter.

—Revelation 9: 10–12

With an host of furious fancies
    Whereof I am commander,
With a burning spear, and a horse of air
    To the wilderness I wander.
By a knight of ghosts and shadows
    I summoned am to Tourney,
Ten leagues beyond the wide world's end—
    Methinks it is no journey.

—ANONYMOUS
"Tom O'Bedlam's Song"

SEVENTEEN
DECEMBER 20
TERROR

GENERAL SAMSON HAD GOTTEN THE summons back in the daily packet from Abaddon. As usual, it had been choked with demands and threats. But this time, on top of the bundle that had been thrown through the small, highly stable gateway that was here beneath the geographic center of the Northern Hemisphere on all three worlds, was a sheet of thick yellow paper.

He had known instantly what it was: a summons from Echidna.

He now sat miserably on a packed bus, on his way to the sort of meeting from which one should not expect to return.

He had come back not only to his own beloved form, the marvelous darkness of his scales, the proud flash of his bright red eyes, but also to a world where he did not need to dose himself with antiallergen, then remained rigidly shifted for hours, all the while itching like mad in every stifled scale on his body.

He didn't want to die. But more, he was afraid of torture. And they would torture him, of course, as a lesson and warning to others. It would happen in some auditorium full of laughing, cheering underclass, delighted to witness the abnegation of an overlord.

They would rip off his still-living skin and make him dance in the cold, and kids would come up and rub salt into his white, exposed musculature. They would roast his haunches and force him to attend the banquet dressed, no doubt, as a clown.

It was she, that damned high-born Captain Mazle, she and her accursed father who had engineered this.

He had hoped that a victory over the humans would bring him real wealth at last, and the power that went with it.

Instead, the starving billions who were marked to go swarming through the fourteen huge gateways when they opened tomorrow would instead have to be kept here, and their rage and their rebellion would only become worse.

And he, of course, would have no souls to sell.

But he wasn't defeated, not just yet. He might be able to talk his way back to earth, because even if he couldn't open the gateways to the people of Abaddon, he could bring back all those millions of souls, full of memories of love and joy, treasures that were not available to anybody here.

But not right now. Right now, he was just another miserable, frightened man riding a rickety bus down the Avenue of the Marches to Government House, one among fifty in the old vehicle. He listened to the gas hissing uneasily out of the tank on the roof—coal gas, supposedly less polluting than the powerful fuels available to the elite. Actually, nobody cared about the brown sky. What they cared about was the fact that coal gas was cheap and, like sails at sea, therefore the best way to transport underworlders.

On both sides of the broad street stood government buildings, and ahead the grandest of them all, where he was supposedly to receive new orders.

There was a lot of traffic in the jammed bus lanes. Occasionally, also, an authority vehicle raced past in the restricted lanes. From time to time, an aircar whistled past overhead. He didn't even look up. He deserved that life. He deserved a place among the elite, even on the Board of Directors itself.

They finally came to the Street of Joy, marking the center of the long government esplanade. The wailing cry of a siren caused the bus to stop with a jerk. Children in white-suited rows sang an anthem praising the achievements of some committee or other. The tune was always the same, but the committees changed with the political climate.

The Standing Space was crammed with as many as five thousand naked underworlders, all bound, some screaming their innocence, others in tears, others stoic. Lawyers in the bloodred hoods that signified their profession moved about among the committeemen and their friends trying to get various orders signed, buying and selling the condemned. Every so often, one of them sent a runner into the rows of prisoners, generally coming back with a young woman to be raped to death at a party later.

The stench of prisoners' vomit was sour on the air. A platoon of Young Leaders in their sky-brown uniforms and black caps marched up to the first row, swinging their arms and singing with the choir, then began slitting throats, causing one and then the next prisoner to spray blood and writhe, then slump. The boys were getting kill badges.

There'd been a battle with the Unionists last night, a ferocious encounter at the wall, which we appeared to have won. Of course, it was always impossible to be certain, but such a cheerful Execution Morning did suggest that the news was true.

The Union was nearly finished, reduced to a few hills, nothing more than a park, really. It was surrounded by the vast planetary city that was the Corporation in all its might, its wealth beyond imagination, its poverty beyond belief.

That was why they had to expand into two-moon earth. That population pressure had to be relieved, or there was going to be an explosion here and Echidna and her class were going to have their own throats slit.

Having each done ten or fifteen victims before their parents' cameras, the boys withdrew. One, who had been urinated on, remained kicking his victim to death. After he went strutting back to the grandstand, a soldier like Samson himself, also a general, squeezed the bulb that activated a Multi Projectile Delivery System that stood on a rickety army wagon. Instantly and without a sound, the five thousand condemned were turned to meat. Then he snapped his whip, and his great orange syrinx warbled and hooted angrily, but trundled off happily enough when it realized they were headed back to the Central Vehicle Pool.

In the bus, total silence. These were all blue-pass people, all from the underworld neighborhoods just like the people who were now being harvested by the bone spiders that had come lumbering up out of their warrens at the first scent of blood. The animals would strip off the meat and leave it behind, and carry the bones into their lairs.

Every underworlder alive was afraid he would end up in the next collection. After all, the executed had been tortured, most of them by having capsicum injected under their skin and into their anuses, or pellets of plutonium pressed into their eyeballs. He'd seen the globular orange messes that had replaced many of their eyes, had watched the steam curling up from their bobbing heads.

You'd say anything, given that kind of pain. And "anything" would invariably include implicating anybody you were asked to implicate in whatever plot might be imagined.

He might have been implicated. Maybe it wasn't political at all. Maybe that was why he was here.

The bus started with a jerk and a loud mechanical whine. The roadside was littered with the remains of exploded buses, inside some of which could be seen the pale green bones of the dead. Behind them, shrill screaming began. The elite had flitted away in their aircars, and now people rushed out of side streets, their scavenging permits flapping on their backs, meat bags in their arms. There would be soup tonight.

The bus shuddered and popped. Would it explode?

He found himself wondering what he wanted more, an end to this misery of a life, or a chance to talk his way out of whatever trouble he was in.

Now came the four tones that preceded Morale Service announcements. Sick though everybody was of Morale Service and its lies, they all clapped and cheered.

The bus's speakers crackled. There was a brief hiss, then a moment of earsplitting feedback. "Are you on your way to your designated earth station?" a woman's recorded voice shrieked, crazed with delight. "Attention please, earth stations are now receiving colonists. You must be at your earth station by midnight tonight."

All the screens on the bus came to life with children singing and dancing in some green fantasy of a world. "Yes, more and more people every day are buying their tickets. Earth is huge and it's rich and there's room for all. Room for all in the new lands. Room to dream."

Samson knew the reality, of course. Much of the existing landmass was being sunk into the sea, exposing vast ocean flats that would be where these poor fools would have to build. The reason was simple—the sea floor was full of methane and sulfur hydrates, which would melt in the air and change the atmosphere to the same richly sulfurous mix enjoyed here on Abaddon.

Cheap terraforming, in other words.

Each family that went would receive a gaggle of human slaves, which would die in a few weeks or months.

At least human meat was edible, if you could manage to get used to that creamy texture.

"Building One."

Samson got to his feet, then stepped out. He hurried across the wide, black tarmac. Somewhere in the depths of the city, there was the roar of an explosion, followed by wailing sirens and the appearance of hundreds of bright red police aircars hovering like great wasps, their grapples dangling ominously. Do anything that appeared menacing, and they were liable to snatch you up and drop you a hundred leagues out at sea. They'd go in low so that you'd drown instead of die of impact, and the press would show up to tape the spectacle. Or they'd drop you amid pleasure craft, and people would use you for target practice.

The reason for all the brutality was simple: fear works. Ten thousand years ago the Corporation had been a loose confederation of free companies, even some tribes and even more ancient political units. But with growth had come mergers, and then the disastrous battle over the two human earths that had been lost, in the end, by all the combatants. This had been followed by long years of population growth coupled with a gradual consolidation of power, until now, when an elite million ruled a land jammed with three billion underclass.

Attempting to seem confident, he strode up the steps, brushing at his uniform, trying to remind himself that it meant something in a government context. Here, a general's service stripes were important. After all, they'd put him in charge of what was arguably the most important project in corporate history.

So why was his craw filling with vomit?

"Samson, General," he managed to mutter when he reached the desk. He handed over his orders, his passport, his clearances. The young clerk was a pureblood, dressed in the blue silk uniform of the intelligence service. He had fine, white scales, and eyes that had been surgically altered from piercing gold to a much more genteel eggshell blue.

He read the documents, then pressed a button on his desk. Two guards appeared, one an underworlder like him in a black uniform, the other upper class and dressed in the lovely green that the fashionistas called Memory of the Sky. In a military uniform, it indicated serious power.

The only place you could still see a green sky on Abaddon was in the very heart of the Union, amid the fields and the streams.

The clerk handed them Samson's papers. He followed them back through the lift area to a private elevator that had an ominous, even legendary, reputation. Many a soldier had ascended to these highest floors and never returned. As he stepped into the pink marble interior, he entered another world, where every detail was sumptuous and perfect. The lift had no controls. It was controlled from elsewhere, and he stood to attention as it rose.

He thought to review his life, but could not stop his mind from imagining torture and how he would fail in its rigors, and they would all see and know the cowardice that, in his most secret being, he felt defined him. He thought about death constantly, wondered at what it would mean no longer to be, and feared above all things the destruction of his soul.

This was why he had risen so extraordinarily high. It was his willingness—which he detested in himself—to do anything he needed to do to prove his loyalty to his betters, even if it involved lies, cruelty, and pointless killing. His journey upward was a desperate flight to safety.

The doors opened and bright light glared into his face. He tried to control his hearts, but could not. The rhythms synchronized into panic mode, and he knew that his state of fear would be flaring alarms in some nearby monitoring center.

What he thought might be a board member came and stood before the light, so that he was a black shadow to Samson, his face unrecognizable. "You have twenty hours before the gateways open. You're not even close to being ready."

Samson took a breath. He thought he knew that voice. He thought it was Beleth himself, the master of all the males, Echidna's husband. In effect, the king of the world. "We're right on schedule, Sir."

"You're a liar, of course."

He thought as quickly and carefully as he could, considering that his mind was racing with fear. "They can't defeat us, they're only human."

"That's your mistake and I'm surprised at you. We knew you were arrogant and venial, but who isn't? I had not taken you to be stupid."

"No, Sir."

"And neither are the earth people. The full-blooded earth human is smarter than we are, as you know. They lack only experience, this new species, to make themselves masters of the three worlds. Remember that they already have two, which we do not."

He seemed to want to engage in conversation. Samson was compelled to respond. He cast around for something positive to say. "They are a more advanced form than us, it's true, Sir. But they have no idea how easy it is for them to pass through gateways. They're ignorant."

"Thanks to the work of our forebears. Can you imagine what a human army would do here? Bringing hope, happiness even, to people who cannot be controlled except by fear?"

"That would be an extraordinary misfortune. But I don't think it's one we need to worry about. They are far from realizing that they can use gateways at will, at any time."

"How about the Union intelligence agent in the one-moon universe?"

"That's going well, Sir."

"In what sense, General? Have you killed him?"

"I expect that to be confirmed on my return," Samson replied.

"But it's not confirmed now?"

"No, it's confirmed, in the sense that we got an assassin through. So, yes, I can confirm that."

"How did you get an assassin into a place that we can't penetrate, General?"

"Well, we are able to, in a limited way. And remember, the closer to the moment of passage we come, the easier it is."

"So the agent is definitely no longer a problem? You can guarantee this?"

Samson forced acid back out of his craw and into his churning stomach. This agent had been placed only a few leagues from the center of the whole operation, and not only that, had somehow been penetrated into the inaccessible one-moon universe where he lived in direct parallel to the single most dangerous human being on the two-moon earth, Martin Winters.

It was quite an achievement. And the problem was, he had no idea at all whether or not the agent was dead. But North was a brilliant achievement, too, and he had to believe that the attack had worked.

"Can you guarantee it, General Samson?"

The only acceptable answer was "yes." Anything less could bring torture and death. "The agent is dead."

"Then let me report the good news to my wife. She's been very concerned about this aspect of the situation."

Samson fought for air. He needed to sit down, but there were no chairs here. As it was supposed to, the piercing light was making him feel naked and exposed. It was forcing him to shiver his scales, lest his body temperature rise and make him slow.

There came, from behind the horrible shadow, piercing female laughter. It could only be her.

Then the light went out. As Samson's eyes got used to the dimness, he had a great surprise: he saw that the entire Board of Directors was present. All of them, even Mazle's father, he noted.

Behind the assembled Board, an enormous window overlooked the Sea of Anubis, and a great longing entered Samson when he saw a ship, a pearl-white jewel tiny in the sun, its red sails rotating slowly in what must be a light breeze. How lovely their lives must be, those simple sailors, even the ones whose jobs would make their time short, the pitch makers and the rope weavers and the scrapers. At least they did not risk their souls, not like a politician or a general.

"Come," Echidna said. She actually took his hand. Up close, she was dazzling, a shimmering complex of the smallest imaginable scales, blushed pink under her high cheekbones, delicate blue around her smiling, sparkling, delightfully pale pink eyes. Her body, easily visible beneath a floating gown of gossamer gold thread, was superbly curved, breathtakingly desirable. She was so vastly, incredibly different from the humble women on the bus with their dull scales, sagging with untended molt, that she might as well have been an entirely different species, not a seraph at all, but something from some grander and more extraordinary world than Abaddon.

He followed her past the boardroom and into the private apartments, feeling her strong, cold hand in his. He forced his neck scales as tight as he could, but the musty scent of his desire still oozed from his

pulsing glands. It made her throw back her head and laugh, and made
Beleth nudge him from behind, and hiss.

Children's toys littered the legendary floor of pure gold, and kids
playing darted between the feet of their elders. In the family shrine at
the far end of the great room, the mistress's women attended their business, some sewing quietly while warming her latest clutch of black eggs,
others listening discreetly to the proceedings.

"He will sit," Echidna called as they approached her ladies.

Chairs were brought by two young fashionistas, so highly bred that
their scales were like white cream, almost as pale as hers.

He found himself surrounded by gorgeous women. These really high
aristocrats made even a highly bred noble like Mazle seem dreary.

He strove not to appear as he felt, thunderstruck.

Some of the children gathered, interested, no doubt, to watch whatever was about to befall him. Because he had only won the first round.

He looked across the impassive faces of the board members. Nobody
was readable. All eyes stared straight ahead. The ultimate power rarely
acted, and when it did, all were silent. Whatever she did, there would
be absolute approval. Debate would end.

She glared down at him, then leaned forward slightly and stroked his
neck. "Such interesting scales," she murmured, and he saw something in
her eyes other than the contempt he had expected. It crossed his mind
that the old Echidna might have died and been replaced by another
clone, and perhaps also another soul, one that might use the memories
stored in the brain quite differently. With the high born, there was no
way to tell who actually possessed a given identity at a given time, so
this might not even be the person who had favored him and promoted
him in the first place. She might consider that her memories of doing
those things represented a mistake on the part of a predecessor.

She looked into his face. "I've seen no lying from you, but I have seen
impetuousness and arrogance. I see that you despise us of good blood.
You do, don't you?"

What should he say? The light was low, so any nervous flittering of
his scales would not be seen.

"Of course I hate you. But I am loyal to you and to us all. I am loyal
to our beloved Abaddon."

She tightened her grip on his neck. He began to feel his throat closing. She knew just what she was doing, the way she dug her thumbs down into the sack of his craw, pressing it up so that it would be sucked down into his windpipe and make the throttling require less force. Easier on the hands.

He could no longer breathe. He waited. His penis stirred. Sex and death were so close. He felt his sheath draw back. Two of the girls giggled. One of them stretched herself. Children gathered closer.

Time passed. She wasn't allowing even a trickle of air. Flashes came into his eyes, and air hunger now caused his body to torsion, throwing his abdomen forward and his head back. Amid peals of childish laughter, his bladder evacuated.

Air rushed in, sputtering as the sac of his craw fluttered in his windpipe, then snapped back where it belonged. He coughed, tried to gain control of himself, then flounced back, helplessly kicking the air.

As he gagged and spat mucus, everybody laughed. Kids ran up and spat on him and slapped him as he crawled to his feet.

"He pissed on us, Momma," one of them yelled. Then another, older one, "Kill him, damn you, you old hag!"

"Nobody kills him," she muttered.

A boy, his face flushing with eagerness, came toward him with a throating knife. "Let me! Let me get blooded, Mom!"

"Stay away from him, you little shit."

"Dad, listen to her!"

"Obey your mother," Beleth said.

"You people are such assholes."

"Watch your mouth, boy," Beleth said. "I'd just love to beat the shit out of you."

"You don't have the right."

"Shut up, both of you," Echidna snarled. She spat. "I'll let your sisters whip you senseless, Marol."

Little girls swarmed her, dancing around her, pulling at her skirts. "Oh, mommy, mommy please! Yes, he deserves it, *please!*"

"Later, we'll talk it over." She clapped her hands once, and all the children withdrew. "Now listen to me, Samson. We need you to go back there and win this thing."

"I will, ma'am."

"*How dare you lie to me!*"

His blood literally dropped to his feet.

"Look at him," one of the fashionistas hissed, "he's scared to die."

He thought he'd passed this hurdle. But the agent was small stuff compared to the larger problem, which was that nothing close to a billion people were going to make it through the gateways, because two-moon earth was not ready, not even close, and that was the real reason he'd been called back. "I will not get a billion people onto earth, it's true. But I have something else that I am going to bring out. Echidna, I have the greatest treasure in history, and I lay it at your feet."

"This had better be good, Samson. Hyperbole annoys me."

"I have human souls in captivity. Beautiful, healthy ones."

Her eyes widened. The only ones Abaddon ever captured were ugly, and had to be sifted for the good bits, a sweet memory here, a compassionate act there—the things that smelled and tasted so good, that could be relived endlessly, like a delicious food that would never be finished.

"A few souls changes nothing." She sighed. "Let's get him stripped. Get the skin off, I haven't got all night."

Somebody grabbed him from behind. The boy who had wanted to kill him came forward, a silver molting hook in his hand. He smiled up at Samson. "This is not gonna be fast, you shit."

"Ma'am! Wait, ma'am. I have more than a few. More, ma'am!"

She gestured toward the eager boy, dismissing him.

"Mom!"

"How many do you have, Samson?"

"Ma'am, I have ten million of them."

The silence that fell was absolute. This was, indeed, the greatest treasure in the history of the world.

"Ten million *good* souls?"

"Ma'am, any one of them is better, more fulfilling, more delicious than the best you have ever eaten in all your memory. Fabulous, rich emotions. Delight, love, sweetness, all the best stuff, ma'am."

He saw the calculation in her eyes. "Where are they?"

He could feel the boy getting ready, could see his scales shimmer with eagerness. He had to be careful, here, or she would kill him for insolence. "Ma'am, they are under the stable gateway, ready to be brought through. I have them connected to two-moon earth's core. They cannot escape. I can bring them through."

She gestured toward the boy, who swiped the air in front of Samson's torso, then hurled the molting hook at one of the board members, who dodged it, hissing and spitting.

The boy glared at him as he adjusted his uniform. "You'll be back, bitch," he said. "And when you get back you an' me, we got a date, do." He ran his fingers across Samson's throat.

Samson backed away, bowing until he was off the gold floor and onto the marble. When he saw its blackness, he almost wept with relief.

On the way down in the lift, fear became rage. How dare they, those grunting, greedy oru. He'd like to tear their living skin off their bodies with a molting hook, even her, yes, especially her. Tear it right off!

The elevator opened and he stepped out into the lobby. As he crossed it toward the great steel doors, he gloried in the fact that the guards were now indifferent to him. Delightfully indifferent.

The doors slid open to the wide esplanade of freedom, and he went through. So beautiful, life, despite the pain, the losses, the struggle, all of it. Life itself unfolding, so sweet.

How dare they throw away his life for the amusement of a mere child! His *life!* As he descended the steps, part of him wanted to cry out to the brown sky, "I lived, I went to the top on a black ticket and I lived!" He did not cry out, though. As befitted a general, he strode.

He was walking toward the bus stop when a wonderful Shu, the best aircar in the world, came swooping down so close that he had to duck, lest he be clipped by it.

It stopped, though, and hung there, its yellow surface gleaming, its black windows revealing nothing of the interior. Then the passenger door went up and a pureblood leaned out. "Hey, you Marshal Samson?"

"I'm General Samson."

"I've got orders to deliver this to a Marshal Samson. You got your number ID?"

Samson produced it.

The salesman thrust the ID card into the slot. Samson heard the car's confirming bell. The salesman hopped out. "She's yours, Marshal. Ever driven before?"

He forced himself not to gape. It was stunning: instead of killing him, she'd given him a gift of one of the finest sports vehicles in the world, a wonderful, beautifully made creation that belonged only to the highest of the upper classes. Merely possessing such a thing raised you into the aristocracy.

He entered the car. The fine interior gleamed with exotic metals, greens and silvers and golds. The leather was pale and as supple as cream. Human, without a doubt, and young.

He glanced across the dashboard, a forest of gleaming gold buttons, none of which he understood. Apparently, the car had every option you could imagine. "I have no idea how to run this."

"You don't need to know. It's ensouled."

He was momentarily too amazed to speak. Shu ensouled perhaps a thousand vehicles a year. Such a car would cost a man like him ten lifetimes of income. Driving it identified him as one of the world's most powerful, most elite people.

"Is the soul . . . human?"

The salesman laughed. "Maybe next time, mister. It's a good one, though. Very smart, very compliant. You need to ride a human ensouled vehicle very carefully, you know. They're fast and really, really clever, but they can be tricky."

Indeed, they'd been known to smash themselves to bits in the hope of getting release. It didn't work, of course. They couldn't release themselves.

But they ran a vehicle superbly.

Experimentally, tentatively, he asked the car, "Are you there?"

There was a pause, then, "Who are you?"

"The new owner. Take me home."

It hesitated a moment as it read his ID. "Yes," it said. He did not ask it why it had been put into a machine. He didn't really care, as long as it did its work. It was his now, that was all that mattered.

As he soared upward, his engines singing, he called Echidna.

"You're welcome," she said into his ear.

"How can I ever thank you?"

"I can think of two ways."

"Which are?"

"Open both human worlds, and I will grant you an entire city. I will break the law of blood, and let you wear Sky."

The car swooped low into the dark streets of the back city, the real city. People looked up, some knelt, all bowed, pulled off hats, raised their open hands to sign loyalty to the Corporation, for nobody but an owner could be driving such a vehicle, a car glowing with the violet light of a soul.

The door opened. He got out. Wide, amazed eyes. Smiles everywhere, then cheering as his neighbors came to their windows, looked down, and saw his triumph. Success honored all.

He climbed the narrow stair, thick with the smell of boiling soup, and went into his apartment. There were meat parties everywhere in the street. The day's executions had favored his neighborhood, and they all thought he was the reason, and he was cheered from every door.

Who knew, maybe Echidna had given such an order.

The gateway was open, waiting. He walked up to it. The stress waves shimmered evenly. It was as clear as he had ever seen. The approaching date was really having an effect now.

Then he realized what he was looking at. Mazle stood in their cramped headquarters space beneath two-moon earth. She was looking down at the autopsy table. On it lay the body of Al North.

He felt sick. That should not be.

He stepped through. "Is the agent dead?"

"You lived!"

"*Is the agent dead?*"

She gestured toward North. "This needs fixing."

"I told her—" His mind returned to the sick, vicious boy, waiting for him with his molting hook. He shuddered. "Never mind what I told her."

"We're going to try replacing the brain entirely," she said. "This almost has to get rid of the residual will. Then it's going to work."

"It had better work."

"Yeah, because if it doesn't Daddy's gonna take away all your toys. And if you ever lie to my aunt again, I'll help my unpleasant little cousin take off your skin, and I'll eat it before your eyes." She smiled. "You're nothing, Samson, you and your ugly little car."

He bowed to her.

EIGHTEEN
DECEMBER 19
ORIGINS UNKNOWN

NICK SAT READING THE PAGES his father had just finished. Over the past two weeks, Dad had slept maybe six hours, but he was asleep now, sprawled like a corpse across his keyboard. Of course, corpses don't snore.

It was four in the morning and two weeks ago he wouldn't have dared to get out of bed and venture into the dark, but things had changed, hadn't they?

"What's going on?"

"Hi, Mom."

"What're you doing up?"

"Dad's written about being an intelligence agent."

"Anything more than what we've already remembered?"

"Not really. When I came in here he was sound asleep and snoring, and he was writing." He gestured toward the laptop. "This. It's a description of Samson going to the demon earth. It's horrible, Mom, really horrible."

"Wylie, wake up."

"Mom, leave him."

"I don't want him like that, he needs a bed."

"Look, if you disturb him, he's just gonna start writing again. He's gonna have a heart attack. Let him sleep."

She leaned over and read a few pages. "God, what a place. Abaddon."

"I googled it, it means 'the abyss.' At least, it does in our language. In seraph, it probably means 'Home,' or 'Nice Place' or something.

They're cannibals, and even the children torture and kill. It's, like, play for them. Like a video game to them, to skin a real person alive. They're loathsome, Mom, and we do not want them here."

She looked down at her husband. "I'm gonna get him a blanket at least." She went to the linen closet and pulled one down. They covered him together, mother and son, and Nick slid the cushion from his chair under his head.

"I'm sober, I swear," he murmured.

"It's okay honey, it's good."

"Let's fuck, baby."

"Sh!"

He gave a long snore and smacked his lips.

"I grew up with him, remember, Mom."

She tried to laugh, almost succeeded.

"Mom, the thing we have to ask ourselves is, not only who Dad is and who we are, but what we're supposed to be doing, because I have to tell you, I am starting to realize that I feel this incredible kinship with somebody in his book, and I want to understand what's going on. Trevor is, like, my soul brother or something. And another thing—this is dangerous. What happened with Al North trying to come in here, and that thing that came after Dad—it's very, very dangerous."

At that moment, there came a thin sound, almost like the wail of a smoke alarm, and for a split instant that's what they all thought it was. Then Nick was running, they were all running. Kelsey stood in the hall outside her bedroom clutching Bearish and making this terrible sound, a noise Wylie had never heard his little girl make before, and which he had not known she could make.

Brooke leaped to her and enclosed her in her arms, and Kelsey sobbed the ragged sob of a child so terrified that not even her mother could comfort her. "There's hands in my room and they were touching me and touching me, and when I threw Bearish at them, I saw a face and it was *awful*."

"Oh, honey, honey, there's nothing in your room, look, it's empty in there, the light is on and it's empty."

"You saw just hands, Kelsey?"

"Yes, Daddy. They tried to grab me, and when they touched me I saw them. Then they were gone."

"And the face, you saw it—"

"When Bearish hit it. It was bloody and awful, Daddy, it was *horrible*."

He looked at Nick. Nick looked back, his eyes steady with understanding. But he said nothing.

No, and that was right. They had to be careful here, extremely so, because there was a person in the house that they could not see, who had one goal, and that was to kill.

"Let's go downstairs and make cocoa," Nick said. "We need some cocoa."

"Nicholas, it's late and Kelsey's tired."

Kelsey threw her arms around her mother's waist. "Mommy, yes!"

"Just one cup, then, and we have to make it quick. Because my girl needs her beauty sleep." She picked Kelsey up, and her little girl snuggled into her arms.

As they trooped downstairs, Nick asked Wylie, "Are we going hunting in the morning?"

"Hunting," his mother said, "on a school day?"

"Not for middle school," Nick replied smoothly. "Teacher's Day."

Wylie understood exactly what his son was doing. He could not communicate openly, not if somebody was in here and they couldn't see him and they were listening. "We could go for pheasant," he said quickly. "Maybe we'll put a bird on the table. The guns are ready, so we can get an early start."

"Let's pull 'em out, then," Nick said.

Wylie could feel the presence in the house just as clearly as Nick apparently could. An invisible something, and it was close, it was right on top of them.

He unlocked the gun cabinet and pulled out one of their birders and tossed it to Nick, then got himself a 12-gauge. "Get behind us," he said to Brooke.

"Excuse me?"

"Mom, get behind us!"

Wylie saw movement, very clear, not ten inches from his face. An eye, part of a face. And he knew something about who was here: it was a man, and he was horribly scarred. Al North was back for a second try.

Then there was a hand around his wrist. He looked down at it, felt the steel of the grip. "It's on Daddy," Kelsey screamed, and this time Brooke saw it and she screamed, too, and not just screamed, she howled.

Nick fired into the seemingly empty space where the figure had to be, and there were a series of purple flashes in the general shape of a man, but the buckshot passed through him and smacked the far wall of the family room, shattering the big front window and leaving a trench in the top of the couch.

The hand had gone.

Nick grunted and he was up against the wall, he was being throttled, and where the body of the intruder touched his, you could see edges of a black, tattered uniform. Wylie was not a huge man, not as big as Al North, but he waded in. From behind, he put his arms around North's neck and pulled his head back, gouging into his face, and as he did that, the face and head appeared, the stretched neck, arteries pulsing hard, and the eyes, surrounded by scar tissue and dripping blood.

Seeing this, Brooke went into the gun cabinet and brought out the big silver magnum she'd fussed and fretted for years about him even having. She waved it, not having any idea how to use it.

WHAM! WHAM! WHAM!

Amid a showering mass of sparks, the figure flew across the room, slamming against the TV with a huge crash. It lay there, the left half of the head and face visible down to the left shoulder. Both hands and most of the left arm could be seen, also, until the hand moved across where the stomach would be, slipping into an envelope of invisibility, then coming out again with blood on the fingers.

The one visible eye was gray, glaring ferociously out of a blood-ringed socket. The surgery was crude and cruel. Until now Wylie had not realized just how poor their doctor had been.

The hand shot toward him again, like the head of a snake, and there was a knife in it, and the knife sailed at him, spinning, flashing metal, and clanged against the wall. There was a spitting, sparking sound and a burst of blue electric fire, and where it hit, reality seemed to peel back.

Where there had been a blank wall, there was now a door with a blue-shimmering frame, and beyond it a kitchen with a twisted, melted countertop, a toaster that looked like melted wax, a Sub-Zero fridge that had been clawed and melted and was hanging open.

There were people there, and one of them looked in this direction. Wylie knew what he was seeing, and it was even more terrible than he had imagined when he was writing about these humanoid reptiles, because it was so sleek, so beautiful with its shimmering pale skin, and so terrible with its empty, hard eyes, quick eyes that focused fast on this room, then came alive with a glitter that could only reflect eager delight.

Seraph, they called themselves, but we had names for them, from every culture in the world, from every time in history, but all these names amounted to the same thing, the one word that described something so exquisite and yet so ugly: he was looking straight into the eyes of what mankind in both human universes had identified as a demon.

Kelsey ran—toward it. She ran with a child's blindness and raw, instinctive hunger to find safety. No doubt, she didn't realize what she was seeing. Maybe she saw a policeman—black uniform, silver buttons, red collar patches—or maybe some other form of deliverance, but she ran to the thing, right through the opening and into the other universe. The dying universe. The place where they tore souls out of bodies and made wanderers of little girls.

Wylie tossed Nick the twelve-gauge. "Blast it," he yelled, "it's getting up."

"KELSEY," Brooke screamed, running after her, leaping, trying and failing to grab her flying nightgown before she went through the door.

—which made a faint, wet sound, a sort of gulping, as she passed through. She stood shimmering with bright violet light, as if she'd been trapped in some kind of laser show.

The creature waiting for her went down and opened its arms, but the smile revealed rows of teeth like narrow spikes, and the golden eyes were not eyes of joy, they had in them the look of a famished wolf.

Wylie dove in behind his daughter, feeling a hammering electrical pulsation over his whole body, followed by gagging nausea as he landed beside her. She was icy cold, her skin gray, and he had the horrifying thought that her soul was already gone.

The demon had white hair, thin and soft, waving around its head like a halo. "Hi," it said, "I'm Jennifer Mazle. It's good to meet you, Wylie."

The words were like blows delivered with a silk-clad hammer, so soft were they, so vicious the tone.

He turned—and faced a blank wall. The door was no longer visible.

"You'll need to come with me," the demon snapped, "you're here to stay."

But Wylie remembered the wisdom that has come down from one human age to the next, the whispered knowledge, and knew that she could only lie, and therefore threw himself and his daughter at the wall anyway.

Behind him he heard a cry, *"Shit!"* and then he was home again, Nick was blasting the shotgun into the assassin, and Brooke was rushing to them, now grabbing her baby, now throwing both of them down behind the couch.

"Stay behind me, Dad," Nick said.

"Use the magnum for Chrissakes!"

"No bullets!"

Another blast of the 12-gauge rocked the world. Behind them there was a crackle and a hiss of rage, and the demon stepped through into the room. As it did so, it became human. "You're under arrest, Wylie," Jennifer Mazle said softly.

What the hell universe did she think she was in? "Not here, sweetheart," Wylie snarled. He'd picked up the empty magnum, and now hurled it at her head. There was a flash of white-purple energy when it struck her. She turned away, her skin spurting red smoke. She gasped, gasped again, put a long hand up to her jaw, then straightened up and produced a weapon of her own. It was blacker than night, this thing that was in her hand, with an ugly, blunt snout.

Somehow he knew that he mustn't allow her to fire it, that it wouldn't tear them apart, not physically, that what it would do would be to splash out that light of theirs, and rip the souls out of the whole family, and hurl them into the control of the soul catchers, and make this little family of his the first wanderers in this universe.

He threw himself at her, and as Nick kept Al North back with blasts from the 12-gauge, he waded into her, his fists hammering, delivering blow after blow to what turned out to be a body hard with some sort of armor. Somewhere in there, he knew there would be something soft and vulnerable, a lizard's delicate meat, and he hit where seams might be, at the waist where she had to bend, and then the face, he hit the face, and it was just as hard, like steel, this structure of scales.

She was like a thing made of garnet or steel, not a living creature at all.

He went for an eye. Grabbing the skull with his fingers, he gouged his thumb into it and found there a softness that made him snarl with pleasure. Beat the devil, Wylie, why do you think you've got that name?

Behind him, *WHAMWHAM, WHAMWHAM.* Nick had had the presence of mind to reload the magnum, and he knew how to use it, too, holding it in both hands to compensate for his size and its power.

Wylie routinely cleared him on all the guns. If they were going to be in the house, the kids were going to know their proper use and safety. Kelsey, too, when the time came.

Whatever he was doing, though, it wasn't helping, because something had just jumped on Wylie's back. Shot up though he might be, Al had one hell of a lot of staying power.

Then Wylie had an eye under his thumb. He damn well *had an eye!* Jennifer Mazle reeled back, hissing like the most enraged possible cobra, *HRRSSTT! SSTT!* Her mouth opened wide, the teeth glittering, the interior as white as a snake's. The tongue gleamed black, was as thick as a finger and as long as a rope, and it came up slowly out of the throat.

He'd never seen anything so menacing. Never imagined menace like this being possible.

Then the thing on his back let go, and he turned and saw Nick and Brooke standing over it. Nick had one of Wylie's superb Abba Teq hunting knives, and was thrusting and pulling expertly, and deep purple guts were spilling, and North's mouth gaped wide.

The general's whole body shimmered, then began flickering like a light turning on and off, and there came great thunder, and outside and inside blue flashing light, and then they were both gone, him and Jennifer Mazle.

"They're here," Wylie shouted, "still here!"

Nick thrust his knife at the air. Wylie picked up the 12-gauge and delivered a random blast into the ceiling, which rained down like the ceiling of Third Street Methodist had when Ron Biggs had emptied his 12-gauge into it, in the two-moon world.

Outside, there was long thunder. Then he heard shouts, voices crying out in an unknown tongue, voices and the clatter of machinery.

"What is it?" Brooke hissed.

"Sh!"

They could see shadows cast on the floor, on the walls, big shadows, but not the people and machines making them. The physical people were in the version of the house that belonged to the Winters family, but as the twenty-first approached, the fabric that separated the universes, in this very unusual corner of the world, was becoming thin indeed.

Wylie listened, he watched the shadows—one in particular as it crossed the wall, something low being moved by two hunched figures. Then the figures bent over even further, and lifted something that looked like a long sack and merged its shadow with the shadow of the object, then moved off.

"What is it, Dad?" Nick asked. "What's going on?"

"I believe that seraph medics are carrying them out on gurneys."

"Oh, Christ, you're right," Brooke said. "That's what that is, all right. My God, what we're seeing here—I mean . . . just, my God."

The shadows were gone now. The house was quiet. The family came together, the children and the parents, struggling each in his own way with a trauma almost too intense to be borne.

"Mommy, can Bearish have a drink? Because Bearish would like an absinthe."

"Absinthe?" She gave Wylie a careful look.

"Be it far from me."

"Daddy has a bottle of it in his liquor drawer in his office."

"Wylie?"

"There is no liquor drawer. There is no absinthe. I mean, it's illegal."

"Come on, baby, show Momma the absinthe."

"Excuse me, we just nearly got killed here!"

As if this return to their old life was the most welcome thing she could know—which it probably was—Brooke marched off to his office, followed by her little girl.

"Oh, come on," Wylie muttered, hurrying after them.

"Dad, don't lose focus now. This is not over."

"Brooke, there is no absinthe!"

"Dad, come back!"

"Watch our backs," he yelled to Nick.

He entered his office behind Brooke, who was opening the desk drawers.

"It's behind the fake back in the file drawer," Kelsey said.

Wylie saw the empty desk. Saw that there was no laptop there. Saw that his old typewriter was melted like the Winters' toaster had been melted, his beloved old Corona oozing down the side of the desk like molten plastic.

"The computer is gone," Brooke said. She looked at him. Her eyes were practically bulging out of her head, tears were flowing.

"Dad, get down here, please," Nick called.

"What do you mean, gone?" Wylie said. "It can't be gone."

But it was, and with it their window into the other world.

He felt suddenly numb. As if lobotomized. As if soul-robbed. "Do you have that copy?" he asked.

She thrust her hand into the pocket of her jeans. She shook her head. "They got it."

"They have blinded me . . ."

Brooke said, "Which is what they probably came here to do."

"Dad, you better get to the front window right now."

Coming from outside, from the front, he heard it, a deep rumbling sound, regular, the unmistakable noise of a big engine.

He went to the window, looked down. Initially, he saw only blackness. Then he understood.

What stood at their doorway was the most ominous thing he had ever seen.

"It's just sitting there, Dad," Nick said.

The huge Humvee gleamed black. Its windows were as dark as a cave, its engine growled on idle.

They had gotten one of their vehicles through the gateway.

The engine stopped. There was movement behind the black windows. The doors began to open, and what they saw coming out was not human, not even remotely.

NINETEEN
DECEMBER 20
GATEWAYS

ALL NIGHT THE LIGHT HAD worked the town and the outriders had patrolled the woods and the rain had come in endless sheets, and the drums had muttered on. The kids were in a trance, Martin thought at first, then later that they were beyond trance, they were in a space that despite all that had happened to him he could never reach. From time to time, though, Trevor's hand would come through the dimness and touch his own, and he would know that there are things that never will change no matter how much we change, that a child needs his parents, that there is love in families that is beyond understanding.

In the late hours he found himself under a pile of little ones, all of whom were trying to be close to the largest male in the place. Mike and George and the other older kids tried to control them, but eventually everybody gave up and he contented himself with holding the little beings in his arms as best he could.

The beauty of mankind touched him as they did, softly with their little hands, and looked at him with their great, admiring eyes. One of them, a little girl called Tillie, who reminded him so much of Winnie that it made his blood ache, said to him, "You have to be our soldier. We need one and we ain't got one." Her eyes had studied his, and he had felt her mind enter his mind, and it felt like smelling flowers feels, or lying in grass. She'd tossed her head, this tiny, perfect girl, then raised her hand to his cheek and tapped it. "Soldier," she had said.

Morning brought new necessities. There were twenty-two human beings here, they needed food and water, they needed decent sanitation and children are not good at sanitation. They were growing up fast, but as nobody could leave the tent at night, they used things like an old plastic bucket they'd brought with them and plastic bags which they seemed to have in abundance, and these tended to get spilled. They were not modest, the little ones, but the poor teens were desperate for privacy, the boys trying to control their vital young bodies, the girls trying to put them at their ease.

It was altogether the kindest, most forgiving, and smelliest group of people Martin had ever known. The roughest dig he'd ever been on did not even begin to compare to this.

There were two kids called flap guards who remained at the door of the tent, making certain nobody opened it after dark and, above all, nobody went outside. The drumming was loud enough to drown the sounds generated by the outriders and the nighthawks, so the little ones might cry for their parents, but they did not experience the kind of fear that would have brought the things leaping down on the tent.

As the hours slid past, Martin felt more and more trapped in the damned thing. The kids absolutely refused to stop their drumming or go outside even for a few seconds, not until dawn. They wouldn't let him leave either, not that he wanted to. Trevor clung to him. His bevy of little ones did, too, and he would never deprive them of that comfort, no matter how illusory he feared that it was.

After they had forced Martin into initiation, and to some extent to be transformed himself, he had found Trevor with strange, pink sweat on his face and staining his filthy shirt. Martin thought he knew what it was—from the stress of sending his father to face that test, capillaries on the surface of his son's skin had burst. His boy had sweated blood.

Over the long night, Martin had tested his new mind and found true changes. He still thought as he always had, but there was new information and there were new things he could do with his thought.

Trevor had spoken of another world he had seen, a world a lot like this one but with other people, and no evidence that it was under attack. He had gone through a gateway, he said, and there had read a book, and it was the book of their suffering and the secrets of their days.

Martin was familiar with the multiverse concept, of course, and he was aware of the recent discoveries at the Four Empires Supercollider in Switzerland that had suggested that parallel universes were real. But that there would be gateways that you could just walk through—well, this was going to be interesting to see.

There was a stirring in the tent as the sun rose. The drumming became haggard, then stopped. Then it got very quiet.

"What's up?" Martin asked Trevor.

"I think something's wrong with Wylie. I think the seraph have broken through to his world," he replied.

Martin realized that he could see, in his mind's eye, a shimmer hanging over the Saunders river. It could as easily be a spiderweb gleaming with dew as an entrance into another universe. He saw, also, that outriders were pacing there, looking for all the world like enormous tarantulas. They had been designed by the seraph to strike terror into the human heart, and even seeing them in this way touched him with fear, and made them lift their forelegs and eagerly test the air.

He withdrew.

"Any thoughts, Dad?"

"It's a gateway. If it wasn't it wouldn't be so heavily guarded."

"Okay," Pam said, "we're gonna take the opportunity to move the tent off this sludge factory, then I'm taking a supplies detail into town." She glanced at Martin. "You stay here."

He couldn't disagree with that.

Martin followed the others into the kind of morning that comes after great storms, when sunlight washed pure seems to cleanse the world. Golden columns of light marched among the pines, and when they walked out and it fell on Martin, he had a shock, because it was just the sun but it felt as if somebody was there.

A couple of the kids, aware of his thoughts, glanced at him. He was going to have to somehow get used to this lack of inner privacy—and the deep sense of belonging that came with it.

Gentle, probing fingers seemed to be touching him, the fingers of a being that was deeply accepting of him, of life, of everything.

Who was this? Was the sun alive?

"It's all alive," Trevor said. "Everything is alive and everything is conscious. All the stars, all the grass, the trees, every little animal there is. And some of them have high consciousness. The bees do, Dad. When you're in a glade with them, you'll see."

"The brain of the bee is microscopic, son, so they couldn't really be all that conscious."

Trevor smiled a little. "Just let yourself happen, Dad. You'll be fine."

Watching the chaos of kids moving here and there with stakes, with boxes and ropes, singing, laughing, you would never think that they were working together, and carefully organized at that. But they were, and exactly at the moment the tent shuddered and collapsed, four of them came out carrying all the bags and buckets of refuse that had accumulated inside.

Not a word was said as it was rolled and folded and carried off, followed, improbably, by a little boy who was completely overshadowed by the huge Cougars bass drum balanced on his head.

Their efforts looked a lot like those of worker bees, Martin thought, and then that a shared mind would naturally be far larger than any single component.

It hit him then—*all* mind is shared. That's the way things work. Just surrender to it. Let yourself happen, like Trevor said.

"Okay, Dad, let's go."

Of course, Trevor could read his thoughts.

"Don't let it bother you."

"But I can't read you."

"Sure you can." He headed off into the caressing sunlight.

Following him, Martin did see into his son's thoughts, which were of that gateway, and going through it. But that wasn't possible, look at the river!

"It's possible, Dad. But you have to not think about it and not worry about it. Concentrate your thinking on your body, the way your feet feel as you walk, your hands, every physical sensation."

—Why?

—This is why, what you're doing right now.

Martin was stunned. The exchange had been so perfect. Of course, he understood the recent advances in mind-to-mind communication that were being achieved at Princeton, but that was with the help of implanted microchips.

—No implants here, Dad.

Trevor headed up the sharpening rise that separated them from the Saunders and the gateway. Martin looked ahead in his mind, and saw the outriders still guarding the gateway, and the water just a literal torrent. As soon as his mind touched them, though, every outrider turned this way and raised its forelegs. Some of them began to march.

"Blank your mind, go to your body!"

He forced his awareness into his flexing muscles, his feet, his heart and lungs. Although he could no longer see the outriders in his mind's eye, he could still have clear awareness of them, and he knew that their alarm had subsided.

To do this successfully, you had to be like animals were, looking out at the world without looking in at your thoughts. Not easy for a professor.

—If you start to hear that rattling noise, stay in your body. Do not let your mind go out to it or they'll be on you.

Why was nobody else coming? This was obviously extremely dangerous and more would be safer.

Trevor glanced over at him. His eyes said it all: *this is my job. Our job.*

At that moment, they came up the rise, and Martin saw that the Saunders, even in just the past few minutes, had risen more. It had been bad before, but now it was a great, surging mass of gray-black water full of trees, roofs, walls, floating staircases, even a car's wheels appearing and disappearing as it went tumbling downstream.

Across the stream, he could see their house, the windows dark, empty, and forlorn. The water extended almost to the front door. And water wasn't the only problem, five outriders lay curled up on themselves halfway down the ridge, ready to spring into action if anybody came into their range. And the ones on this bank still patrolled.

"This is impossible," he said aloud.

He was confused to see the water getting closer, looming up toward him. Then he realized that he was seeing it through Trevor's eyes. His son was scrambling down the bluff right toward the patrolling outriders and the thundering river.

Martin raced down behind the last of his children, throwing himself forward, trying to reach him, to at least get his attention—whereupon one of the outriders on this bank turned from its patrolling and came straight toward him . . . but past Trevor, whom it did not seem to see.

And indeed, Martin felt a surge of fear, he couldn't help it. The thing's metal fangs moved so fast that they sparked.

"Run downstream, son," Martin bellowed. He picked up a rock and threw it at the thing. It bounced off the head, causing it to rear back and hiss, and making two more of them come prancing toward him.

To his utter horror, Trevor walked right into the flood. "Son! SON!"

He could not escape the outriders and Trevor was about to be killed. But he *could* escape, all he had to do was to leave his fear, leave his mind, let himself happen. He paused in his headlong dash, closed his eyes, and emptied his mind. He put his thought on his roaring blood and the roaring water. His prayer came to him then, Franny's prayer, and joined itself to the whisper of his blood.

When he opened his eyes, he found himself face to face with an outrider. Its eyes stared straight at him, its jaws moved slowly. Carefully, he stepped around it, then past another, so close that he could see that there was venom caked to its abdomen, and a stinger tucked in the size of a butcher's meat hook.

Trevor was now well out into the flood. Martin threw himself in and began swimming.

The water grabbed him as a giant would, and he saw a great oak, stately, from somebody's yard over in Harrow, no doubt, come sweeping toward him and with it death in the tangle of branches, drowning as he was swept away.

Trevor still waded forward, though—and then seemed not to be wading but walking. He was visible inside the water—but not affected by it. Walking inside it. "Trevor!" Martin forced himself to dive to avoid the oncoming tree, forced himself to swim, felt the water ripping at him—and then saw Trevor beside him walking easily as water and limbs and pieces of cars and houses and bodies and drowned cattle went not only around him, but *through* him. In the other world, of course, the stream wasn't in flood, so crossing this way would be easy.

He looked down at his own body, and saw that a great limb of the tree was moving through him, and a human arm, white and bloated, and a spatula and dozens of poker chips, all passing right through him and leaving not the slightest sensation. A lawnmower went through him, then theater seats, a TV, a tangle of shrubs.

He took another step forward and the flood was gone. Instead, he was on the far side of the Saunders. Behind him, the little river flowed quite normally, tinkling faintly where it hurried across some stones.

"Be very, very careful, Dad. I don't know what's going on up there."

"I can't hear your thoughts."

"Not over here, it doesn't work."

Martin looked back toward the Saunders. The bluff was there, but everything was quiet, washed with golden early sun. It was a view he'd looked at a thousand times, and on summer Sundays heard from here the faint bells of the town.

They had gone through the gateway, and on this side, in this universe, the Saunders wasn't in flood.

"Come on, we've gotta see what gives with that Hummer."

"It looks like typical army issue."

"Their military's Hummers are all camouflaged. This is something the seraph brought here."

"They're here?"

"Apparently."

Trevor started off, moving quickly up the familiar hill toward the familiar house. As he walked behind his son, Martin experienced a sense of déjà vu so powerful that it was actually disorienting, even painful. This looked like home and it felt like home but it was not home. It was *not home.*

Trevor stopped. "They're noisy," he said.

"It's dead quiet."

"That's the problem. His car is in the garage, but it's just really quiet." He saw what looked like a Saab in the open garage. "It's *blue.*"

"Their cars have all sorts of different colors. Blue, red, white."

Martin had never heard of anything so outlandish. Who would be willing to drive around in a colored car? Cars were black. This Wylie must be an eccentric, which fit the literary pretensions, he supposed.

Trevor approached the place cautiously, moving up the steep hill, his eyes always on that Hummer.

Martin whispered as loudly as he dared, "Trevor!"

His son motioned at him furiously. The message was unmistakable: *Shut up!*

Trevor dropped down on all fours, then onto his stomach. The Hummer was between him and the house, but he could almost certainly be seen if anybody looked closely enough. From the Hummer, definitely.

Then he motioned again, this time indicating that Martin should come forward.

Eagerness flashed through him. He jumped to his feet. Trevor's eyes widened and his mouth dropped open—and then there was a terrific crash and something went whanging off into the woods. "Get your ass outta here," a voice crackled. "We got you in crossfire, shitheel!" A shot whipped past him so close that he felt a hot blast of wind.

He threw himself to the ground. "No," he called, "we're friends!"

Another shot kicked up gravel beside his head. He tried his best to back away, attempting to reach the brow of the hill so that he could slide back down.

But then a shot rang out behind him, and this one was closer, much closer. There was only one thing to do. He stood up and raised his hands. "Okay," he said, "okay."

From the woods came a boy's voice, "It's a guy, Dad. A guy and a kid hiding by the Hummer. Back wheel."

Silence.

"We mean no harm," Trevor called. "Please, we need to talk."

The boy appeared coming up the far side of the driveway. He carried a big rifle, hefting it expertly. Martin realized what was happening here, that this was an historic meeting, the first contact between human beings from two different universes.

"Hello," Trevor said as he stood up. He walked out from behind the Hummer, into full view of the house. "Mr. Dale, I'm Trevor."

"You got the laptop?" Wylie Dale asked.

"No."

"This is my dad, Martin," Trevor said. "We need to look at the book again."

"The laptop was stolen. Plus, it's been rough around here. Real rough. I haven't even thought about writing."

Martin realized that the smell he had been noticing was meat, and it was coming from the Hummer. As he walked closer, he could see blackened ruins in it, the shattered bodies of seraph. And then, around the side of the house, one of the outriders. For a moment, he froze, but then he understood that they had destroyed it, too.

"So you're Trevor," Wylie said. "Hey, Brooke, here's the people from my goddamn book, come to life!"

The boy had walked up to Trevor. "Hiya, Nick," Trevor said.

"Hey." Nick put his hand out.

Trevor looked at it. "Can we?"

"Dunno."

Martin watched. Wylie watched. His wife Brooke watched. A little girl's voice said from behind the very lovely mother, "Bearish thinks it's okay."

Bearish! Winnie had called her stuffed toy Bearish, too. As the mother and daughter came closer, Martin saw that her Bearish wasn't a zebra but an elephant.

"He's cryin', Mommy."

"They've lost Winnie and Lindy," Brooke said, "you know that, honey, you know what they've lost."

"What happened here?" Trevor asked.

"You better get inside with us," Wylie said.

The house showed signs of a terrific fight. Martin was quietly astonished. These people were unhurt, obviously, but there had been a lot of killing around here, a lot of it. The rugs had blood on them, and he thought he saw a bloody body wrapped in a sheet behind the couch.

"There's been a spot of bother around here, boys," Wylie said. "But me an' mine, we did 'em." He drew a long brown object out of a pocket of his heavy leather jacket. "Cigar?"

Martin watched in silence, unsure of what, exactly, was meant. The intonation of the unfamiliar word had suggested a question. Was it some sort of offering? There must be differences between the universes, obviously there would be—look at the colored cars—but this was perplexing. Surely it wasn't a sacrificial offering, they must be past that.

"I think I've earned house rights," Wylie said.

"Wylie." Brooke strode to him, threw her arms around him. "You are the most amazing damn man," she said, "smoke your lungs out, lover."

"*Ew*, Mommy!"

He inserted the thing in his mouth, produced a book of matches, and lit the free end of it. He gave Martin another glance. "It's a Partagas straight out of Fidel's humidor."

"It's tobacco," Trevor explained. "They burn it and eat the smoke."

"But . . . it's powder. Snuff is powder."

Nick said, "Dad, I don't think they have cigars." Nick regarded Martin. "You, do you know what he's doing?" Then he frowned. "Jesus, look at their eyes."

"You haven't read my book as well as you imagine, son," Wylie said as he ate smoke. Or rather, breathed it. Martin enjoyed snuff, but he didn't care to join the hordes with cancer of the sinuses, so he'd sworn off. No doubt this method eliminated that problem. They could smoke the tobacco, he guessed, without fear of health problems.

"Your friend Fidel makes those things?"

"Well, he's dead, but yeah, they're genuine Cubans, imported all the way to Kansas City."

"Tobacco is legal in our world, but it's dangerous. It's sold in a powder called snuff."

"Dangerous here, too. These suckers are really cancer sticks. But I do love 'em."

"Ask him about Fidel Castro," Brooke said.

"I have no idea who that would be," Martin replied. "Do you know, Trev?"

"No."

Nick said, "Cuban dictator, died a few years back. Communist."

"Communist, as in, uh—Trev, can you help me, here?"

"A nineteenth-century philosopher called Karl Lenin invented a system of labor management that became a huge movement in this universe. Dad, they've had total chaos here for over a century. That's why they're so tough. It's why there are dead seraph and outriders all around this house and these people put fire in their mouths. In this universe, human beings have been at war so long they've become incredibly strong."

"No wars in your universe?" Wylie asked.

"No, Wylie, not really. The British and the French bicker over their African holdings, of course. And the Boer Contingent is an irritant for the British in South Africa. The Russians had a war with the Japanese."

"Wait a minute." He puffed on the cigar. "Sarajevo. Mean anything?"

Martin couldn't think what it might be. He shook his head.

"World War One?" Wylie asked. "World War Two?"

Martin was mystified.

"Dad," Trevor said, "they have huge wars here." He pointed to a blood-spattered bookcase. "War books," he said. "I've read some of them."

"Look, we've been at war on this little earth of ours ever since the Archduke Franz Ferdinand was assassinated in 1914."

"An archduke? Assassinated? That's hard to credit."

"You still have them, don't you?"

"Of course. And Cuba is an American colony and there is no Fidel in the colonial leadership, and this business of an obscure historical figure's gimcrack philosophy meaning anything—"

"Communism was the scourge of our world for seventy years," Wylie said. "It took half a billion lives, and the world wars three hundred million more. It's been carnage."

Martin looked at the wall of the family room, dominated by its gun case. "We have too few of these."

"You're not wrong there," Brooke said. "Violence attracts violence."

Nick picked up what looked like a hand cannon that was lying on a table. He blew on the barrel. "Doesn't it, though, Mom?" he said.

No child would ever address an adult like that at home, least of all one of his parents. "Wylie," Martin said, "I'm wondering if you have any specific ideas about what we might do? Given your own toughness."

"The shitheels are tough, too, and we're likely to take a beating from 'em, big time. And soon."

"But you'll—you'll shoot."

"Buddy, I seem to recall that your president tried a hydrogen bomb on Easter Island and it didn't do jack shit. That isn't exactly a lack of aggression, there, not by my definition. But the fact that it didn't work—when I wrote those words, I have to tell you that I felt sick. Real, real sick. Because a hydrogen bomb is the best we've got, too."

"However, if your world is at war all the time, you won't have a British Battle Group demanding an explanation, will you? Not like us. By the time we got the superpowers to take an interest, it was all over."

"The first wanderers were in England."

"It takes a big empire like that a long time to act. In this case, too long, even if there was anything they could've done."

"Wylie," Trevor asked, "do you know why we're here?"

"You had a conference last night and decided that you wanted to open up direct communications. Problem is, I have no more idea than you do what's gonna help. I mean, you are already looking at one hell of a megadisaster. I don't see how you can do anything. I have to tell you, I think you folks are done."

Trevor asked, "Without the computer, can you still write?"

"No kid, I cannot. I tried using Nick's laptop and Brooke's laptop and Kelsey's pink Mac, and nothing came. Nothing at all. Whatever magic there was, there ain't."

"Which we sensed," Trevor said, "and why we came. Because we knew that things were going wrong for you."

"You people are so—I don't know, *precise*. The way you go about things, moving slowly from A to B to C—do you think you might be a little slower than we are? Mentally. Not quite as smart?"

"We're not as aggressive," Martin said. "Obviously, given all your wars, the communists, the smoke breathing, which I interpret as domination-symbolic—"

"Speak Greek. Your English is for shit."

"Actually, I do have a little Greek. I've done some dig dating there, you see. Dating the Acropolis, which turned out to be noncontroversial, unlike some of my other work."

"Which I know all about, of course. We have strange ruins here, too. Same ones. Plus very similar legends. A war in the sky, a great flood, all of that."

"Meaning that they were here, too."

"Momma," Kelsey asked, "when are we gonna kill the man in the crawl space?"

"What man?" Trevor asked quickly.

"Dad's got this really fucked-up guy from your universe trapped in our crawl space. He's human, so we have this cop we know, he's on his way to take a look."

"It's Al North, isn't it? General North?"

"He's in rather iffy shape," Wylie said. "But I'm not gonna go killin' people without the cops say it's okay. If you get my drift."

"Could we question him?" Trevor asked.

"Sure, waterboard the fucker, for all I care." He sucked on the cigar, pulled it out of his mouth. "Use this on his eyes. Make 'im chatty as hell, be my guest."

Trevor took the thing from him, held it. "How would we?"

Nick laughed.

Wylie said, "Waterboarding is a form of torture, makes the chappie you're curious about think he's drowning. And as far as that cigar you're holding is concerned, boy, you stick the business end of that thing in the sore eyesocket General Al is nursing, my guess is he'll tell you more than his address."

Trevor thrust the thing away from himself.

Wylie caught it before it could touch the floor. "Cuban, remember?" He sucked it, made a great cloud of smoke. "A thing of beauty." He got up and strode across the room and into the kitchen.

Martin reflected that he might be a writer by trade, but he had the speed and power of a soldier about him. The boy did, too, and with her hard-set lips, the woman looked as if she could kill a man as soon as look at him. Only the little girl seemed vulnerable, or perhaps that was just because her cuddle toy was also called Bearish, and Winnie had been such a gentle child.

Wylie opened a trapdoor. "Howya doin' down there, General? We're gonna torture you in a min', just wanted to let you know." He closed the trap. "It's called softening 'em up."

"He's not playing with a full deck, Dad," Nick said.

"Always remember this son, if they're just playing with a half a deck it don't matter as long as it's your half, or even one card, if it's the card you need."

"We have no idea how to deal with Al North," Nick said. "And neither do they."

Silence followed. It was true enough.

Wylie opened his cell phone, dialed. "Where in fuck's name are you, Matthew? I just finished your last Partagas, incidentally." He listened. "Well, I'm telling you, the weirdness index up here has just shot through the roof. You need to put the fricking donut back in the fricking box and get your ass moving." He hung up. "You know, I'm not saying a whole lot on the phone, so he thinks I'm bullshitting him some way, but I gotta tell you—" He stopped. Suddenly the bravado blew away like so much sea foam. He closed his eyes. Shook his head. "I saved my family," he said softly, "me and my boy did." Then he sat down. He took a long drag on the cigar.

A truck came bounding up to the house, its gears grinding as it negotiated the steep driveway. It came to a stop. "Ah, wait until the gentleman of the law does his body count."

A tall man in a police uniform opened the front door and came in, using the same striding, aggressive walk that, it seemed to Martin, characterized them all.

"What in hell kind of a Hummer is that," he said as he entered. Then he sniffed the air. He looked toward Brooke. "He dope you up or something?"

"He's getting a reward for saving our lives."

"From what? Some drug dealer's fancy Hummer? Man, that's a U.S. Army vehicle, full scale. You don't see many of those puppies around. And in limo paint, no less." He looked at Wylie. "Don't tell me you purchased that thing? Buddy, that is gonna piss me off."

"Matt, I want you to turn around and look at that man standing in front of the fireplace trying not to wet his pants. I want you to look into his eyes and tell me what you see there."

The lean, narrow-faced man turned, and as he did, Martin saw that he did not carry a small firearm like Bobby, but a gun almost as big as the family's hand cannon. Martin looked to the pistol and the great ham of a hand dangling beside it, then, reluctantly, up to the face. He let Matt look into his eyes.

"What happened to you?"

"I—it's—"

"It's a rapid evolutionary change induced by extreme species stress," Wylie said. "That would be correct, wouldn't it, Martin?"

"I would say so."

"But, uh, excuse me, I don't think we've been introduced." He thrust out his hand. "I'm Matt. Uh, hi."

"Hi."

"You—" He motioned with his chin, an expressive gesture.

"That's right, we're from over there. This is my son, Trevor."

"So you're the one lost Lindy and Winnie. Oh, Jesus, you poor guy."

"Matt, I would recommend a very stiff scotch, but we don't have time. What we do have is one of his compadres tied up in our crawl space. A very weird, very altered piece of work that used to be a general over there in their version of the U.S. Air Force, but is now a sort of monster designed to be able to function freely in both universes, apparently by being made into a cut-up mess. You wouldn't believe it. I mean—you remember the guy downstate with the mutilated face?"

"Nunnally. Sure do."

"The missing pieces have been sewn onto this man."

"*What?*"

"Sewn onto him to provide a physical connection with our universe. Give him greater freedom of action. The theory. In fact, bullshit. It's the seraph who have trouble moving around in our universe, not people. And he's people. Was."

"Okay, I'm getting an occasional word. There is a man in your crawl space that has—Nunnally—Nunnally's body parts—"

"In a misbegotten attempt to enable him to function more freely in our universe."

"And this is Martin and his kid."

"Yessir."

Matt looked at them again. He held out his hand. Martin shook it. "Wow," Matt said. "You sure this is for real, Wylie?"

"Oh, yes, and what we need is for Frankenstein down in the cellar to tell these people something—what, Martin? What might he know that would help you?"

"If we could stop the seraph coming through, that would help us. If we could understand how to close their gateways, that would help us. Anything at all."

"You've read the part about Samson's journey to Abaddon?" Wylie asked. "Do you see a vulnerability there anywhere?"

"They're in a hurry. So we need to slow them down," Martin replied.

"Thing is, I also keep seeing an ending to my book, and in it I see these filthy huge cities full of starving seraph, and they are in your world. I do not see New York and Washington and London. Sorry, fellas, but I just don't. What I see there is open ocean. Right now, looks like you lose."

"Can this man extract information? Does he know these techniques?" Martin asked.

"He knows 'em, Martin," Wylie said. "He's served in the Mideast in his time."

"So you'll torture General North for us?" Martin asked.

"I can't do that!" Matt burst out.

"You gotta, buddy," Wylie said. "Because once the seraph finish with these guys, we're next."

"We'll cut their hearts out," Matt muttered.

"What we've been through here, believe me, it will be mutual. No, we don't wanna have them show up here, believe me. And this North cat is the key. So you are gonna help us. You are gonna devote five minutes to this effort."

"It's totally illegal!"

"He doesn't exist in this universe, therefore has no legal standing. Therefore, Nick, go get your skateboard. I think we can do this with a skateboard and a towel."

"I am not going to waterboard a goddamn general in any goddamn air force!"

"Yeah, you are." Wylie pulled the trapdoor open. A stench of urine and blood rose from the crawl space. He looked inside. "Good morning, again, General. Visitors!"

General North's eyes stared. His chest did not move. Wylie knew it at once: Al North was dead.

TWENTY
DECEMBER 20
THE GOOD SOLDIER

GENERAL AL NORTH HAD NEVER experienced pain like this. Although he had seen torture in Lebanon—men getting phosphorus splinters jammed under their fingernails and lit—he did not think for a moment that their pain, as awful as it was, approached this.

He was screaming, he knew that objectively, as if from a distance, but he also knew that no sound was coming out. He'd come into this strange place—a parallel universe, he had come eventually to realize—faithful to his orders, to carry out an assassination. He'd never expected to be asked to do such a thing, but this was war and we were desperate and the military and intelligence communities were in chaos, so, yes, he got why he had been called upon, and he resolved to do his duty.

Something is wrong!

He lay listening to the voices overhead. The man he had been sent to kill had proved to be a tiger, and his son was just as ferocious. Very frankly, they had overpowered Al, who was not a small man, and had excellent personal combat skills. He had not expected an adversary ready, willing, and able to gouge out eyes with his bare hands, or a child who would pick up a damn handgun the size of an anvil and just literally blow a grown man's guts out. A child!

They're not the enemy!

What was that? It was like part of his mind was yelling at him from behind a closed door. He had to get the hell up and get back out there, because those folks needed killing and they were still walking around. He was going to do them all. Massacre them, the women, too. Kill them all.

Don't!

Yeah, that's great, disobey a lawful order transmitted to you in person by your commanding officer, who also happened to be the acting commander in chief. He did not like Tom Samson, never had. The president had made a grave mistake giving him his appointment. But this was wartime and they'd just about had it, and under such circumstances you have no choice but to trust your superior officer.

You trust your own soul!

That voice—it was saying something. "Soldier," perhaps. "Soldier, you're dying," that's what it was saying.

He had not completed his mission and he had to get out of this hole and do the damn deed!

He fought to rise, could not. He closed his working eye, took a breath, then pressed downward with both hands. Rivers of agony swept up and down his arms and through his bubbling chest. His head went light. He fell back. His heart was thundering. Below the waist, no sensation at all.

He'd seen others in the house, he'd seen a Hummer come up.

It was them. THEM!

It had been some kind of an enemy unit, he could see that, but even they had taken a hell of a beating from these people. The mother cut up some of their exotic weaponry with a damned axe, and the little girl— what, seven, eight—stood there watching and laughing. "Mommy's killin' a big spider." Tough sonembitches.

That was an outrider and outriders belong to the enemy, soldier, and you are working for them, and you need to FACE THIS!

The trapdoor was opened again. Light swamped his eye for a moment. Then he saw a silhouette.

"This man isn't dead! This man is breathing!"

Another head appeared, disappeared. "Fuckaroo, he's right."

The woman's voice: "Kill him!"

"You can't do that, Brooke! I gotta call EMS, I gotta try to save his life. And—Kee-rist, you got a man all shot to hell in your crawl space, so nobody leaves. Got that? Nobody leaves!"

"It was self-defense, he attacked us."

"I know that, but I got procedures, buddy. This is serious."

"He's from our universe," another voice said.

General North listened to them up there, murmuring together. Those bastards had figured out how to get through a gateway, and they were gonna mess this whole operation up.

You're not sad about that! You're glad! It's good, it's a triumph, for God's sakes, listen to your soul!

His mind cast about, trying to find a way to carry out his orders. There had to be one, there always was.

There were guns upstairs, plenty of them. But down here there was nothing, only dirt. His own gun was long gone. So, did he have anything else that might cause damage? Belt—sure, but he wasn't going to be able to garrote anybody. Pins on his medals, big deal. Teeth. He could bite, maybe damn hard. So there was that. He could bite through one of their cheeks. And clutch with his left hand. He tested it. Yes.

So he needed them to pull him out. He'd take it from there.

He waited. Nothing. No more voices that he could hear. Stomping that faded, then faint shouts. They were looking at whatever the intelligence unit had done.

So they'd called EMS and now that was done, they were showing the cop the rest of the damage around the house. Not good. He needed them to pull him up before some EMS bunch showed up to spirit him away.

He took a breath, deep as he could, and let his pain possess him. He knew how to manage pain, and he'd been doing that, but now it was time to change his approach. As he let out the breath, he made himself scream.

It worked amazingly well. Damned well. He took another breath, did it again. The sound was odd, a lost, bansheelike howl, and it caused the river of pain to start flowing again.

It also caused the trap door to open. "EMS'll be along directly," the new voice said.

Then that other voice again, somehow gentler, thinner, "He's from our world and he's evil, you have to let us—"

"I don't have to let you do one damn thing, Doctor Winters! This man is shot, he is here, and what *you* have to do is let me do my job."

"He's a criminal in our world. Wearing a military uniform but working for the enemy. He belongs to us."

"Don't you push me," Matt said.

"Hey, guys, knock it off," Wylie responded. "Martin, you've got gumption, after all."

"We need to take that man back with us," Martin insisted.

"Sounds like you need to take the whole damn Marine Corps."

"We had a Marine Corps, too, did you know that? And they are gone. Gone! The military was done in the first wave. Worldwide. Done. So unless we can stop the seraph, they are coming here *tout de suite*."

"Matt—"

"Fellas, I'm gonna show my piece here in a second, and I do hate to do that."

"Did you know that you have an equivalent in our universe? Who is also a lifelong friend of mine, just like you are of Wylie's? His name is Bobby. He's disappeared and we think he's wandering—alive but without a soul."

"And you will be, too," Trevor added, "if they come here. Wandering with your soul locked up just like Wylie has seen—or worse, you'll be like that man down there, so twisted and turned around that he works for the enemy and thinks he's working for his own kind. You'll be just like that, and possibly within days."

"Look, this shooting is the most serious thing to happen in this town in my entire career."

"You should see the one my mommy shot. It looked like a big spider and when she blasted it, it sent out hot stuff that smelled like when you burn bacon."

Listen to them! They're your friends.

He sucked another breath, howled another howl.

"Let us take him back," Trevor pleaded. "Let us find out what we need to know."

"You can question him in the hospital," Matt offered.

Wylie laughed scornfully. "Oh, for shit's sake, Matthew, this cat needs to be waterboarded at the very least. He needs a live rat stuffed in that eye socket. At the *very fricking least*. Hospital. Do you put a goddamn cobra in a hospital?"

"If you're me, you sure as hell do. In an animal hospital. Departmental requirement, all injured animals are provided treatment."

"That is not what I meant."

The ambulance was coming soon, so Al had to make a maximum effort here, a supereffort, or this was not going to come out right. He had more than one job to do, he knew that now, because he had to kill every one of these damn people, especially the ones from the his own universe.

How had things gone so wrong? He had to kill them and get back and warn General Samson that things were out of control, they were *way* out of control.

Then the cop came down into the crawl space. Just like that, he was standing over him. This was his chance, his only chance.

As the fool bent down, he reached up and pushed the pistol out of the holster with the heel of his hand.

It hit his thigh with a thud that shook him but which he didn't feel.

"Excuse me," the cop said, reaching down.

Al was faster. Al got the butt of the weapon between thumb and forefinger. He felt along the side of it, and got his finger around the trigger.

He raised the weapon.

"Shit, he's got my gun! He's got my fucking—"

He shot upward wildly, through the floor. There were cries from above. He had no way to know if he'd hit anybody, so he shot again and again, until there was only one bullet left.

By now, the cop had skittered back up there, too, and they were all yelling.

He knew what he had to do because he knew the stakes. They needed information that he did indeed possess and it sounded as if they were going to drag it out of him with pliers. They would succeed, too. Our expertise at torture was child's play compared to what these bastards sounded capable of.

Give it to them! Tell them everything!

There was one gateway they knew nothing about. But he knew about it, because he'd been taken through it, and they were not going to find that out.

They couldn't destroy the seraph, not even close, but they might slow things down, and that was the issue, wasn't it, because every day after the twenty-first, things were going to get harder, and around the twenty fifth, the gateways would once again close, and Abaddon would be denied all but minor access for another thirteen thousand years. They'd have to go back to sending through agents provocateurs to derange human civilization, cause wars, spread starvation and greed and confusion, and keep the bastards weak.

Keep YOUR people weak, you mean. Listen to yourself, General, you're thinking with the enemy.

He got the barrel of the gun nestled under his chin, prayed to the good lord above that he had killed the man he'd been sent to kill, and pulled the trigger.

Then he climbed up out of the crawl space and into the kitchen. Wylie, whom Al had been sent to kill, was unhurt. They were all unhurt.

And Al was elated.

The next second, he understood that the person still lying down there in that crawl space with a splayed head was him. And, all at once, he realized what he had done. "Uh, hey! Oh, Jesus, I'm sorry. *Sorry!*"

He remembered the Mountain, going down into the rock with that woman, Captain Mazle. He realized that she had been seraph. Samson was one of them, too. They were heavily disguised and they used drugs to enable them to live in our air, and they had stolen his will.

Needles, sharp scissors, clipped flesh wobbling in silver trays—brain being removed, brain being installed.

They had stolen his memory. They had subverted his honor.

This soldier owes his duty to his country, NOT TO THEM!

He'd been working for the enemy.

As he watched, EMS technicians came running in. He watched them jump down into the crawl space.

"I can tell you what you need to know," he said.

The cop hurried out behind the EMS doctors. Wylie and his family came together, holding each other. Martin and Trevor left, and began to move off down the hill.

Al ran outside. "Wait! Listen to me! I made a mistake, but I can help you!" He went up to them. He shouted into Martin's face, "Listen to me! I can help you!"

Nothing. He grabbed Martin—and his hands went through him. Martin shuddered and said, "I feel like a goose just walked over my grave."

"Dad, we have a problem here, because when we go back, we're gonna hit really fast water. Remember, in our world, the Saunders is in flood."

Al could hear every word. "Can you hear me?" he bellowed.

"Yeah, that's right, we can't cross, not with the flooding on the other side."

"What about the Hummer?"

"Yeah!"

No! NO! You fools, it'll float right down the river!

They started back up the hill. "It's full of dead seraph."

"Take 'em with us, save Wylie and Matt a lotta trouble."

"Plus, the back's caked with venom. They must've brought that busted up outrider with them in it."

Al had followed them. He was right with them, just inches away.

LISTEN TO ME! LISTEN NOW!

They set about pushing reptile bodies into the back of the Humvee.

Al inventoried his situation. You still exist, you can think, you can see and hear, you can move effortlessly wherever you want to go. *But how in hell do you communicate?* A quick review of his knowledge of ghosts and such, and the answer was immediately clear: you don't.

He was a damn ghost, was what he was.

But no, this ghost was no cute little Casper and—he hoped—no raging banshee. He had a much larger vision of his life than before. His conscience was very, very powerful now. He saw deep into the arrogance that had made him who he was, the entire falsity of it, and how profound feelings of worthlessness were the foundation of the ego that had led him across all his life, all the way to this final predicament.

He knew now who he was, he knew the mistakes he had made, and he knew just exactly how to help the people of his world turn everything around. They could completely defeat Abaddon—these people, this man and this boy, if only they knew what he did. He had to tell them— *but he couldn't make them hear him or see him.*

Martin and Trevor opened the doors of the Hummer and shoved two gray, lifeless seraph bodies into the back, then, as an afterthought, Trevor pocketed one of their hand weapons. Al knew those weapons, electrical-centrifugal handguns that could propel thousands of lightweight plastic rounds at five thousand clicks an hour. The only sound they made was the crackle of the rounds breaking the sound barrier, but they could slice a man in half a mile away. Or a dozen men . . . or a thousand.

"How do these work?" Martin asked.

"Let's test 'em."

Holy shit, be careful!

"It doesn't look very lethal," Trevor commented.

Martin held one of the black disks away from his body, pointing its three short barrels in the direction of some trees. He pressed the two triggers, top and bottom. There was a brief snarl, and three of the trees literally flew apart, a foot-wide chunk of their trunks turned instantly to sawdust.

"What is this thing?"

The U.S. military has the same thing. Bigger, vehicle mounted.

"It's a seraph weapon," Trevor said, producing a dark blue box with seraph hieroglyphics on it. "Here's some ammo."

"Wylie and Nick would love this."

"You like them. Their macho and their guns and all."

"They're winners, Dad. This whole universe—it works better than ours, it's more dynamic."

"It's been at war with itself for a hundred years."

"And we live in a world of kingdoms and empires where nobody's really free."

"We're free."

"We are and the French are and the English are, at least at home. But look at the rest of it, Dad, it's a vast system of slavery—orderly, easy to live in, but—"

The Hummer roared to life. Al watched, no longer trying to stop them. He knew that he couldn't. The dead did not communicate with the living. Just didn't.

So when you finally understand and you can tell them everything they need to know, this happens.

They closed the doors and drove the Hummer down toward the bank of the Saunders—here, flowing gently. There were places where you could jump across it, even, but certainly not into another universe.

They needed to know about the seraph headquarters, deep underground and just a few miles from here, had to be told what he had remembered about being in there.

If they could enter it, they could free millions of trapped souls, they could wreck the power systems, maybe even stop the lenses from functioning. They could cause core damage to Abaddon's plans, maybe kill Mazle and Samson, even.

He raced down to the Hummer, shot into it right through one of the windows. "Hear me! HEAR ME!"

"There's the gateway," Martin told Trevor.

"Is it big enough for this thing?"

"They got it through."

Maybe this was good, maybe the gateway was too small, maybe the Hummer wouldn't fit and they wouldn't kill themselves, the damn fools.

"Do we just aim at it or what? I'm not sure I know how to go about this."

"I'm not sure, either, Dad."

Don't try, please.

"We have to try."

Please.

As Martin backed the Hummer up, Al did everything he could think of, attempting to project his thoughts into Martin's mind, actually going *inside* his body where his organs were sloshing and his blood was surging. He went directly into the brain, but even that didn't help. He could perceive the gray matter like a pulsating, sparking fog all around him, but he couldn't do anything to affect thought from in here, either.

The Hummer went roaring toward the gateway. Al saw the diamond-shaped crystalline object much more clearly than he'd been able to in life, and saw it expand smoothly, almost obediently, to accommodate the Hummer. So it was going to go through, they were going to be in it, and they were going to be drowned.

He saw black water, roiling, churning, and in it what looked like people, swimming hard. Then the Hummer hit with a huge splash, and the gateway closed and was gone.

He was moving fast, and sailed right across the stream and into the woods beyond. But he was still in this universe.

He rushed back across the river, looked for the gateway, could not find it. But he didn't belong here, this wasn't right.

He rushed up and down the river bank, trying to find a flicker of the gateway.

Even when he'd seen the president die and known—*known*—that Samson had somehow done it, he had not acted. Instead, he'd gone to Cheyenne Mountain to take a new job, because he'd wanted the promotion.

What had he been thinking? How could he have so blinded himself?

In this state, he was finding that he was becoming naked to himself, seeing past the self-deception that had defined his life.

He was seeing how loveless, how empty it had been. A useless, silly journey, his wife dead early and no further attempt to find love, and love all that mattered.

In this state, he was revealed to himself, and he saw clearly that his willful blindness had led to a great catastrophe, and there was no way for him to justify himself.

He found himself back a very long time ago, sitting on the side porch at home on a night in July, with music drifting across the evening air. He saw a girl he had known then, a girl called Nellie, who had been full of love for him.

Had he let himself accept her, had he chosen the humble life that being with her offered, he would be soaring now, flying above all these cares instead of sinking into this pit of regret.

He wasn't just sinking into despair, either, he was becoming involved with the actual ground. He was sinking into the earth itself. Above him, he could sense realms past imagining, where things like the walls between universes had no meaning and time itself was only a memory.

He was falling, but he wanted to rise.

He had to rise, it was heaven, he was seeing heaven and he had to rise!

Then he thought of the souls Samson had trapped. They belonged there, they were part of heaven, but they had literally been stolen from

God to be bought and sold, their memories and emotions stripped from them like ripe fruit and consumed into the darkness of demon hearts.

It was the greatest of all evils, to kidnap the good into hell, but that's what they were doing—or rather, trying.

He would fight. He would do battle with Samson.

But he was already lower, sinking into the grass, and below him he could see black halls and hear desolate cries.

He strove, he struggled, he fought. Above him, love and forgiveness shimmered, above him freedom beckoned. He tasted the greatest agony there is, that of being unable to rise to heaven.

But then, he thought, perhaps he could save himself. There was something he could do, perhaps. One thing. Wouldn't work, probably. But he could try.

TWENTY-ONE
DECEMBER 21, DAWN
THE DEPTHS

AS SOON AS MARTIN AND Trevor had left, Wylie had found himself able to write again. He and Brooke read over what he had just completed.

"Did they drown?" she asked.

"God forbid. The key thing here is that Al North knows something that can help them but his soul is here, still on this side, so if he thinks about it clearly enough, I'm going to pick up on it, I think."

She sat reading the screen, scrolling, then reading more. "Is he . . . what's happening to him? What's he sinking into?"

"My best guess is the core of the planet. Maybe the way you live makes your soul weigh more or less. If you weigh too much—have too little love and too much greed, essentially—you sink. And then I guess you just stay there, trapped. Cooking, given that the core is hot."

"But the universe has an end. What then?"

"I think the evil are forgotten."

"But we need him. We need him now!"

Outside, dawn was breaking. The last phoebes were calling, the last tanagers chirping. Winter, such as it was, would drive them south any day now. They were very late to leave this year. But there was not much winter now, so they would return by February.

She came closer to him. He closed the laptop.

"Nick?" she called softly.

No answer.

"Kelsey?"

Silence.

But then she moved away. "I can feel him. He's not going down. He's here."

"The world is full of watchers. We're all on stage all the time."

"I want privacy."

These past days had isolated them from each other. But he had learned something from what he was seeing of Al North's miserable afterlife. Love is the great treasure, it is what we come here to feel, and every bit of it that can be taken must be taken, because it isn't like the other acts of life. Most everything is forgotten in death. The names, the facts, the achievements, the failures, all are left behind. But love is not left behind. Jacob's Ladder has another name in heaven. It is Love.

She folded her arms, their signal that it wasn't the right moment. "I feel too exposed," she said.

"We are but players," he said.

"I can't do it onstage! Anyway, I'm—oh, my mind is blown. Martin and Trevor, my dear God, what's happening to them now?"

He took her in his arms. She lay against him, and it was good for a time, in the quiet.

Soon, though, he felt something other than the beat of her heart. He raised his head. "What is that?"

"Trembling. I think, uh . . . the fridge?"

But it got stronger. Things began to rattle.

"Dad!"

"All right, everybody stay calm," he shouted.

In her room, Kelsey began crying.

"Hold on, Honey!"

He wasn't going anywhere, the house was now shaking and shuddering so hard that he couldn't take a step. There was a tremendous crash from downstairs. He thought that the chandelier in the dining room must have collapsed, or the gun cabinet gone over in the family room. "Try to get out," he shouted. Behind him, Brooke vomited. He grabbed her and forced one foot in front of the other, dragging her toward the bedroom door and the stairs.

Nick appeared—incredibly, with Kelsey in his arms. The sight of them galvanized Brooke, who took her little girl, and they went lurching down the back stairs. The family room was in chaos. It had indeed been the guns.

Now windows began shattering, their glass exploding into the house. Nick got the back door open, and they struggled out onto the deck, which was soaked because the pool had heaved most of its water out and the rest was splashing crazily. The woods presented a chilling spectacle, with all the limbs swaying, and a continuous thunder of cracking trunks and the sighing rumble of falling trees.

They got to the middle of the backyard, well away from the house, well away from the woods. The quake had been going now for at least two minutes, maybe three, but it felt like years, it felt like forever. There was another crash from inside the house, and the lights in Nick's room flickered. Wylie put his arm across his son's shoulders. His bunk bed had just collapsed.

Just one sound, then—choking, astonished sobs. Brooke. Staring at her house in horrified amazement.

The quake had ended.

"This is Kansas," she said, her voice an awed whisper.

"Bearish had a heart attack," Kelsey announced. Then, her voice careful, "I'm quite concerned about him."

Wylie was looking back into the woods, where he was seeing flickering. "I think we have a fire going back in there," he said.

"Call the fire department," Brooke responded as she headed toward the house.

He watched his family go in, heard Brooke scream her rage when she saw the mess, heard Kelsey start to cry, then Nick's calmer voice giving instructions.

The flickering was along the draw that drifted south down from the ridge they were on. For their view, they had paid a price, because if there was ever a fire in that draw, it would be here in minutes. Knowing this, he had prepared himself with a portable water tank, which he kept in the garage. He'd tested it and it worked well, but it was not huge, so the key was to reach the fire early.

The tank was behind his car, wedged against the wall. Worse, the garage door was jammed. Fine, he was ready for that, too. He strode across the garage and got his axe, which was lying in a heap of other tools. When he'd bought this, he'd imagined that he would take out a few trees himself, thin his woods by the sweat of his brow.

Not.

He hefted it and smashed it into one of the doors. The mechanism shook, and Nick appeared. "What're you doing?"

"I gotta get down to that fire."

"Here—" He reached up and pulled a lever Wylie hadn't even known was there. Then he lifted the door. The mechanism had been locked up because the power was out.

Nick began pulling the fire pump out.

"Look, you stay with the girls. I'll go down."

"Dad—"

"Nick, please. You have to. They need one of us."

"What just happened, Dad? We don't have earthquakes here."

"I know it. Whatever it was, it's got to do with that fire down there."

Nick went in the house, reappeared immediately with the magnum. "Take this, Dad. I've got everything loaded up and we're gonna be in the family room."

Wylie took the magnum, stuffed it in his belt, and headed out to fight the fire. He loped down the rough little draw, the pumper bouncing along behind him on its two bicycle wheels. As he got closer, the glow became more distinct. Would fifty gallons of water be enough? And in any case, what was burning? The electrics came up the road on the other side of the ridge.

He pushed his way along a jumbled path, slowing down as he got closer to the glow. When he broke through into the clearing, he didn't even bother to unhook the hose, let alone pump up the tank.

For a good half minute, he had to struggle to make sense of what he was seeing. It looked like a doorway into a little room. He walked closer, his feet crunching in the dry autumn grass.

It *was* a little room, he could see it clearly. But what the hell was it doing out here? It was like an opening into a tiny cottage, and he thought maybe he knew where the stories of the witch house in the forest came from.

It had come with the earthquake, this strange opening. Perhaps because of the quake. Or maybe its coming had caused the quake.

It was about six feet high and three wide. From inside, there glowed hard light that came from a single bulb hanging down from the room's ceiling. He went closer yet. He was now standing directly before the room. Another step, and he would be inside. On the right, he saw a rough table with a bowl on it. The bowl was filled with hot soup, he could see it steaming. To his left was a narrow bed covered by a gray, damp looking sheet. On the opposite wall there was a window, which was blocked by a thin drape. Beyond it, he detected movement, but could see no detail through the frayed cloth.

It seemed very sad, the little room. Somebody's little hutch. But . . . where was it, exactly?

Experimentally, he pushed his hand in the doorway. There was a faint *pop*, nothing more. Immediately, though, his hand felt warm. It felt damp. Slowly, he moved it back and forth, and observed what was without question one of the most bizarre things he had ever seen. His hand moved more slowly than his wrist, meaning that, when his moving arm reached the center of the doorway, his hand was a good two feet behind it. There was no pain and there was no sense of detachment, but the hand simply did not appear to keep up with the arm.

He snatched his hand back.

Was he, perhaps, looking into a room in Abaddon?

If so, then this might be a major opportunity. There were controls in Abaddon that kept the fourteen huge lenses that were the main gateways open into the other human world. Tonight, the seraph would pour through them in their billions.

Disrupt those controls, and you would set the seraph back. The gateways, which would be wide open tonight, would begin to close. By the twenty-fifth they would be closed entirely, not to re-open again for all those thousands of years.

The secret of Christmas was that the birth of goodness came on the day that the door to evil was closed.

This was a gateway and that little room was in Abaddon. He knew where, of course. It was General Samson's apartment.

The "earthquake" had been local. It had involved the opening of this gateway.

Should he go through? Dare he?

It must be a trap. A temptation.

Then he noticed that the glow was less. This very unusual gateway was closing.

It could be an opportunity.

It was here that the seraph had originally attacked him.

Except, no, there was something wrong with that picture. As soon as his memories flitted back to that night, he saw Brooke and Nick and Kelsey coming up from the draw with him. And everybody was happy. They were thrilled. He was thrilled.

What?

He'd been raped by seraph marauders in this draw, trying to claw their way into a human universe that had rejected them.

The glow was dropping fast.

He stepped up to the gateway. The room on the other side looked now more like a photograph than an actual opening.

He stepped forward—and found that the surface was now thick, that it felt like stepping into a molten wall. He pushed against it, pushed harder. It was like squeezing through a mass of rubber.

And then he was stumbling forward. He tried to check himself, but windmilled across and hit the far wall hard. He sank down, feeling as if all his blood had been drained right out of him.

Then the noise hit him. Coming from outside was the most ungodly screeching and roaring he had ever heard in his life. Machinery howled, voices squalled and screamed, high and rasping and utterly alien—but not the voices of animals, no. They were shouting back and forth in a complex language, oddly peppered with any number of human words, English included. Worse, they were close by. This was a ground floor apartment.

A greasy stink of sewage and boiled meat came from the bloodred soup. The fact that it was still steaming worried him, of course, because whoever's dinner it was would be back for it at any moment. It must be Samson's food, meaning that he was here.

Recalling the story of the Three Bears, and the little girl who had entered their woodland cabin and found their meal ready to eat, he thought that others had passed through gateways like this before. In fact, if you read it right, you could reconstruct the entire fairy-faith of northern Europe as a chronicle of contacts with Abaddon.

He could either leave here now and try to make his way to Government House, or he could lie in wait for that monster.

Maybe he should try to steal Samson's car. But it had a soul, didn't it, so maybe it wouldn't be so willing to let itself be stolen.

The safest thing would be to lie in wait.

There weren't many places to hide in the room—just a curtain that concealed a still toilet full of puke-yellow goop that was being swarmed by flies as fat as ticks and as red as a baboon's ass. Or no, look at the things, they weren't flies at all, they were tiny damn *bats*.

He could not hide in there. He could not be near that toilet, which had, among other things, part of a rotting seraph hand in it. He knew that they were cannibals, of course, he'd seen this place before, had heard Samson think to himself that the execution fiesta he'd witnessed from the bus would mean lots of soup.

So this was some of that soup. But where was Samson? It had to be getting cold, even in the jungle heat they had here. Maybe he'd been arrested. Could've happened in a heartbeat. Maybe he was being tortured to death right now by that sociopathic kid of Echidna's.

The shrieking rose, and with it came thudding from above. There were crunching noises, more cries, then a sound outside the door of somebody running downstairs. The sobs were unmistakable. A short silence followed. Then, more slowly, a heavier tread. It moved past the door.

This was not good. If somebody came in here, they'd raise the alarm and—well, he dared not allow his imagination to go there.

He decided this had been a fool's errand. The soup was a trick. Samson was actually on the other side, and he was going to be menacing Brooke and Nick and Kelsey.

It was obvious, and what a damn fool he'd been.

He turned to go back through the gateway.

Except there was no gateway. For a moment, he simply stared at the blank wall.

The door clicked. He watched the crude wooden handle rise slowly. There was a flicker and a sputter, and he realized that the sharp light wasn't even electric. It was carbide, a type of gas that had been used at home a hundred and fifty years ago.

They didn't even have electricity.

The door swung open.

A gleaming creature stood there, shimmering purple-black. The vertical pupils in its eyes were bright red, the irises gold. It had in its hand a small disk with two barrels on the business end. Wylie knew what that was, and he decided not to show the magnum just now.

Slowly, carefully, he raised his hands.

The creature smiled a little, a tired smile. "I've been waiting for you," it said in a rasping voice. Its English was good enough, but spoken with a curious singsong lilt that made Wylie think of the voice of a car.

Wylie had been outmaneuvered.

"Where's Samson?"

"He is with your loved ones, Mr. Dale."

Wylie knew what the phrase *to die a thousand deaths* really meant. In a situation like this, it was no cliché, but a dark expression of truth.

The creature made a very curious sound, a sort of smacking. It watched him with ghastly eagerness. He thought that they might be allergic to human dander, but they could eat human flesh, and this thing was hungry.

"At this time, come with me."

What else was there to do? Wylie followed the creature down a steep, narrow staircase that reeked of something that had rotted dry. The walls were covered with graffiti—squiggles and lines that looked at first meaningless . . . and then didn't.

They were drawings, all at child level, but done with the light and dark backward, like photographic negatives. For the most part, they were scenes of torture and murder and orgy. Some drawings showed male seraph with sticklike penises, others females with bared teeth guarding black eggs.

And as they came to the street, he saw some of them. One that looked up was the same color as Jennifer Mazle, creamy and pale, her scales glittering. Her eyes were the same as those of his captor. She gave Wylie a long, melting look as she slowly ran her tongue out and touched it with her fingers.

"A whore," his guard said. Then some boys appeared, wearing hugely oversized T-shirts painted with images of crocodile-like creatures so perfectly rendered that they seemed about to leap off the cloth and into his face. Some of them. One had a New Sex Pistols T-shirt obviously from home, another a shirt with a big green fruit on it in the shape of a bitten apple, and in the bite, an image of a squeezed human face. This one carried a brutal weapon, an Aztec sword made of steel with obsidian blades jutting out of it. The squeezed face was instantly familiar. It was Adolf Hitler.

They watched him with their brilliant, dead eyes, their heads moving with the clipped jerks of lizards. As he walked, he saw that the street was made of wood—in fact, of cut tree trunks fitted together with an Inca's skill. Before them was a vehicle looking something like a horse-drawn hearse, but with a tiny barred window in the back instead of glass to reveal the coffin.

Standing in its equipage was a brown animal with fearsome, glaring eyes and purple drool dripping from its long, complex jaw. The jaw itself was metal, and appeared to be partially sprung, the way it dangled. The animal was smaller than a horse by half, but seemed made entirely of brown, wiry muscle, with the narrow, ever-twisting neck of a snake. When it saw them, it began to burp and stomp pointed, spikelike feet, which made it look as if it was dancing. Others just like it, pulling various wagons and carriages, moved up and down the street.

The door at the back of the wagon was open, and his captor made a brisk little gesture toward it and bowed. A twisted smile played on his almost lipless mouth, and his spiked teeth glittered in the brown light.

There was a hissing sound overhead, and he saw soaring past, a gorgeous green machine shaped like a horizontal teardrop with a gleaming windshield at the front of its perfectly streamlined shape. It was so different from the miserable mess in the street that it was hard to believe that it even belonged to the same world.

Then he got a terrific push, which caused him to bark his shins painfully against the edge of the wagon's floor. He tried to turn toward his assailant, but a powerful blow brought whizzing confusion.

The door shut behind him with a dry clunk. For a moment, he could see nothing. As his eyes got used to the dimness, he examined the space he was in. It was like nothing so much as the interior of an old, zinc-lined ice chest. It was at most three feet high and five long. There were claw marks gouged in the roof and walls, and in the wooden floor, places—many of them—that had been gnawed.

He drew out the magnum, cradling it in his hand as he would the rarest diamond. This was hope.

He twisted himself around until he could see out one of the tiny, barred windows. They were not going up the great esplanade he had seen through Samson's eyes, but along the city's back streets. There were neon hieroglyphics everywhere, and flags overhead with more unreadable slogans on them. The place was ancient Egypt on steroids. Martin would have loved it, but he wasn't the sucker on the spot, was he?

No, indeed, and the fear had a funny quality to it. The fear had to do with more of the knowledge he had gained. He had a soul. These people could take out your soul and put it in a damn glass tube. They could re-move your memories and graft them into their own souls—eat them, as it were. They could use you for crap like running a car, and God only knew what else. In this place, the phrase *the soul in the machine* had a ghastly new meaning.

They went around the corner—the animal was not fast—and began to pass what appeared to be a restaurant. Behind the lighted windows, he could see gleaming red walls and a gold ceiling. Balls of light floating in midair provided illumination. Sitting in large chairs were seraphs in beautiful, shimmering suits, tight against their bodies.

Then he got what could probably and with accuracy be called the surprise of his life: there were human beings in there, too. As they trun-dled slowly past, he strained to see more. There was a man in a fur jacket and a white ermine fedora, not recognizable to him but obviously some kind of entertainer, maybe a rapper or rock star, there were women in silks and furs. Other men wore tuxedos, some business suits, others caftans and gallabias. Then he saw a cardinal, distinguished by the red zuchetto on his head and the red-trimmed black cassock.

On the tables before them were golden dishes beautifully decorated with garlands of greenery and white flowers. Heaped on them were roasted body parts, both seraph and human. The diners were eating busily.

Then it was gone, replaced by more of the endless gray city and its hurrying, oblivious hordes of seraph.

A stunned Wylie Dale sank down to the floor. For a time he lay there listening to the creak of the axles, feeling the steady swaying of the wagon. His blank mind held an image of that cardinal. Of the men in tuxedos, the women in evening gowns.

Who in the name of all that was holy WERE THEY?

Rich, to be sure, compared to the starved horde that crowded these streets. Human beings, movers and shakers all, living large in hell.

Or was that the whole answer? The seraph were chameleons. So maybe these weren't human beings at all, but seraph spending time at home. Two-moon earth must have been plagued by them. It had totally ignored air pollution, and global warming was running wild there, even worse than at home.

Shape-shifted seraph had probably been running the place for centuries. They were the cardinals, the big personalities, the ministers and the kings. Like Samson. He'd ended up in control of the United States itself, and he was a shape-shifted repitilian seraph maintaining himself on drugs.

He wondered, Who in his own world might be a seraph in disguise? Who sought the ruin of souls? Who encouraged greed? Who lived by the lie that pollution didn't matter?

Who, indeed?

He realized that he was not far from insanity, here. His mind just wanted to go inside itself. Walk in the green fields of dream, smell the flowers, above all shut this horrible world out, scrub his brain free of all knowledge of it and memory of it.

Every trembling cell of his body, every instinct that he had, every drop of his blood said the same thing: *You are not supposed to know this, you are not supposed to be here, and you cannot get away, and to keep their secret, they are going to kill not just your body but your immortal soul.*

But now that he had fallen into the trap, he must not freeze, he had to do everything possible to turn their trick back on them. He had to try.

Oh God, he prayed, *what is the universe? How does it really work? Above all, how can I save this situation?* A memory came to him of Martin and his ceaseless prayer, and he began to pray that way, also. He prayed to the healing hand that had raised Osiris after his brother had cut him to pieces, and Jesus after his passion had ended. The unseen one who bound the good by the cords of love.

They were arriving somewhere, the wagon turning, stopping. He looked out first one window and then the other, but saw only skeletal trees, huge once, no doubt rich with leaves and life, now gray and dead, clawing at the brown sky. "Mr. Dale, if you don't mind?"

As Wylie came down, the creature added, "I was wondering if you'd autograph *Alien Days* for me?"

For the love of Pete, it had a paperback of the damn book and a pen in its clawed hand. Too stunned to do anything else, he took the book. Opened it to the title page. "Do you want me to personalize it?"

"Oh, hey, yeah. Make that out to me."

Confused, he looked up, to find himself staring into a very human, and very familiar face—Senator Louis Bowles, chairman of the Senate Intelligence Committee, senior senator from Utah.

Senator Bowles smiled, then shuddered and shifted back into a long-faced vampiric horror, its scales glistening, its eyes glaring with evil energy.

He finished the inscription—*to Senator Bowles* . . . and as he did so, saw the hand that was doing the writing, and then also the hand that was holding the book. He saw long, thin fingers of the palest tan, ending in black claws, neatly manicured.

He saw the wrists where they were visible outside the sleeves of his jacket. Narrow, scaled, shimmering with the gemstone sheen of snakeskin. He looked at the hand that held his Mont Blanc, turned it over, watching the light play on the scales. Then he raised his fingers to his cheek, and felt beneath their tips the delicate shudder of more scales.

He hadn't come to an alien earth at all.

He was a shape-shifter himself.

He had come home.

PART FOUR
THE BLUE LIGHT

He found the blue light, and made her a signal to draw him up again. She did draw him up, but when he came near the edge, she stretched down her hand and wanted to take the blue light away from him. "No," said he, perceiving her evil intention, "I will not give you the light until I am standing with both feet upon the ground." The witch fell into a passion, let him fall again into the well, and went away.

—THE BROTHERS GRIMM,
"The Blue Light"

How long, Yahweh?
Will you forget me forever?
How long will you hide your face from me?
How long shall I take counsel in my soul,
Having sorrow in my heart every day?
How long shall my enemy triumph over me?

—Psalm 13: 1-2

TWENTY-TWO
DECEMBER 21, EVENING
THE CHAPEL PERILOUS

OUTSIDE THE TENT, THE NIGHT bellowed. Earthquakes had started right after they had come back from Wylie's universe and were continuous now, a low shuddering that never stopped. On other parts of the planet, Martin and Trevor knew from reading Wylie's book, this meant that hell was unfolding. The seraph were racing to sink the great human cities and most of the human lands, and raise the ocean floors that would be their new continents. They had only hours left until the fourteen artificial gateways they had constructed around the world opened wide and a billion hungry seraph came swarming through.

Three times now, the little band had heard the unearthly scream of tornadoes in the sky, then the bone-shaking thudding that followed when they hit and went marching off across the prairie.

Pam and George had had the presence of mind to locate the tent close to the foot of a small hill, meaning that they were unlikely to take a direct hit from a tornado. But if a big one should sweep this clearing—well, then it was over for them.

Thunder snapped, the wind screamed, and Ward and Claire James drummed on their drums. Outriders chuckled and rasped nearby. Martin believed that they probably didn't even want to attack the tent at this point. They wanted this little band of evolved humans right where they were, because as long as they were here, what problems could they cause?

He and Trevor had almost been drowned when the Hummer passed through the gateway and hit the flood on this side. But the other kids had anticipated what might happen, and were waiting with ropes in the slow water near shore. It had been a near thing, but the both of them had managed to ford the swollen, raging river.

Trevor slept with his head on his dad's shoulder. Another kid had the other shoulder. Two little ones shared his lap.

And he thought, working in his mind with Pam and George and Mike. The kids were getting expert at this, their minds racing much, much faster than his. The change had affected children and adolescents because their minds were more supple and less informed with the weight of civilized knowledge.

There was a name for the state they were in—many names, in fact. It was called *bhodi*, *satori*, many things. But it was not as if the soul was lit from a higher power—enlightened. They weren't enlightened, they simply *were*.

Man had left the forests of Eden an animal, but these kids had found their way back, bringing none of the debris of civilization, but all of its compassion, its consciousness of the value of the individual, its ability to balance personal and collective need. They had returned to Eden as true human beings. They understood how to be as lilies of the field. For them, it wasn't impossible to live in the rain. They had each other. They had love.

But they were still just this tiny, little band in a great and frightened world.

It had been this way, before, he thought, in the lands of southern France and northern Spain thirty thousand years ago, when the spirit had been on the children, and adolescents had begun to paint the walls of caves with the magic animals of the mind.

Pam shook him. She frowned at him.

He'd allowed his mind to drift while they were reading his memories of Wylie's book.

"See them?" Trevor asked suddenly. His voice was curiously flat, as if he was dreaming.

"Are you asleep, Son?"

"I'm out of my body, and if I keep having to talk, I'm going to be back in, so come out, I need to show you something."

Pam nodded. They could read the information stored in his brain in peace if he wasn't there, so he took a deep breath, let it out and with it let his soul out of his body. When he moved out of the tent, he found Trevor and some of the other kids together. The rain whipped through them, the outriders did not react to them. He saw them as their ordinary selves, but knew that this was only his mind filtering their essences into familiar forms. Their bodies were still inside the tent.

Trevor pointed, and he followed the direction. Moving slowly, he tried to clear himself of all expectation, to so empty his mind that the actual appearance of the world over which he was flying would come through.

It was hard, though, in this state, to see anything except what you expected to see, or wanted to. He saw cities brightly lit in the night, Wichita and Kansas City, and the smiling prairie farther on dotted here and there with the lights of smaller communities.

He saw, in other words, a safe world, and so one that was not real. So he told himself, *You will close yourself to this. You will blank your mind. And when you look again, you will not see your memories or your hopes, you will see only what is part of the actual, physical world.*

He saw Lindy. He was right in front of her and she was still walking, but she was so thin and tired, she looked like she had only a few more steps left in her. Her eyes were glazed as if dead, but still she walked, and not far ahead were lines of fourteen wheelers, Continental Van Lines, Murphy's Stores, Gap Leaders, an ad-hoc assembly of vehicles. Other wanderers were getting into them and she was eager, he could see it, because it would mean no more walking on her blistered clumps of feet.

Soldiers, some of them in standard issue G.I. uniforms, others thin and sleek, seraph in gleaming black, their hands gloved in white, their heads hidden by visored helmets, were separating the arriving wanderers into two groups. Seraph and human soldiers worked together, and he knew that the human soldiers were themselves wanderers.

There was a crackle, and a group of wanderers who had just been moved into a small field blew apart, their legs, arms, and heads flying in every direction.

Sitting in the back of a nearby pickup was a soldier manning a peculiar, disk-shaped weapon, and he knew what that was, too, because back in the tent Trevor had the smaller one he'd taken from Wylie's house.

As he watched, more wanderers approached the ruined bodies with knives and saws and began harvesting the meat. The ever-thrifty seraph must be feeding their captives to themselves. It made ugly sense. How could you find a cheaper way to keep them going than that?

He tried to scream at Lindy, but his voice could not be heard by her or anybody else. And look at her poor feet, surely she wouldn't be set to work, surely they would select her. And his poor Winnie, God only knew what had become of her.

The sorrow was so great, the helplessness almost enough to drive him mad.

A warmth came over him, then, so kind, so surpassing in protective compassion that he allowed himself to hope that at last the deity he had been praying to constantly for all these days had come. But it was not God, it was another soul. He had a sense of a soldier's heart, determined, disciplined, and a soldier's face, tight with effort.

When he tried to open himself to this soul, though, the way you do when you are practiced in out-of-body travel—and he was getting somewhat okay at it—the other soul threw up a memory from its childhood, a boy riding a bicycle up a driveway on a summer's night, a yellow porch light with moths flying around it, an elderly dog standing up on the porch, then coming down to greet the boy, his tail twirling.

Martin recognized it as an attempt to say, in the multilayered language in which soul speaks to soul, that this visitor who was trying to contact him now had been a boy beloved of an old dog. And with the high-speed insight that characterizes thought unencumbered by the electrochemical filters built into the brain, Martin saw that this meant that he had once been good and gentle, but it was a long time ago. But he had seen his error and now longed to return to his boyhood state.

He had done evil, this interloper, but he was trying to say that he was not, himself, evil.

Then Martin saw hieroglyphics. They were extremely vivid, but were they coming from the soul or were they in the physical world? Telling the difference took an expert, and he was no expert.

Trevor's mental voice said, *This is what I wanted you to see. Let General North continue to guide you.*

Martin saw the face of their guide again, just the eyes. The eyes were pleading.

Martin could, of course, read hieroglyphics. But there were over two thousand hieroglyphic symbols, and translation could be an extraordinary challenge, and the farther back in time from the date of the creation of the Rosetta Stone, which was the basis of all hieroglyphic translation, the less accurate translation became. He saw immediately that these were Old Kingdom if not even older, and that they were a mix of words and numbers, with bits of quickly scribbled hieratic notes here and there along the edges.

These were the most complex hieroglyphics he had ever seen, but as with all complex texts, there were simpler words, and he thought to start with these. They were lovely glyphs, really well executed. He read *ur*, the swallow glyph, then *udjat*, the Eye of Horus that has become the familiar ℞ of modern prescriptions. He read on, recognizing the name Narmur, the first pharaoh of the Old Kingdom. Then a bit of the hieratic text became clear: *the connection*. This was followed by an unknown number that had been scribbled beside the hieroglyphic for copper.

Incredibly, this appeared to be a set of instructions about making electrical connections.

The souls of the kids were filling the chamber now. Pam had come, and was signaling an image of a long tunnel with some kind of a car in it. Then George showed a picture of the Rockies, then the entrance to the Cheyenne Mountain facility, easily recognizable by its huge steel doors.

This image agitated Al North. Martin could feel his sorrow. But why? They knew that somewhere the human souls were stored, and maybe what they were learning here was that it was under the Rockies.

A map was thrust into his mind as if into his hand, accompanied by a red flush of anger. It was a Google map centered just west of Holcomb.

A shock went through him. "Zoom," he said. "Again." The map now pointed to a particular crossroads.

And he at once understood why the seraph had scoured this part of Kansas the way they had. It wasn't only because he was there and the gateway to the other human world was there, it was because the repository where the souls were hidden was there, at the geographic center of the continental United States, which was a few miles from the town of Lebanon, just over the county line from Holcomb, just at the crossroads he was looking down at right now.

This spot must be of enormous geomagnetic significance. But the men who had made the casual measurements that had located it, had been innocently playing around with a cardboard map.

But they hadn't. They had been under seraph mind control and doing the work of seraph engineers.

He could feel Al North's delight as a sense of dancing. Music came out of him, joyous chords. He had been working and working to communicate this. He had been struggling to be seen, to be heard, but until now nobody had noticed him.

Martin had not noticed that they'd gone down into the earth to find this place, but they had, they'd gone deep, and as they returned, traveling through so much stone was eerie, to feel yourself in the pull of it, to feel your sensitive electromagnetic body negotiating the smaller spaces in the dense matter—it was claustrophobic and they were deep, very deep.

Without warning, he burst up into the storms of the night and went rocketing into the sky. For an instant he saw the wide plains of Kansas whirling beneath him, then the clouds, then he was above the clouds and the second moon was high, its soft light making castles of the cloud tops from horizon to horizon.

He felt a pull upward, strong, and he saw laughing, singing children looking down from a tower above him, pleading with him to come. But he looked only for one face in the tower of song, and he did not see that face, he did not see his Winnie.

Above the tower were spreading mansions and roads in the high sky, great, flowing blue spaces, and the clouds were gone and the moons were gone and waves of pure pleasure were pouring through his body with such intensity that he could not believe that he had anything even approaching such a capacity for delight.

It was the pleasure of great love, mature and rich and filled with the resonance of long companionship, an exalted version of the love he had known with Lindy, but also there was somebody there who wanted him and to enter him and become him, too, and there was the laughter of children, and the perfect voice of a great choir.

Then something stung him. Hard. On the cheek.

"Dad! Dad!"

What *was* that? Well, it wasn't heaven, so he wasn't interested.

Another sting, harder. No, go away.

Another one, harder still. "Damn you!"

"Dad!"

Trevor was there. Physically there, because souls don't have beads of sweat running along their upper lips. Trevor shut his eyes tight and *whap*, Martin saw stars.

"What the hell, you hit me!"

His son fell on him sobbing and laughing, hugging him. "Finally! Dad, you almost didn't come back!"

He had never in his life felt as heavy as he did now. Returning to your body was putting on a lead overcoat.

"How long have I been . . ." He bowed his head. He could not bear to say it. He had been in heaven.

His son's hand touched his shoulder. "I went there, too, Dad."

Martin shook his head. He didn't want to think, to talk, to listen to those damn drums anymore, to be here in this awful place, he wanted to be *there*, where flowers that bloomed forever never stopped surprising you. Eternity was not living in the same old world forever, it was discovering the world anew forever.

"Where's the monument," Trevor asked. "Who knows where it is?"

A few hands went up. "It's off the roadside, near Smith Center," Tim Grant said. "There's a chapel there that can seat, like, twenty people. It's all sort of nothing, actually."

"Except for the millions of souls that are trapped under there."

"According to Wylie's book, it's where General Al North was taken," Trevor said. "It might be under Kansas, but the entrance is in Colorado, at that base."

Martin felt that Cheyenne Mountain didn't matter. It was just another seraph trick, a diversion.

No, the chapel would be the key. If they went there, they would find the vulnerability that the seraph were trying to hide. "Thing is, the way they've scoured this part of Kansas, how interested they are in us—and we're just a quiet little corner of the world, after all—I'd say that if the monument is right above the center of their repository, then that's where we need to go to reach it. That's got to be their weak point."

The atmosphere in the tent became electric. "It's not very far," a voice said.

"We have to go in the physical," George added, "or we won't be able to do anything in the physical."

From outside came the chuckling clatter of the jaws of outriders. The drummers started drumming.

"I'm going with you," Trevor said softly.

Martin did not reply, not verbally. There would be no way to keep Trevor here. He stood up, and so did Trevor and so did Pam. But the others did not stand. He could sense something among them, a kind of mutual agreement, but it wasn't clear exactly what was in their minds.

Mike stood. His girl cried out, but stifled her cry. She came to her feet and threw her arms around him. They stood like this, the young couple, and Martin saw that their hearts were married.

She stayed behind, though, surrounded by the little ones.

The woods were quiet now, the outriders having gone off when they failed to smell fear here. To the west, lightning flickered. Would the storms never end? No, not as long as the seraph tortured this poor earth, Martin knew. All of that seafloor that had risen would be gushing with methane from hydrates and billions of tons of dead marine life, and hydrogen sulfide and other gasses he couldn't even name. In a matter of days, it would change the atmosphere, and the seraph would be able to breathe easily here, and all the humans and most of the animals and insects would die.

First moon now rode in the high sky, its light bright and bitter, and the night was so still that you could hear the whisper of grass when breezes touched it. It was a sound familiar in Kansas when the crops were high and the night wind ran in them, sighing and whispering.

"Stop," Mike said softly.

Sensing trouble, Martin drew his prayer back into his mind.

Trevor pointed upward. For a moment, Martin saw only the sky. Then, against the moon, a flash of darkness, ugly and ribbed like the wing of a bat. Then he saw another and another, and as his eyes began to track the movement in the sky he understood that there was not one nighthawk circling up there, but dozens, no, hundreds, in a soaring column that seemed to go up forever.

Thousands in the moonlight.

Something slid into Trevor's hand, and Martin knew what it was, that seraph gun, even more fearsome than Wylie and Nick's arsenal.

"All right," Mike said, "right now, you're thinking away as usual, Doctor Winters, and the rest of us are absolutely not afraid. And the reason is, we're doing what you keep thinking about doing. You have to use the prayer, Doctor Winters, you have to keep it in your head all the time—and now you're about to think about the Valley of Death and comfort yourself with the psalm but please don't even do that."

He recalled Franny's prayer, took it to his mind, and began repeating it. Of course, he was not even a believer. If anything, he was a Jeffersonian Christian, an admirer of the man but not a believer in the resurrection. And, in any case, Zooey had been right, had he not, that the prayer was itself a form of egotism?

He realized that Mike was looking at him. They were all looking at him.

—The fourteen parts of Osiris.

—The fourteen Stations of the Cross.

—The fourteen sacred sites.

—The fourteen black lenses.

"Do you understand now, Doctor Winters?"

He nodded, but he did not understand. The great magic number of the past was seven, the number of a completed octave and a completed life. So what was fourteen?

"The number of resurrection, the key to heaven," Trevor said, "and it's the resurrection energy that the seraph hate, because it's what they can't have. That's why they steal souls, to find in their goodness a taste of heaven. That's why they're really here. It's not for bodies and land, it's for souls."

They walked through the wrecked forest, past uprooted trees, through the yards of ruined houses, and he could see the white steeple of Third Street Methodist still standing. Also, they walked out from under the great column of nighthawks, which could not see them because they could not see any fear.

They reached Pam's yard, and he saw that her house had been torn apart just as theirs had, by seraph who had not anticipated that some of their victims would gain power from the attack, and sought any crumb of information they might find about these dangerous little viral particles.

Pam broke into a run, and disappeared into the house. Martin saw in his mind's eye a flashing image of a car key, but knew that her heart was taking her to her old room, and the rooms of those she loved, and he saw her looking at the melted, deranged ruin of her home and knew that she was feeling the same horror that he had, the same anguish at seeing something so much a part of herself made so ugly.

Nobody spoke, nobody needed to, they could hear her rage in their minds, even Martin could hear it, and a moment later could also hear the increasing roar of wings, and the forlorn, eager cries that grew louder as the nighthawks, seeing her terror like a bright star in a void, found them again.

From the house, then, silence. She'd become aware of what her emotions were doing.

Nobody moved. Not a hundred feet overhead, the creatures swarmed. And from the dark woods all around now came the chuckling of outriders. They had begun marching this way, working their steel fangs.

The truck stood in the drive, but when they drew near it, they found that it was peppered with tiny craters. Farther down the driveway were heaps of something—the remains of people, there was no way to tell.

As they got into the double cab, Pam tried the key. "We need a miracle, thanks," she muttered.

The truck's engine growled.

There was a huge crash and the ceiling was crushed enough to knock Martin's head forward—which was fortunate, because enormous claws came ripping through the metal, ripping and clutching.

"Keep down, Dad!"

The engine ground again. "Come on," Pam said.

It was a double cab, and Trevor and Mike had gotten in the back. Trevor came forward between the seats as more of the huge nighthawks landed around them, their great heads thrusting, their beaks, lined with narrow teeth, opening wide when they bellowed, then snapping closed with a lethal crack.

More landed, and more, until Martin could smell their breath, a mixture of hydrogen sulfide and rotting meat that made your throat burn.

Then one of the heads thrust forward and crashed through the windshield, and the teeth slashed toward Martin. From between the seats, Trevor fired the disk-shaped weapon.

There was no report. The head simply flew apart, the upper and lower halves of the beak whirling against the opposite doors, the eyes exploding into a dust of glass and gelatin, and the tongue fluttering in the ruined face as the creature shot backward and ended up squalling on its back in the driveway, its fifty-foot wings flapping furiously, hammering the ground so hard that the truck rocked with every great convulsion.

With a thunder of howls, the rest of them took off, rising as mayflies do from a spring brook, but monstrous.

"Thank you, God," Pam said as the truck finally started. She put it into drive and accelerated toward the street, driving over the creature, which snapped and crackled and squalled beneath the bouncing vehicle.

"Sorry about that," she said.

They went down to Harrow in the ravaged truck, and changed there to another one—Bobby's police car, which stood open on Main and School. The keys were still in the ignition, and it had a quarter tank of gas. Also, between the front seats, a sawed-off shotgun. They got in, Martin behind the wheel.

They rode in silence down an empty Highway 36, passing an occasional motionless car, but otherwise meeting not the slightest sign of life. "That's a terrible weapon," Martin said to Trevor.

"It's nearly empty," Trevor replied.

"The light is coming," Mike said. "We need to hurry."

Martin scanned the sky, looking for some sign of an orange disk. He saw nothing, but he stepped on the gas, driving the police interceptor up to a hundred and twenty, then a hundred and thirty. Bobby kept the thing in good shape.

"Take a right," Mike said.

"I thought it was in Smith Center."

"The monument's on 191."

Martin turned north on 281. The fields were fallow, the country totally empty.

"Left," Mike said.

Another mile and Martin saw the little monument just off the road. A short distance from it was a small building.

"Okay," Mike said, "you got it. Now what?"

They got out. Martin carried the shotgun.

Mike took it. "That's an eight-shot semi," he said, "not seven."

"It's loaded?"

"I know that."

Martin went to the chapel, a white portable building, its siding weathered. The door was unlocked. He pushed it open. Inside were a few pews, a table, and a cross on the wall behind it. He noticed that this was not an ordinary Christian cross. Christ lay upon it, but the four limbs of the cross were of equal length. He wondered who might have done that in rural Kansas, made it into such a very ancient symbol, for the solar cross marked the solstices and the equinoxes, and related to the greatest depths of human memory and knowledge, from the time when we did not think like we do now, but made wonders in the world because we were surrendered to God, and thus acting on exquisite instinct, not plodding thought.

"Who is she?" Pam asked.

For a moment, Martin was confused. Then he saw her, too, a shadow standing in the corner of the chapel, so still that she at first appeared to be little more than a thickening of the dark. But he could see her eyes there in the corner of the room, her gleaming eyes, and her slimness.

Jennifer Mazle sprang at him. One second, he was wondering if the figure was even alive, the next he had been slammed to the floor.

Her hands came around his throat, closed. His head felt as if it was going to explode. At that same moment thick light surged in the windows and the door with the force of a tidal wave, causing the glass to shatter and the door to slam all the way across the chapel, where it hit the wall and dropped the cross to the floor.

Martin looked directly into Mazle's face, into eyes that bulged until the contact lenses popped out, revealing the reptile eyes of the seraph.

In the light that was all around them, he could see the kids moving with method and direction, and could hear the whispering of their minds.

Mike pulled Mazle's head back. Her mouth opened and her long, black tongue came out as she screamed. Trevor thrust the shotgun into her mouth and pulled the trigger, and her lithe body shot backward in a shower of green blood. The head burst.

"But the light!"

"Don't think, Martin!" Pam yelled.

"Just let yourself happen, Dad!"

As he took his attention away from his mind and into his body, he felt his soul return also, and knew that the light had been taking him so stealthily that he hadn't even realized it.

Then Pam marched into the corner where Mazle had been standing and simply disappeared.

For a moment, Martin thought she'd gone through a concealed gateway, but when he heard echoing footsteps, he understood. Cunning doors like this were seen in some Egyptian temples he'd worked on, but especially in Peru, where there were many of them in old Cuzco, doors that to this day only the Inca knew. But to find one here in Kansas— well, he would have been surprised once.

Concentrating on his breath, on the way his body felt as he moved, leaving his thoughts and his fears behind, he found that he could move through the light easily and without danger. The kids weren't even concerned by it.

He crossed the ruined chapel with the others, walking straight into the corner, feeling it give way, seeing the darkness, then finding his footing on steep black steps.

They had defeated the light, and if only mankind had recognized his own soul before it was too late, the whole world would have been able to do the same thing. But the seraph had infiltrated us with the lie that we were a body only, that there was no soul that was admissible to understanding and to science, and that science itself was a strange exploration having nothing to do with the kingdom of God, when, in fact, there was no real science that did not address heaven and *satori*.

As they went down, the air changed, growing thicker and warmer, beginning to smell stifling. This was the air of Abaddon, air as it would be everywhere in this world of theirs very soon. It was heavier, their air, and would be filling low places first.

He was last in line, going down the iron steps. Faint light came from below. From above, now only darkness.

They went down for a long time, and Martin remembered the part of Wylie's book about Al's descent. He had been taken miles into the earth.

As the light from below got brighter, it took on a blue cast, and the narrow shaft they were descending became more distinct. "It's our guide," Mike said.

Martin knew that the blue light of souls was also the color of good worlds, and that Abaddon was brown, but the human earths were palest blue, the color of their waters and their skies, and the glow of their dead.

"Are we sure?" Martin asked. They were a good two hundred steps down, and he was beginning to feel a distinct sense of claustrophobia in the narrow space. He forced himself not to think of the depth or the closeness. He'd found reading Wylie's description of Al's descent beneath Cheyenne Mountain to be almost unendurable, so vivid was the sense of being enclosed in rock, and he could never forget the feeling he'd had here earlier.

"Oh, my God."

It was Pam, calling up from below. "What?"

He reached the bottom of the steps. At first, he was only aware of color—gold, green, red, tan. He couldn't understand what he was seeing. Then he could. "This is the most extraordinary room in the world." He'd seen it before, of course, but not in the body, not with all the vividness of his living eyes.

"Back down, Dad. Try to put your mind away."

"I can't put my mind away! Don't you see what this is? It's where we saw the hieroglyphics. But now we're here in the flesh, and it's all so— so vivid and so real. This is the most superb example of Old Kingdom bas-relief on the planet. And it's in the middle of the United States!"

"Dad, listen to me. If you don't just let *it* take you over, we're in trouble. Because we're not in the United States, dad. This is Abaddon, and the second they realize that we're here, we are done."

"We've come through a gateway?"

"We're still on earth, but in the physics of Abaddon."

"Come on," Mike said. "We've got work to do. Stuff to figure out."

Martin followed him across the room where Al North had been deprived of his life and his soul. He followed them through a low doorway, which was the source of the light, which was a living light that penetrated the flesh and made you weep to feel it upon your body.

Then he saw why. He was in a cavern, blue-lit like a submarine cave just touched by sun from the surface. Before them stretched a sea of glass tubes, each three feet long, all plugged into huge black sockets, all living, exact replicas of the images on the wall of the temple of Dendera. Except these tubes were sparking with life, and you could see the lights inside them leaping and jumping and struggling, causing the whole room to flicker continuously.

Slowly, Trevor, then Pam and Mike went to their knees. Martin followed them, because the light shining on them was not just alive, but richly alive, and they could see millions of summer mornings, dew on the flowers of the world, signs of struggle and happiness, and hear, also, a roar of voices that was vast.

The flower of mankind was here.

"What do we do now, Dad?"

"I have no idea."

TWENTY-THREE
DECEMBER 21, THE FINAL HOURS
ON ABADDON: THE UNION

WYLIE HAD REALIZED THAT HE was being dieseled when he saw that they were crossing the same sodden shopping street again. There were piles of yarn, there were farm implements, there were baskets and paint-brushes, and hatchets polished to a high shine.

He might be a shape-shifter like the rest of them, but he was not on their side. No, he was a Union man, he had remembered that. They were right about him being an intelligence agent. He was, but not a very good one, given that he'd gotten his sweet ass caught just when that was the worst possible thing that could have happened.

Wylie had examined every inch of the wagon, but it was made like a fricking safe. The goddamn driver would open a little hatch from time to time and shit and piss into it. Wylie stayed well back, but the place stank. He wondered if his own shit was yellow now, too?

The wagon had been stopped for some time before he understood that it wasn't going to be moving again. There was a series of clicks, and the door went hissing open. Even in this place, with its dirty brown sky, coming out hurt his eyes.

He was coming to the crisis of his failure now, he knew.

"Ready for lunch," his captor said. "Your hands are comin' to me and mine, I hear."

His *hands*. What a place. Trapped in the wagon with nothing to do but think, he had remembered more of his real life. If you looked—*really* looked—you wouldn't find a trace of Wylie Dale before December 26, 1995, the day he'd made his transition into a human life that had been painstakingly constructed for him to enter. "Wylie Dale" had already been established as a novelist by the organization that had sent him to the human earth, but the first book he'd written himself was *Alien Days*, his story of his abduction, which had actually been a looking-glass memory of his arrival on one-moon earth.

As Wylie's eyes adjusted to the light, he found himself standing before a gigantic version of a building familiar to him. It was the model for the Tomb of Skull and Bones on the campus of Yale University. But the Tomb was not large. This building was two hundred feet tall, a great, ugly monolith.

Compared to the rest of the city, which echoed with roars, screeches, discharges of steam, the rumbling of wagons, and various unidentifiable hoots, laughs, and howls, the silence here was total.

Bones had been founded by William Huntington Russell, whose stepbrother Sam had carried opium into China for the British when they were trying to get back the gold they'd spent on Chinese tea. British captains hadn't been willing to do it. It might have been the 1850s, but drug running was still drug running. Russell had no problem with addicting the Chinese.

"Are you happy?" he asked his grinning captor.

"Yeah, I'm happy."

"Then fuck you."

"Could I season your fingers?"

"You going to two-moon earth?"

"I should be so lucky. No can afford."

Wylie thought of the shithole the seraph hordes were being sent to. "What does it cost?"

"Whatever you have. Which assumes you have something. They don't consider an artificial syrinx with a busted jaw and this old wagon worth a ticket. I live in it, you know. When it's not otherwise occupied."

"So you're poor?"

"Poor as shit, which is why—" He stopped. He listened, so Wylie listened, too. Keening came, heart-freezing, getting louder fast. "Knees!"

Wylie didn't argue. As he went down to the hard earth and little knots of mushrooms like small, exposed brains, a line of flying motorcycles with silver fenders, ridden by figures in gold metallic uniforms and gleaming gold helmets and face masks, came speeding out of the sky and hung dead still a foot or so above the ground, their motors revving as the riders worked to keep them stable.

This was followed by a smooth whoosh of sound, and a jewel of an aircar appeared.

He knew who it belonged to, of course: Marshal Samson. His escort bowed, and he bowed, too. There was a click and he could sense somebody getting down, coming over.

"Hello, Wylie." The voice positively bubbled. "I knew it from the first. It had to be this. Actually, I'm impressed. I'll never tell *her* that, of course, but it was a brilliant operation."

"Thank you."

"I just came from raping your wife, incidentally. Bring him."

He was kicked from behind, and ended up scuttling through the huge doors, which had opened soundlessly and now presented the appearance of a gaping cave.

As Wylie walked through the darkness of the anteroom and Samson opened the inner door for them both, the enormous golden floor struck him with a powerful sense of remembrance. That floor had been a source of scandal at home, a symbol to the Union of the greed of the autocrats who ran this side of the planet.

A tall woman loaded with jewels, her hair sleek and white, dressed in the richest clothing Wylie had ever seen, came striding forward. Her face was so white that it glowed, the scales attractively tiny, the features delicate. He knew that this was the infamous leader of this world, Echidna, whose family had held controlling ownership of the Corporation for uncountable millennia.

All the females in the line were called Echidna. When one wore out, a new clone replaced it seamlessly, without any public awareness. There was never an issue of succession, unlike the Union, which was a simple democracy and in turmoil all the time.

"Come, Spy," she said, "I want to gloat before dinner."

As they crossed the great room, he saw Lee Raymond, Robert Mugabe, and Ann Coulter playing a game involving dice on what appeared to be a table made of emeralds, rubies, and a great, gleaming expanse of pure diamond. He recognized the game. It was senet, the Egyptian predecessor to backgammon. In the human worlds, the rules of senet had been hidden away by the seraph, but here, where they had not, players at senet gambled for souls.

He was not sure if they were human, or simply proud of their achievements as human, and showing off their forms.

"I had no idea your penetration of human society was so extensive."

"But not of both human worlds, not as much as I hoped. This time around, we're only getting the one, I fear." She shot him a twinkling glance. "But we *are* getting it, you Union shit!"

Coulter now shifted into a sallow reptilian form with big, beady scales. Her black tongue darted behind spiked teeth made yellow from too much tobacco. Wylie realized that she was lusting after him. Mugabe, who was apparently her seraph husband, scurried behind her, trying to keep a cloak around her.

"Ann wants to bed you before we eat," Echidna said. "It's a particular pleasure of hers, to fuck her food."

They arrived at a tall window, curtained. "Open it," Echidna snapped at Samson. "I just want you to see this, Union man."

Wylie realized that she had brought him close to a great, black wall with huge levers on it. Scalar controls, he knew, that worked the gigantic lenses that were deployed on two-moon earth. But then the curtains swept open, and he saw a lawn so bright green it must have been painted, awash in splendid people, some of them reptilian, others human, or seemingly so. There were politicians, of course, great, grinning hordes of them, military officers in the uniforms of a dozen countries, representatives of various royal families, rock stars, CEOs, television personalities, preachers, mullahs, gurus—in fact, every sort of human leader and person of power. Among them strolled naked seraph girls and boys, their scales bleached so white they looked new-minted, carrying trays loaded with barbecued fingers, ears and toes, and flutes of hissy champagne.

To one side was a line of elaborate gas grills, all black and chrome. He recognized that they were Strathmores from home, the brand he had on his own deck, except that these were limousine models, with twelve burners instead of the usual four. Most of them were rolling spits, and on them some of the victims still twisted and squirmed. Behind each grill hung a complete body molt on a tall spike, a pale skin attesting to the youth and therefore tenderness of the person under preparation.

Echidna pointed to an empty grill. "That'll be you," she said.

He wanted to try to run, anything to avoid what seemed inevitable. But there was more, because he saw that this party was not to celebrate his capture, or not only that, it was also to celebrate an enormous event that was unfolding in a valley behind the building.

In the center of this valley was a gigantic circular lens of purest black, its surface reflecting the wan midday sun. And around it, stretching to every horizon, were what must be millions and millions of seraph, ready to pour through the moment the signal was given. He saw men, women, children, heard the booming of syrinxes, the chatter and whoops of other animals, and above it all the excited, argumentative shrieking of the seraph themselves as they jostled for position and accused one another of trying to break the baskets of black, oblong eggs the women all carried.

He assumed that he would die here today. He'd been living for years in an extremely dangerous situation with a wiped memory, and that made you vulnerable—so vulnerable, in fact, that it was probably just a matter of time before you ended up going through the funny little door in the woods. He loved his poor family, though, his striving, brilliant, lovely family. What would happen to them? Could they shift, he wondered? Did they, perhaps in secret, the children under their covers at night, Brooke in the privacy of her early mornings?

Ann had sidled closer, and he thought maybe he could cause a little confusion. In this class-ridden society, she was bound to have some prerogatives. Time wasn't on his side, obviously, but distraction might be.

He turned to her. "Must I?"

She squared her shoulders. "Of course you must."

He went toward her, and thus also toward the wall behind her.

"Guards," Echidna said mildly. "Stay with him."

Samson came, and with him his heavily armed escort.

Wylie was still bound, of course, but he came to Ann Coulter and looked down at her. Her scales fluttered and surged, and a black substance that smelled of sulfur began to ooze from under her eyelids.

"Ann," her husband hissed, "you're compromising yourself."

She was really steaming. She loved a man in bondage, that was clear.

Wylie saw that he had a moment, and only one, and it was this moment. He opened his mouth and drew his tongue along the backs of his teeth in the best imitation of a whore that he could imagine.

She tittered. Her breath had in it the flat muskiness of death.

"Will somebody please remove these children?" Mugabe shouted. A number of them had foregathered to watch the fun.

"Part of their education," Echidna said. Her husband now joined her. Wylie had forgotten the name of this huge being, but he was peerlessly imposing in his sleek black suit, with his shimmering skin and brilliant, watchful eyes. Another ancient ruler riding the ages on a foam of clones.

He tilted his head and felt Coulter's kiss invading his mouth like a soaked chaw of somebody else's tobacco.

With all the power in him, his every muscle singing, his whole heart and soul and mind devoted only to this one movement, he sprang upward. These lizard forms were not as earthbound as human bodies. They didn't feel as much, either, not pain, not love, not pleasure. But they were ferociously strong, and he was strong, he had kept himself well, understanding now the obsessive hammering away he had done at Gold's in Wichita. He'd scared people, the way he would swim laps like a machine. He hadn't known why his body was like this, just that he needed the swimming, the running, the boxing, the karate, all of it, needed it and devoured it.

The guard had made one mistake, early on. He'd seen him as human and bound him as human, careful of the delicate skin of a much more fragile creature than a seraph. He ripped his arms free with ease.

Unfortunately, the gun had gone. They'd left it with him only to amuse themselves with his disappointment when it was taken. "These sell for a nice price," the guard had said as he removed it.

For a moment, there was nobody between him and the great control panel. He grabbed a lever, pulled it. Grabbed another, did the same. The action was so damn satisfying that he growled, he screamed, as he pulled another and another.

Echidna roared, her husband—Beleth, that was the name—leaped toward him—and came crashing into Mugabe, who threw himself into his path. Samson turned, and Ann Coulter slashed him with a molting hook, drawing his skin open and revealing the muscles beneath. He shrieked in agony. It felt good to draw off dry molt, of course, but raw like this, it was torment.

Coulter Union! Her human disguise was brilliant—a spokesman for the aims of the Corporation so extreme that she made them look ridiculous.

Wylie leaped, giving Beleth a head kick that he could feel smash the skull. Gabbling, his brains flying, he pitched back into his own onrushing guards.

"Samson's aircar," Ann shouted. "Go!"

"It's ensouled!"

"Of course it is, you damn fool, go!"

There was a whispering crackle and Ann flew into a thousand red chunks. One of the guards now turned his weapon toward Wylie, who hit the floor as he pushed Echidna into the line of fire.

Her legs and bottom half, spurting fountains of blood, ran a few steps and collapsed at the feet of the surprised guard, while the top half, which had hit the floor smack on its bloody, waist-level base, uttered whistling gasps, waved its arms, and tore at its hair as shrieking, laughing children, who had mistaken the whole thing for a game, surrounded it, running in and pinching and squealing and then running away.

As Wylie crossed the floor, he heard the snicker of more guns. Then a dozen outriders came swinging down from above on webs like thick ropes dripping with glue. But he was outside now, and the aircar was waiting there, its now unattended motorcycle escort lined up neatly on the ground.

He kicked them over and dove into the interior. Expecting the car to resist the entry of what would be a known enemy, he yanked the door down with all his might.

"Hello, Brother," the car said, and the voice hit Wylie with a shock like freezing water and the joy of the first morning of the world.

He hadn't heard his brother speak aloud in over thirty years, but he recognized his voice instantly.

When Wylie was just a tiny boy, his beloved older brother had been killed by Corporation marauders and his soul kidnapped. His brother had been a great soldier. They'd kept his Medal of Valor and his various orders in a glass case in the family room, proud mementos. Wylie had gone to the human world because it took courage, and he wanted to show that he, also, had the ability to fight well for the Union.

They swept into the air. "Brother," he said, "did they steal your soul?"

The car did not answer, and a flash of unease went through him. Abaddon was a place of deceptions, so maybe—

But then he looked down at what they were circling, and saw that the lens below him was now surrounded by as vast a crowd as he had ever seen. But things were not going well. The blackness of it had turned angry red, and it was boiling like a lava pool, and the surging crowd, in trying to escape, was instead falling in from all sides. Smoke and steam rose from the massive pyre.

"Are they dying?" Wylie asked.

"I think they're going through. But it's not right. It's very not right."

"Brother, has your soul been trapped in this car all this time?"

"Hell no, I stole the car yesterday. I've got a lot of bodies. I use them like scuba gear, to dig into the physical whenever I need to. And—uh-oh!"

There was an angry rattle against the vehicle, which proceeded to shoot upward so fast that Wylie blacked out momentarily. When he came to, flashes were speeding past the windows. "Pulse/Strider," his brother said.

This was a weapon that delivered pulses of discrete superexcited electron plasmas that could instantaneously incinerate a car like this.

"Fly me, Brother."

"Me? I don't know how!"

"You were a hell of a pilot as a boy."

"How could you know? You were . . . dead."

"I'm an operative just like everybody else in the family. They were tricked into believing they'd captured my soul."

Mean red light filled the car, and it tumbled wildly through the air.

"Brother, I need you to remember your piloting skills! Do it now!"

The words cause memory to flood Wylie's mind, of being at the controls of a machine like this, of handling the twin sticks, of firing its weapons at sky targets, of having a glorious time in mock dogfights and evasion training.

He'd expected to be a pilot, but his aptitude tests were what had gotten him dragooned into intelligence. That, and he now also realized, the fact that his brother was already an agent. He remembered it all now, his whole life as a Union kid, his training . . . and something so poignant that he could almost not bear the recollection. He'd had a girl. He'd married her. He had a wife here on Abaddon, in the Union, the one good place that remained.

The car rattled, there was a flash, and this time the cabin filled with smoke and the fire alarm started.

"Fly me!"

Wylie gripped the controls. He swung the car from side to side, spotted the telltale sparkle of the Pulse/Strider installation on the ground. He turned hard, thrust the nose down, opened the throttle and slammed both sticks hard over.

The car shot like a diving eagle straight toward the installation. Pulses poured out. They would be forced to go on continuous triangulation, and his random jigging of the controls meant that not even he was sure of the trajectory.

He was nearly on top of them when they began to try patterns. Now, this was bad, this might work for them. "Are you unarmed?" he asked his brother.

"Of course I'm unarmed, I'm a sports car!"

"Just asking. Hold on!"

"My keel hurts, I can feel my keel going!" If an ensoulable machine's nervous system was properly designed, the soul inhabiting it would sense it the same way it did a body.

Wylie leveled out. He was now speeding across open land, directly toward some aristo's hunting estate. It was fashionable, he could see the house like something out of the English countryside. His brother said, "I see twelve bogies coming down on us."

Wylie went into the forest, among the trees.

"You'll wreck me!"

He took some advice from Martin's son, Trevor. Just let yourself happen. His hands moved as they shot down a forest path, then up a stream. This far from the city, it wasn't so polluted, not even on the Corporation side where mentioning global warming drew a death sentence. But then again, practically everything drew a death sentence. Executions were not only a form of population control, they kept the masses both entertained and fed.

Then he saw a wall. *The* wall, the one the Corporation had built around the Union. It was gray, immense, and dead ahead. He pulled back on the sticks and hopped it, and suddenly everything changed.

Here were fields of swabe and borogrove and orchards full of trees heavy with lascos and spurls and nape. Everything was green, the sky was dusty blue rather than dirty brown, and he knew that there would be stars at night, a few stars. Here, it was illegal *not* to mention global warming.

"I'll take me back," his brother said.

"Yeah, since I don't know where I'm going."

"I'm pulsing our code but we could get a look-see from the Air Force, so if we do don't take evasive action. We are home, Brother."

Wylie's heart ached as he watched the rich green Union land speed below them. Home. And look at the houses, he could even see pretty shutters. Most unionists farmed. He had farmed, and he could see that the harvest was still coming in here and there. "Harvest is late."

"Winter's late, it's too warm. If only an eighth of the planet fights the good fight, we can't win, we can only lose slowly. The Gulf Stream stopped for four months this year. Avalon nearly froze while here in Aztlan, most of the maize crop burned."

"What about the Corporation? They must be feeling it, too."

"Farming's illegal there now." He paused for a long time. "I suppose you noticed what they're eating."

"I noticed."

They came down on a pebble driveway before a modest old sandstone, its worn carved serpents of luck and joy barely visible in its ancient walls. But this was home, all right, a place he now realized that he had felt as an absence in his spirit for his whole time away.

He got out. "I wish you could come in, Brother."

"When this tour's over, I go back to my natural body forever, and I am looking forward to that, Wylie."

"I don't want to rattle around in the house alone!"

The arched wooden door opened. A figure stood back in the shadows, one lovely, tapering claw on the doorjamb.

Oh, it was impossible.

"Talia?"

"Aktriel?"

"Yes." His response was so automatic that it required no thought. Aktriel was his real name, and he was a Department of Defense information officer. After pilot training, his work had been involved in the issuance of directives and proclamations, and he'd been sent to the human world because of his writing ability and his communications skills.

As she came out into the light, the car's horn beeped twice and it took off into the sky, turned, then raced back toward Corporation territory. For a moment, Aktriel watched it go, watched sadly, wishing that his brother would come out, understanding why he could not bear to live in the freedom of his real body even for a short time, only to have to return to that miserable thing and go back to his hellish work.

She came to him, her eyes lowered, tears flowing. He took her in his arms, and truly he was home again, and from such a far, far place. "I'd forgotten everything," he said.

She nodded against his shoulder.

"But where's your husband, Talia? Your family? Surely you have one. It's been years."

Arm in arm, they went into the dim, comfortable interior of the house. Memory flooded him as he walked into the broad central room with its white walls and sky blue ceiling, and the climbing flowers painted everywhere. His mother's hearth was here, his father's tall harvest boots still by the closet where he'd always kept them. Beside them, smaller, shorter boots. When he'd waded for the tender swabe, he'd worn them.

"Do you still farm?"

"It will always be a farm."

"Of course." The Union's goal of environmental balance meant that changing land use patterns was not done without major reason.

She took his hand. "Do you want me?"

He threw his arms around her, felt her heart beating against his. This love—how had he ever managed to leave it? She was his dear, dear one, the alpha and omega of his soul. When he could have farmed here forever and never left her side, why had he ever gone?

Then he remembered his little Kelsey and proud, strong Nick, children of two worlds. His kids, and they were out there on the front line with their mom, and if he stayed here they would be abandoned.

It was as hard a moment as he had ever known. The beauty of his wife was stunning, her scales so tiny and so pale that she looked like a doll, her hair a wisp of delicate white smoke around her head, her eyes bluer than a fine earth sky, and deeper than the deepest ocean.

How he loved this woman, his friend of his youth and childhood, his dear companion.

But there were vows of the lips and vows of the blood, and his vow to those children on one-moon earth was a vow of the blood.

"I'm so glad it's over," she said. She gazed into his eyes. The Corporation seraph were remembered by man as nephilim, as archons, as demons. Mankind called Union folk angels or daikini, sky dancers.

"I'm glad it's over, too."

"But you sigh, husband."

He drew her close to him. These were simple houses, a central great room, with kitchen, dining, and storage in one wing and sleeping quarters in the other. They had been living in these houses forever, almost literally. They had no age, nothing here did. The Union was with God. There was nothing to count.

But he had forgotten how good a woman's hair could smell, sprinkled as hers was with the dust of flowers. It fell, sometimes, on that brilliant, glowing brow, that was almost as soft as human skin. She was almost as beautiful as Brooke, really, but the truth was that even to seraph, the humans were incredibly beautiful. It was why Corporation types had gone to rape them in the first place. It was why Unionists cherished and protected them as best they could. There was something about the humans that was close to God, very close, and you felt toward them both a desire to protect and a desire to worship.

Kelsey, Nick, Brooke. His buddy Matt. Cigars and absinthe. The fun of it all, of being in the human form, of looking like them and being able to kiss human lips and walk their pretty streets, to look up into the sacred blue of their skies, to lift his face to clean rain and listen to wind in the night, to watch TV, to go to the movies and eat popcorn, to feel warm human hands on his human skin, to sink into the dark of her.

"You're far away," Talia said.

"I'm just in shock. Seeing you again. Remembering you. Realizing—oh, my Talia, all that I've forgotten." He took her again, held her close. "All that I've missed."

She saw the truth, though. She knew him so well. They had been children together, born in the same basket, their eggs warmed by the same egg ladies. Their families had entwined their destinies long before they were born.

Trying to hide his tears, he turned away from her. "I belong to you," he said, feeling the twin pulls of his fiercely divided loyalties. Again, he hugged her, and again felt Brooke's absence in his arms.

Her eyes met his. The question that flickered in them now was a dark one. Then she held up her hand.

Her Electrum ring glowed softly. His ring. He took her hand and kissed it. She laughed a little, deep in her throat, and he wanted her. He wanted her so badly that he began to exude from under every scale on his neck. She brought a towel and wiped it gently. Her hands touching him evoked desire so great that it seemed beyond his trembling flesh, beyond belief, beyond body itself, a longing that was literally fantastic.

But if he did this then he could not leave her, not a second time, it was too cruel. And yet he had the children, the vow, and the other dear wife. And he knew, as soon as he was with Brooke again, he would lose himself in the wonders of human life and human love.

"It's only a few minutes," she said softly. She drew up the wooden blinds, and he saw in the evening light a diamond hanging in midair. In its facets, he could see another house, lights just coming on in the windows, and a small form at one of those windows looking out.

Kelsey was waiting for her daddy to come back.

"I have the permanent salve," she said. "Choose."

He took her hands. "We always knew the danger of the mission. I have a life there, now. I have children who need their father." And he wished—he just wished.

"You won't remember me."

"You'll find somebody else," he said.

"Don't mock my love, please."

He would leave her forever wanting him. If only he had known it would be this hard.

He had known. She had known.

She began to apply the salve, and he let her. It sank deep into him, into the most secret corners of his deepest cells, and as it did, this old homestead began to look stranger and stranger. He noticed that blinds closed up here, that there were no chairs but only these strange, three-legged stools. He saw the spinning wheel and the loom, ancient and obviously heavily used, but who used looms nowadays? And the grate and the big iron cook pot, so strange and archaic, and candles instead of electric lights, all so just plain weird.

But then she did an odd thing. She applied salve to herself.

"But no, you mustn't."

"Look, the sun is setting and Kelsey's gotta be getting scared. And Nick's liable to blow our heads off if we come up in the dark."

"Brooke?"

"Yes? Hello?"

Talia had been with him all along. Now, as they changed from seraph to human, fixed by the DNA salve, he threw his arms around her. "It's you, it's always been you! Did you know?"

"Not until I followed you through Samson's little gateway. Then I knew."

"But you escaped from the Corporation, you came home, you came to meet me even though you could've stayed back."

"To protect you. Remember what I am."

"The Guardian Clan." He laughed a little. "You really are a guardian angel."

"Who you need, Mr. Drinker and Smoker and hell-raising daredevil—the idea that any sane person would volunteer for an assignment like this!"

"It had to be done."

"Which is why I love you so." She smiled up at him, and as she did, her face shimmered, the scales smoothing in blurry waves, the brow widening, the cheeks growing less narrow, the eyes deeper, less wide, more human, the nostrils opening more, the lips softening and becoming red, the

teeth thickening into human teeth. And he could feel by his own inter-
nal shivering that he was doing the same.

This was not shape-shifting. This was fundamental DNA transfor-
mation. When his brother ended his tour of duty, this would be his
house. He would reenter his old body here, he would find his wife and
bring her here, and there would be eggs here, and the egg ladies would
brighten the house with their laughter again, in the coming years, in
the ages.

But Talia and Aktriel were dying into the human form.

She took his hand more firmly. "Ready?"

"How do I look?"

"Perfect. Or no, you're missing that mole under your left ear."

"Whose gonna notice?"

"You know your daughter. She's inherited your following and watching instincts."

"Do we need to take salve for them?"

"Born of earth as they were? They have the DNA to shift, but not the
skill. They'll stay as they are, with their good seraphim hearts in those
lovely human forms."

"Are you gonna be on my case again?"

"Always."

Then they were in their familiar woods, and for a fleeting moment
his soul was in both worlds. Brooke said, "I've got something on the tip
of my tongue."

He shook his head. "I feel like I just woke up from a dream I thought
I'd never forget."

"Which was?"

"I forget."

She came to him and kissed him. "We've all been through too much.
And it has to end. It ends here." She looked toward the house. "It's time
to return to normal life."

"Can we?"

"I think we can. I mean, have you noticed that it's six and nothing's
happened yet? No 2012 shift here."

The moon was yellow in the eastern sky, coming toward full now, rising in splendor.

They both fell silent, and both for the same reason. "Why are we out in the woods, Wylie?"

"We're—" He stopped. Why *were* they out here? "I came looking for you," he said at last. "That's it."

"And I came to find you."

"I was in the cave?"

"Well, you're here."

"I feel like I was on Mars or something. A million miles away."

Suddenly she threw herself on him. In the gathering dark, he felt very alone. Odd. Homesick even, but for where? His house was a quarter of a mile away. His only house.

"I think our kids are gonna be missing us," she said.

They headed up the hill.

The love that is so great that it cannot be seen, that seems not even to exist, but is in fact the silent binding that confirms the world, followed them, lingering close as if to enjoy the warmth of what they had found together.

"Where have you guys *been?*" Nick yelled as they came up out of the woods. "It's getting darker and darker around here!"

"I got lost," Wylie said.

"And he got found."

"You got *lost?* How? I thought you'd been killed." Nick threw his arms around his father, and Wylie felt his surging youth and his love for his dad and then Kelsey's, also, from farther down by his knee, holding Bearish up like an offering to her household god.

As he entered with his children into the calm light, he heard the calling of another father whose desperation began pouring into his mind the moment he was inside the house.

He remembered the book and Martin and Trevor, and their quest to recapture their invaded world. "I've got work to do," he said.

Nick followed him upstairs. "They're in terrible trouble," he said. Then he added, "I've written some."

Wylie stopped. He turned to his son. "Oh?"

"Do you imagine that I don't know what I am, Dad? After what I've been through? What I've done for you?"

He looked at his son, he thought, as if for the first time. "What you are?"

"What we are, as a family. We're not the same, Dad, we're in communication with other worlds, we have powers and I know it and you can't say otherwise. That's why they tried to kill us, and why they failed. I defended us, too, dad, and I'm owed."

"Owed what?"

"You have to take me into your confidence, and you will *never* go into a gateway again like that without me to help you!"

A memory flashed, of a cottage in the woods. Funny memory, like a dream. Less than a dream, just a daytime imagining, the stuff of a story, no more.

"I, uh—"

"The solstice is coming and Martin and Trevor need us, Dad. But you're, like, lost in your own mind all of a sudden, and right now is the worst possible time for you to lose the thread." He paused. "Actually, I've written a lot. I've written the entire story of what you and Mom just did on Abaddon and who you are, and you can read that later, because right now we have a huge emergency and Dad, *there is no time!*"

He went into the office.

From downstairs, Brooke called, "What's going on?"

"Nick just wrote his first short story." He sat down at the laptop. "Talia," he said, "it's a beautiful name. But who's this Aktriel? You've got to find a better name than that."

"Dad, you'll read that later. Right now, it's time to write, because when you do write, something new is gonna happen."

"Nothing's there. I can't write."

Nick grabbed his hands, thrust them onto the keyboard. "Do it!"

After a moment, there was a whisper in his mind. He typed a few words.

"Trevor, Dad, you need to write about Trevor."

It was as if lightning had blasted him and shattered him, and he had a vivid image of a vast room lit by a curiously affecting, even disturbing, glow, a light that was blue and very alive, and communicated more clearly than any scream that it was in terrible trouble.

His fingers moved on the keys, then sped.

"At last," Nick said. "Trevor, buddy, listen up."

Wylie was at his desk, but at the same time in another place deep underground, and there was heard as another voice. "And the seventh angel poured out his vial into the air; and there came a great voice out of the temple of heaven, from the throne, saying, 'It is done.'"

But it was not done, not for the seven people who were struggling in that dark underground hell for their lives and the life of an entire world.

"There's a gateway down there and they don't see it, Dad."

"I know."

"Then write it! Say where it is if you know!"

"But they can't come here, they can't read this!"

"Just do it!"

Silently, in the dark of the great cavern where Martin and his little band struggled to break the soul traps, the hidden gateway to Abaddon slid slowly into focus, and began to open.

TWENTY-FOUR
SOLSTICE 2012 ON THE TWO EARTHS
A TALE OF SEVEN SOLDIERS

AS MIDNIGHT APPROACHED, THE FOURTEEN great lenses ranged around two-moon earth shimmered darkly. There was nobody to see, though, but for a scattering of seraph soldiers, and gangs of wanderers lined up, waiting to conduct their new masters into the cities that still stood, and out into the flats of the new lands, where enormous shantytowns were still under feverish construction, amid heaps of dead sea creatures and dead wanderers.

"Dad!"

He stopped. Came back to the world of his office. Turned to Nick, tried not to shout at him, which was what he wanted to do, to tell him to just shut *up!*

"Dad, you need to focus on Martin and Trevor."

"Sorry."

"Don't be sorry, just do it!"

His fingers shot back to the keys, began flying.

Downstairs, little Kelsey also ranged across the night of the other world, looking for Winnie. Lindy, Brooke had found. She was on a truck that was running down to Denver, which was intended to become a major resettlement area for the Corporation's starving billions. There her destiny would be simple: like all wanderers, she was to be worked to death.

On the sunlit side of the earth, the gigantic flats that had replaced much of the mid-Pacific were covered by an impenetrable fog, as trillions of tons of gasses boiled up out of the drying soil. Where India and

China had been was a new ocean, stormy and unsettled, floating with what appeared to be islands that were actually made of furniture and ice chests and logs and carpeting and toys and siding and plastic doors, flowerpots, Styrofoam cups, shipping beads, any container that was closed and would float, and on these islands were rolling hills of the corpses of cattle and dogs and monkeys and all manner of beast, and human corpses with pale-glazed eyes, and swarming masses of gulls and crows, and hordes of pelicans flying from place to place, their craws bulging.

They all saw this, the Dale family, in their new free minds, and as she watched, Kelsey sang softly to Bearish, whom she cradled as if he was the whole world. She sang the ancient lullaby her mother had taught her, "Dereen Day," that had come up from the quiet hearths of the Union and into the quiet hearths of Ireland a very long time ago, a song shared between angels and men. Her voice came up the stairs from the lonely pool of light where she sat carrying in her arms not only Bearish but all the dead of a whole world. She hummed to them and sang in her little voice. "Dereen Day, the nightjar calls upon the heath . . ."

Outside, night swept on and the evening star shone on the peaceful horizon.

She had been sending her mind down the roads of the other earth for a long time, had this very private child called Kelsey, for she shared with Winnie the same bond that her brother did with Trevor. So she sang not only to her Bearish but to Winnie's, whom she had found in a cradle of snow, the night flakes whispering along his fur, as they whispered across all the little corner of Nebraska where Winnie had given everything she had to give, and laid down.

Now, as Kelsey sang to Bearish and Winnie's Bearish, she sang also to Winnie, to the silver of the ice that crusted her cheeks, and her red car coat that was being worried by the winter wind, and to all the little lumps in the ocean of little lumps that were left everywhere on earth that wanderers had passed, each one somebody whose strength had not been enough to meet the Corporation's cruel test. Survival of the fittest—the Corporation's way—was not the way of the true of heart, human or not.

In the office, Nick and now Brooke along with him, struggled to get

Wylie to concentrate on the place that counted, the soul prison where Martin and Trevor and their few struggled for the life of their world.

"The souls," Brooke whispered, "can you see?"

Wylie sighed like a weaver does working on a difficult knot. The only sound in the house was Kelsey's singing coming up from below.

"Okay," he said. He began to type again.

But he saw the lens that stood in the ruin of the Giza plateau. It glowed angry red now, and red light leaped out of it, a huge column that reflected off the shattered city and the desert, making it appear as if the whole landscape was on Mars.

With it came a sound, at first a crackling like the rattling of a great curtain, and then another sound, a *snap*, then another louder one, and the lens seemed to shimmer, to shudder within itself, and seraph were suddenly walking away from it, each carrying a little bundle or a suitcase, some carrying briefcases or rolling bags, some in black, some like hurrying officials in hats and coats, some carrying their babies or baskets of eggs, or with their childrens' hands in theirs. They came clutching receipts for the tickets they had bought, and began to stream out past the Mena hotel toward Cairo, and up and down the banks of the Nile.

Another sound came, then, the gigantic spitting noise, a volcano makes when it vomits lava. Some of the colonists turned, others kept on, intent on getting to whatever corner of the new lands they had bought. Already, some were boarding buses that had been smashed in the explosion of the pyramid and trying to get them started, while others threw out the skeletons of the tourists who had died there, and marveled over their delicate, colorful clothes.

With a roar so huge that it would over the next few hours echo around the entire world, a massive red column of material shot out of the hole where the lens had been. The lens itself arced into the stratosphere, turning over and over, and as it turned changing shape, twisting and melting and then falling and becoming black, then blacker still, and landing in the Arabian desert not far from Mecca, a city of corpses of those who had died praying, surrounded by a desert coated with wanderers who had fallen beneath the sun.

None saw it strike, but Wylie and Brooke did, and Nick and so also Trevor and Martin. Deep in their traps, the souls of Lindy and Winnie sensed some signal from the outside, and for the first time since she had been pulled from her body, Lindy realized that she was not buried alive in a coffin, hideously and inexplicably unable to die. She began to call the name of the strongest and most trusted person she knew.

"I hear my wife," Martin said. "Lindy is calling me!"

At the same time, though, diamonds began to appear in the air, shimmering black, as Samson prepared to move the souls that would make him rich in Abaddon.

Winnie, who had been alone and cold and feeling drawn to some great joy she could not reach, now felt herself in the arms of her friend Kelsey, and heard a lullaby her mom had sung her every night of her life, "the nightjars calling upon the heath . . ." and rested in the knowledge that somebody was at last saving her from the monsters who had bound her here.

In Mecca, a new black stone now lay not far from the Alhajar Al-Aswad, and of the same material and the same shape and color, for the last one that fell here had started from exactly the same place thirteen thousand years ago, as Abaddon failed in its last attempt to steal the human worlds, and the raw hole it had left had been filled, and the pyramid built to close the wound, and remain as a warning—one that Abaddon had spent thirteen millennia tricking and deceiving mankind into forgetting.

The rest of the material that had blasted like lava from the huge gateway came to the top of its trajectory and began sailing back down. Far below, the seraph began to see arms and legs of their own kind, torsos, heads, shoes, falling around them, striking one and then another of them and causing their yellow brains to splash out. Heads bounded along like great hailstones, or rocks catapulted down by a siege army. As they bent to protect children or possessions or eggs, they were smashed, they were all smashed in a maelstrom of destruction from above that seemed never to end, a storm made of body parts.

A roar of terror and woe rose up from their throats, but was quickly buried in the wet thudding, as the living seraph disappeared beneath the mountains of their own dead.

Brooke lay her hand over Wylie's for a moment. He glanced up at her, and in that glance they shared exultation, perhaps also sorrow at the suffering that was being experienced, but it was nothing compared to the rage of battle that was breaking out in the lands of the Corporation, gnashing so intense that it was shaking even the pearly walls that enclosed the Union, and rustling the leaves in the peaceful lands they protected.

They were being torn apart, the minions of Echidna, who had ruled for so long. Wylie looked for Samson, but did not see him. He wanted to identify him, because Samson, who knew human customs and understood gateways, was not defeated until he was destroyed.

"They need us," Nick said from behind closed eyes. "They need us *now*, Dad."

"I can't help where the story goes."

Nick pushed his father away from the laptop.

"Hey."

"Dad, it's another deception! They're fascinating you with their own destruction, so you won't go where you're needed."

He began to type, and when Wylie tried to stop him, Brooke intervened with a sharp shake of her head.

Nick's eyes closed. His fingers flew.

Before him was a huge room. It was lit by faint blue light that dwindled in the massive space to a blue haze on the distance. The haze flickered slightly, and then he saw why. It was coming from millions upon millions of lozenge-shaped tubes, each emplaced in a socket that was connected to thick, black cables that ran between the hundreds and hundreds of rows.

Martin was quite familiar with the large cartouches that were depicted on the walls of the Temple of Hathor in the Dendera complex. He had not dated this temple, but he had known since he'd read of Al North's ordeal, that the accepted explanation for the oblong cartouches, that they were simply borders meant to enclose hieroglyphics, was not correct.

In each one, a multicolored light flickered along a copper filament. It twisted and turned, flying now against the glass of the tube, now twisting itself around the filament, now flashing in a million colors.

The light was souls, and he understood now what Abaddon's ageslong propaganda had done to us. It had made us forget the science of the soul so that we would be helpless when the three earths again crossed the plane of the galaxy and they would have their chance—this chance—to return. It had made us forget what these tubes were, which were soul prisons. It had given us generations of scientists who considered the soul a "supernatural" idea and so stayed away from any study of it. But there was no supernatural, there were only phenomena that had been understood, quantified, and measured, and phenomena that had not. That the patterns induced in fields of electrons by changing conditions in a body would persist after death and become a sort of plasma, conscious and richly aware of its memories, had never been imagined. It had been assumed, if it was thought about at all, that any electromagnetic activity in the nervous system simply ceased when the body died.

And so Martin's earth had been defenseless when the seraph returned—as ours will be, also, on the inevitable day when in their greedy, starved fury, they come bursting in on us in whatever cunning new way they may devise.

Above the ocean of Samson's soul traps, the long lines of gateways were sparking and shimmering. It would only be moments before it was too late. The souls, seeming to sense this, flickered frantically in their prisons.

There came from along the narrow path between two rows of soul traps, a clanging. It was young Mike in the gloom, hammering at one of the tubes with a rock he had found on the way in.

The sound echoed up and down the great space, rising in intensity until it was the ringing of a great bell, then falling again as he grew tired, finally stopping.

Trevor said, "I think there's a seam here." He was down between two rows, where the tubes were connected to the sockets that held them.

"What's next, Dad?" Nick asked has father.

"You're the writer now, son."

"They're running out of time!"

"And you're frozen. It happens."

"Dad, pick it up."

"I can't pick it up, it's yours now!"

Nick sat. Nothing happened. Wylie waited. His mind remained blank.

Brooke said, "What about Al North?"

That did it. Nick's fingers began to type.

Al North had done wrong and been wrong, but he had never wavered from his duty as he understood it. He knew where his fault lay and what it would inevitably do to him, but also as long as he had consciousness in him, he would strive to right the wrongs he had created.

Even so, those wrongs had led to a horrible catastrophe and billions of deaths, and no small act of heroism could rectify such a tremendous mistake. He could no longer reach the surface of the earth, but this desperate place was far beneath it, and here he could still maneuver.

"Look!" Martin pointed to what appeared to be a star in the vault of the space. At that same instant something rushed past beneath his feet. He looked down in time to see scales, iridescent purple in the blue light, but then the thing was gone.

An instant later Mike screamed as coils surged up around him.

Al North saw all this with the clarity—and, indeed, the peace—of somebody who had accepted his life in full, and was prepared to pay the debt he had incurred. He understood the secret of hell, that souls who go there forfeit their right to be. They no longer have a place in this universe or any universe, not until time ends, and a new idea comes to replace the one that is the present creation.

And then, maybe.

He who had done evil accepted the rightness of this.

Still, he wanted to repair what he could, and there was something he could do here. They had all forgotten, in their terror, to just let themselves happen, to trust the grace that was immediately and always ready to support them. He forgave them. He hoped for them.

Which was a very great thing, that he could surmount his anger and his disappointment and his arrogance long enough to do that one tiny thing, to feel hope.

It seemed small, but the energy of such an act on the part of a lost soul is huge, and the tiny spark of goodness that was still within him was easily enough to open ten million soul traps in one flashing, electric instant.

A roar of voices burst out, the faint blue light became a million times brighter. Memories, thoughts, pleas, cries of relief—a huge, gushing roar of human surprise and joy—flew at Martin and his little band in the form of pictures of happy moments, loving in the covers, running by the sea, leaves whirling in autumn, Christmas tree lights, girls dancing, men in blue water, hamburgers, the faces of happy dogs, and song in a million verses of hallelujah.

In this mass, a thousand great serpents came screaming up from the depths of the place and down from the shuddering gateways, their bodies burning from the goodness around them that they could not bear, and they flew into the air like great pillars of fire, writhing and screaming in the sea of song.

They were another design like the outriders and the nighthawks, especially fashioned to terrify human beings, but they had been unleashed too late to save Samson's wealth. No doubt, the huge snakes were a rental, and he hadn't wanted to spend the money unless he had to.

The song ended. The hot bones of the serpents tumbled down through the ruined masses of shattered tubes. The gateways shimmered and went out.

Samson's enormous cry of rage echoed, faded, and died away. He dropped to a stool in his simple room, his narrow head bowed. Outside, the city roared. Another revolution, another aristocracy burned, and now this, his fortune lost.

So it went, in the unsettled misery of this age.

Unnoticed by the raging crowds, the hour of midnight had passed. The weak had won the day.

With a quick swipe of his hand across his face, Samson shifted into his human form. Outside, torches flared. Feet pounded on the stairs, fists pounded on his door.

He stepped through his quickly closing gateway, but not into his old world, not into Martin's world. He had a plan. If there was vengeance to be tasted, he intended to drink deep.

"Dad, he's in our woods!"

They got their shotguns and took off after him, both of them, and Brooke and Kelsey agreed that they'd gone mad.

The woods, though, were empty. From along the ridge above the house, they could see the lights of Harrow. Faintly, one of the church bells sounded. Snow was falling, whispering in the woods, drawing pale lines along the dark branches of the winter trees. The peace here was so deep that it seemed impossible that Samson could have passed this way.

They went back to the house, the two of them. They lingered on the deck.

"The Belt of Orion," Wylie said, gazing up as the snow clouds made a window for the stars.

"And his bow," Nick said, pointing.

"You did good, Nick."

"Thanks, Dad. Dad?"

"Yes?"

"Is it real? The book?"

"I thought Samson was in our woods. But he wasn't."

They went inside, then, and made a fire for the girls. Popcorn was popped, and hot chocolate produced, and Wylie even managed to slip a goodly shot of whiskey into his.

They spent the remainder of this quiet night speaking of the things of ordinary life. "Past midnight," Nick said. "I think we won."

Nothing more was said, and after a time, Nick played cards with Kelsey and Wylie, and Brooke broke out the celebration cognac, a hundred-year-old bottle that was sipped at moments of victory.

Tomorrow, Christmas vacation began for the kids, and in the very late hours, Wylie went into his wife's arms for what felt like the first time in an age.

At breakfast, the radio said, "The world ended last night, but it seems that nobody noticed. New Age gurus from China to Scotland stood on mountaintops and chanted, but guess what, Chicken Little stayed home. We are now living on the first day beyond the end of the ancient Mayan calendar, a date that has no number in their measurement. But then again, they went extinct a long time ago."

Later in the morning, Nick found boot prints back in the woods, where Samson's gateway had been.

"Could've been left by us," Wylie told him.

"I was wearing sneakers when we came out here. You had on a sock. One sock."

"I went out in the woods without shoes? In the dead of winter?"

Nick nodded. "We did not make these tracks, Dad."

They'd put a throw rug over the bullet holes in the floor above the crawl space, and they both looked at it at the same time, and for the same reason. It was now gone and the floor was unmarked.

"Brooke, what about that little rug in the kitchen?"

"I put that horror back in the mudroom where it belongs and leave it there please. In the future, if you want to rearrange my house, submit your request in writing."

"Dad, it was all real! It happened! And we're—" He stopped. Frowned a little, shook his head. "I lost it," he said. "It was right on the tip of my tongue."

Wylie called Matt, but nobody had reported anybody strange wandering around in Harrow, or anywhere in Lautner County, for that matter.

"What about the body in my crawl space? Is that resolved?"

"You want me to come out there with a net?"

"I thought you were gonna arrest me."

There was a silence. Then, "Oh, yeah, you've got that absinthe, not to mention the cigar theft issue."

He had no memory whatsoever of Al North, then.

They talked, then, about the state of the pheasant population, which was excellent. "Matt wants to hunt tomorrow," Wylie called to Nick, "you game?"

Nick looked at him. "He doesn't remember a thing, does he?"

"You want to go or not?"

"'Course I do."

Wylie made plans to meet with Matt before dawn, and go to some of the walk-in land over in Smith County. "You sure there's been nothing odd, Matt? No cars stolen around here, say?"

"In your neck of the woods? There hasn't been any crime of any kind over there at all, ever. What the hell's the matter with you today, anyway? Is this some new insanity? I don't hunt with crazy people."

"Read me the blotter for last night."

"The *blotter*?"

"Look, it's not gonna kill you, now read the damn thing!"

"Okay! 16:32, Miss Wicks's chickens are in Elm Street again. Ticketed. 18:05, car fire, put out by occupant. 20:22, kids smoking and playing loud music behind Wilson's Feed and Seed, sent home."

"That was it? That was what we paid you for last night?"

"We got a possible stolen truck. Jim Riggs can't find his farm banger. But it's probably gonna be that Willie of his, hid it for a joke. That kid's got an unfortunate sense of humor."

So nothing strange had happened in this quiet little corner of Kansas for a long time, unless it was Samson who had gotten that truck, of course.

Or no, there was one thing: the miserable accident that had befallen poor William Nunnally.

"So, what's new in the Nunnally case?"

"Nothin.' Coroner's report says it was exposure. He was high, it seems. Got a lotta meth heads down that way. Damndest thing. The family's not gonna sue you, for some strange reason, going down there and terrorizing them like you did."

"So it was just one of those things?"

"That would be true, crazy man."

The night passed uneventfully, Wylie and Nick got up at four-thirty, and as the sun rose, they were hunting. True to form, Wylie over- or undershot every rise he got, and all his pheasants lived to see another day.

Nick, however, bagged Christmas dinner.

EPILOGUE
THE INHERITORS

NEW WORLDS ARE MADE IN two places: the ruins of the old and the minds of the survivors.

The captured souls had instantaneously returned to their wandering bodies—all but those of the dead, who had begun another kind of journey.

Those who returned to life found themselves waking like sleepwalkers are known to do, in unaccustomed and impossible places. Lindy discovered herself riding in a jammed truck that was being driven by people who were equally mystified by where they were going and why.

At the first town they came to, they stopped the truck. Everybody was thirsty and hungry, and many of them were hurt, mostly with injured feet, which Lindy certainly had. They pulled over in Lora, Colorado, which they found empty. There was no power. All phone lines were dead.

Lindy remembered up until they had entered Third Street Methodist. The rest—she just had no idea. None at all. But she knew who she was and where she was from, and she also knew that she was going home. No matter what, she was returning to Harrow and to Martin and Trevor and her dear little Winnie.

This was far from impossible, as there were abandoned cars and trucks everywhere. She found a serviceable-looking hybrid that was full of gas. Her idea was that she was about three hundred miles west of home, so the hybrid would get her there with gas to spare.

She and some of the others from the Truck Gang, as they called themselves, broke into a place called the Lora Cafe. The milk was rotted, the eggs were higher than a kite, and there was no gas to cook with, so she contented herself with Cheerios washed down by water. They shared out the breakfast cereals, the cans of beans and soup, and took off in their various directions, all of them obsessed with the same thing: home.

Lindy did not care to travel with anybody else. She wasn't sure what might happen. The world had collapsed. Then, for whatever unknown reason, her coffin nightmares had ended and here she was. She had obviously been walking for miles and miles, but she had no memory of it at all.

The car had a GPS but it didn't manage to pick up any satellites, so she simply drove east on 70. Frequently, she had to go around abandoned vehicles, some of them in lines miles long, and travel cross country in the bounding car. It held together, though, well enough, and soon she was heading into familiar little Harrow.

There were people here and there, looking for the most part like they'd just come up after a tornado had passed, to see what was left.

Winnie said, "I can come back."

The voice was so clear that for a moment she thought that her daughter was sitting in the backseat. She shook her head. Seeing Third Street Methodist, she experienced a surge of terror so great that she had to stop the car right there in the middle of the street.

"Mom?"

She did not open her eyes. She'd lost her kids, her husband, everything. There was no more Winnie and that voice had not been Trevor.

Then the car door opened.

She looked up into the smiling face of the most beautiful, most wonderful man in the world. She could not get out of the car. She tried, but she was shaking too hard, her hands just went out and went clutching toward her Martin, and then his arms were coming, they were strong around her, they were taking her and lifting her, and she felt his lips upon her lips and heaven came and lifted her.

There were a thousand whispered words, but no words could express the meaning of this meeting. Her husband's and her son's eyes were strangely dark, and hers were, too, they told her, and they told her that this was good, it was a miracle, it was the future of mankind in their eyes, dark still, but there would be light.

"What happened to us?" she asked as they drove out toward the Smoke Hills and home.

"There was an earthquake," Martin said at last. "That affected the entire planet. And we're not out of the woods yet. But we're learning how to work in new ways. How to fix things."

"A lot is wrong," Trevor said.

Home was one of them, she soon discovered, and it was very wrong, so wrong that when she saw it, she burst into tears. "We can't clean this up," she wailed. She looked in disbelief at the melted, crazy furniture, at the twisted ruins of her kitchen. "What did this? This was no earthquake."

"2012 came and went," Martin said at last. "It turns out that the old Maya knew a lot. They calculated the return of—well, of—"

"Evil," Trevor said simply. "Evil was here, but it failed." He paused. "And it had a good effect, because fighting it transformed us. I guess that's why you're supposed to love your enemy."

He fell silent, then, and in his silence and with it, she could hear something that was a voice and yet not a voice. It was more than a voice. She could hear engineers and physicists like herself and architects and workmen all gathered in a great chorus of plans and work and effort. "We're going to put the world back together again," she said.

Martin said, "We've changed. The human mind is not the same, and a lot of people—the bad ones, I guess—are they gone? Could they be gone?"

They knew, then, that this terrible attack had also been a cleansing, because they could feel by its absence that the weight of wicked souls had been lifted.

Lindy was the first to utter the words that had been on all of their lips unspoken, from the moment they had found each other. "What about Winnie?"

Martin shook his head. "We believe that she didn't make it."

"What do you mean?"

"Mom, you just need to let yourself happen. Don't think. Just—be with us. Part of us."

"My daughter is missing! Where's Bobby? Where are the state police, the FBI? The FBI gets involved in child disappearances. And what about our Jenny Alert? Where's our Jenny Alert!"

He came to her and she didn't want to do it, but she let him hold her because she had spent what seemed like an eon trapped in that strange somewhere-or-other tying to find him and to feel him where he ought to be and wasn't. "My baby's not bad, there's nothing wrong with her, she's hardly had a chance to live!"

She had to accept. But it wasn't going to be easy, because it was unfair that her dear little girl suffer the same fate as the wicked, it was just really, really *unfair!*

Night fell, and Trevor made a place for himself on the floor of their little office, because his room was destroyed, and they did not want to disturb Winnie's room.

It was cold and without electricity it got dark early on the twenty-second of December, and as it got dark, Lindy agonized over her lost child. But under their quilt that she had made when she was first married, it was wonderfully warm. They were dirty, though, and the warmth was ripening them. There was no water to wash but that, also, did not prevent her from being Martin's wife again, and their bodies in the night were glad.

Mommy?

Lindy's eyes flew open. She cried out. Martin's hand caressed her cheek. "Sleep, my love." He came close and kissed her. "From hell to heaven," he murmured. Her whole heart, her blood, her soul took deepest joy in those words.

Mommy?

She leaped from the bed, ran to the window. "It's her!"

Martin came to her, put his arms around her waist from behind. She pulled away from him. "Honey—"

"Shut up!"

Hi, Mommy.

"Oh, baby, my baby, I hear you! Where are you?"

Silence.

"She's out there somewhere! Martin, she's out there and we have to find her. Martin, the nighthawks—"

"Sh! Sh! There are no nighthawks, they're gone."

"How in *hell* do you know?"

Martin tried again to hold her, but she pulled away. "Listen!"

"Lindy, love . . ." She was hurt. Everybody was hurt. So hurt.

Then Trevor was there. *Listen to her, Dad.*

He turned around. Trevor came to them, nodded toward the window.

Then Martin heard it, the ticking of an engine out in the dark. An electric surge of fear went through him. They had no gun. They still had no *gun*!

Then he saw it, moving slowly closer to the house, a rattling old car with only the single light.

"That's Bobby," he said.

Then she was running, Lindy was running, and Martin, and behind them Trevor.

The car stood in the driveway, its engine guttering. Then the driver's door opened, and Martin saw in the light from within a tiny form prim in the passenger's seat.

Lindy leaped at Bobby's car, threw the door open and there was her little girl, who came out into her arms, and Lindy danced, whirling round and round with her child silent in her arms, her child smiling a soft smile.

"Baby, baby, baby," Lindy cried, then cradled her and covered her with kisses.

Hi, Winnie said, and it echoed like a song in them all.

"Buddy, she came in half an hour ago."

Martin looked at him. Embraced his old friend. "I thought you were a goner for sure."

"I thought you were." He looked at Lindy and Winnie. "I don't know how to tell you this, or even exactly what I am telling you."

"I know she's dead," Martin said. "I saw her body."

Daddy, it's all changed. Winnie and Trevor's thoughts echoed as one.

He had a son who could read minds, now a daughter returned from the dead. They took her inside, loving her, touching her, and she was full and normal flesh in every way.

Bobby lingered. "Boy, they did a number around here."

"Oh, yes."

"I don't know quite what happened, but I know you were a big part of it. I can hear people thinking. Thinking about what happened, and a lot of them are thinking about you, Martin."

We can all hear each other, Trevor said in their minds.

Gonna be interesting times for cops, Bobby thought. He glanced around, then laughed a little. He took Martin aside. "She isn't the same," he whispered.

I'm all different, Winnie added. Then, *This house is a mess!*

They—Lindy threw a picture of the glaring reptilian features of Mazle into their minds—*did it*.

Winnie reached into the air, and her old friend Bearish came flopping into her hands. He was soaked and crusted with ice and mud. *You got lost.*

As she moved through the house, everything she touched came back to its previous condition. She opened the fridge. *We still have to go to the store.* Then, in words, "Except for these apples. I din steal 'em. They were grounded."

She brought out five small apples. They were cold, a little old, obviously falls. Martin was famished, they all were, and they ate silently. He wondered where they'd come from, and saw in his mind a picture of the Wright's apple tree, it's fruit all fallen.

She came and hugged his legs. He lifted her and thought that she was not quite as heavy as she had been, not quite as solid. He knew that he held a great miracle in his arms, and that there must be millions of such miracles over all the earth right now. He kissed his miracle and she laughed, and he thought he was holding the promise of the whole future in his arms.

You are, Trevor said as he crunched into his apple.

The little family was taking a journey into a new world, and this journey was being repeated all across the planet, as a new mankind rose up from the ruins of the old, and the risen and the living joined together in a new chorus, and the long ages of illusion that there is a curtain between the living and the dead were ended.

The undiscovered country had been discovered, and the explorers were returning.

Winnie settled into the deep comfort of her father's arms. Bobby reached out and touched her, and she felt the energy in him that was a little sharp in places, and smoothed it out. Tears came to his eyes. He stared at her, drank her in. She let him clutch her, she laughed, she had been on such a long journey. "You smell like roses," he whispered.

She ate her apple, thinking of what life is—what it really is. She thought of her old body still lying where it had fallen, giving itself back to dust and memory. *Life is the mystery of the world*, she told them.

The minds around her fell silent.

Death had ended, they just didn't know it yet. She understood what had really been done here, and who had done it, and the real reason, that only the good remained, because only the good could find the next secret, the true meaning of life without death.

Over time, she would tell them everything, that there was a new humanity born and a whole new way of living to be discovered, but now she laid her very tired head against her daddy's shoulder.

She would sleep on this night the sweetest of all sleeps, deep in her home, surrounded by her family, at one with their love and all love, in a world that had been saved.

A little while, and the wicked will be no more;
though you look for them, they will not be found.
But the meek will inherit the earth and enjoy great peace.
—Psalm 37: 10–11